OLDER

By: Jennifer Hartmann

For Megan Lick.
Fifth-grade laugh attacks and Wonderwall sing-a-longs are never far from
my heart.

TRIGGER WARNINGS

This book deals with heavy themes, including childhood abuse and neglect. It also depicts a large age gap between the leads. While I always put delicate care into my words, this story may not be for everyone. XOXO.

PROLOGUE

Halley

I GRIPPED the edge of the mottled mattress as a leather belt whipped across my bare back.

My punishment was ten lashes and an early bedtime with no supper.

My crime?

Love.

I loved more than I should have. I loved all things, big and small. Today I'd loved a biscuit-colored bunny with an injured leg that had scampered across our driveway. I had loved it enough to carry it into our one-car garage and tend to the wound with a purple Band-Aid I'd snuck from the hall closet while Mom was sound asleep with an empty bottle of gin clutched to her chest.

Father had come home from work thirty minutes early and caught me wallowing in that love, holding the trembling bunny in my arms and humming my favorite song to calm its quivering. Blood had oozed all over the garage floor, the same shade of red as his angry face when he'd discovered the mess.

"In the house. Right now." Violet veins had popped in his neck, meaty fists clenching at his sides. "Meet me in the den."

I'd obeyed.

And now my body jerked with each flog.

Father made me count out loud as the ruddy-brown belt slashed down on me and painted fiery lines across my skin. Tears burned behind my eyes, but I refused to let them fall. He hated emotion. Hated weakness. Crying only made him more furious.

Mom slept through the whole thing.

Not that it mattered—she wouldn't have stopped it, anyway. My mother turned her back on me whenever my back was beaten to every shade of blue.

Maybe it was out of fear. Maybe it was out of unlove.

Father didn't love me; Mom didn't love me enough.

I guess that was why I loved too much. I had a lot of loveless holes to fill.

When the punishment was complete, I lowered my dirt-stained T-shirt and tipped my chin as Father relaced his belt through the belt holes of his worn jeans. "I'm sorry, Father. I'll go clean up the mess now." My feet itched to rush past him toward the garage, but I waited for permission.

Father eyed me, his icy gaze sliding down my bony frame as I folded in my lips to keep them from quivering. "You'll go straight to bed, that's what you'll do."

"But it's only four o'clock. It's too bright and sunny to fall asleep, and—"

"You want to lose supper tomorrow, too?" He thwacked me upside the head with a flat palm. "Do as you're told, you smart-mouthed brat."

"Yes, Father." I slunk past him with defeat as my cotton shirt scratched at the nasty welts blooming on my spine.

"You know what? Think I changed my mind," Father said before I slipped out of the den. "I'll bring a hot plate of supper to your door."

My stomach grumbled with anticipation.

Was he lying?

Father was never kind to me.

Maybe he saw how upset I was. How petrified and sad. There had to be a spark of humanity buried inside his jet-black heart.

Pivoting around, a flicker of hope jumped between my ribs as I stared at him with wide eyes.

Father smirked and latched the belt buckle into place. "I'll leave a nice helping of rabbit outside your room in a few hours. My treat."

It took a minute for his words to sink in.

And when they did, they sunk me.

My bottom lip wobbled as dread pitched in my stomach, overriding the hunger pains. All I wanted to do was throw up. "I'm not hungry."

"You'll eat what I give you and you'll be grateful. Now go to your room."

I spun on my heel with lightning speed, just so he didn't see the waterfall of tears erupt as I choked back a sob.

But he stopped me one more time.

"Oh, and Halley? Don't you go sneaking into the garage to save that pesty rodent. You'll fail. And you'll suffer the consequences for disobeying me."

The back of my neck pricked with icicles. "Yes, Father," I choked out.

"Wouldn't matter, anyway. You've never been good at doing hard things."

He was right, I decided, as I holed up in my bedroom that afternoon and slid beneath the starchy covers, tucking myself into a ball as my body shivered in the aftermath of my beating.

I was a late walker, a late talker, a late learner in so many chapters of my life.

I was never able to earn my father's affection, no matter how desperate I was, how needy and fraught.

I couldn't put my fractured family back together.

I couldn't even save that little bunny.

Father was right...

I wasn't good at doing hard things.

Life is like photography. You need the negatives to develop.
—Ziad K. Abdelnour

CHAPTER 1

Halley

June, 1995

"ARE YOU LOST?"

That was the first thing the guy in the Soundgarden T-shirt and leather jacket said to me as my ankles kissed the lake water.

I tilted my head over my shoulder to assess the stranger who was standing just inches from the waterline. "Lost?" Curling my toes into the soggy muck, I gave him a onceover. The man was older than me; probably too old to have come from the house party a few yards away that reverberated with loud grunge music. "Do I look lost?"

Moonlight carved him out of the darkness, outlining a tall, muscled frame and a mop of inky-brown hair, its hue approaching black but not quite reaching the deepest shade.

"A little." He shoved both hands into denim pockets and slanted his head toward the house. "I mean, you're out here all alone, standing in a lake."

"Maybe you're the one who's lost," I volleyed back. "Unless you're here with unsavory intentions. You know...watching a girl standing all alone in a lake." My gaze slowly panned down his body like I was checking for weapons. But I knew well enough that a man only needed two capable hands and a sharp tongue to inflict harm. Sometimes less. A single look could do me in.

His brows bent at my implication. "I'm looking for someone."

"I'm probably not who you're looking for."

He peered back over at the house, marinating in the statement before deciding it was true. "Yeah," he replied, the response just loud enough to carry over the deep bass seeping out through an open window. "Sorry to bother you. Have a good night."

"You're not bothering me." I watched as he faltered mid-swivel. Still wading in the shallow water, I took a small step forward and confessed, "Maybe I am a little lost."

The man glanced at my chunky heels tipped sideways in the sand, then panned his gaze out to the stretch of water that appeared endless as the surface bled with dark sky. "You don't live here?"

"I live on the other side of town." *Live* was a tragic elaboration, but he didn't need to know that.

He nodded. "I'm Reed."

"Halley. Like the comet."

We locked eyes.

He was too far away for me to make out the color, but they looked light. Lighter than my hollow hazel, even through the gloom of nightfall.

"The party was lame, so I came out here to get some air," I continued. "The person you're looking for is probably inside doing body shots with Jay Jennings."

Reed rubbed a hand over his jaw, the other returning to his left pocket. "I really hope not." He took a step closer to the water. "Do you need me to call you a taxi or something?"

"I don't need a ride." I ducked my chin before spinning back around and staring out at the lake. "Unless you have a boat."

"Fresh out of boats."

"I suppose I could swim."

My back was facing him, but his voice sounded closer. "Swim to where?"

"Anywhere." I shrugged. "Everywhere."

"Mm," he mused. "Bad night?"

Bad day. Bad night. Bad life.

"Something like that." Cool water sloshed at my bare ankles before I plopped down and crossed my legs. "Anyway, I hope you find your person. Maybe they're the one who's lost and they're waiting for you to find them."

Silence answered for a few breaths before his voice broke through. "What are you doing?"

"Sitting in a lake." I planted my hands in the sludge and wheeled around on my butt to face him, stretching out my legs. Off his baffled look, I frowned. "What?"

His fingers continued to coast over his stubbled jawline as he studied me. "This is a strange encounter."

"You're welcome," I said, pulling a smile.

"I never thanked you for anything."

"You might one day." Leaning back on my palms, I danced my legs up and down, my red-tipped toes peeking out through the water's surface. "One of my fondest memories is that one time I stumbled across a weird girl sitting fully clothed in a lake in the middle of the night."

His eyebrows were so furrowed, he was actually scowling. "Really?"

"No." I smiled again, and the upturn of my lips was foreign but pure. A priceless feeling. "You could join me. We could be weird together."

"Think I'll pass. Maybe another time."

"Liar." My smile faded, but the zippy feeling inside my chest refused to ebb. It sizzled and churned, crawling up my throat and sparking my tongue with more conversation. "How old are you?"

"Thirty-four." He took another step forward until the water almost touched the toes of his worn black boots. "You?"

"Twenty-one."

He was a lot older than me. Aged in that rugged, seasoned way, like he had stories to tell and experiences to share, yet an abundance more still to come.

He was good-looking, too.

Strikingly so.

Even the shadows couldn't veil his angled cheekbones, strong jaw, silken waves of dark hair, and full lips that quirked with the barest smile when he took a seat in the sand.

We faced each other. Stared.

Reed bent his legs at the knees and dangled his hands between them, leather-encased forearms pressed to his thighs. My body was halfway submerged in water, his bone-dry, but the crackling charge in the air upstaged the elements that separated us, while pearly starlight blanketed him in a soft glow.

Sky, water, earth.

Him.

His gaze held with mine, and for a moment, time seemed to suspend as we allowed the silence to breathe, the thump of music from the party serving only as a distant heartbeat.

"So, Halley Like the Comet," Reed finally spoke, his voice a gentle ripple in the summer breeze. "Do you have a story to go along with the name?"

I continued to flick my toes in and out of the water as droplets splashed along my lower legs. "My mom was a stargazer. A dreamer."

"Was? Past tense?"

"Yes. Now she's just an alcoholic."

Too dark. Too deep.

I chomped down on my tongue like I could chew through the spoken words and swallow them back down.

His expression wilted. "Sorry to hear."

"Who were you looking for?"

He tugged his bottom lip between his teeth and made a hissing sound, processing my swift subject change.

I tried not to focus on the action but failed.

"My daughter," he said.

I blanched at the admission, my bobbing legs ceasing all motion. "You have a daughter?"

"Yes."

"A daughter old enough to be at a party?"

Shifting across from me, he sighed as the soles of his boots drew imprints in the muted sand. "Thanks for that stone-cold reminder. I'm still getting used to the concept of her having a social life that doesn't involve Disney movies and bedtime stories."

Oh, boy.

I was way out of my league with this guy. Something told me I should remove myself from the conversation with dignity before the curious allure of him eclipsed my logical thinking.

Unfortunately for both of us, I ignored the nagging tug of sound judgment.

"Her mom said she'd be here, but this isn't really her scene," he added, scratching his jaw. "She likes beachy bonfires and country music, not the grunge scene with rowdy douchebags. Thought she might've come outside."

"Nope. Just me out here." I dug my toes into the lake floor until they were wholly hidden. "Sorry to disappoint."

He paused, his eyes returning to mine, twinkling with what looked like pale-green flecks now that he was closer. "I'm not disappointed."

My smile returned, less foreign this time. I'd smiled more in the last few minutes than the last few years and we'd hardly exchanged more than a handful of sentences. "Well, then. Cheers to random, strange encounters behind Jay's house." I lifted my invisible flute in the air.

A half-grin twitched on his mouth as he moved an inch closer to me in the sand, his boots teasing the water. "How do you know him?"

"Through Becky." Everybody knew a Becky. I didn't, but he probably did. "She left a little while ago and I don't know anyone else here."

"Sure you don't need a ride?"

Our eyes snagged when my chin tipped up.

I considered his intentions again, wondering what was going through his mind—after all, he was a much-older man. Was this about sex, or was he just being nice? Acts of kindness were a far-fetched concept to me, especially when it came to the opposite gender. It was hard to imagine this man offering me a ride home with no strings attached.

Then again...maybe I wanted strings.

Something to tether me. To anchor my floundering heart.

I envisioned this mysterious stranger taking me home in his car or truck, warm wind whipping through the open window, his scent mingling with the breeze. I wondered what he smelled like. Mint, pine-steeped mountaintops, cheap cologne. He was too far away for me to pinpoint the soap on his skin or the shampoo in his hair, and I found myself instinctually scooting forward in the water to get a whiff of the compelling unknown.

Temptation teased me. An escape.

But I shook my head at the offer.

If Father caught a strange man in our driveway, he'd come barreling out of the house with his shotgun and scare Reed away for good. He'd probably shoot him. "I can walk."

He glanced back down at the sand. "Are you in college?"

I honed in on his strong jawline and the way his throat rolled when he swallowed. Then I stiffened as his words registered and peeled a water-soaked leaf off my ankle. "Not yet. I'm still figuring out what to do with my life."

"I get that. Took me a while to figure it out, too."

"What do you do?"

"I used to be a paramedic. But then I sort of switched gears and got into jiu-jitsu training and made a career out of it. I specialize in self-defense."

My eyes popped.

That was...impressive.

I didn't take Reed with his messy hair, casual clothes, and pretty, probably-green eyes to have such a respectable occupation in both the medical field and martial arts. "Do you teach locally?"

"I do now. I lived in Charleston for a while and opened up my own studio. Then my daughter and her mom moved back to Illinois. So, after another year passed, I handed the business reins over to one of my employees, then followed them here. I opened up a second studio near-by." Reed pursed his lips, masking a sheepish smile. "Sorry. That was probably more than you wanted to know."

I gawked at him, transfixed. "No, that's amazing. I love the idea of helping people in that way."

"Yeah, it's my passion."

"I bet your daughter is really proud."

"Hard to say." He drank in a long breath, scuffing the loose stones near his boot. "Somewhere between her scowling, pouting, and scathing sarcasm, I'm hopeful there's some pride tucked away." Chewing on his bottom lip, he glanced back up at me. "What about you? Any grand ambitions?"

Disappointment flattened my lips, then it traveled south, settling in my heart. "I wish I had a grand answer, but my ambitions are kind of scattered and hard to catch. I think the thing I love most doesn't really have a title. Doesn't fit into any sort of box, you know?"

He didn't know, judging from his creased browline.

Or...maybe that was interest.

Reed leaned forward and skimmed his fingers across his lips, his attention fully fixed on me. He was waiting for more. There was a curious glimmer in his eyes that kept me talking.

"I enjoy capturing the intangible," I explained. "Flashes, flickers, the in-betweens. I want to immortalize them forever. I write in my journal, draw, sometimes I paint. But I'm not very good at any of those things. Far from career-worthy." An insecure laugh slipped out, and I flicked my foot out of the water, splashing us both.

A spray of droplets danced across our legs. Reed smiled.

Warmth infiltrated my chest, my cheeks, my lungs. "Sorry...that doesn't make any sense." Cringing, I wished I could erase my rambling. "I guess I just love moments."

"Moments," he echoed, nodding slowly. Processing. Allowing my words to sink in. "Blips."

"Yes...exactly." My response floated over to him like a whispery daydream as an organic smile crested on my mouth. He understood. No one else had ever understood, because nobody bothered to listen. "Life's fleeting blips. The ones that seem insignificant at the time, but later on, they mean everything. You know, like when you're watching a movie, and you pause it to grab a snack? You stop it at this random scene, and the frame freezes on someone making a weird face that makes you laugh, or an extra is caught smiling in the background, or a dog is running through the park trying to catch a butterfly with its tail in motion..."

The crease didn't unfurl from his brows; in fact, it only deepened. He looked contemplative, completely engrossed.

My skin heated, despite the chilly water lapping at my skin. "I'm getting carried away," I said through a chuckle. "I just love moments like that, but in *real* life. I wish I could solidify them. Prolong them. Make them last forever."

Reed drank me in, the glimmer in his eyes brightening with tenderness while he seemingly mulled over my long-winded dissertation on blips. "What about journalism?"

I shrugged hopelessly.

That would never happen—I had no money for college and I wasn't good at doing hard things.

Becoming a journalist would be really damn hard.

"Putting thoughts into words isn't my strong suit. As I'm sure you've noticed." I shot him a weak smile. "My Nana always wanted me to pursue business, but my heart was never in things like numbers and quotas."

"Sounds like your heart already knows what it wants. Go with the blips."

"I wish it were that simple."

"It is. People always overcomplicate shit."

"That's because life is complicated," I countered, peeking up at him through water-dotted lashes.

"Is it, though?" He held my gaze. "Life is living. If you're not living exactly the way you want to live, then what's the fucking point?"

My chest fluttered.

I thought about my sad life that lacked the vibrancy and purpose Reed was so well-versed in. Everything was hollow. Everything except for my heart. And having an abundant heart in a hollow world was an affliction I was helpless to overcome.

I chewed on my cheek and fidgeted my feet back and forth.

And somehow...our toes touched.

My naked, wet toes brushed the leather of his boots, and I realized we were a mere waterline apart. Within the interplay of words and the stretch of frozen-in-time seconds, he'd moved closer to the water, and I'd moved closer to the sand.

Reed's gaze flickered over my body, scanning up my lightly bronzed legs, soaked denim skirt, and landing on my band tee. He swallowed again, blinking up to meet my eyes. "You like the Gin Blossoms?"

Nodding, I licked my lips that were sheathed in my favorite color of lipstick—Copperglow Berry. The makeup, paired with my five-foot-seven height, made me look older than I was, which was always the desired intent.

I thought maybe Reed liked the way I looked. He kept studying me in a way that made my skin itch. But not like spiders crawling down my spine in the same way Father's voice boomed through me and tangled me in cobwebs, but like little fireflies with streaks of light skittering across my chest.

I rubbed my bicep, glancing down at my T-shirt showcasing the

New Miserable Experience album cover. *"Found Out About You* is my favorite song. Have you ever listened to the lyrics? They're beautifully tragic."

"Huh." He tilted his toes forward, pressing them to mine. "Can't say that I have."

Do you like tragic things? Are you drawn to the ghosts in my eyes?

Stupid, fruitless thoughts.

If he ever sat down with my ghosts and had a heart-to-heart, he'd be running for the hills.

"Are you going to join me on the shore?" He leaned back on his palms and tipped his face skyward, squinting at the stars.

"Nope. Are you going to join me in the water?"

He shook his head. "No."

A few quiet drumbeats rolled by, our toes still touching, our connection simmering and awaiting the strike of a matchstick.

I rubbed my lips together. "What's your daughter like?"

Endearment shimmered within the tilt of his lips as he continued to stare up at the twinkle-studded sky, his Adam's apple rolling. "She's perfect, but I could be biased. We used to be really close, but this new phase—centered around boys and hormones—have been tough to navigate. And my absence over the past year hasn't helped. Sometimes I wonder if I made the right choice...staying behind, miles away, at such a vulnerable time in her life." He glanced at me, almost like a silent plea, a question that demanded an answer.

But I had no answer to give him. I wasn't armed with any tools to deconstruct his doubt. All I had was a sad smile that stretched with shadows, and it was enough to keep him talking.

"Anyway, I knew she'd be in good hands with her mother," he finished, looking away. "We exchanged letters, talked on the phone. She's thriving in school and sports."

"Are you and her mother divorced?"

"No, we never married. Just didn't work out."

"I'm sorry."

"Don't be. We get along great and have the co-parenting thing down." Reed studied me through the moon's lowlight. "Do you have a boyfriend?"

My stomach pitched at the question. I'd had my share of boys, but none of them friends. Truth be told, I only had one friend—Tara. She lived two streets over in a little brick house that felt warmer than mine. Her mom was kind and attentive, and her dog, Ladybug, always greeted me with face kisses and happy, eager paws.

I guessed I had three friends.

Tara, her mom, and Ladybug.

Shaking my head, I played with the drenched hem of my shirt. "No."

"How come?"

"Relationships are overrated. Love is nothing but a building block for collapse. A stepping stone for tripping and stumbling into a black hole you can't climb out of it."

Reed lifted up in slow motion, returning to a sitting position across from me and folding his hands. "You're too young to be so jaded."

"Am I?" Our gazes tangled and snared. "I wish that were true. But being jaded doesn't come with age; it comes with hardship. And hardship can blow through like a stormfront, destroying everything in a blink. Five years old, fifteen, fifty. Doesn't matter. Once you're caught in the funnel, you never stop spinning out."

God, I was depressing.

My black hole was a reach away from snatching him up and taking him down with me.

I needed to pivot. "Do you like peanut butter?"

Reed blinked at me, multiple times, before dipping his chin and breathing out a laugh. "Sure."

"I don't. It's the texture, I think. Smooth, crunchy, runny, lumpy. It's not straightforward."

"So, you hate peanut butter, house parties, and love. What do you like?"

"I like you."

The glint in his eyes sparked, the quirk of his lips buckling. He'd moved in closer, and so had I. My knees were drawn up, matching his position, and the rough denim of his jeans was a finger's-width apart from grazing against my slick calves. He could part his legs, stretch them into the shallow water, and he'd cage me in.

But nobody moved. Only the water rippled and danced around us while Alice in Chains serenaded us from yards away.

When Reed spoke, his voice was rough. "You don't know me well enough to like me."

"Yeah." I stared at him, held his gaze. "Maybe that's why I do."

Something flashed in his eyes. Curiosity, temptation, uncertainty.

He unfolded his hands, cupping both knees. One foot drifted toward me in a slow slide that was filled with all the same sentiment shining in his eyes. His knee unbent, the sole of his boot closing in near my hip. I knew that a single touch would pull me from the cold lake and drop me in his lap, and I'd be forever lost to this moment beneath the full moon.

But then a high-pitched squeal carried over from Jay's house.

He tugged his foot back with a light splash.

We both looked over at the property teeming with twenty-some-things out on the patio, a girl being hauled over some guy's shoulder as a glass bottle shattered on the pavement.

Sighing, I tucked my legs closer to my chest, wrapping my arms around my knees like a hug. Or a shield. "You should go find your daughter," I said, watching as he stared off over his shoulder, deciding on his next move. He could stay with me, teasing this connection and weaving it into something with knots and barbs.

Two strangers on a lakefront, destined for nothing.

No good story ever started that way.

Reed nodded slowly, returning his attention to me. We seized, held, and nurtured the interval for what it was.

A fleeting moment.

A blip.

Then he blinked, rose to his feet, and towered over me as he gazed down at my lake-laden form. My hand was linked around my opposite wrist, cradling both legs as I pressed my chin to my kneecaps and peered up at him.

His eyes swirled with misfire before he glanced away. "Goodnight, Halley Like the Comet."

I smiled softly. "Goodnight, Reed."

Hesitation gripped him for one more heartbeat before he scrubbed a hand over his face, through his hair, and spun around to retreat.

I tracked him as he stalked away, over the hill, and past Jay's house.

Out of sight. Out of reach.

Forever on the distant side of the waterline.

CHAPTER 2

Halley

AN HOUR LATER, my back was pressed to a stale-water-blue couch in the main bedroom as my hand loosely curled around a plastic cup of warm beer. *Black* by Pearl Jam blasted from a speaker across from me, mingling with chaotic laughter, clinking glassware, and someone shouting "chug, chug, chug" from the adjacent living area.

I scanned the room, my gaze landing on the shelving units next to the bed, filled with hundreds of CDs.

I'd ventured off by myself after deciding there was nobody here of value to me. Not anymore. No connection to foster, no friendly face, no compelling man to take me home and offer me a few hours of surface-level solace. Regardless, I needed a place to sleep for the night, so I'd settle for Jay's tattered blue couch. I could pretend I was passed-out drunk, then head home when the sun crested.

Cold, wet, and alone, I nursed my beer and stretched out my legs, trying to get comfortable as I zoned out to the song.

But I wasn't alone anymore.

A shadow loomed in the doorway, and my skin prickled with awareness. Familiarity. I lifted my chin, glancing right, and my breath caught like a rock in my throat.

I never expected to see him.

Not again. Not ever.

Leaning against the doorframe, hands shoved into his pockets and leather coat draped over his broad shoulder, Reed stared at me, his features illuminated with bulb light.

Our gazes met, tangled, and clenched. I couldn't hide my wide-eyed expression or steady the newly erratic beats of my heart.

He was devastatingly attractive.

The stars and moon had done him no justice, and I resented them for that.

People always said that in the harsh light of day, the rose-colored glasses fell off and you saw things for what they really were. I'd experienced my fair share; a few random hookups to dull the stab of loneliness and heartache. It had felt so warm and fulfilling at the time, heady in the moment. But then the sun would rise, casting new light on the guy sprawled out naked beside me, drooling into a starchy pillow. Nose too big. Hair too short. Skin too sallow. Whatever connection had bloomed within the shadows, burnt away to ashes come sunrise. Warmth chilled, and fulfilling moments never stretched long enough for me to fully embrace them.

Temporary.

But beneath the brassy light fixture overhead, I was able to finally get a good look at Reed as he pulled up from the frame and sauntered toward me.

Rippled, corded arms and flexing muscle. Long legs attached to heavy black boots. A tousle of dark hair, thicker on top and shorter on the sides—not brown, but not quite black either. Overgrown bangs hung over his eyes in careless waves, and he pushed them back as he approached. There was even a tattoo roped around his right bicep that hinted at a past I was curious to uncover. Something that ventured beyond self-defense training and domesticated Dad life.

Reed tossed his leather jacket on the bed and took a seat beside me against the couch, his hand fisted around a beer bottle. I folded my arms as our shoulders brushed, my golden-blonde hair contrasting the jet-black color of his T-shirt. His scent finally traveled over to me, making me think of fresh grass, open skies, and bonfires in the fall. A hint of amber, too.

It was just as seductive as I'd imagined.

"Are you still lost?" He looked my way, pinning me with the prettiest pale-green eyes I'd ever seen.

I dipped my gaze to his mouth to avoid getting consumed by those eyes, but that wasn't any safer. "Not anymore." My tongue poked out to wet my lips. "Why? Are you here to save me?"

Reed brought the nozzle of the beer to his lips and took a lazy pull. "Saving you would imply you're in peril," he noted, stretching out his infinitely long legs. "Are you?"

"Maybe." I shrugged, glancing at his legs. They were cased in distressed dark-gray jeans, tapered to fit properly, unlike the dumb baggy kind that most boys wore. "See the guy in the overalls over there?" I jutted my pinkie finger out at the open door, pointing toward the edge of the living room, while hanging on to the red Solo cup. "He came over to me earlier and said, 'You got a real pretty mouth' in a *Deliverance* voice, and then he gave me a wink like his eyeball was trying to make a break for it."

"Unsettling."

"I know. You got here just in time."

The truth was, I was in peril.

Father had locked me out of the house, making this party three blocks down the road sound more appealing than sleeping in the back-yard. The summer had been so blistering hot, we hardly had any grass. It was nothing but naked patches of dry straw. My twenty-something neighbor, Marnie, had mentioned the party earlier while speaking ten octaves above normal to her roommate on her front porch, and I'd made a mental note of the address belonging to Jay Jennings.

But I kept that truth from Reed.

He stared out the doorway to where Unsettling Overalls was doing a terrible job of pouring beer into his glass as liquid sloshed over the rim. "Good thing I came back when I did."

I blinked at him, curious. "Why did you?"

"Why did I come back?"

A nod.

Reed shifted beside me on the floor as our shoulders grazed, and then he gave me a look as undecipherable as his response. "Don't know."

"Same reason I stuck around, I guess."

"You're still wet." His gaze flitted down my body and met with my soaked-through denim skirt that touched mid-thigh.

"Hazardous side effect of sitting in a lake. I've made a mental note of it for future bouts of spontaneity." I flicked my finger in the air, mimicking a check mark. "Always bring a change of clothes."

A chuckle vibrated through him as he took another swig of beer. The way his lips parted to wrap around the nozzle was momentarily mesmerizing, so I took a weak sip from my own cup, leaving a berry kiss behind.

"I feel like we haven't been formally introduced," I said on a thinning breath.

Running a tongue over his top teeth, he skimmed my face. "No?" A slight frown wrinkled his browline. "I know your name, your hopes and dreams, and your favorite song. Not a terrible start."

"I have a lot of favorite songs." I glanced across the room at a giant speaker, as if trying to see the chords and notes pouring out of it. "This is one of them."

He followed my gaze. "Pearl Jam is good. This one's kind of depressing."

"You say depressing, I say expressive. It makes you feel…right here." I pressed a curled fist to the space between my ribs where my heart pounded with mournful beats. My eyelids fluttered closed as I savored the closing lyrics, then I sucked in a breath and twisted toward Reed to extend a hand. "I'm Halley. Like the comet."

He glanced at my hand with a confused expression. "I think we did this already."

"Nope. We never shook hands before."

"Is that how we make this introduction official?"

"Yes." I bit back a smile.

Nodding, he reached out and wrapped long, warm fingers around my palm. "Reed."

My airways narrowed to a stifling pinpoint. Palms clasped, grip soft yet soul-churning, I felt heat flare from the tips of my fingers and whiz up my arms, staining my neck in a pink flush. I didn't want to let go. A single touch was like a sunbeam neutralizing my blackened veins.

When we finally pulled apart, it felt like a heavy loss.

We both took a sip of our drinks at the same time, eye contact still holding. I racked my brain for more words, something to break the silence, something to keep him talking. To keep him interested in a broken, directionless girl like me. "Want to browse through Jay's CD collection?"

Reed hesitated, the beer bottle mid-journey to his lips as a spark of interest glowed in his gaze. "Sure."

"Okay."

A grin hiked up his lips. "Okay."

Chugging back the rest of the beer, Reed rose to his feet, then leaned over me as my curious eyes lifted to his.

He was so handsome.

Taller than I'd first noted when he'd been standing at the edge of the shoreline.

Even more staggering than he was five seconds ago.

"Come on, Comet." A hand extended toward me to help me off the floor. "You can tell me the rest of your favorite songs."

The name processed like a drain trying to swallow down the swampy lake water.

Comet.

Something happened to me.

Something devastating and beautiful unfurled inside my chest.

No one had ever given me a sweet nickname before. Father called me a brat. A waste of space. A disease, a low life, a worthless nobody. Even my mom never referred to me by my first name.

I wondered if maybe she'd forgotten it.

But Reed had just called me Comet, and that was exactly what it'd felt like as the name soared past his lips. A bright, cosmic phenomenon lighting up my insides and colliding with my heart.

I sucked in a breath, discarded my cup, and raised my hand to his.

Our palms locked.

Warm, tingly, transcendent.

Reed didn't realize it, but as I took his hand and he tugged me up from the ugly brown carpeting of Jay Jennings' bedroom floor, he took my whole life in his.

I felt it.

I was certain of it.

I stumbled on my clodhopper heels, to which he planted a firm hand to the center of my back to steady me. I had to force back the wince after Father had left me with painful stripes of slow-healing bruises from his belt.

"You good?" A frown creased his forehead when I stiffened at his touch.

"Great."

Eyeing me for a beat, he bobbed his chin, then dropped his hand before turning toward the shelving units crammed with CDs.

I followed, my focus aimed at his back.

The Soundgarden T-shirt was glued to his body like a sinful second skin, his biceps bulging and straining against the short sleeves. He clearly worked out to stay fit for his job, and I imagined him on his back, hauling a giant barbell overhead, every cord and vein dilated as he sweated through the movements.

I was in trouble.

Padding over to where he was standing, I watched as his fingers grazed over a collection of album spines.

"Tell me why you're here," he said. "At this party."

My cheeks heated as my father's twisted, snarling face flashed through my mind. *If you want to be a filthy whore, I'll treat you like one. You'll sleep in the shed tonight.*

I may have been filthy, but I wasn't a whore. I was dirty because my home life was a steaming pile of shit I couldn't scrub off my skin. I'd only been with a few guys, mostly as a way to try and siphon the poison out of my blood, but it never worked, only serving as a small comfort at the time. A short-lived purge. But my father had caught me making out with some guy in the driveway and banished me to the backyard for the night.

"You look like you went to a dark place," Reed noted off my delayed response.

I didn't *go* there.

I lived there.

"I was just bored." Shrugging away the gray cloud, I forced a smile. "It's Saturday night."

"You were sitting all alone in here."

"Maybe I was waiting for someone."

"Hmm." Eyes on the shelves, he made a humming sound. "Did you find him?"

"Verdict is still out, but I'm optimistic. Did you find your daughter?"

"Yeah. She's sleeping over at a friend's house."

I reached for a CD and plucked it out, glancing at the face. Garth Brooks. "Do you like country music like she does?"

Reed shook his head. "No."

"The optimism rises." A playful cadence stole my tone as I inched a step closer to him and pulled out another CD. "Collective Soul."

"They're good. I saw them in concert last year."

We continued to peruse the CD collection, both of us wiggling out handfuls and carrying them over to the queen-size bed. I took a seat beside him on the edge of the mattress as we sorted through our haul, commenting on the different bands and genres. Jay had everything from Mariah Carey to Metallica, and even some do-wop from the fifties and sixties.

I fingered an album by The Drifters and sing-songed in a floaty voice, "*Save the last dance for me...*"

Reed looked up, his eyes following the climb of my smile. "There's a really good cover of that song by Harry Nilsson."

"Oh, yeah?" My smile brightened even more. "Do you dance?"

"Aside from those cutesy daddy-daughter dances from a decade ago, no."

My mind spun with images of Reed and a little girl dancing in a gymnasium filled with balloon arches and a crooning Bette Midler, while his daughter danced on the toes of his big boots. "I love to dance. Movement is art. Motion is freeing." He stared at me, and I wondered if he was imagining our bodies in motion, swaying and bending in infinite ways. Clearing my throat, I tried to tamp down the tension hissing temptation into my ear. "Do you think Jay would notice if we borrowed one of his CDs?"

He glanced down at our pile and gave his head a slight shake. "He has enough."

I sifted through them, making a separate reject pile as our knees angled and touched.

"Which one?" Reed held up CD after CD, the covers glinting off the ceiling light. "Green Day?"

I made a face.

"That's a no." He chuckled, discarding it.

"Alanis Morisette?" I suggested.

He shook his head, his nose scrunching up. "Radiohead?"

"Oasis."

He grinned. "I'm kind of feeling Radiohead."

"I'm feeling Oasis." I knocked his knee with mine. Warmth trailed up my leg, my thigh, blooming with fireworks in the pit of my stomach.

Reed held up both CDs, eyes panning between *The Bends* by Radiohead and *Definitely Maybe* by Oasis.

I rubbed my lips together. "We could figure it out the old fashioned way."

"How's that?"

"Rock, paper, scissors."

He considered the proposal for a second before dimples popped on his cheeks and his eyes glittered. "All right."

Hands in position, we slammed our fists to our opposite palms twice before we both shot out two fingers on three, making scissors.

We tried again.

Scissors.

We tried again.

Scissors!

"Oh, my God." I laughed. "Stop that."

"I figured you'd switch it up by now."

"I was thinking the same thing."

"No more scissors. Let's try again."

One, two—

Scissors.

Still laughing, I tilted forward, my forehead brushing his shoulder and my hair splaying out like a golden waterfall down his inked upper arm. "Well, we suck at this."

As I lifted back up, I realized how close we were. Sitting on a bed in a dimly lit room. Music as our backdrop, unseen heat as our firelight.

I swallowed. Our thighs were smashed together as we sat on the mattress amid piles of CDs, our faces inches apart. The Foo Fighters played, a distant hum to parallel my revving pulse.

Our eyes caught along with my breath. I wondered for a heart-stopping moment if he would lean in and kiss me. I bet his lips were as soft as they looked. His hair, too. I wanted those lips on mine, his tongue in my mouth, his hair spilling between the cracks in my fingers.

Electricity sizzled as I fidgeted beside him, uncertain, but so goddamn sure. I considered how late Father would be working tonight and if he'd notice I was gone. If he did, I'd be punished. But the consequences seemed worth it when Reed's eyes panned to my parted lips, gleaming with mystery, intrigue, and living. God, how I wanted to live. True living *was* steeped in risk and adventure in *spite* of the consequences. Ten lashes to my mangled back felt worth it as Reed's gaze slowly drifted back up and snagged with mine.

His Adam's apple rolled in his throat, his irises flickering in the lowlight, almost like they were trying to brighten every shadow inside me.

He inched forward.

Leaned in.

I inhaled sharply. "Is this why you came back?" Our mouths hovered a millimeter apart, his warm breath coasting over my lipstick stain in shaky bursts. "For a kiss?"

Lifting his hand, he grazed the back of his knuckles up my jaw to my cheekbone. "I was curious."

"I was waiting."

A smile twitched as he moved in.

Our lips touched. Just barely. But the air left me like I'd toppled off a twenty-foot cliff and landed on my back.

Reed sighed, his other hand lightly sliding up my leg, underneath the hem of my damp skirt, and skimming along my inner thigh.

My legs parted on pure instinct.

He reacted to the silent invitation, his eyelids fluttering as the pressure on my thigh tightened, and he squeezed me, just an inch below my underwear.

A whimper left me, colliding with his sharp intake of breath, and then his tongue poked out to taste my full bottom lip. That was all it took. I shivered, shattered, and leaned all the way in until our lips crashed together and his tongue filled my mouth.

Remnants of wintergreen chewing gum and a hint of beer.

One kiss, and I was already addicted to the taste of him.

I gripped his T-shirt, vibrating with need. This felt different. It wasn't an awkward, stumbling kiss with a high school boy that left me empty and questioning everything. I questioned nothing. All I did was savor as he memorized my mouth with his skilled tongue, angling and deepening.

Heady moans tangled as Reed pushed me backward on the bed and collapsed over me, one hand cupping my cheek and the other still squeezing my thigh.

I wanted more.

As our tongues thrashed and tasted, I tugged at the hand hidden under my skirt until his fingers flew all the way up my thigh and roughly cupped the space between my legs.

He groaned, rough and virile.

Holy shit.

I arched with a whimper as he stroked the fabric of my underwear that was soaked with lake water and desire. As our tongues drove deeper, I reached down and found his erection. Steely, huge. Straining against denim. He broke away from my mouth to let out a strangled sound and nicked his teeth along my throat.

It was the only bruise I'd ever beg for.

"I don't do this." He ground against my palm as I squeezed him through his jeans. "I'm not that guy."

My back bowed off the bed as his fingers stroked me, faster, with more pressure. "I want you to be that guy."

He dragged his tongue up the side of my neck and fumbled with the elastic of my underwear until two fingers snuck inside and sank into my flesh. *"Fuck."*

"Reed..." I was boneless, gasping, a ragdoll beneath him. "Please."

His fist was in my hair, fingers pumping, his tongue lashing against mine while we moved and writhed and moaned, and that was when Jay Jennings stumbled into the room with a woman on his arm.

We both shot up, my cheeks flushed, blood pumping hot with unresolved lust.

The door had been wide open, people just a few feet away.

Oh, God.

"What are you fuckers doing in here?" Jay slurred good-naturedly, his arm slung around the woman's waist. "Buddy, this chick looks too young for you."

We stood from the bed, the tension severed. My face burned as I inched my skirt back down and rearranged my T-shirt that was halfway up my torso.

Reed blew out a breath, stabbing a hand through his hair. "Sorry."

"You're welcome to fuck on my bed." He winked. "After I'm done with it."

"We were just leaving," I muttered, slipping back into my heels.

Jay's attention trailed over to me, his gaze sweeping up and down my body with approval. "No need. I like an audience."

The nameless woman swatted him on the arm. "Don't be gross."

Reed placed his hand on my lower back. This time, I hid my flinch and bit back the hiss.

"C'mon." He dropped his hand and walked ahead.

Jay waggled his eyebrows at me, ogling my legs as I swept past him with a quick apology. And as Reed came to a halt halfway down the hall, I almost slammed into him as I reached for the wall to maintain my balance.

He spun around to face me.

We were an inch apart. He towered over me by half a foot, his proximity wrapping me up in a tight hug. My heartbeats jackknifed, the fever between us far from snuffed out.

"Did you want to get out of here?" he asked, low and dark. "Go back to my place."

The invitation shot tiny firecrackers between my ribs. Between my legs.

Pop, pop, pop.

Explosions, colors, and shimmery heat.

Instinct had me clenching my thighs, my mind reeling with implication. With images of continuing what we'd started in his warm bed, tangled in sweat-slick sheets.

"Yes," I said on a quick breath. No hesitation.

Reed's eyes were glazed and heated as his focus dipped to my thoroughly kissed lips. He swallowed. "Let me grab my jacket. I'll meet you in the living room."

"Okay."

It was a shame he had to grab his jacket.

I think a part of me would never understand why he'd brought a jacket in the first place, considering it was the dead of summer in northern Illinois and even nightfall came with eighty-degree temperatures.

But he just had to grab the damn jacket.

And the moment he stalked back over to me waiting for him in the center of the living room with a wildly racing heart, everything imploded in my face.

"Halley Foster? What the hell are you doing here?" barked a pitchy, shrill voice. "You're only seventeen years old. Christ, honey. Your daddy's gonna blow a gasket if he hears you were here."

Marnie LaRue...*my neighbor.*

Time froze.

My chest seized, heart buckled.

A slow-motion haze swirled around me as I tilted my head and found Reed's eyes as he stood at the base of the hallway.

He was staring at me.

Stopped dead in his tracks, his leather jacket slung over one shoulder and the Oasis CD gripped tightly in his opposite hand.

For a split second, he looked expressionless.

Numb.

Processing.

And then a flicker of something like grave disappointment settled in his gaze. Maybe even a dash of betrayal. He went ashen, almost sickly-looking.

I'd lied to him.

He knew I'd lied to him.

He'd been a heartbeat away from taking home a seventeen-year-old girl. A girl who was probably his *daughter's* age.

I stood there, a few feet away from Reed, Marnie's tirade battering the wall I'd thrown up around me to keep everything out but him. Her words were a fog. Mindless drivel. Attention fixed on the man across the room, I mouthed, "I'm sorry," my shoulders slackening with defeat and heartache.

Reed's dark eyebrows furrowed as he scrubbed a hand through his hair, his throat bobbing while our eyes continued to hold.

Then, jaw ticking, he dropped his gaze, slowly turned, and disappeared out through the front door, slamming it behind him.

I flinched.

He'd left without a backward glance.

Without a goodbye.

I stood rooted in place, even though every part of me wanted to run after him, apologize, and beg him to wait for me.

After all...

I would only be getting older.

CHAPTER 3

Halley

December, 1995

I TUGGED the hat over my ears and zipped my winter coat all the way up to my chin as I raced through the parking lot, dodging ice patches and hurried shoppers.

I hated Christmas Eve.

It was never the warm, magical snow globe of wintry dreams that most people associated with the holiday. Christmas was nothing but a reminder of everything I lacked. Everything I'd never experience.

But this year, I wanted to change that.

I was desperate to sprinkle a little magic into my life.

Armed with a generous tip from my animal shelter supervisor, I kept my head down as I veered toward the grocery store entrance, hoping to gather enough ingredients for a feast with the fifty-dollar bill crumpled in my coat pocket.

Tara had invited me over for dinner tonight, and the notion was appealing. I'd met her in the springtime at a nearby park that I often visited to clear my mind and escape the violence between my four walls. She lived in my neighborhood and went to my school but was one year behind me. A junior to my senior.

I'd spent a lot of the past week at her house catching up on late homework assignments while we gossiped about the winter break adventures I'd never be allowed to fully enjoy.

I smiled anyway.

It was hard not to smile when I was at Tara's house. Her mom smelled like spiced cake and her golden retriever never left my side, making me feel like I was part of the family.

Like I was a part of something, period.

In the living room, their Christmas tree glittered with multicolored bulbs and tinsel, while hand-wrapped gifts were stacked underneath the pine-fresh needles.

It was a wonderland; a home life I craved.

But I was determined to turn my own home life into something more than drunken outbursts, belt lashings, and cruel words. Father had smacked me hard enough to rattle my teeth after I'd gotten home late from Tara's house the other night. Now a bruise painted my jaw in hues of violet and blue, and I'd had to piece together a lie to tell people when they gasped at the colors on my face.

I fell down the stairs.

We didn't even have stairs, but what else could I say?

A cold gust of wind brought me back to the parking lot. Lost in my dreary thoughts, my eyes on the pavement, I yelped when I accidentally collided with a hard body. "Oh, sorry, I—"

My eyes lifted.

My mouth snapped shut.

A very familiar man stood before me in a leather jacket and a knit cap that shielded waves of dark hair I never got to sweep my fingers through.

His lips parted, a breath of recognition hitting the air in a plume of white. Blinking a few times, he swallowed. "Hey. You're—"

"Halley," I provided, because there was probably no way he remembered my name like I remembered his. Then I waited for the residual anger to crease his brows and shadow his eyes.

But all he did was nod once as snowflakes splashed across his navy hat. "Like the comet."

My heart jumped, lashes fluttering.

It was nine degrees, but my skin sizzled with telltale heat as I pressed my lips together in an attempt to flatten the smile. "Reed."

Reed, the man with green eyes and golden words.

Reed, the man I'd been dangerously close to going home with six months ago.

Reed.

The man I'd lied to.

I was confident he hated me, and he had every right to. I'd tricked him. I'd been so desperate for comfort, for connection, for more of his tender looks and touches, that I hadn't cared about the consequences. Not even a little. I was selfish, and now he was wholeheartedly aware of that.

"Yeah." He stared at me, bouncing on the heels of his boots, a reminder that the temperature was in the single digits. Popping his thumb toward the store entrance, he pivoted around and started walking. "Last minute holiday shopping?"

I took the question as an invitation to follow.

"Sort of." Keeping pace on his right, I failed to give him all the details of my spontaneous Christmas Eve grocery store stop. "You?"

"Same."

"I'm grabbing some ingredients to cook dinner tonight."

"Cutting it close."

I shrugged and peered down at my raw-bitten cuticles as we passed by a weathered-looking Santa Claus ringing a copper bell.

Reed shoved a hand in his pocket and plucked out a twenty-dollar bill, popping it in the man's bucket.

Santa gave us prayer hands, his eyes alight with gratitude. "God bless you."

As we stepped through the entry doors, I glanced at Reed, my bottom lip caught between my teeth. "That was nice of you."

"It was decent," he said, grabbing a shopping cart. "Bare minimum, we should all strive to be decent, don't you think?"

I wasn't sure if his comment was a thinly veiled reference to my awful lie, but because his eyes remained soft under the fluorescent store lights, I didn't stew in the potential implication.

Then I cursed those bright lights when Reed's focus zeroed in on my bruise.

"Whoa. What the hell happened to you?"

His hand lifted but faltered halfway to my face. He tucked his fingers in and slowly dropped his hand, the contact seemingly too inti-mate for this spontaneous grocery store meeting with a teenager who'd betrayed him.

I swallowed hard, gritty shards of shame scraping the back of my throat. "I fell down the stairs. Clumsy."

He frowned. "You sure?"

"Hard to forget face-planting at the bottom of a staircase." Touching two fingertips to the ugly canvas of colors, I wished I could erase the evidence with one quick brushstroke. "You saw those clunky heels I wear. They're a death trap."

Reed ran his tongue along his upper lip, studying me. Analyzing another lie.

I stared at his tongue, and he stared at my tarnished face.

Someone bumped into me, and I stumbled forward against Reed, catching myself by latching onto his bicep.

The guy mumbled gruffly, "Sorry. Need a cart."

Reed placed his hand on the small of my back to steady me, and I soaked up his warm touch like it was the sun on my skin after a yearlong winter. Then we both moved away from the collection of carts as he finally lowered his hand.

I hovered beside him, clearing my throat and pulling off my hat to smooth down my hair.

His eyes flicked to the golden tresses spilling over my shoulders before he dipped his attention away and hunched over the cart, his fore-arms on the handlebar.

He started walking.

I reached for my own cart and pushed it in the opposite direction, an awkward goodbye teasing my tongue.

But before I could say anything, he gestured toward the produce aisle with a quick head-nod. "We can shop together."

The invitation froze me. I hesitated for a beat before my legs found their courage and carried me toward him. My eyes lingered on the back of his leather coat as he pushed forward, swerving between frenzied shoppers tossing last minute items into their carts. I wasn't sure what to say. My internal thoughts were a web of apologies, conversation starters, and more apologies.

I went with something dumb. "Do you like pierogies?"

Reed glanced at me over his shoulder as I attempted to maneuver my cart to his right side. "Almost as much as peanut butter."

Apparently, he recalled my penchant for random food-inspired questions.

"I love them. My mother was Polish, so when I was a little kid, my Nana would make pierogies every Christmas Eve." I blinked, catching myself. "I mean, she's still Polish. That doesn't ever go away."

I was rambling and we both knew it.

"Anyway...she died, so it's been a while since I've had pierogies." My cheeks puffed with a full breath. "Nana died. Not my mother."

I was a mess.

Cheeks heating, I clenched my teeth to keep my mouth from opening again. I should cut my losses, apologize to him, and scram.

Reed swung his cart toward the frozen food aisle. "Let's grab pierogies. Then you can help me pick out a gift," he said. "It's for a girl. I already got her a purse, but I felt like I needed something else...maybe a gift card?"

All I heard was *girl*.

My heart wilted pathetically. "Okay, sure. That would be cool."

It wasn't cool.

It felt like a rusty nail had been hammered through my stupid, infatuated heart, which was beyond delusional. I was seventeen years old and he was thirty-four, and just because we shared one night together at Jay Jennings' lake house, didn't mean he was waiting around for me, checking off the days on his calendar until I became old enough to pursue in good conscience.

Refusing to let him see what a ridiculous teenager I was, I held my head high and pretended to be immune. "What does she like?"

He scratched his head as we stared at a row of fog-laden freezer doors, eyeing the Tombstone pizzas and TV dinners. "She really likes her dog."

"I love dogs." It was pointless to say—this wasn't about me. "You could get her one of those photo-frame ornaments shaped like a dog, and she could put his picture inside."

"That's a good idea." Reed nodded as he grabbed one of the door handles and pulled it open, reaching for a few boxes of frozen pierogies. "How are these?"

I smiled. "Not homemade like Nana's, but I can improvise."

He popped the boxes in my cart and we ventured down more aisles. I tossed in an array of items—instant mashed potatoes, canned green beans, jellied cranberries, and a few sticks of butter.

Reed's cart was still empty.

"How's your job going?" I asked, watching as he reached for a box of Rice Krispies with holiday colors, thought about it, then put it back.

"Grueling. Rewarding."

"Self-defense training, right?"

"Yeah." He glanced at me like he was surprised I remembered. "A past client from my east-coast location sent me a letter the other day, telling me I saved his life with training. It was a great feeling."

"Wow." My chest was heavy with warmth. Saving lives was no small feat; I didn't even know how to save my own. "I'm sure you've made a big difference in the world."

A smile twitched on his mouth. "What about you? Have you been capturing any blips lately?"

Every jaded piece of me shimmered at the question because I knew he'd been paying attention to my words that night. My mess of hopes and dreams. "Just in here." I tapped my temple. "But I'm volunteering at a local animal shelter for the holidays. We did a photoshoot with the dogs and cats up for adoption with one of those disposable cameras. I dressed up like Rudoph—which was basically just a headband made of antlers and a red nose—but they turned out great."

We headed out of the cereal aisle, but I made a last-minute decision and snagged the box of Rice Krispies, tossing it in my cart before we moved to the next aisle.

"Rudolph, huh?" He glanced at me, his eyes trailing over my face like he was imagining me with reindeer ears and a red nose. "Cute."

I relished in the sentiment, my pinkening ears hidden by my hair. "It was."

As we finished shopping and inched closer to the checkout lines, my chest strained with trapped emotion. I wanted to give him the apology he deserved, even though he didn't seem to be holding a lifelong grudge. Which was strange. I probably would have.

I reined in my nerves and took in a breath. "You know...I'm really sorry about that night at the party," I blurted out, refusing to look at him.

His head tilted toward me in my periphery while I chewed on the inner lining of my cheek. "I didn't mean to lead you on. It was stupid and in poor taste. I was just lonely and lost, and I thought you'd stop talking to me if I told you my real age. And...well, I liked talking to you."

Silence festered.

It spanned so many seconds, I wondered if I should ditch my cart by the gift-wrap display and make a clean break while I still had a fragment of my dignity intact.

Finally, he spoke. "I liked talking to you, too, Halley."

My face was hot, my cheeks as rosy as jolly ol' St. Nick's.

Did he like kissing me?

Touching me?

I heaved in a shaky breath, the sound of my name on his tongue sprinkling goosebumps all over my skin. "It wasn't right. I lied to you. And I'm really sorry—"

"Hear that?"

I blinked, his question cutting my words short as I frowned, confusion settling in. "Hear what?"

A smile hinted as he leaned forward on the cart with both leather-clad arms and glanced up at the ceiling. "Listen."

The clamoring of squeaky carts, busy shoppers, and checkout beeping drowned out as I focused on whatever it was he wanted me to hear.

And then my belly pitched, a sharp breath leaving me.

A song filtered into my ears.

Oasis.

I looked at him, looking at me, while he awaited my reaction. I couldn't contain the genuine smile I sent him, and it only brightened his. "*Wonderwall*," I whispered.

It was their newest smash single.

I'd be lying if I said I didn't crank up the volume dial every time the first chords rang out through my boombox.

I'd also be lying if I said I didn't think of him every time it played.

"You like this one?" he wondered.

"Yes. It's my favorite."

He nodded, then pushed his cart forward.

We passed by glittering red-and-green kiosks as we surveyed the long checkout lines and the song continued to play from the store's speaker system. I felt on top of the world in that moment. Shopping alongside Reed on a blustery Christmas Eve, my favorite song playing overhead, and my cart filled with a holiday feast of pierogies and tasty sides I couldn't wait to cook for me and Mom.

But the bubble burst when my eyes landed on a display of colorful Beanie Babies.

It burst because Reed's cart was still empty.

I stopped in front of the stand and pointed at the plush toys. "You should get her one."

Reed glanced to the right. "You think?"

"Yes. She'd love it." I gestured at a little tan puppy with floppy chocolate ears. "Get her that one. He's adorable."

He peered over at me, his lips twitching, before he reached over and snatched the Beanie Baby off the shelf. Peeling open the heart-shaped attachment, he read aloud, "Bones."

"Bones is a keeper."

"Bones will do." He sent a dimple-steeped grin my way and plopped the animal atop the child seat of the cart. "Thanks."

"Sure."

My heart sank further as we found a line, my gaze panning to the stuffed toy.

The song was over.

Reed would be a distant memory in just a few more minutes.

As we creeped up the line and approached the counter, Reed stepped in front of me. "Let me pay for those."

I barreled forward. "No way. I got it."

I wasn't *actually* sure if I had it, with the amount of items I'd panic-grabbed off the shelves, but I couldn't allow him to pay.

"It's Christmas."

"And I'm sure you have plenty of friends and family you can spend your hard-earned money on." My voice cracked. "And your girl, of course."

I wasn't a friend or a family member, and I certainly wasn't his *girl*. I was just the googly-eyed, barely-legal girl who'd lied to him and spoiled his evening six months ago.

Reed sighed as the cashier slid item after item over the scanner and the total escalated. "Guess we'll settle it the old fashioned way."

Chewing on my fingernail, my gaze wheeled to his. "How so?"

"Rock, paper, scissors."

My eyes lit up as I fought back a smile. "Okay."

"Okay."

Our hands went into position and I tried to think it through.

One, two—

I was about to make a fist for rock, thinking he'd do scissors, but then I second-guessed it at the last minute, wondering if he was thinking the same thing.

I did paper.

He did rock.

I was right.

"A plot twist." I covered his fist with my flat palm while trying to ignore the feel of his warm skin against mine. "I win."

"I suppose fair is fair."

I glanced at the total as it continued to rise, my insides twisting with anxiety. Thankfully, the universe spared me the humiliation of coming up short and the number froze at $47.22. I let out a relieved breath and handed the cashier my wrinkled fifty-dollar bill as another clerk bagged the items.

Reed paid for Bones and followed me out of the store after we discarded our carts.

Freezing-cold air snapped into my lungs as fat snowflakes floated from a dark sky. I stopped short of the crosswalk and felt Reed brush up along my puffy coat. My chin lifted, our eyes catching for a beat that felt far too long yet not nearly long enough. Sparks swirled between us until the coat started to suffocate me. It was nine degrees and I was sweating.

Then I remembered something.

"Oh! I got you this." Linking the shopping bags around my wrist, I reached inside one of them and pulled out the cereal box. "Here. I saw you eyeing it."

He stared at the box with a furrowed brow, then flicked his gaze up to my face. "You didn't have to do that."

I shrugged, pulling my lips into a small smile. "I wanted to."

"Thanks." The word fell out as a whisper as he tentatively took the box and slipped it in his plastic bag. "I appreciate it."

I studied him one last time, drinking in his stubbled jaw, tufts of dark hair poking out from underneath the navy cap, and his light, light eyes, sparkling green and grateful.

Nodding, I turned away with a small wave and pretended it was the cold that was clogging my airways and not the knot of sadness at the thought of never seeing him again.

I didn't make it very far when his voice reached my ears.

"Halley," he called out as I heaved my three grocery bags through the parking lot, an icy wind whipping me in the face.

I turned toward him.

I stared at him standing there in his leather jacket and wool hat, holding his singular bag filled with a box of holiday-themed Rice Krispies and a Beanie Baby meant for a girl who wasn't me.

He smiled before stepping backward and retreating. "Merry Christmas."

I couldn't get a response out before he disappeared into the cold, black night.

But I still said it, hoping, somehow, he could hear me.

"Merry Christmas, Reed."

"Mom." I nudged her shoulder with my palm, and she didn't even flinch. "Mom, wake up."

It was only seven o'clock, but it wasn't out of the ordinary for her to be passed out before suppertime. I sighed, glancing around the dark room, the windows blacked out with ratty quilts attached to curtain rods with plastic bag clips. Her limp, coarse hair fanned out across a once-white pillow that was now the color of my cousin Lizzy when she was born with jaundice last summer.

It was silly to assume Mom would put me first on Christmas Eve. I was her daughter, sure, but the empty bottle of gin lying beside her was far more precious than the child she birthed and promised to protect. I should've known better. Holidays, jingle bells, and family traditions would always be secondary to these drunken stupors.

Sometimes I was jealous that Mom was able to float away from it all so easily. I bet she spent most of her life in a dreamworld, while I was forced to live in this one.

I tried one more time to wake her from the alcohol coma. "Mom," I said, my voice loudening over the hum of a rusted pedestal fan in the corner of the cluttered room. "Mom, please..." The words cracked as tears welled in my eyes. "It's Christmas."

That didn't matter.

I don't matter.

Wholly defeated, I finally withdrew from her bedside, sparing my mother a final glance. She was a shadowy lump underneath the frayed, dirty blankets, and a phlegmy snore slipped from her throat, telling me the alcohol hadn't stolen her away for good.

I slipped from the room and shut the door. The tiny ranch house smelled of pine, thanks to the single candle I'd found in one of the cabinets, the one I'd lit with a Zippo lighter in hopes of brightening my spirits and luring Mom into the kitchen.

No such luck.

As I padded over to the counter in my fuzzy socks patterned in frogs wearing Santa hats, I blew out the candle, tidied my mess of dirty dishes and empty wrappers, and retreated down the hallway to my bedroom with a plate of pierogies. They glistened with butter under the ceiling light as I sat cross-legged on my bed and swiped away tears.

Pink walls lined with posters and magazine clippings were my only company on what was supposed to be the most magical night of the year. Father wasn't home yet, and I supposed if anything good came from tonight, it was that I might avoid a berating or a lashing.

I turned my radio on to a holiday station and let Bing Crosby serenade my sorrows.

The food was good.

My heart was lonely.

I imagined Tara and her mom sitting in front of the fireplace, sipping hot cocoa and telling tales of Christmases past.

I pictured Reed and his girlfriend opening gifts by the tree as the nameless woman clutched Bones to her chest with joyful tears in her eyes.

I wished the cold night would only go as far as my ice-glazed window pane, but winter always had a way of sneaking through the cracks and burrowing in my bones. It was a permanent chill. One I'd never warm to, no matter how many layers I tried to add.

When I finished my one-person supper, I changed into snowman-themed pajamas and went to hang my coat that I'd tossed on the floor. I shoved my hand in one of the pockets to grab the spare change, then carried it over to my bedside table for safekeeping.

And when I glanced down, I froze.

I did a double-take.

My heart constricted, pulse jolting as I stared at the extra money mixed in with the crumpled dollar bills and coins. Shock and awe coursed through me.

No way.

With a deep ache in my chest, I crawled into bed that night, my warm, wet tears sticking to my cheeks.

And when Christmas morning dawned, I found myself still clutching the one-hundred dollar bill Reed had snuck inside my pocket; a precious gift I would never forget.

It was the only gift I received that Christmas.

CHAPTER 4

Halley

January, 1996

"YOU'RE A LIAR." Saliva dangled from my father's chin as he towered over me, his eyes glowing with menace. They were dark brown, but with the way his pupils swallowed his irises, they looked black. "I may have raised a whore, but I refuse to raise a liar. Who were you with?"

I inched down my crop top while simultaneously trying to cover the hickey with my hair. "Nobody," I lied. "I was working late at the shelter."

The latter part was true.

I was working late at the shelter, making out with Jesse the kennel attendant in the women's bathroom. He was ten years older than me and an aggressive kisser. If I'd closed my eyes long enough and zoned out, I could have almost pretended that his lips belonged to a mid-thirties single dad who smelled like ivy leaves and sandalwood.

"You smell like cheap cologne. You were whoring around with some boy," Father roared, getting right in my face. "Tell me the truth."

I didn't flinch, didn't blink, as I locked eyes with my disgusting sperm donor who'd had the audacity to bring me into a world so ruthless and soul-draining.

I was numb.

Deadened by dysfunction and never-ending abuse. I wanted to run away, disappear, jump off a goddamn bridge and let the water have its way with me.

Surely, it'd be more humane than him.

Folding my arms beneath my breasts, I cocked my head to the side and glared. "That is the truth, *Dad*."

His wild eyes widened at my sass.

And then he walloped me with the force of a hurricane. The blow sent me sprawling backward, crashing against the wall. Pain shot through my body, a searing reminder of the chaos that had become my life. A reminder that I wasn't quite as dead inside as I'd thought.

I fought to steady myself, staring up at him through tear-blurred vision. His anger loomed like a storm, unpredictable and destructive. The room felt smaller, suffocating, and the scent of alcohol on his breath hung in the air like a bitter aftertaste.

I was being punished for a kiss.

For *affection*—something that I'd never once gotten from my father and hadn't felt from my mother in years.

"You think lying to me is acceptable?"

"None of this is acceptable," I managed to say, my voice trembling but resolute. The truth was my only ally.

He scowled at me, searching for a sign of weakness, but defiance clung to my every word. "You enjoy toying with me, don't you?" He sneered. "You're a disgusting disgrace, just like your mother."

"Maybe I am." The metallic tang of blood sluiced across my tongue. "You raised me on a diet of beatings and cruelty. If I'm anything like her, it's because that's the only example I had. Congratulations."

His fists clenched and his face contorted with a mix of anger and frustration. He was a monsoon, and I was the unfortunate soul caught in its path. A swollen beer belly heaved with the weight of his wrath, and muscles clenched beneath his sleeveless white tank stained with grease.

And then, with a new surge of fury, he raised his hand again.

I should have been ready for it.

But nobody could ever properly prepare for annihilation. Human beings were hard-wired to triumph and rise above, no matter what.

Father yanked me forward by the front of my crop top, then back-handed me so hard, my feet lifted off the floor and I flew backward, straight into the glass coffee table.

I screamed.

I wailed with raw, bone-crumbling *pain*.

My skin was pierced with jagged shards, my arm taking the brunt of the fall and shattering on impact. I wanted to run away, find a tree to curl up underneath, and die, just like an old dog savoring its last breath. But as I rolled across the strewn glass and begged my legs for steadiness, I knew I had a safe place to go. One last chance at pulling myself from these ashes I was constantly choking on.

Gritting my teeth through the pain, I staggered to my feet and inhaled a fractured breath. Something inside of me hardened with resolve. I couldn't let this be the end.

With determination fueling my steps, I stumbled toward the faint glow of the front door, my battered body yearning for the only home I knew could offer refuge.

"Where're you going?" Father demanded, stalking me. "Get back here!"

I ran.

I flung myself at the front door and slipped out into the blizzardy January evening, cradling my broken arm and broken heart. Lamplight ushered me forward. The tempting draw of safety and warmth possessed my dizzy steps. My father's final hollers pushed me the rest of the way down the sidewalk, and I didn't look back. He didn't follow me because he didn't care enough to.

And for that I was eternally thankful.

Minutes later, I found myself shivering and wrecked on Tara's doorstep, my tears turning to fragile icicles on my cheekbones.

I rang their doorbell.

Ladybug barked.

I collapsed the moment the door swung open, revealing my wide-eyed, gasping best friend.

"Mom!" Tara screamed over her shoulder before yanking open the screen door and wrapping her arms around me. "God, what the hell happened?"

I cushioned my splintered arm with the other as blood dribbled into my eyes. "He...hit me..."

"Shit, Hals." Tara gaped with disbelief.

As I sobbed against her fuzzy blue sweater, snot bubbles and blood oozed through the fabric. I was mortified. Tara and her mom didn't deserve this. They didn't need the extra burden of me and my abusive home life landing on their doorstep.

And now Tara's fuzzy sweater was ruined.

"Oh, my God."

Sniffling, I lifted my head and my eyes met with Ms. Stephens' horrified gaze.

"Halley...what...?" She shook her head back and forth, her long brown hair fluttering in the cold wind. "Get in the car. I'm taking you to the hospital."

"No," I croaked. "I'm fine. I'll be fine."

I wasn't fine.

My arm was broken. It probably needed pins to keep the bones in place.

Pain sliced up my forearm, all the way to my eyes, and I saw stars. My body trembled and swayed as Tara held me to her chest.

"Mom is right." She stroked back my blood-crusted hair. "You need a doctor. And you'll be staying with us for a while." Glancing up at her mother, she confirmed, "Right, Mom?"

Ms. Stephens swallowed. "Did your father do this to you?"

I couldn't hold back the lie any longer. I was confident they'd already suspected as much, thanks to all my mysterious bruises. "Yes. He's a monster and I never want to go back there."

Her expression hardened. "That son of a bitch. I'm calling the police."

"No, please. He'll take it out on me." Panic inched its way through me, lacing my plea. If the cops got involved, my father would come for me. He'd find me and end it, once and for all.

I wasn't *actually* ready to die. Hope still lingered.

"Halley, listen to me." Tara's mother fell to her knees beside me and placed a loving hand on my shoulder. "I'm getting you out of there. I'm not letting you step foot inside that house again if I have any say in the matter. Look at what he's done to you, sweetie."

There were tears in her eyes.

And an awful, twisted part of me relished the sight of them.

She cares.

She cared about me, and that was a good feeling. Almost good enough to overpower the slices of pain shooting through my shipwrecked body.

I let them take me to the hospital.

I didn't need pins, but I did get a hot-pink cast that Tara quickly signed with her name ringed in doodle hearts.

My mother dragged herself into the hospital room a few hours later, her face gaunt and chalklike and her eyes gleaming with alcohol glaze. She'd given the receptionist my medical card then landed at my bedside, unable to make direct eye contact.

"Mom." My eyes begged for her to see me. To really *see* me.

I loved her so much.

Despite neglecting me and acting as a stagnant bystander to Father's violent attacks, I still loved her. She was my mother. And she wasn't evil like him; she just *wasn't*. She was broken, too. Frozen and dangling between being brave and going unseen. He was vile to her, and I never understood why she stayed with him.

"I spoke with Whitney Stephens." Mom scratched the back of her hand, where a dark scab crusted over her knuckles. "I think it'd be best if you stayed with her for a little while. You're about to turn eighteen, after all."

Frowning, I blinked at my mother, taking in her delicate nose, sunken-in cheeks, and limp blonde hair, a shade lighter than mine. "You want me to live with them?"

"I said for a little while. You'll be safer."

"You…" A wall of tears blanketed my eyes, and I tried to swipe them away with my cast. "You're getting rid of me."

"Don't be dramatic," she scolded, her focus aimed at the itchy white sheets. "I'm trying to protect you. Your father has a temper. This is for your own good."

"But we could go somewhere. Together. You and me. It doesn't have to be this way. Leave him. Let's start over again."

Once upon a time, we'd been close. I still clung to fading memories of gliding on a swing at the playground, watching my legs stretch and bend as warm summer air kissed my face and my mother pushed me from behind. I was five or six, and she was my whole world. I was hers, too. We'd take walks, go grocery shopping, bake cookies, and read storybooks until the stars became my nightlight and guided me toward a peaceful sleep.

Those were the days when clouds were pillowy shapes in the sky that I'd love to count and name. Colors stood out through the monochrome swirl. Birds chirped and sang sweet songs, while innocence and fairy tales overpowered all the evil things in the world.

Yeah.

We had a few good years together before Mom took my father back and chose him over me. Chose booze over me. Chose everything over me.

Choose me, my eyes pleaded with her. *Please, please, pick me.*

She shook her head.

Just one little headshake and my world crumbled.

The truth was as obvious as the giant pink piece of plaster weighing down my left arm: she didn't want me anymore. Didn't love me enough. Had no desire to fight for me.

I let the tears fall.

"I'll come visit you some time."

That was all she said before the chair legs squeaked along linoleum and she stood to wobbly feet, disappearing through the curtain.

Mom hadn't come to visit me.

Not once.

"My dad is coming over for dinner next week."

At least Tara had parents who gave a shit.

I sent her a weary smile in the mirror as we got ready for school. Sun seeped in through the window while music played from a neon-pink boombox covered in years-old stickers.

Tara chomped on a piece of bubblegum, studying her reflection in the glass. "Dad's really cool. You'll like him."

She gathered her wavy chestnut hair into a high ponytail and secured it into place with a blue scrunchie. Tara loved the color blue. Her bedroom walls were blue, her wardrobe was eighty-percent blue, and her fingernails were blue as she picked at the chipped polish.

I hadn't met her father yet. Her parents weren't together anymore.

To be fair, Tara and I had only become close this past year when I was at the park, and her dog, Ladybug, escaped her leash and came barreling toward the picnic bench where I'd been aimlessly doodling. I'd seen Tara in the hallways at school, but I was more of a loner. She was fun and popular and always had a beaming smile, while my smile was halfhearted, at best. I stayed in the shadows, nursing my wounds and hiding my bruises from teachers and classmates.

But Tara was bright.

Luckily, Ladybug had seen something worthy in me and dropped right onto my sandals for a belly rub on an early-spring day, claiming me as her new best friend.

Five minutes later, Tara had claimed me, too.

I used my mobile hand to apply a layer of berry balm to my lips as I glanced over at Tara. "Are you and your dad close?"

"Yeah, I guess." Her eyes flickered with something I couldn't pinpoint. Melancholy, maybe. "It was rocky for a bit, but we're kind of getting to know each other again. He works a lot and was out of town for a while. But as far as dads go, he's one of the good ones."

I must've winced, because Tara immediately backpedaled.

"Shit. Sorry."

"It's fine." Eager to change the subject, I capped the lip balm with my teeth. "So, are you still seeing Rob?"

She let out a dramatic sigh as she flopped backward on her baby-blue bedcovers. "Maybe. Sort of." She shrugged. "I dunno."

"What does that mean?"

"It means Josh Cicero asked me to the winter fling and I'm leaving my options open."

My brows winged up. "No way."

"Way. What about you? Rumor has it, you might be getting an invitation from Eric Soloman."

Her eyebrows waggled, while mine collapsed into a frown.

"Okay, okay." She giggled. "He's no *Prince* Eric, but he's no sea urchin either. You should think about it."

"Think about trying to dance in a packed gymnasium with my mammoth robo-arm clocking people in the face? Sounds like a nightmare."

Tara covered her burst of laughter with both hands before peeking at me between her fingers. "That would be classic. I vote yes."

I didn't want to go to the winter fling.

I was only two weeks into wearing this eyesore on my arm, and the doctor said I'd likely be wearing it for *at least* another four weeks, and that was if the bone healed properly. The dance was in three weeks. Besides, the only person I wanted to go with was well-past high school age and had probably long since forgotten about the girl in the Copper-glow Berry lipstick with cartoon hearts in her eyes, lies on her tongue, and *Wonderwall* flowing through her veins.

I sighed as Ladybug came skipping into the room wearing her red-and-black collar decorated in ladybugs. She dropped at my feet and promptly rolled over for the best tummy rub she'd ever received. I was good at those.

But it wasn't hard to be good at tummy rubs.

"So...has your mom called you at all?" Tara wondered, her tone bitten back with hesitation as she pulled up on her elbows.

Mom had Whitney Stephens' phone number, but so far, no calls had come through.

Part of me wasn't surprised.

Part of me wanted to die.

"Nope." I focused on Ladybug's warm, soft fur, instead of on that cold, hard truth.

"I'm sorry, Hals. That's crappy."

"How long do you think I'll be staying with you?"

"I dunno. Mom hasn't said much about it, but you're almost eighteen. I guess your mother hasn't put up a fight, so maybe you can live here until we both move out. We'd be like sisters. That would be something, huh?"

"Yeah, it would be." My decrepit heart glimmered at the thought. Growing up as an only child in a loveless household gave me an extra appreciation for family. Tara sure felt like family. I glanced at her with a soft smile, her light-brown hair extra teased, wavy, and loaded with chunky barrettes.

We both loved Gin Blossoms, the color blue, and *My So-Called Life.* Jared Leto was a babe.

And...

A thought struck me.

Reed kind of looked like him but with green eyes and shorter hair.

Heat fizzed inside my chest, a feeling I had to snuff out before it sparked, ignited, and burned me alive. It was stupid to still be thinking about him. He was twice my age and probably had a horde of beautiful, worldly women at his disposal.

Ladybug dashed from the room then, and I straightened from the floor, peering at my image in Tara's photograph-lined mirror. Polaroids and magazine clippings had been taped to the oblong frame, my favorite one being a picture of us together last summer as we sucked on cherry Blow Pops while leaning against her seafoam-green Saturn.

My eyes were closed with a frozen-in-time moment of contentment and her head was tipped to my shoulder while we smiled for her mom's camera.

I had felt like I belonged.

It was one of my favorite blips.

Skimming my fingers through my blow-dried hair, I grinned when Ladybug came bounding back into the room, her butt shimmying, a prize clutched firmly between her teeth.

But that smile buckled when my attention locked on the object she was holding.

"Um...what's that?" My voice shook as I pointed to the item in her mouth.

Tara leaped off the bed. "No, Ladybug! That's not a dog toy." She raced over to the pup as Ladybug's tail wagged, happy and oblivious. "My dad gave me that for Christmas, you mangey mutt."

Christmas.

Dad.

Tara's dad.

I blinked half a dozen times, stitching the pieces together. Wondering if I was imagining things. "What's your dad's name?"

Tara struggled to pry the item away, but Ladybug held firm as she dodged her flailing hands. "Reed." She sighed, shaking her head and swiping her palms down her blue jeans. "Gross. Now I'm covered in dog slime."

An imaginary rug was yanked out from underneath my feet.

I smothered the choking sound with one hand and turned to face the wall, my heart shattering to smithereens.

There, hanging from the dog's mouth...was Bones.

CHAPTER 5

Reed

"AGAIN." Two fists came flying at me, and I smoothly sidestepped the attack, feeling the onrush of air as they missed their mark. I signaled for the eighteen-year-old boy in front of me to keep the momentum going. "Circles, Scotty. Stay light on your feet."

The studio was my sanctuary, a haven where the echo of footsteps against blue mats reverberated with fire. While my career had been rooted in the medical field at first, being a paramedic had come with a front-row seat to the horrors of humanity.

I'd seen a lot of shit.

I'd *experienced* a lot of shit.

When I was in my twenties, I'd signed up for self-defense classes and worked my ass off to obtain a black belt in both Taekwondo and jiu-jitsu, mostly to help me cope with a violent attack I'd suffered in my late teens that had left me with a near-fatal stab wound. As the years pressed on, the desire to help fellow victims find their strength and to shed their self-limiting beliefs had only amplified.

My job tending to medical emergencies had triggered something deeper in me—a passion for tending to the wounds that lingered long after the sirens had faded.

The dual roles had intertwined seamlessly for a while, until the passion took over, becoming my full-time career. My calling. I knew that trauma didn't disappear once the physical injuries had healed, and that notion had fueled my commitment to pursuing this new profession.

Standing in my breathable performance tank and dark athletic pants, I assessed Scotty's form. Mirrors along the wall behind me reflected the look in his eyes, a flicker of uncertainty fusing with fierce resolve. I threw a controlled jab, a test to gauge his reflexes, and Scotty responded with a crisp block. He was learning to read his opponent, to anticipate the next move.

"Keep that guard up," I encouraged, guiding him through a series of kicks and strikes. The scent of effort-fueled sweat filled the room, blending with the muted thuds of limbs making contact.

I was in the zone; my happy place.

Sparring was a form of therapy for me, and the difference I was making in the lives of motivated kids and adults mirrored the impact it had on mine.

Twenty more minutes flew by as we finished up the session, and I swiped my forearm across my hairline as I gave him an accomplished nod. "Good job. Big improvement from last week."

"Yeah?" Scotty grinned, hands planting on his hips, breaths measured. "I've been practicing. My dad set up a punching bag in the garage."

"I can tell. Just remember, it's all about the mindset." I grabbed a clean towel to dry my face before tossing him one of his own. We both reached for our water bottles and took a swig as the adrenaline petered out. "I can teach you every technique in the world, but it's nothing without confidence. You second-guessed yourself a few times."

His flushed cheeks puffed out as he exhaled a breath. "I'm working on that. Why does it feel impossible?"

I leaned against the studio wall, my head tilting as I studied him. He was gangly, close to six-feet tall, with shaggy brown hair and a gnarly scar inching up from his upper lip. "Confidence is like a muscle," I told him. "It needs consistent exercise. The more you practice, the stronger it becomes. It's not about eliminating self-doubt entirely—it's about pushing through it."

Scotty chugged down the rest of his water and fisted the empty bottle in his hand, the plastic crinkling. "What can I do to strengthen that muscle? There's always this stupid fear that creeps in, no matter how focused I try to be."

I gestured to the mats. "Start by visualizing the win. Before you even throw a punch, see yourself executing the techniques. Flawlessly. Build that mental image of yourself as a capable defender. It makes a world of difference when you step onto the mats."

His expression turned thoughtful as he sighed. "Yeah, I'll keep working on that."

"Progress is a journey, not a destination." I stepped forward and clapped him on the shoulder. "You're doing good. Keep at it, and you'll see the difference."

"Thanks, Coach Madsen." Scotty swept past me, heading for his duffel bag before waving me off with a goodbye. "See you next week."

"Yep."

The sound of the heavy door closing echoed through the studio, and my eyes lingered as I licked a stray dollop of sweat from my upper lip.

Scotty was a good kid, and his story had left me rattled.

He'd been jumped by four teenagers on a suburban sidewalk while taking his little sister trick-or-treating last Halloween. Thankfully, his sister had run off to get help and avoided injury, but Scotty had been brutalized, left sprawled and unconscious on someone's front lawn.

The assailants had been quickly captured and brought into custody, determined to have been high on something.

Their motive for the attack?

They'd wanted his sister's fucking candy pail.

The absurdity of the reasoning had left me sickened. Scotty's injuries had been severe—internal bleeding, scarring on his face and torso, and a grade-three concussion that'd confined him to a hospital bed for weeks. In the past, I'd been trained to separate personal interest from my profession. Now, in this new line of work, I was able to harness empathy and education, offering his parents the assurance that I would provide self-defense courses for Scotty at no cost.

When he'd walked into my studio in December, his drive had been palpable. I found fulfillment in knowing I was contributing to his recovery, offering a tool to rebuild his sense of security.

I'd been in his shoes.

I understood.

Running my fingers through my still-damp hair, I slung the towel over one shoulder and sauntered over to the far wall to snatch up my keys and wallet. Although my work shift had ended, the self-defense session complete, there was one final commitment awaiting me.

As the clock approached six p.m., I smiled, tossing my keys in the air before pushing through the main door and into the crisp winter night.

I had a dinner date with my favorite girl.

"Hey, Reed."

Whitney leaned in for a hesitant hug the moment the bright-blue door swung open. I teetered on the front stoop with a bouquet of roses for Tara as my other arm loosely wrapped around my ex-girlfriend. "Hey, Whit. Smells good in there."

"We have a great chef tonight." When she pulled away, a smile teased her lips. "Come inside. Tara's really been looking forward to dinner."

I followed her through the threshold as sauteed garlic and rosemary wafted under my nose. The house looked the same. Lots of blue pops and splashes, thanks to my daughter, and a coastal, nautical theme reminiscent of the years they'd spent living near the beach in Charleston before laying roots back here at home, just outside of Chicago.

Photographs decorated the walls, featuring one of my favorite pictures of Tara. She was three or four at the time, perched at the top of a big red slide as her little hands reached for the sky, her smile stretched just as wide. I stared at the image for a few beats, memorizing her light-brown pigtails and crooked grin, lost in the reverie. Craving the innocence and magic that had come along with early childhood.

I'd never liked being in pictures, and it was a feeling I semi-regretted as I panned my gaze around the canvas-laden walls, feeling like a ghost in my own memories.

"Tara's in the shower, but she'll be down in a minute." Whitney snatched the white roses stained cerulean blue, breaking into my reveries. She gave them a whiff and her smile bloomed brighter. "These are great. She'll love them."

"I miss her."

Somber undertones breached the space between us as Whitney glanced down at her sock-covered feet and nodded slowly. "She misses you."

I'd been back home for eight months now, but work had kept me busy and school and social commitments had kept Tara distant. "Is she pissed at me?"

Sighing, Whitney glided over to the dining room table and replaced a fake flower arrangement with the fresh roses in a decorative vase. Then she swiveled around and leaned back, her hands curling around the edge of the tabletop as she stared at me. "If she is, it's in that moody teenager way. It's no different with me."

I sniffed, hands sliding into my pockets. "I fucked up. I should have packed my shit and left the moment you told me you were moving back to Illinois."

"You had a thriving business you'd just built from the ground up. You were making a difference in the world. Changing lives. She knows that."

"Making a difference in *her* world is my priority."

"Reed," she said. "You gave her your entire world for years. You were always dedicated. Present. She doesn't hold it against you."

I looked away, jabbing the side of my cheek with my tongue to keep the self-loathing at bay. Guilt gnawed at me. Whit and I had been high school sweethearts, her being one year older than me. I was eighteen and she was nineteen when Tara came into our lives. While our relationship had crumbled under the strain of becoming parents at such a young, immature age—and a shit-ton of external stressors—we were *good* parents.

When Whitney had scored a temporary position in the social work field out in Charleston, I'd followed. But when she'd moved back to the Chicago suburbs, our home base, after nailing down something permanent...I'd hesitated.

Opportunity had been dropped in my lap, something I craved, something that really fucking mattered to me...

And I'd stayed behind.

I'd been away from my little girl for an entire year. I'd missed out on moments, on high school milestones, and on that vulnerable phase in every teen's life when parental guidance is needed more than ever. I was trying my best to make up for lost time now, stopping by for regular family dinners and taking her out for coffee and lunch dates, but there was a nagging tug inside my chest, telling me she hadn't appreciated my twelve-month absence.

"Anyway..." Whitney sensed my runaway thoughts and cleared her throat, popping up from the table. "Let me introduce you to Tara's friend. She's going to be staying with us for a while."

I toed out of my boots, sliding them out of the entryway and moving toward the kitchen. "All right."

Whit had told me about the neighbor girl they'd taken in—Tara's new best friend, one year older than her—who had come from an abusive home with two parasites for parents.

The notion warmed me. For as different as my ex and I were, we both shared a soft heart. Compassion for the unloved and forgotten. Whitney was a dedicated social worker, and I'd always admired that about her. She worked hard making a difference in the lives of those kids.

I could only hope we were raising Tara right.

Pretty sure we were.

A clattering of pots and pans seeped out from the galley kitchen around the corner as I followed behind Whitney with my hands still tucked inside my denim pockets.

"Reed, this is Halley." She stepped aside, revealing a girl standing at the stove with a wooden spoon in her hand. "Halley, I want you to finally meet Reed—Tara's father."

I came to a careening, heart-stopping halt at the edge of the kitchen.

I froze.

Blanched.

Something Whitney had once told me swept through my mind like a storm-charged wind.

Everyone gets a moment.

A moment that tested us, defined us, shaped us. One that showed us who we really were. The *real* us, down to the marrow. Not that superficial bullshit we flaunted to meaningless passersby who filtered in and out of our lives like transient ghosts.

Every goddamn one of us got a moment.

And this was mine.

I wasn't prepared.

Nothing could have prepared me for when the girl I'd met in the Gin Blossoms T-shirt and bright-berry lipstick spun around, her honeyed hair tossing over her shoulder as she looked right at me.

Our eyes locked together.

My heart pounded as my fists clenched at both sides. I fumbled for something to say before the moment spanned too long and Whitney interrogated me as to why I was paling before her eyes, every muscle locking up.

I cleared the soot from my throat. "Hey."

"Hey." Halley forced a weak smile and turned back around to face the stove. It was like she'd already known it would be me walking through the front door tonight and had come to terms with this fucked-up twist of fate.

Whitney pressed a hand to my corded bicep. "Do you two know each other?"

I could have lied, could have said no, no, we'd never met before, and the seventeen-year-old girl in her kitchen who often trickled into my mind only reminded me of someone else.

But I knew that even the smallest white lie could grow teeth and I'd end up burying myself deeper than I already was.

I loosened my fists and chewed on my tongue. "Yeah, actually. We ran into each other at a party last summer."

"A party? You always hated parties." Curiosity flickered in her dark-chocolate eyes as she gazed up at me. "Small world, I guess."

Yeah.

Small fucking world.

I scrubbed a hand over my face, forehead to jaw, hoping to erase my ashen look of disbelief. "It was that night in June when you said Tara had snuck out. You were worried. You thought she was going to Jay's, so I went over there looking for her."

She nodded slowly. "I remember that. She ended up sleeping over at Marissa's."

"Right. Halley was there and we chatted for a bit."

My gaze lifted to the source of my turmoil, but she kept her attention on the saucepan, refusing to meet my stare.

Halley's name hadn't come up, or, if it had, I hadn't noticed. Nothing could have ever led me to believe that *she* was the girl Whit had taken in.

What were the goddamn odds?

Probably the same odds as running into her at the grocery store on Christmas Eve, a cruel reminder of that maddening connection that had seeped in when my guard was down, her eyes were soft and vulnerable, and her full, wine-stained lips looked like they were made for kissing mine.

Shit.

This was a nightmare.

She was seventeen, completely out of the question by default, and now she was the temporary foster kid of my ex—*and* my daughter's new best friend.

I was a serial killer in a past life.

That had to be it.

Halley continued to ignore me, stirring some kind of marinara in the pan. "Dinner's almost ready," she said, tucking a golden strand of hair behind her ear. "I set the table already."

"Thanks, sweetie." Whitney dropped her hand from my arm, then guided me to the dining room. When we were out of earshot, she looked up at me, her eyes narrowing with scrutiny. "You were being weird. Did something happen?"

Happen?

Yeah, something fucking happened, and I was damn lucky it hadn't turned into more.

But that was only because I'd discovered her real age right after I'd been a heartbeat away from taking her home to my apartment and sinking inside her.

I stumbled for an answer other than the aforementioned internal thought. "It just took me by surprise. We talked for a while and I never expected to see her again."

"Right. Makes sense." She breathed out a laugh like the notion was absurd. "Sorry. The mood just got tense or something."

Nothing made sense.

I was fucked.

Tara's footsteps clamored down the wooden staircase a few seconds later, graciously tearing through the moment. "Dad!" she chirped.

The tension momentarily rolled off me at the sound of her voice. I sent her a small wave as she trotted toward us in an oversized T-shirt secured at the waist with a hairband, and a genuine smile lifted on my mouth. "Hey, Squirt. How's school going?"

"Oh, you know, learning about quadratic equations, the anatomy of frog guts, and Shakespearean insults. Stuff I'll surely use in daily life after graduation." Then she made a face. "Don't call me *Squirt*. I'm not five anymore."

I was about to respond when Halley interrupted, emerging from the kitchen with one arm linked around a salad bowl, the other encased in a neon-pink cast.

"Thine face is not worth sunburning," Halley quipped.

"Thou is a scullion!" Tara shot back.

The girls giggled.

Halley glanced at me and her smile fell.

And when she sat directly across from me at the dinner table, looking far older than her actual age and more beautiful than I last remembered, I snatched the glass of wine Whitney handed me and chugged the whole thing, while the devil on my shoulder leaned in and whispered in my ear:

Thou is royally fucked.

I was marginally buzzed on red wine when dinner wrapped up and Halley shot up from her chair like a fire had been set underneath her ass.

Clearing my throat, I dabbed my mouth with a napkin after inhaling the best manicotti casserole I'd ever eaten. "That was great. Thanks." My gaze trailed to Halley as she dashed into the kitchen, her hair bouncing mid-back. "I'll help clean up."

Tara snickered. "So domesticated, Dad. Can you do my laundry, too? I have, like, seventeen piles in my bedroom."

"Nice try." I pushed my chair back. "No."

Whitney reached for my shoulder. "You don't need to clean. I'll do it."

"I can be useful on occasion." Sending her a tight smile, I stood and headed toward the kitchen.

Halley was eyeing me from the sink, but quickly returned her attention to the pile of dirty dishes when our eyes caught.

With her arm buried in soapy suds, she attempted to scrub a dinner plate one-handed with a yellow sponge. I tentatively approached, searching for something to say. We hadn't spoken much at dinner, but her light-hazel eyes had burned holes into me whenever she thought I wasn't looking.

I noticed.

She was impossible not to notice, and that was a problem.

"You're a good cook," I said, coming up beside her. "Best manicotti I ever had."

A smile flitted across her lips as she kept her eyes on the sink water. "Thanks. I love cooking."

"Yeah?"

"Mmhmm. Keeps my mind busy. Besides, it feels good making other people feel good," she told me. "My Nana always said that the best way to a person's heart was through their stomach."

If she was trying to breach me, it was working. All I could do was pray there was no deadly takeover and I'd come out of this in one piece.

I idled beside her for a beat before joining her at the sink and reaching for a dish. "I'll help."

"You don't have to."

"I want to. Besides, I'm not sure how you plan on doing the dishes with one hand." I took the plate balancing on the edge of the counter and toweled it off, setting it aside. "Listen, I'm hoping we can keep what happened at the party between us," I murmured, schooling my voice to stay low as I glanced toward the dining room. "For Tara's sake."

"Sure. That's fine." She stole a glance at me, her slender throat working through a swallow. "Nothing happened."

That was a lie and we both knew it.

But I was the adult here. There was no other choice but to be *fine*. And while we might have gotten swept up in a physical reaction that night, no fatal lines had been crossed.

Fine was doable. Fine was possible.

"All right. Good." My eyes settled on her profile, then on her broken arm that I wanted to mend with just a look. "That bruise on your face on Christmas Eve...that was from your father?"

The thought alone was a lethal invader, and my body tensed up imagining her own father hurting her like that. I couldn't fathom it. He was a fucking bastard, and I was glad Whitney had given her a safe place to stay, despite the circumstances.

Halley faltered, blinking down into the soap bubbles as her lips thinned. She nodded once. "Yes. Sorry I lied again, but there was nothing you could do. There wasn't any point in bringing it up."

"I could have helped you."

"How?"

"I..." I didn't know. She was just a pretty girl I'd met at a party. A stranger, essentially. "I could've done something. Called the cops. Given you a place to stay for the night."

She made a huffing sound. "You would've taken a teenage girl back to your place on Christmas Eve after we'd already..." Looking up at me, her eyes glazed over, muted caramel and a dash of emerald. "Never mind."

"Yeah." My lips flattened. "I would have."

"I don't need you to save me, Reed. I'm not actually lost." Her eyes dipped back to the sink. "I'm stronger than you think."

That had been the first thing I'd said to her as I searched Jay's property, on the hunt for my rebellious daughter, before spotting her standing all alone in a shallow lake with her hair lit up like a halo under the moon.

Are you lost?

She'd looked it.

Lost, searching, a split-second away from disappearing underneath the water for good.

I wasn't prone to one-night stands or random hookups, but as the evening had pressed on, something about her had me wanting to toss her in my truck to take her back to my apartment, just so I could memorize the look on her face when she screamed my name and came apart beneath me.

She had told me she was twenty-one, and I'd stupidly believed her.

She looked older. And even though younger women had never appealed to me, a strange connection had bloomed in those first few minutes while we talked about music and dreams, facing each other, just a waterline apart.

Seventeen.

Everything unraveled when the truth had spilled out. Shock, horror, a sickening pang of disappointment. I'd been this-close to sleeping with a fucking teenager and the notion was deplorable.

My daughter's best friend.

I'd managed to bury the lust-driven thoughts fairly quickly, but she had still crossed my mind. I'd wondered where she was, how she was doing, and if she'd captured any new blips or found another favorite song.

As if reading my mind, Halley changed the subject and reached into the sink for a serving bowl. "Have you listened to their new CD?"

I swiped the dish before she tried to wash it herself. "What CD?"

"Oasis."

"Yeah." I smiled softly. "It's good."

She stared at me, unable to hold back the flickering of light that inhabited her eyes. "I don't have it yet. I'm trying to save my money for necessities."

I wondered if she'd discovered the extra cash I'd slipped into her coat pocket that night outside the grocery store. It wasn't supposed to mean anything beyond an impulsive act of kindness. Her coat had looked old and tattered, her shoes full of holes. And I'd noticed the worry coasting across her face with every item that had dinged along the checkout scanner.

She cleared her throat. "Anyway, I should thank you for—"

Before she could finish speaking, Halley moved the wrong way, and her cast knocked one of the dishes off the counter. We both watched it shatter across the tile at our feet in slow motion.

She paled.

Tears glistened in her eyes as she carved out a sharp breath and dropped to her knees.

"Shit. Sorry...I-I didn't mean—"

"It's not a big deal." I grabbed a towel to help contain the mess, my attention locked on her panicked face. "Hey, it's all right. I got it."

"I just...I'm sorry." Shaking her head, she fell back on her haunches. "It was an accident."

"Seriously. It's fine."

She stared blankly at the mess. And then the color slowly made its way back to her cheeks as her breathing steadied. When the fear dissipated, she let out a self-deprecating laugh. "Yikes. That was an overreaction."

I studied her as I held a dishrag over the scattered glass.

And I understood.

She'd probably been beaten for dropping a plate before, and the thought was like acid to my veins.

Whitney raced into the kitchen, reaching for a dustpan and falling beside us. "A casualty," she teased, easing the tension.

Halley inhaled a breath, composed herself, and climbed back to her feet. "I'm really sorry, Ms. Stephens. I'll try to be more careful."

"You can start by not doing my dishes, you goofball. You should be resting that arm." Dusting and scooping, she collected the loose shards and added with a smile, "Also, please call me Whitney."

"Okay. No problem."

Whitney shot me a look before she disappeared out of the kitchen. Turning to Halley, I watched as she picked at the hem of her pale-yellow blouse and fidgeted in front of me, her eyes on the ground.

I took a step closer and leaned in. "At least it's not your rock, paper, scissors hand."

A beat passed.

And a smile finally broke free.

She chewed on her bottom lip, cheeks flushing a similar rosy shade, as her eyes lifted to mine. "You should sign my cast," she said, the cloud of unease dissipating. "All the cool people are doing it."

"That so?" I blinked down at the pink beacon attached to her left arm. "Got a marker?"

"Sure. One sec." Halley returned a moment later with a Sharpie.

I took it.

Our fingers brushed together and my jaw ticked as I sawed out a breath.

Then I scribbled my name on her cast with a black marker, telling myself it would be the only thing she'd ever claim from me.

CHAPTER 6

ON THE MORNING of my eighteenth birthday in mid-February, I woke up with what felt like a colony of fire ants taking up residence in the back of my throat. If someone was in need of a dragon, I'd volunteer. I was confident I could breathe hellfire.

My head pounded.

My eyelids felt like they were stuck to my eyeballs with masking tape.

I was trying to stay coherent by skimming through a collection of photographs I'd developed in the school's dark room, the pictures blurry and distorted as I shuffled through the pile.

A plate of blueberries in the cafeteria. Kids laughing against their lockers. Our real-life mascot, Nibbles the Rabbit, munching on a carrot stick. The principal checking out my science teacher.

I should probably hide that one.

But the more I tried to focus, the more the images jumbled into fog. My brain was failing me. Everything was failing me.

Tara threw a pillow at my face. "Get up! It's your birthday."

Her voice was too loud. It sounded like she was screaming in my ear, but she was at least few feet away, given the trajectory of the pillow.

"Ugh." I groaned, flopping backward and using the pillow as a tool to block out all sunlight. "Think I'm sick."

"No, you're not. You're just trying to get out of going to the winter fling with Eric tomorrow."

She could be right.

Maybe my body was deteriorating at the thought of awkward, mechanical slow-dancing with Eric Soloman, who was two inches shorter than me and came to school with a giant, face-eating pimple on his forehead yesterday.

My stomach curdled.

I honestly wasn't sure if it was because of the memory of that pimple, or the flu.

"I'm actually sick, Tara. My bones are disintegrating and my brain is dribbling out of my ears."

"Way too dramatic."

"That's what it feels like. I'm dying." My voice was muffled by the pillow.

"You're lying?"

"*Dying,*" I repeated, tossing the pillow back at her. My strength was that of a newborn baby, and the pillow hardly made it over the edge of the mattress. "I want soup."

When my eyelids finally peeled open, one sandpaper eyeball at a time, I watched as Tara yanked a baggy sweater over her head and pulled a mound of shower-damp hair from the collar. "Damn, Hals. You do kind of look like my Grandpa Harry on the day of his funeral but with way better teeth. I'll tell Mom to make you soup."

I muttered something unintelligible.

Then I must've drifted off to sleep, because when I jolted awake again, Tara was gone and Whitney was sitting beside me on the bed, stroking back my hair. "Happy birthday, Halley."

Unlike Tara's booming voice, her mother's voice sounded a million miles away. Soothing, peaceful, nurturing. I sunk into the comfort of her words and soft touch as I burrowed into the blankets, shivering with fever.

"I made you soup and brought you some fever reducer. You feel like you're burning up."

"Hmmph."

"I'll call you out of school today," she said. "I have to leave for work... do you think you'll be okay? Should I call in?"

No way.

She'd already sacrificed so much for me. Too much.

I forced myself to perk up, peeking over the edge of the blankets and smiling at her blurry, pretty face. "Go to work. It's just a little cold." My focus trailed to the bowl of steaming broth on the nightstand. "Thank you for the soup."

"Of course. I'll come by on my lunch break to check on you."

"Okay."

That was the last thing I remembered before fever dreams stole me away...

"I can stick around for a bit. You should get back to the office."

"I don't know...she doesn't look good. Should we take her to the hospital?"

A big, cool palm pressed against my forehead, lingering softly and smoothing back my sweaty hair as a swirl of amber and earthy woods swept me up in a cloud of contentment. "I think we just need to get this fever to break. I'll make sure she takes the meds."

"Are you sure?"

"Yep. It's my day off and I know you're busy with that upcoming court case. I'll take the dog for a walk while I'm here."

A long pause.

A sigh.

"You're a lifesaver," she said softly. "I'll call to check in."

"All right."

Footsteps retreated from the room as my mind spun, a haze of reality and a faraway dreamland. Reed was here. He was sitting on the bed beside me, his hand returning to my forehead as his thumb gently grazed my hairline. I forced my eyes to flutter open until his handsome face became a fuzzy shape above me; a smog of dark hair, kind eyes, and full lips creased with tenderness.

"Hey. We need to get your fever down."

The pills Whitney had left for me were still sitting next to the bowl of cold chicken soup, untouched. I couldn't move. The simple task of reaching for the medication sounded like a Herculean feat. I burrowed deeper in the bedcovers, my teeth chattering. "Are you real?"

"Pretty sure."

"I was...dreaming..."

He continued to brush his thumb along my forehead. "What did you dream about?"

"Dancing...songs." I wasn't making sense, but it was hard to make sense of anything when Reed was near, and the fever wasn't helping one bit. "There was music."

He hesitated, the mattress shifting beneath his weight. "Want me to turn on some music?"

I managed a nod.

I must've dozed again when I felt him return, his fingertips touching my lips as my favorite Gin Blossoms CD filtered from the boombox speaker.

Am I still dreaming?

I didn't know, but part of me didn't want to wake up.

His fingers felt like butterfly wings against my dry lips, and I yearned to go back in time to when our lips were hot and wet, tangled together amid thigh-clenching moans, and he was breathing fiery light into my soul.

"You need to take these. You'll feel better."

Two tiny pills coasted along my tongue. They tasted like bitter sawdust and I gagged.

"Here, sit up."

His arms were around me, guiding me into an upright position. My pulse hammered in my head like a power drill as I attempted to move, falling against the crook of his shoulder, my body no stronger than a raggedy teddy bear.

Reed was warm, firm, and safe.

I'd live with this fever till the end of time if it meant he'd stay here with me.

"C'mon, Halley. Swallow."

His fingers were on my jaw, closing my mouth to keep the medicine inside, right before the rim of a glass poked between my lips. I parted them and drank. I choked down the pills, coughing and sputtering when the water clogged my sore, parched throat.

He rubbed a tender hand down my back until the coughing ebbed.

It had been a while since Father had whipped me with his brown belt, so I didn't flinch away at the contact. Reed stroked his hand up and down my spine, his palm landing at the nape of my neck and cradling gently. Long fingers sifted through my knotted hair as his sigh whispered along my temple.

When he inched away, it felt like he'd tossed me in a freezer and sealed it shut.

But then his words traveled over to me, warming me again. "Did you take these?"

"Hmm?"

"These pictures."

I tried to blink away the film as I slowly twisted my head to face him. Reed was holding the stack of photographs I'd taken at school. "Yes," I croaked. "They're crap."

"They're not. They're really good."

The compliment sent more fuzzy heat straight through me. "I was just practicing."

He was silent for a few beats and it felt like a lifetime. "You have something here."

"Yes. A pile of crap."

"Halley." Reed fell quiet again, studying each picture like it was a rare portrait hung on a gallery wall. "Even these blueberries. The way you framed the picture and blurred the background."

"I was hungry."

A sigh coasted along my temple, reminding me of his proximity.

He discarded the photos and moved away.

No.

I needed him closer. I craved comfort.

"Can you stay..." I nuzzled closer to him, already feeling the pull of sleep threatening to yank me back under. It had been nearly a decade since I'd been cared for like this. When I was ten years old, I'd come down with a sinus infection that had kept me fever-ridden for a week. Nana was still alive, and she'd taken care of me. She'd sung lullabies by my bedside, read me storybooks, and reminisced old-age stories to comfort my restless mind.

And then she'd died.

My lifeline had been severed.

"Please," I rasped, snuggling closer to him.

Reed stiffened at my plea.

There was no response.

I was about to withdraw it, take it back, but after a few seconds passed, Reed lowered me back down to the bed and pulled the blanket up over my trembling body, tucking me inside.

I felt him lay down at my left. Not too close but close enough to bring me the most peace I'd felt in a long, long time.

"I'm sorry...I lied to you..." I stuttered through the dizzying daze of sickness, fever, and Reed. "I'm an awful person."

"Don't. It's in the past."

I swallowed down a bone-dry boulder in my throat. "Lots of things are in the past. Doesn't mean they don't matter."

Leather belts.

Mean, acidic words.

Loveless looks that were forever tattooed on my heart like a hot iron brand.

Selfishly deceiving a good man.

A few quiet seconds rolled by before he spoke. "I don't hold on to grudges, Halley. I'm too old for that shit."

He was subtly reminding me of his age, and even in my weakened state, I knew that. Forcing a small nod, I fell further against him, my temple pressed to the hard ridges of his shoulder. "That night didn't mean anything...right?"

"Right." The response was strained, just a whisper, almost like he didn't believe it.

I licked my lips, my eyelids drawing closed. "But...maybe it could've meant something. If I'd been older...and less lost."

He didn't reply to that, and I hadn't expected him to. I should probably be embarrassed, but the sickness was possessing my tongue, clouding my reality, so I allowed the words to dangle between us, unbidden and unwelcome. I focused on the feel of his warm body pressed to mine, knowing I'd soon drift away to a kinder world.

We could meet at the lake again, and everything would be different. He'd venture into the water, or I'd slip onto the sand.

Until I Fall Away echoed in my ears, mingling with his steady breaths, and sleep soon stole me away. But I swore I heard him mutter one last thing before I sailed into darkness...

"Happy birthday."

Hours later, I awoke, drenched in cold sweat. A warm body was beside me, but when my eyelids flickered open, I discovered that Reed was gone.

Ladybug was curled up near my legs.

I reached a hand down to pet her fur, and she sighed contentedly at the attention, inching closer to me and giving me added warmth. The room was dim, the sun having already set. I pulled up on my elbows, shaking damp strands of hair out of my eyes as I glanced around the quiet room.

The CD had run its course. All I heard was commotion from downstairs—Tara laughing, dishes clattering, and Whitney chatting with somebody with a cheerful lilt in her tone.

I listened for Reed's voice; I didn't hear him.

But as I turned to face the nightstand, my empty stomach grumbling and craving that soup...

I saw something.

I blinked.

Smiled wide.

And for as sick as I was, I had never felt better.

Resting on the nightstand was the new Oasis CD, topped with a little pink bow.

CHAPTER 7

A WEEK after my forty-eight hour flu bug had run its course, I was sitting out on the back deck, bundled up in one of Tara's pale-pink North Face puffy coats and a pair of fuzzy earmuffs. Ladybug skipped around the backyard, leaping across the stubborn patches of snow as she chased a red rubber ball.

I lived for these moments: the crisp February air biting at my cheeks, a big wooden deck with a charcoal grill I couldn't wait to use when springtime surfaced, and a golden retriever with a swiftly wagging tail who loved me like I was part of the family.

Smiling at the scene, I reached for my mug of coffee that sat beside me on a glass table. I curled my legs up on the white plastic chair and palmed the still-warm ceramic, savoring the quiet Sunday afternoon as Tara and her mom reorganized Tara's bedroom.

I glanced up when the patio door rolled open.

Expecting Tara to come bounding out, I had my grin ready, but it wilted to a flat line when Reed stepped out on the wooden deck planks, instead.

It didn't wilt because I was unhappy to see him, or because the sight of him brought me something other than spine-tingling heat and heart-clogging joy.

It wilted because those feelings were going to be the goddamn death of me.

And I'd *finally* started living.

"Aren't you cold?" he inquired, decked out in his customary leather jacket that I equally loved and hated.

Loved because it looked so good on him.

Hated because it was the reason Marnie LaRue was given the opportunity to stick her nose where it didn't belong and ruin a night I'd forever wonder about.

Truthfully, the jacket was just an excuse to not hate myself.

I glanced away, panning my attention over to Ladybug chewing on a bone she'd uncovered in the yard. "Not really. The sun feels nice."

It was in the upper thirties, but the sun shone brightly in a cloudless blue sky, warming my frosty bones.

Reed's hands were already turning pink against the chilly air, so he shoved them in the pockets of his distressed jeans. I tried not to trail my gaze down his legs. He wore the jeans as well as he wore the jacket.

And he wore both of those things almost as well as he wore a tiny smile that sent my heartbeats into topsy-turvy turmoil when he took a seat beside me in the adjacent plastic chair.

Stop it, Halley.

"Feeling better?"

"Good as new," I replied, trying to ignore him and failing. After all, I was never any good at doing hard things.

"We were worried about you. Your fever was high."

"It was just the flu. Are you sticking around for dinner?" I brought the mug of coffee to my lips with my free hand, peeking over at him as I took a sip.

He nodded. "I took Tara out to lunch, and now Whit's finishing up her pre-spring-cleaning extravaganza. Looks like a bomb went off in there."

"I tried to help, but she shooed me away." Popping my cast-heavy arm in the air, I made a sour face. "Can't wait for this hideous thing to be cut off of me."

Reed's expression dimmed as he stared at my pink arm scribbled with names and doodles. "Your father is a despicable piece of shit."

My chest spasmed.

I blinked at him, my throat tightening with bitter memories. I didn't know how to respond. Reed was right, of course, but Reed was also Tara's dad, which made him the last person I should be confiding in.

Swallowing, I stared down into my lukewarm coffee.

"If he ever comes around you again, you'll let me know?" There was a gravelly undertone to his voice.

The request made my breath catch. "That's not your job. I'm not..."

He faltered. "You're not what?"

Shrugging, I cleared my throat as I stared up at the ocean-blue sky. "I'm not your responsibility."

Silence spanned between us as he leaned forward in the chair, elbows to knees. He scratched at the stubble along his jawline, simmering in my words. I'd tried to make them sound indifferent, but I was certain he knew that the pink flush blooming on my cheeks and neck was not from the cold.

Reed glanced at me, his expression unreadable. I was envious of his ability to do that so easily. I was an open book; a colorful canvas of thoughts and wishes. If he looked long enough he'd discover everything he wanted to know about me.

Along with everything he didn't want to know.

"Thank you for the new Oasis CD." I picked at the wooly outer lining of my left boot. "I love it."

"Sure," he said, voice dipping. "You're welcome."

"You didn't have to get me a birthday present. Especially after every-thing..." I trailed off again, not wanting to purge anymore of my toxic truths. I couldn't hide behind the fever excuse this time. "It was sweet. I appreciate it."

"Sweet," he parroted, rubbing a hand over his jaw.

He said it like the word tasted anything but.

And I supposed I was playing with fire every time I opened my mouth, caught his gaze, or melted against the warmth of his proximity. Part of me just couldn't step away from the flames.

Reed steepled his fingers at his chin, his green eyes flicking to me and looking a shade lighter in the hazy daylight. A few heavy heartbeats stuttered between us while he stewed over his reply.

I thought maybe he was going to say something that would fan the flames. A response that would keep me warm and hopeful.

He didn't.

"I got it for a friend." His jaw ticked through his words. "Turns out, she's not really into their music. I figured you'd get better use out of it."

Ouch.

I ground my teeth together as my heart perished, my chest suffocating on the ashes.

Reed looked away, something unsaid flickering in his eyes. Then he stood from the chair and walked inside, backing away from the fire I was so eager to dive into, head first.

It was for the best.

No point in both of us burning.

Family game night.

It was a foreign concept to me, considering the only game I'd ever played with my family was Hide and Seek. I would hide, and my father would seek. When he'd find me, I'd lose.

Game over.

As we waited to pull out Pictionary while Whitney cleaned up the kitchen, Tara roped me into a round of Dream Phone, mostly to laugh our way through the cheesy clues given through a bulky pink phone. I'd never played it before. It seemed like something I would have liked five years ago if I'd had friends, freedom, and the luxury of being a carefree kid.

Instead, I'd been learning how to pick my bedroom door lock before my boobs had even grown in. I'd been educating myself on the best, affordable makeup brands to mask my welts and bruises. When I'd needed a friend to confide in, I'd stare up at my cracked popcorn ceiling and whisper secrets to Nana, imagining her seated among the clouds and stars on her throne of wisdom. She'd always listen. Even in death.

I glanced up at Reed as Tara and I sat on the living room floor, the board game spread out across the wooden coffee table amid half-eaten bowls of ice cream. He was lounging on the couch across from us, his brows pinched together, knees spread while one bounced repetitively.

His eyes were pinned to the game like he was trying to understand the point of it.

We hadn't spoken much since our brief interaction on the deck earlier, and I understood why. What was there to say?

Hi, it's me, the girl currently living with your ex-girlfriend and teenage daughter—the one who lied about her age in a deceptive ploy to spend more time with you. Let's be friends.

Stupid.

Lost in my dark thoughts, I dialed in a phone number listed on one of the playing cards.

"You're right! I really like you," said a too-eager voice coming from someone named Jason through the speaker. Blinking, I pulled the phone away from my ear and stared at it, frowning.

"Jason likes me," I announced.

Tara made a face. "Too bad no one likes Jason. His is an unrequited love."

Reed leaned forward, eyebrows still wrinkled with a look of concern. He started flipping through the pile of cards, huffing at all the photographs attached. "Dan. Mike. Gary. Zero creativity in these names," he mumbled, pausing on another card. "Bob? Bob is in his forties. He looks like the stick-in-the-mud chaperone at a junior high dance."

Tara busted out laughing, ripping the card from her father's hand. "He's just mature," she said. When she pulled out another card, she flipped it around to show her dad. "Thoughts on Matt? I see potential."

His eyes narrowed. "Matt is a former pastry chef turned balloon artist. After a freak accident involving a giant cream puff, he decided to embrace his new life traveling the country making balloon animals at children's birthday parties. His wife left him for the cream puff."

Tara doubled over with laughter before pulling out another card.

Reed scratched his chin and sniffed. "Scott started dating George shortly after this game was released. They share an apartment in Los Angeles and have a dog named Marshmallow."

We both giggled as Tara grabbed another card.

"I see you, Spencer," Reed said, glaring at the image. "A former small-time criminal turned born-again Christian. Once entangled in a world of check fraud and tax evasion, Spencer found redemption through the church. Spencer is proof that change is possible, even though I'd still never allow him within a ten-mile radius of my daughter."

I couldn't breathe, I was laughing so hard.

Whitney poked her head out of the kitchen, a half-smile turned up on her lips and a dish rag in her hands. "What am I missing?"

"Dad is profiling the Dream Phone dudes," Tara managed to say between bouts of belly laughter. "He doesn't like Spencer."

She glanced at the card. "Spencer looks...nice."

"He's not nice," Reed cut in, tone teasing. "C'mon, Whit. It's our job to protect these girls from the Spencers of the world."

These girls.

Plural.

My laughter tapered off as I sank back down to my knees, my gaze catching with Reed's for a beat before I cleared my throat. "Don't worry, Spencer's not my type. I prefer Bob."

Tara swatted my arm. "The forty-year-old school chaperone? Yikes, Hals. I need to get you out of the house more often and broaden your potential dating pool. There's a party next weekend I plan to lure you to."

"Will Bob be there?" I yawned, leaning back on my good hand.

Tara cringed. "Trust me. You don't want Bob."

There was a strange, subtle undertone to her statement, but I let it slide.

Whitney joined us in the living room a few minutes later with a handful of loose-leaf paper and pencils. "I couldn't find Pictionary. I think we sold it in the garage sale last spring," she said, plopping down beside Reed on the couch. "We can make our own version. Kids versus adults."

My stomach soured.

I hated being called a kid. I was a legal adult, and I knew I didn't *look* like a kid. Not to mention, I'd seen far more in my eighteen years than most adults had.

Reed tossed a piece of chewing gum into his mouth, and the trace scent of spearmint traveled over to me. "I've got about thirty minutes before I should head out. I have a client tonight."

We took turns drawing pictures.

Nobody was very good, but for thirty minutes, the world fell away. Warmth filtered its way inside me. Laughter echoed louder than my demons that hummed and sneered in the back of my mind. Ladybug sidled up against me, her soft fur grazing my thigh as I scratched her belly in contentment.

I was the last one to take a turn drawing before we wrapped up the game. The mustard-yellow hourglass plucked from a different game spilled tiny grains of sand into the bottom of the piece while I jutted my tongue between my lips in concentration.

A long step. Little buds. Blossoming petals.

"A flower!" Tara yelled as I waved my hand to keep her guessing. "A pretty flower?"

I pointed to my tank top, a vibrant shade of blue.

"A shirt. A blue shirt. A sunflower shirt."

"Sunflowers aren't blue," I practically growled.

"You're not allowed to talk!" she shouted back. "Um, shit, this is way too specific." She chewed on her lip, deep in thought. "A tulip?"

I sighed. Attempting to redirect, I started drawing a boombox with little musical notes circling it. I jabbed the tip of my pencil to the radio, then back to the flower, then back again, leaving scuffs of lead dots behind.

Tara shook her head with frustration. "What the hell is that? A singing flower?" she questioned. "Oh! A Venus flytrap!"

"Morning glory."

Reed's voice had all three heads whipping in his direction. Silence followed as he stared at the picture, then flicked his eyes to me.

I couldn't help the smile that bloomed like the subpar floral sketch. We blinked at each other as I dropped my pencil and nodded. "He got it."

Tara finally spoke, frowning with dismay. "What? How did you know that?" Then her eyes thinned as she glared at her father. "You're not even on her team. Way to go, Dad."

Whitney glanced between the three of us, confusion etched across her face. "Nice guess."

"Why is it singing?" Tara wondered.

My gaze panned back to Reed and held. "The new Oasis CD. *What's the Story, Morning Glory?* is the album title."

"I never would have gotten that." Tara pouted, tossing her pencil aside. "Jeez. You're fired."

Silence stretched between us as I collected the used pieces of paper and made a pencil pile, my cheeks warm and my heart skipping.

"I should get going." Reed cleared his throat and stood from the couch, sweeping a hand through his unruly dark hair. "Same time next week?"

"Sure." Tara stood from the floor and stretched her arms over her head. "I'll brush up on my horticulture knowledge in the meantime. Lots of late nights at the library are in my future."

Ladybug started running circles around me as I stood, her tongue lolling and paws dancing. "Can I take her for a quick walk?" I glanced at Whitney. "I won't be long."

"You can just let her out back. It's dark."

"But she has so much bottled-up energy," I said, bending to scratch between her ears with a wide grin. "Don't you, girl? You want to go for a walk?"

Ladybug bounded toward the front door where Reed was slipping into his combat boots and sliding his arms into the sleeves of his leather jacket. I followed, reaching for my own coat and shoes.

"All right," Whitney relented, crossing her arms, attention on Reed as he opened the front door. "See you next week, Reed. Tara has a parent-teacher conference on Friday if you can swing it."

"I'll be there." He glanced at Tara before heading outside. "See you, Squirt."

She huffed. "Bye, Dad."

Crisp wind blasted me in the face as I secured Ladybug's leash and let her lead me out into the star-freckled night. Reed strolled over to his red pickup truck in the driveway, tossing a quick goodbye over his shoulder.

I swallowed, wavering briefly, then tugged Ladybug over to him. "Reed."

His gait slowed until he came to a stop beside the truck, palming the back of his neck before he half-turned to face me. "What's up?"

As Ladybug sniffed a patch of grass, I glanced at my fingernails that Tara had painted cerulean. "I went to the library after school last week and looked up what morning glories symbolized."

Reed stared at me, brows furrowed, both hands sliding into his coat pockets. His eyes glinted in the soft glow of the nearby street lamp, resembling two pearly stars. "Why did you look them up?"

I worried my lip between my teeth, glancing skyward. "I was curious. Naming an album is a big deal, so I wanted to know the meaning behind the flowers. They represent love. I thought that was kind of beautiful." I shrugged, embarrassment trickling in at the random confession. "I don't know. The singer is probably a romantic."

I wasn't going to tell him that the flowers primarily represented *unrequited love* and that my heart had shriveled up like petals under a scorching sun the moment I'd read those words.

The irony.

When a smile hinted, Reed rubbed his lips together, shaking his head back and forth as he leaned against the side of the truck. "I'm about to burst your bubble, Halley."

"What? How?"

"Pretty sure it's a reference to drugs."

My eyes popped, my grip tightening on the leash. "Really?"

"Yeah, really."

We stared at each other through the shadowy night, my eyes wide and stricken and his glimmering with telltale amusement.

A burst of laughter fell out of me.

I cupped a leash-roped hand over my mouth, giggling into my palm as the golden retriever plopped down on the toes of my sneakers. "Yikes. I guess I'm the romantic."

The laughter fizzled out, and Reed blinked at me before ducking his head. "You say it like it's a bad thing."

"Feels like it is sometimes. It makes a person soft and hopeful in a world that's hard and painful."

"Maybe the world needs more people like you."

I wanted to smile at the sentiment, but I wasn't sure I believed it, so I just shrugged and stared at my fingernails again. "Do you have a favorite flower?"

His brows slanted when I looked back up. "Not really my forte. But I do have a favorite video game."

"What is it?"

"Mortal Kombat."

My nose crinkled. "Typical guy."

"However, it might be defeated when Resident Evil comes out."

"You sound excited about it."

"I am. We'll have to play together," he said. "I saw you kicking ass at Donkey Kong earlier. I'm sort of intimidated."

A feeling sailed through me, a dusty trail of light and shimmer crash-landing in the pit of my stomach. "Okay, sure. Sounds fun."

He nodded slowly, then popped a thumb over his shoulder. "I should go."

"Right. Sorry to keep you." I stretched a smile, wishing for time to slow down so I could have more minutes with him. More moments. And also wishing for time to whoosh by like a shooting star so he didn't see me as a child anymore. "Goodnight, Reed."

"Yeah," he answered softly. "'Night."

When I turned away, giving the leash a light tug, Reed called out to me one more time.

"Photography."

I stalled my feet, my back to him. My breath fell out like a feathering of white against the cool air. I swiveled around, staring at him from a few feet away as he straightened from the side of the truck.

"You should do photography." His eyes were soft as they held with mine. "For your blips."

For my blips.

My moments.

A silly wall of tears blanketed my gaze as I watched him break our stare and turn away, moving around the front of the truck to the driver's side. A lump stuck in the back of my throat. My vision blurred as two headlights rolled out of the driveway seconds later and Reed sent me a final poignant look through the windshield before reversing all the way out and pulling onto the quiet street.

I memorized that look.

I pressed an imaginary button inside my mind, capturing it in vivid color and imprinting it on my heart.

Click.

CHAPTER 8

"GROSS, YOU'RE SWEATING ON ME!"

I sat on a park bench after school, a textbook in my lap and Ladybug snoozing at my feet. Inky words warped across the pages, my attention stolen by Reed and Tara sparring a few yards away on the blacktop. March had rolled in, bringing with it fifty-degree temperatures, morning rain showers, and midday afternoons drenched in sunshine.

I craved springtime more than most people. During the colder months, I'd have nowhere to escape to when Father was on a rampage, the sting of the winter air feeling just as cruel as he was.

A particularly haunting memory stood at the forefront of my mind.

I had painted a canvas for fifth-grade art class. A wintry backdrop with sparkling snowfall and white-capped mountaintops. It hadn't been a masterpiece by any means, but I'd been proud. My mother had been staring blankly at the television screen, sipping on a glass of straight gin, the laugh track from the show sounding like a muddle of sniggering cruelty in the back of my mind.

"Want to see this painting I made?" I'd asked her, settling beside her on the rust-tattered sofa and blocking her view of the screen.

A slow blink was her only response.

"I got a good grade on it. The teacher loved it."

She robotically moved my arm away. Said nothing.

Pain and insecurity had swelled in my chest. "Mom," I'd tried, a threadbare demand. "Will you look at it?"

"Your father is home."

My lungs had squeezed with fear when the tires of his truck had rolled over gravel. Then the door had barreled open. Father had stomped inside, his bristled face streaked in grease and oil from a long day at the mechanic shop.

I'd cowered, hoping to blend into the cushions, covering myself with the canvas.

"Dinner?" Father had swiped his hands down his grimy jeans, tracking dirt through the house as he'd trudged through the living room. His eyes had landed on me, narrowing with disgust. "I don't smell food. What have you two been doing all day?"

I'd shrunk back when Father had ripped the gin glass from my mother's hands. She'd hardly flinched, reaching for the half-empty bottle beside her and taking a long swig. Deadened eyes gazed at the flickering images on the television screen.

Popping up from the couch, I'd tried to make an escape to my bedroom but was stopped by a snake-like hand slithering around my elbow.

Bruising. Cruel.

"What do we have here?" Father had snatched my canvas, his dark eyes flitting across the colors and brushstrokes. "A toddler could have drawn this."

"It was for school." Effortlessly, he'd dodged my attempt to take it back. "Please."

"Please?" A sneer had tipped his lips. "Please is right. Please, give me a fuckin' kid who can hold a goddamn paint brush, instead of this pathetic little lamb. Please, send me something more than this braindead child who doesn't know her place. You've been doodling all day when dinner should be on the table. The house is a goddamn mess. What's wrong with you?"

Tears had fogged my eyes. "Nothing is wrong with me. I just got home from school."

"Sing-a-longs on the playground, no doubt. Circle time and jump ropes with your little friends." He'd hocked up a loogy and spit it on my painting, the image smearing with vile yellow saliva. "This is all you'll ever be. Daydreams and wasted potential. Embarrassing."

I'd stared catatonically at the ruined creation, the colors running away with my backbone. Mom had sat like a vacant lump on the couch, only a bark of laughter leaving her lips when a character on screen made a stupid joke. She'd blocked me out. Blocked everything out.

"That wasn't easy to make." My crestfallen eyes had returned to the picture. "I worked hard on it."

Father had nearly choked on his laughter. "You never work hard. All you do is take up space and overcook my supper. Nothing hard about that." With a nasty flick of my hair, he'd stormed past me, tossing my painting in the trash can.

Heart in torn-up shreds, I'd run from the house, landing at this very park that overlooked a lake, wishing I could dunk underneath the ice-clumped water and drown.

My skin prickled with memory as I stared out at the glimmering surface. So calm. So peaceful.

Spring would become not only a season of renewal but also a true lifeline for me. The milder weather would provide me with the opportunity to venture outside, away from the abuse I'd sustain inside my own home. On the warmer days, I'd seek refuge at this same park, a place where the vibrant blooms replaced the drab hues of my daily life. Nature would allow me to breathe freely.

And as the temperature rose now, so did my determination to break free from the icy grip of my past.

Tara's brown ponytail swung in every direction as she bounced around on both feet, dodging her father's carefully executed jabs.

And, apparently, his sweat.

Reed regarded his daughter, slightly winded. "If I happened to be a creep lurking in a dark alleyway, I'd be doing far worse than sweating on you. Your defensive maneuvers need work."

"I'm good at being defensive."

"Physically. If someone grabs you, it's all about leverage. Twist your body like this to break free."

I watched as Reed instructed Tara through the maneuver, my nose wrinkling with curiosity. My left arm pulsed, encased in a navy sling, the cast having been removed the week prior. I couldn't wait to put this injury behind me for good.

If someone were to grab me in a dark alleyway, I'd be as proactive as a sack of rice.

Reaching into my open backpack, I pulled out a disposable camera that was almost out of film. The little wheel made a grinding noise as I flicked it to the right with my thumb before aiming the camera at Reed and Tara.

Click.

Tara huffed and puffed, bending down and clasping her hands around her knees. "You smell like a locker room."

"I smell like someone who could ruin your life if you don't take this more seriously."

"This is boring. I'm hungry."

Reed's hands were loosely planted on his hips as he sighed through a defeated headshake. "Fine. We can reconvene next week."

Tara whirled around, lifting her fingers to make air quotes as she approached me on the bench. "*Reconvene,*" she parroted. "Such a Dad word."

I quickly stuffed the camera in my backpack as Ladybug perked up, tail in full swing when Tara leaned over to scratch her ears.

"Do you guys practice a lot?" I wondered, gathering my text books.

Tara gulped down a bottle of water and shrugged. "Sometimes. I'd rather burn my calories playing volleyball. Dad gets over-the-top serious when it comes to this stuff."

"He probably saw a lot of awful things when he was a paramedic."

"Yeah, but he's overprotective. If I move the wrong way, he gets all quiet and his face does this." She rearranged her face into scrunchy scowl that made me giggle. "Just add in a few more age lines."

I glanced at Reed as he stalked toward us, his bronzed skin glistening under the early-spring sun. His hair was dark and damp as he threaded his fingers through it, his flexing biceps on full display. The sleeveless top he wore had a midnight-navy hue in direct sunlight, and the fabric stuck to him like a second skin.

Our gazes tangled briefly before I pulled away and peered over at Tara. "Dinner?"

"Yes, please. I was thinking we could go to Dad's apartment and order pizza. Mom's working late."

"We? As in, I would go with you?"

"Yeah, why not? Do you hate pizza?" She gasped with mock horror. "Oh, my God. You hate pizza. This friendship is officially over."

Laughing, I shook my head. "I love pizza. I just don't want to intrude on your time together."

Reed took a seat beside me, his own water bottle dangling between his spread thighs.

He didn't smell like a locker room.

He smelled like what I imagined salt clinging to seaside air would smell like, fused with whatever bodywash he used. Something clean and crisp, hinting with the warmth of amber.

My skin buzzed at his proximity.

"My apartment is a mess," Reed noted, after chugging down his water. "Another time."

"Buzzkill."

"My apartment is a buzzkill."

"True." Tara widened her legs as if she were about to do the splits. "You need some color pops. Everything is black and gray like your heart."

He grumbled under his breath. "You clearly get your dramatics from your mother's side."

She popped back up. "Speaking of Mom, you should bring her over to your place to help decorate. It could use a woman's touch."

There was a subtle implication hidden in her tone.

I worried my lip, silently watching the interaction as my eyes ping-ponged between father and daughter.

Reed tensed beside me. His thigh was gently brushing mine, so I felt the way his muscles tightened. Before he could respond, a voice called out from behind Tara.

"Stephens!" a boy from school shouted. "Catch."

A basketball whirled through the air, landing in Tara's outstretched hands. She glanced at us, a tiny grin tipping her mouth. "That's Josh. Be right back."

She skipped away with the basketball tucked underneath her armpit.

Ladybug lay back down on my feet.

I forced my attention to stay locked on Tara as she reached the blacktop and dribbled the ball, skillfully sidestepping Josh and taking a shot.

Swish.

"I saw you taking pictures earlier," Reed said. "How's that going?"

I braved a glance at him. "It's just one of those disposable cameras from the convenience store."

"Gotta start somewhere."

"It was a good idea. Thank you."

He nodded, and I slid a hand into my bookbag to pull out the camera. I tilted it toward him, my index finger hovering over the capture button.

"I don't like being in pictures."

I faltered. "Really? Why not?"

"Don't know. I guess I prefer the fluidity of experiences, the way they come and go without being confined to a frame."

Lowering the camera, I studied him through the lens of two curious eyes. "That's an interesting take." Then I held up the camera again, waving it around with a cheeky grin. "Sounds like an excuse to me."

He stared at me for a beat, looking thoughtful, before pursing his lips with a light shrug. "Fine, but just one. Better make it count."

"No pressure or anything." Inhaling a breath, I lifted the yellow-and-black Kodak camera and placed it in front of my right eye. I watched him through the cloudy lens as he stared straight ahead, expressionless. This wouldn't do. I bumped my knee against his, trying to get a reaction. "Smile or something."

"No."

"Reed, come on. There are literally no pictures of you at Tara's house."

He said nothing.

I bumped his knee again, and still nothing. I pinched his arm. He frowned, glancing at the contact before sliding his gaze up to my face.

"Are you ticklish?" I wondered.

"Nope."

"There has to be something. I've seen you smile before."

"You sure?"

Sighing, I dropped my arm and fell back against the bench. Ladybug jumped up to all four paws at the sudden movement, and her leash tangled with the strap of my backpack, sending it toppling forward onto the grass. Contents spilled from the open zipper pocket: notebooks, pens, lip balms.

Bones.

My cheeks burned as I stared down at the evidence of my godawful crush, lying at our feet in broad daylight. Tara had given it to me after Ladybug kept slobbering on it because she thought it was a dog toy.

Reed's eyes followed and quickly landed on my source of embarrassment. He blinked twice, then bent over, picking up the Beanie Baby toy he'd purchased for Tara three months ago.

Humiliation rocketed through me.

I was certain he saw me as a silly little girl; a dreamy-eyed teen carrying around a stuffed animal in her backpack for comfort. "That's nothing," I choked out. "Tara gave it to me."

I tried to snatch it away, but he dodged me.

Ugh!

I wanted to disintegrate and melt into the park bench.

Reed turned the toy over his hand, slowly, brushing his thumb along the soft fur as his throat rolled.

Then his eyes flickered with something I suddenly felt compelled to freeze in time.

Inhaling a jagged breath, I raised the camera.

He looked at me.

Reed lifted his chin, glanced my way, and his eyes glittered in the sunshine as half his mouth tipped up with the tiniest grin.

Click.

I snapped the picture.

I made it count.

"Grab the bananas!" Tara shouted through her laughter as we battled through a level of Donkey Kong Country 2 and cruised to the finish line.

My thumbs danced over the controller, my tongue pressed between my teeth in concentration. Dixie Kong leaped through the air, her yellow ponytail trailing behind her, and flew across the banana arch before landing on the target.

The level completed, celebrating our win with dancing, victorious monkeys.

"Yes!" Tara dropped her controller and high-fived my right hand. "Even with that sling, you're better than me. So not fair."

Whitney was sprawled out on the loveseat behind us, her ribbons of brown hair blending with a cocoa-colored pillow. "How about that movie?" Yawning, she glanced over at Reed who was seated on the opposite couch. "My work day is catching up to me. I'm fading fast."

My smile slipped as my focus snapped to Reed and held.

He stared back.

We looked away at the same time and I rose to my feet. "I'll make popcorn."

"I got it," Reed cut in, pulling up from the couch and sweeping past me toward the kitchen without a backward glance. I watched as he rubbed his shoulder, wincing slightly before he disappeared out of sight.

Tara stretched her arms over her head. "I'm gonna call it a night. I've got that chem test tomorrow. Yuck."

"I'll be up soon." I moved to the couch and plopped down, curling my feet up beside me.

"'Night, Dad," she called out, heading up the staircase.

"Goodnight, Squirt."

She scowled at the nickname.

Whitney flipped on a movie while the aroma of buttery popcorn drifted out from the kitchen. Reed returned a few minutes later with a giant yellow bowl, his attention on me before sliding to Whitney.

She waved a hand at him. "I'm still full from dinner. Share with Halley."

My throat went dry.

I wasn't hungry either, but I wouldn't turn down sharing a bowl of popcorn with Reed, even if the salty kernels tasted like heartbreak as they slogged down my throat.

Stiffening, I kept my gaze on the television screen as it glimmered with opening credits to a movie I didn't catch. Reed hesitated, fisting the bowl in two big hands, before stalking toward me and taking a seat to my left. There was a gap between us, but my body ignited with what felt like another fever the moment he was near.

He extended the bowl to me. "Extra butter."

I shoved my hand inside, popping a fistful into my mouth as a few pieces slipped through the cracks in my fingers and landed in my cleavage.

His eyes dipped to the space between my breasts and lingered for a single potent second.

Then he popped his chin up and rubbed his shoulder again, eyes darting to the screen.

I plucked the stray pieces out of my tank top and clenched my thighs, inhaling a deep breath as I tried to get comfortable.

Images burst to life, brightening the dark room.

Characters conversed.

A soundtrack played.

I hardly noticed anything but the man beside me. All I could think about was the split-second when his eyes were on my breasts and how his tongue would feel sliding over the swells.

Has he inched closer to me?

Maybe I'd inched closer to him.

Twenty minutes whirled by and soft snores mingled with the television noise. When I glanced across the room at Whitney curled up on the loveseat, I noticed her eyes were closed, both hands tucked between her cheek and the throw pillow.

Reed sighed and massaged his right shoulder.

"You okay?" I asked softly. The bowl of popcorn was discarded, placed on the cushion to his left. He tapped his foot, one knee bobbing up and down. "You keep rubbing your shoulder."

"I'm fine."

"Did you get hurt?"

Finally, he looked at me. His handsome face was bathed in television glow as distant images reflected in his eyes. Those eyes lowered to my lips for the swiftest second before lifting, his jaw ticking as our gazes met. "Not sure. Must've pulled something with Tara earlier."

"Let me help." I scooted closer to him.

"No." Reed inched away, shaking his head. "I'm good. Not a big deal."

"Don't be stubborn. I may be down a hand right now, but it's an effective hand."

He glanced at my hand when I held it up and wiggled my fingers.

Then I thought about those thirty seconds when that same hand was gripping his denim-sheathed erection.

"For a massage," I clarified, neck breaking out into a flush. "I used to give my Nana massages when I was younger. She said I had magic hands."

Dammit. Nothing was coming out right.

Reed sucked in a breath, his jaw clenching tighter as his eyes closed for a beat. When they fluttered back open, he sent me a nod. "Yeah, sure."

"Really?"

He didn't reply to that. He wasn't sure, and I didn't want to give him the chance to take it back. Climbing to both knees, I moved into his bubble as he pivoted slightly and provided me with his injured shoulder. We both looked across the room at Whitney when her snores amplified.

My exhale was shaky as I got into position and placed a palm near the crook of his neck.

He made a sound like a hiss.

I reeled back, worried I'd made it worse. "Shit. Sorry."

"I'm good."

"Did I hurt you?"

"Said I'm good, Halley." The words sounded gritty, like he was chewing on rocks.

I let out another breath and it whispered along the shell of his ear. I felt him shiver when I touched his shoulder again, curling my palm and giving him a gentle squeeze. "Right here?"

His chest heaved in and out as he fisted both knees in a white-knuckled grip. "Yeah."

I pressed harder, maneuvering behind him for better access. My breasts coasted along the planes of his back, pebbling my nipples. Hoping he hadn't noticed, I inched back and gnawed on my bottom lip as my hand worked him harder, fingertips gliding, the heel of my palm digging into the tender muscle.

He groaned.

The sound sent a shot of wetness straight to my underwear.

He leaned back into me, his breathing sounding unsteady as his eyes closed. The scent of him was intoxicating; amber and sun-warmed earth. I tried not to focus on how silky his hair looked and how I'd do anything to go back in time and graze my fingertips through it, if only for a second.

But I kept going, kept massaging, trailing my hand a little lower to selfishly feel the hard bulge of his bicep as it flexed beneath my touch. I imagined both of those arms on either side of me, caging me in, muscles straining as he hovered over me, hips moving, forehead cased in a sheen of sweat as he panted and moaned.

I squeaked out a whimper, then covered it with a cough.

My hand journeyed back up to the correct spot and continued to knead. "Is this okay?"

He nodded once, his hands still clamped around both knees.

I continued, pressing forward, my chest to his back. Soft curves to hard muscle. His body heat infiltrated me, staining my skin with blotches of pink to match the cast that had been cut off me.

As I worked him, my thumb burrowing deeper, he made another soft groaning sound and tilted his head toward me. His lashes fluttered, irises glazed over. Our eyes hooked and held, a surge of electric smoke and unsaid words funneling between us.

My lips parted to say something.

He glanced at them.

Then Whitney shifted on the couch and the TV remote tumbled to the floor.

I jolted away, my heart pounding.

Reed jumped to his feet.

I fell back on my haunches with wide eyes as I stared up at him, my heartbeats ricocheting and limbs quivering as I pressed my hand between my knees to erase the lingering throb of heat.

Reed ran his fingers through mussed, disheveled hair. He let out a hard breath, glancing down at the floor and slamming his eyes shut.

Grinding my teeth, I watched as he gave his hair a squeeze then dropped his arm before swiveling toward Whitney, refusing to make eye contact with me.

He approached her with a nudge. "Hey. Whit."

She mumbled something incoherent, her head popping up. "Huh?"

"You fell asleep. Tara's upstairs, so I'm going to head out."

A drowsy smile pulled at her cheeks as she reached for his wrist and yanked herself into a sitting position. Smoothing down her sleep-tossed hair, she offered, "You can stay the night if you want. I know it's late."

I grabbed the bowl of popcorn, dropped to my butt, and pretended to be lost in the movie while my heart plummeted to concrete.

Stay?

In her room?

"Crash on the couch," Whitney added.

Relief swept through me, and I deflated.

"I should go. I have an early client."

"That's right. No problem." She yawned, standing from the loveseat and stretching out her arms before sweeping past me with a kind smile. "Goodnight, Halley. Don't stay up too late."

"Goodnight."

As she trudged up the staircase, Reed moved toward the entryway and slipped into his combat boots, the leather faded and worn. He caught my stare as he faltered by the front door, and his eyes glinted with something foreign. I didn't know what shined back at me—conflict, loathing, anger. It was only a half a second. A drumbeat.

Whatever it was, it prickled a cold chill along the back of my neck that lasted far longer.

He yanked the door open and stalked out, slamming it shut behind him without a backward glance. Squeezing my eyes tightly, I collapsed down to the couch the moment he was out of sight and curled up into a little ball of despair.

I was pretty sure I knew what that look was.

Regret.

CHAPTER 9

MARCH ROLLED INTO A SPRINGLIKE APRIL, and Whitney had taken the day off work to celebrate the warmer weather by accompanying Tara and I to the mall.

Patches of ice and snow gave way to green grass.

The air was balmy.

The sun was bright and warm.

And it was just what I needed.

Schoolwork was weighing me down as my mind spiraled, my thoughts in constant disarray. Part of me never wanted to leave the house in case my mother called or came by to see me, but part of me wanted to run far, far away, because the house was constantly filled with Reed.

He'd been spending more time at the Stephens' residence, stopping over for dinner once a week and occasionally picking Tara up for father-daughter bonding time. They had a monthly routine of Pizza Hut and a movie at the local theater. Tara had invited me the prior week when they went to go see *Happy Gilmore,* but I didn't want to infringe on their quality time together. I wasn't his daughter.

Fate had made it so I'd never be his anything.

And it was best if I gave myself space so I could batter my heart into submission while I tried to stomp out the invasive feelings trying to drag me down like quicksand.

Tara and I walked together, trailing behind Whitney as her hands curled around bags of department store purchases. I slurped a mocha Frappuccino through a wide straw, my eyes panning from window to window. Colorful clothing and knickknacks tempted me, reminding me that I didn't have an income for such things.

Tara and I planned to start job-hunting during spring break.

"Did you girls want to shop by yourselves for a bit?" Whitney turned around as Tara and I strolled through the mall with our arms linked. She reached into her purse and pulled out a wad of bills, handing each of us a handful of twenties. "I can meet you at the food court in an hour."

"What? Oh, my God, this is awesome!" Tara's eyes bulged at the offering. "I had my eye on some makeup a few stores back."

My heart soared with gratitude, but rational thought pumped the brakes. The money trembled in my hand. "This is too much," I told her. "You've done enough for me already. I can't accept this."

Whitney pressed a hand to my upper arm and squeezed. "You deserve it, Halley," she said with a flash of white teeth. "Enjoy."

I shook my head, handing the money back to her. "No. I don't deserve it. I'll never be able to repay you for everything you've done for me. I eat your food, use your utilities. You've given me a safe roof over my head and a warm bed to sleep in. I don't need anything else."

Tara fidgeted beside me, eyes aimed at the shiny floor.

A crestfallen look coasted across her mother's face as she stared at me, ignoring my extended hand clamped around the money. "Halley... you can't think like that. I want to help. I'm *happy* to help. You deserve to be a regular teenager, to go shopping with your best friend at the mall. You do a lot for us, too."

"Not nearly enough."

"*More* than enough. You cook, you clean, you take care of Ladybug," she countered gently. "More importantly, you bring warmth to our household. Laughter and light. And that's something money can't buy."

My eyes glazed over as a melty feeling trickled through my veins like honey syrup. I wasn't used to feeling worthy or appreciated; I was used to feeling like the opposite. A burden, a nuisance, a strain.

I was a shadow, not a light.

But as Whitney smiled with affection and Tara linked our fingers together with tenderness, those intrusive thoughts dissolved and all I felt was loved.

"Okay." I dropped my arm at my side. "Thank you."

Nodding through her smile, she whirled back around with a wave. "See you girls soon. Don't forget—one hour."

"Got it!" Tara grabbed my hand and yanked me back toward the beauty store. "Okay. There's a bonfire next weekend to celebrate the kickoff of spring. I need you."

My nose scrunched up. "Need me for what?"

"You know..." Feet still in motion, she waved a hand over me from head to toe. "You've got that thing."

"That thing," I echoed, still confused.

"Yes, that *thing*. That thing that makes guys' heads turn, that makes you look a thousand times older and wiser than me."

"I was forced to grow up fast, Tara. That *thing* is made up of nothing good."

She sighed. "It's more than that. The way you carry yourself, your 'I-don't-give-a-shit' attitude."

"I do give a shit. I give an infinite amount of shits."

"For the people you care about, sure. But in the hallways at school, or at a party, or a day out at the beach? Zero shits."

Sighing, I glanced around at the abundance of shoppers and colorful store windows. A group of guys passed us with a whistle, one of them checking us out.

Tara beamed.

I scowled.

The oldest guy with reddish hair puckered his lips at me and made a kissing noise, rattling off a crass comment about the way my ass looked in my jeans.

"See?" Tara glowered after they'd whizzed by, sounding bummed out that she hadn't been on the receiving end of sexual harassment. "I mean, that one guy was way too old to be looking at you like that, but still."

"Maybe I prefer older guys."

"What?" She sent me a disgusted look. "No. That's creepy. Just because you're supermodel-pretty, all long legs and cute butt, and your waistline looks as if calories turn to dust the moment food hits your tongue, doesn't give old dudes the right to leer at you."

I rubbed two fingers to my forehead. "First of all, I hardly ever have an appetite, thanks to my emotional trauma, so that is nothing to be jealous about. Secondly, your boobs are bigger than mine. Third...you're perfect the way you are. Stop comparing."

Tara pursed her lips, sighing through her nose, then glanced at my chest. "I guess my boobs are a little bigger." Her gaze darted back up. "Are you a virgin?"

My neck heated, the flush traveling to my collarbone. "No."

"Oh, shit. I totally thought you were." Her eyes popped, her pace slowing. "How many guys have you been with?"

"A few."

"Like, a few-few, or a few dozen?"

"Just a few. And I've fooled around a little." I wasn't proud of it. I'd lost my virginity just shy of my fifteenth birthday in a desperate attempt at finding companionship and connection. An escape from my mother's cold shoulder and my father's hard-knuckled fists. "It's not a big deal. I'd rather be in a relationship than have meaningless sex."

"I'm thinking about having sex with Josh."

"Do you really like him?"

She popped a shoulder. "Yeah. It feels right." Off my silence, she added, "I wonder if my mom is seeing anyone."

I blinked at her as we turned a corner. "Does she go on dates?"

"I don't think so. All she does is work, work, work," she said. "I'm wondering if she's still hung up on my dad. She made a comment the other day."

The air whooshed out of my lungs and I had to hide my reaction with a cough. "What comment?"

"She mentioned how she missed having him around."

"Well, mowing the lawn sucks when you're the only one doing it. Maybe that's what she meant. And there's so much laundry. I can hardly keep up."

Tara snorted through a laugh and a side-eye. "Valid. But this was after I caught them being all cozy in the kitchen, doing the dishes together. And he's been coming over to the house more and more lately." Tara pulled a pack of gum from her pocket and plucked out a piece.

"Mom is lonely, so maybe they can work it out. Everything's been really good between the three of us, but they have history—and if there are still feelings there, why not? Life's too short to wallow in the past."

I tried not to choke.

Tara wanted her parents back together?

Does Whitney want that, too?

That was a bomb I wasn't competent enough to keep from detonating in my face once I tried to defuse it. Scratching at my cheek, I fumbled for a reply but came up empty. Guilt sawed through my bones. Stomped all over my heart with steel-toed boots.

If Tara ever found out that I'd had an intimate encounter with her father—and failed to tell her about it—she'd write me off for good. And she was like a sister to me.

As we skipped down the crowded mall aisle in silence, something caught my attention in a passing store window, causing my breath to catch. My heart did a little pirouette inside my chest and I came to a stop.

Tara followed my stare. "Those look expensive."

"I'm going to take a look. Want to come with?"

"Too many buttons. I'm not good with technology." Her nose wrinkled. "But I know you've been interested in photography lately, so take your time. I'll be in the nail polish section."

Pulling away from her, I started walking toward the camera store. "I'll meet you over there in a few minutes. I won't be long."

My pulse thrummed as the sea of electronics glittered through the glass window, beckoning me forward. And it wasn't the cameras themselves, per se—after all, I wasn't great with technology either. It was the possibilities. The art I could create, the moments I could capture.

I felt a dream unfolding.

Winding my way through the entrance, I scurried over to the far wall showcasing dozens of different film cameras, ranging in price from the upper one-hundreds to over one-thousand dollars. I sighed, knowing I wouldn't be able to afford a nice camera until I had a regular income flowing in. In the meantime, I'd have to continue making use of the photo lab and dark room at school, along with the convenience store cameras.

Sunk with defeat, I left the store, my mind spinning with ways to earn some extra cash. Dog walking, babysitting, maybe a waitress job at a local diner.

I could do it.

With my thoughts scattered, I strolled down the mall aisle and did a double-take when I passed by another store that caught my attention.

I stopped, glanced up at the sign.

Then my heart started thumping again.

Not overthinking it, I walked through the entrance and marched over to a kiosk that was brimful of video games. I grinned, scanning the new releases.

Resident Evil.

The game came out last month, and Reed had told me he'd wanted it.

Plucking one off the shelf, I headed toward the checkout counter and handed the clerk three twenty-dollar bills to pay for the fifty-dollar game. As he went to place it inside a bag, I stopped him. "No bag, please. I'll put it in my purse."

"Kay," the teenager said.

Ten minutes later, I was browsing through multicolored nail polishes with Tara, the game hidden at the bottom of my purse.

"Did you buy anything?" she wondered, her palms full of nail polish selections in every shade of blue. Midnight, pastel, periwinkle, and even a color that resembled the bright blossoms of morning glories.

I shook my head through the lie. "Nope. Everything was too expensive."

"Bummer."

"Yeah." I forced a smile and grabbed a lipstick off a shelf. "What do you think of this color?"

She glanced at the deep-plum shade. "Sexy," she decided.

"I think I'll get it."

As we browsed eyeliners, mascaras, and brow palettes, Tara kept stealing glances at a girl beside us who was tossing glosses into her shopping basket.

"Do you know her?"

Tara frowned, blinking at the girl, then shook her head and moved down the aisle. "I thought I knew her, but that's impossible. She lives in Charleston." She took me by the hand. "Come on."

"Was she an old friend?"

"Yeah, I guess. Some weird stuff went down shortly before we moved here. Creepy teacher stuff."

"What do you mean?"

She sighed, her expression darkening in the same way mine probably did when woeful memories snatched me up without warning. "One of my teachers was being gross. It was this whole big thing. I don't really want to talk about it."

I went to protest, to ask for more context, but I understood not wanting to live in those dark moments. Pursing my lips, I nodded and let it go.

We paid for the makeup and met Whitney at the food court a short while later, eager to gorge on heaping plates of Chinese food that always tasted so much better at the mall.

"You look happy, Halley." Whitney popped a plastic fork in her mouth as mall browsers chatted around us and Jewel's *You Were Meant For Me* echoed through the food court. "Did you find something to buy?"

I squeezed my purse in my lap and sent her a shrug as my heartbeats skittered between my ribs. "Just a lipstick."

CHAPTER 10

Halley

REED JOINED me in the kitchen that night as I put together a Mexican casserole, stirring the ground beef mixture in a saucepan. My sling had finally been removed, allowing me to really dive into one of my favorite pastimes: cooking.

"Whit's been calling you 'The Casserole Queen,'" he said, coming up beside me.

His tone was light, and I was grateful for that.

After a handful of tension-filled interactions earlier in the month, the awkwardness had started to ebb, and it was like the shoulder massage had never even happened.

Erased. Poof.

It was for the best.

Whitney sat out on the deck with a glass of wine, chatting with Tara, after I'd volunteered to make dinner. It was our routine. I'd make dinner and take on as many chores as I could, while Whitney opened her home and her heart to me.

I had a lot of catching up to do if I wanted to even the score.

Glancing at Reed, I trained my eyes not to linger. Lingering too long always led to heavy eye contact and a slow-build of anticipation that had the ability to swallow me up in one greedy gulp. "Thanks. You know I love it."

"I'm surprised you haven't made pierogies yet."

My fingers tightened around the wooden spoon and my heart kicked up speed. I feigned nonchalance. "You remember that?"

"Sure. The mother of your still-Polish, not-deceased mother would make them every Christmas Eve."

My wide eyes panned over to him and I almost dropped the spoon.

He remembered the entirety of my awkward, rambling spiel as we'd rolled our carts through a busy grocery store on a blustery holiday evening, and that did something dangerous to my heart.

Swallowing down the knot, I forced a weird-sounding laugh. "Good memory."

Reed smiled as he hopped up on the countertop next to me. He was wearing a band tee, and it was the same color as his dark hair that had grown out and was close to teasing the collar. There was a logo scrawled across the front, so I latched onto the easy subject change.

"What band is that?" I nodded at his chest.

He peered down at the logo. "Screaming Trees."

"I don't know them."

"They're a little harder than the Gin Blossoms, but you might like them."

"I've been on a Toad the Wet Sprocket kick lately," I confessed, sprinkling taco seasoning into the meat concoction. "*All I Want* is my favorite song."

"You have a lot of favorite songs." He smiled again, his eyes softening with a sentiment I refused to agonize over.

A line in one of their songs talked about the air speaking of all we'd never be.

I refused to agonize over that, too.

"You've been quiet lately," Reed continued, swinging his legs. The heels of his boots bumped the lower cabinet with each movement. *Tap, tap, tap.* "You good?"

I glanced over at him.

Then I made the grave mistake of lingering too long.

The look in his eyes was still there, burning heavily into mine. Electricity churned between us with nowhere to go. I wasn't sure if he felt it, too, but I supposed it didn't matter. "Sure," I said softly. "I've just been busy with school, and..."

Tap, tap, tap.

I didn't know if it was my pounding heart or the cabinets thudding against his boots.

"And what?" he probed.

Tap, tap, tap.

The tapping sound was making my brain turn to mush, so I let my heart bleed all over him. Screw it. "And...it's just been hard. Being here. Relying on someone else's family for everything because mine didn't want me. It's hard to live," I confessed. "Living is really *hard*, Reed. School is hard. Trying to make friends is hard. Getting through each day with all these scars and bruises is so goddamn hard. I'll be graduating in a few months and I have no direction in life. My grades are slipping. My dreams are dangling by a thin thread. Where will I go? How will I survive? And you..." Choking, I snapped my mouth shut before any catastrophic words dribbled out like water. "Everything is just... *hard*."

He stopped swinging his feet.

But the sound still pounded in my ears, so I guessed it was my heart, after all.

I froze, regretting the depressing monologue instantly. "God, I'm sorry. I didn't mean to say all that." I started furiously stirring the ground beef mixture as I fought back tears.

Reed dropped his chin to his chest, his jaw going tense as his fingers curled around the edge of the countertop, and he blew out a long breath. "Tell me more about your dreams," he said softly.

I shook my head. "It doesn't matter."

"It does matter. Sounds like you need someone to talk to."

I wanted to talk to *him*, but that was a terrible idea.

Spending alone time with Reed while I ambushed him with my graveyard of ghosts and brittle bones, forced to stare at that look in his eyes that would haunt me till the end of time?

It sounded more like a death sentence; like I'd find myself buried six feet under in that graveyard when all was said and done.

Flipping off the stove, I transferred the mixture to a casserole dish. "I didn't mean to lay all that on you. Like I said before, I'm not your responsibility."

"Doesn't mean I don't care."

I faltered, the saucepan tipped sideways as the ingredients sloshed across ceramic. "Are we friends?"

"I don't know." He frowned, pondering the term. "I guess."

Friends.

I was eighteen, and he was almost thirty-five.

Friendship was debatable, but I wasn't opposed to the title. In a way, it gave me permission to talk to him, to spend time with him, without the nagging tug of guilt.

Nodding slowly, I added a layer of crushed tortilla chips to the meat and reached for the freshly grated cheese. "I've been dabbling in photography at school," I finally told him. "Our principal has a pet rabbit in his office. Nibbles. She's a friendly lop-eared rabbit, a little overweight and extra squishy." A smile crested as I thought about Nibbles and the feel of her soft sooty-gray fur. "When I was a little girl there was an injured bunny that found its way into our yard. It was bleeding, and all I wanted to do was take care of it."

Reed listened, his gaze intense as he watched me layer the casserole while I unlayered myself. "Did you?"

My heart squeezed with residual heartbreak as I recalled the smell of cooked rabbit that night. A cruel message from Father. "I tried," I said, pressing a palm to my chest to curb the pressure. "My father found me tending to the bunny with blood all over his precious garage floor. He whipped me with his belt ten times. And then he made dinner out of it."

"Jesus." Reed's face hardened, a contrast to the soothing, heart-mending look in his eyes. He lowered himself from the counter and moved in beside me, lifting his hand for a split second before second-guessing whatever comfort he was about to provide. He just stood there, his shoulder brushing mine, and it was enough. "I'm sorry, Halley."

The way he said my name had the power to piece all my broken bits back together, but I tried not to show it. "Anyway," I continued, spreading sour cream with a spoon and topping the casserole with a final layering of cheese. "I've been taking pictures of Nibbles to add to the school newspaper. Our principal is really nice and lets me take her out of the cage during lunch. It would be cool to do something like that for a living one day." I shrugged and pulled open the oven door. "But I know better than to believe something like that is actually attainable."

"It'll happen," he said.

"Doubtful."

"It will. You have a fire inside of you. You just need to find the spark to ignite it."

I let out a self-deprecating sigh and placed the casserole on the rack. When I popped the door closed, I swiveled to face him and discovered that the look in his eyes had lightened even more, morphing into something almost playful. "What?"

"We can make a bet."

I huffed. "No."

"Rock, paper, scissors. If I win, you're going to chase your dreams—wings spread, eyes on the sky, no looking back. If you win..." His face fell. "Then I guess you're right."

My cheeks warmed, my insides fluttering like my tiny, weakened wings. "Okay."

"Okay."

His smile returned, and our hands went into position.

I didn't overthink it this time.

One, two—

I did scissors.

Reed did rock.

My eyes panned up to his, while his shimmered with victory.

And then he bopped my scissor fingers with his fist until that fist unclenched and his palm opened, covering my small hand. His touch lingered. It lingered like his eyes always did as he brushed his thumb up and down the length of my index finger.

I swallowed hard, all breath stalled in the crux of my throat. I stared at our clasped hands, wondering why fate had to be so wicked and make it so they'd have to part. His touch was warm, thumb calloused yet gentle.

Everything inside of me turned to sunlight.

A fireball, a blaze.

And then the patio door clapped shut, ripping him away from me.

Reed jumped back, spun around, and shoved a hand through his hair as he cleared his throat. Whitney strolled into the kitchen with an empty wine glass.

Her eyes were glazed with Merlot as she sent us both a wide grin. "Smells amazing, Halley."

I twisted back to the counter and began to clean. "Thank you. It's a lot easier now that I have two hands," I replied, showcasing my arm, sans the sling.

It was a lie, though.

I didn't have two hands.

One was swiping sour cream dollops off the counter with a dishrag...

And my other was still tingling with the memory of being locked with his.

Evening crested, and I tiptoed out onto the deck after Whitney and Tara had gone upstairs to bed. Reed was outside, watching Ladybug run around in circles as he tossed her a rubber ball and the string lights on the veranda bathed him in a soft yellow glow.

I swallowed down my jitters and approached as he sat hunched forward in a plastic patio chair, elbows pressed to his knees.

Reed glanced over at me when the patio door rolled open and shut. He blinked, a frown wrinkling his forehead. "Hey."

"You're still here?" I was wearing my new lipstick and my Gin Blossoms T-shirt, while my hands clung nervously to a gift hidden behind my back.

"Leaving in a few. I had some wine with dinner, so I was waiting for it to wear off before I drove home." He watched as I inched closer, his gaze slowly trailing over me before settling on my plum-stained lips. "Are you going out?"

"No."

Confusion settled into the creases of his forehead as his focus snapped up to my eyes. He blinked again, waiting for me to voice my intentions. "Did you want to talk?"

I shook my head. "I have something for you."

"You do?"

"Yes." My reply caught on a spring breeze. "I never thanked you for the gift you gave me on Christmas Eve." Rubbing my matte lips together, I studied his reaction as he continued to stare at me. "The money you snuck in my pocket."

When the memory registered, his pale-green eyes softened against the bulb lights. "It wasn't a big deal."

"It *was* a big deal. You didn't have to do that, but you did. And it meant a lot to me."

Reed nodded and glanced down at the wooden planks beneath his feet as he scuffed them with the toe of his boot. "You're welcome, Halley."

I took another step closer and his head slowly lifted, his eyes even slower to catch up as they skimmed up the length of my body. My pulse revved, and I fought back nerves as I dallied in front of him, words jumbling on my tongue. Before I could overanalyze, I exhaled a big breath and unraveled my arm from around my back. "I got this for you."

I handed him the video game.

It took a second for his eyes to leave my face. They lingered in that dangerous way, in the way I'd been trying so hard to avoid, and in the same way his palm had lingered on mine earlier.

But when they lazily dipped to my outstretched hand, his shoulders tautened. Went stiff. His throat rolled, and the seconds slugged by in itchy silence.

"Here." I pushed it closer to him with a smile. "It's for you."

Gravel stole his voice. "Why?"

"Because I wanted to do something nice for you. You told me you were excited about the game."

His head swung back and forth as he palmed the nape of his neck and released a sigh. "No. I can't accept that."

My smile wilted. "What? Why not?"

Reed stood from the chair, its legs scraping along the planks like a rusty gate closing on my heart. He swooped past me, headed for the patio door, then stopped just short of it.

Hand still squeezing the back of his neck, he whirled around to face me. "You said you were trying to save your money. You shouldn't be buying me things."

"Whitney gave me some extra cash at the mall. And besides, we're friends. You said so yourself."

"I shouldn't have said that."

Anger and confusion coursed through my bloodstream as I stomped toward him on the deck. "No," I shot back. "You don't get to do that. That's not fair."

"I'm not trying to be an asshole." He steepled his hands at his chin. "I do care about you. I want to be a shoulder for you to lean on when you need support. You've been through a lot of terrible shit that no one should ever have to experience. But I feel like I'm giving you mixed signals."

"Don't patronize me." Tears breached my eyes as my chin quivered. "I'm just trying to be nice."

"Why are you all dressed up when you're about to go to bed? Why are you buying me expensive video games? It's not my birthday. It's just a random fucking day, and I'm the thirty-four-year-old father of your best friend. You're a teenager, Halley."

"I'm an *adult*. And what does my age have to do with it?"

"Everything. If you had actually been twenty-one like you told me you were, you'd be—" His mouth snapped shut.

My breath stalled, my heartbeats a stampede threatening to crush my fragile ribs. "I'd be what?"

I waited, holding on to that breath.

His eyes glinted, wild like his breeze-flung hair, and he just stared at me, the rest of his words trampled by the beats of my galloping heart.

"Nothing." He looked away. "Never mind."

"Reed...tell me."

"Go to bed."

I gaped at him, fury igniting in my chest. My lungs. Everywhere. His tone was condescending, like I was some sort of child who'd been banished to her room for the night.

Hands fisted, I took another deliberate step toward him as he stared off to the side, avoiding my gaze. "What were your plans for us that night?"

A heavy beat passed.

And then his head slowly canted back to me.

Every muscle tightened. His fingers clenched and splayed, his biceps twitching in response. He shook his head back and forth as if trying to eradicate the question from the space between us. "Don't ask me that."

"Why not?"

"Don't ever ask me that," he repeated, rasping out the words like they were tiny needles pricking him on the way out. "Please."

"We should talk about it."

"There's nothing to talk about."

"Yes, there is. Maybe we should—"

"You fucking *lied* to me!"

He shot forward like a predator in the night with balled hands and anger in his eyes.

My own traitorous instincts kicked in.

Memories unfurled. Flashbacks assaulted me.

I shrank before him, cowering back, my arms lifting to block my face.

Reed froze.

Stopped dead in his tracks.

"Christ," he breathed out.

Slowly, I lowered both hands from my face, my eyes wide and glassy as reality came tumbling back.

Oh, God.

I shook my head, humiliation sinking in.

"I wasn't going to hurt you. I would never hurt you."

"I-I know. I'm sorry," I stammered, my headshake morphing into a frantic nod. "I know."

He reached for me, cautiously extending both arms, his gaze gleaming with torture and remorse. "Fuck. Come here, Comet."

My nickname.

He'd only said it once, and I wasn't sure why he ever stopped.

I inhaled a shaky breath.

That awful apologetic look he sent me dismantled whatever it was that had taken me over. Images of my father's evil eyes and meaty fists evaporated into distant fog as I stepped closer, then closer, until the heat from his body melted away the remnants of my misplaced fear.

His arms wrapped around me.

Gentle. Careful.

The shot of adrenaline receded and I became a ragdoll in his embrace. I felt his warm breath skimming along the top of my head as his scent enveloped me, bathing me in a wash of pure peace.

"I'm really sorry," I murmured against his chest. "I feel like such an idiot."

"No. Don't apologize." One big palm stroked the length of my spine, up and down, slow and tender. "I'm sorry for scaring you. I swear you're safe."

I wanted to explain further, tell him it wasn't *he* who had spooked me—but I couldn't put the irrational feeling into words. I couldn't spin my bone-deep trauma into anything that made sense.

And I think he already knew.

He'd figured it out.

Reed pressed his cheek to the top of my head, exhaling a long, shuddery breath. I shivered, inching as close to him as I could get and listening to his heartbeats flicker through the Screaming Trees T-shirt. He felt so safe. Like the last thing in the world that would ever bring me harm.

We stood together beneath the veranda lights and half-moon, my arms dangling at my sides because I was too afraid to hold him back. Too afraid that my hands would never loosen their grip once they curled around his waist or pressed along the hard planks of his chest. I would never want to let him go.

But I had to.

Reed would never be mine to keep.

When I stepped back, I looked up at him, tipping my chin as tears bloomed in my eyes. "Keep the game," I said, pressing it to his chest until he finally took it. "It doesn't have to mean anything."

He swallowed hard, staring at me, lips parting like he wanted to say something.

I didn't give him the chance to.

I walked away, pushed through the patio door, and stole a final glance at him before heading toward the staircase.

He was holding the game in both hands, head down, eyes closed.

Looking just as torn up as I was.

CHAPTER 11

Reed

I GLARED at the guy with a pimple scar smackdab in the middle of his forehead as I parked my truck in the driveway, hopped out, then shut the door behind me.

The kid was tall and willowy, void of muscle mass and charm, and he was leering at Halley like he wanted to devour her.

She glanced my way as I approached, and I tried to hide my exhaustion.

I'd just finished up a series of grueling back-to-back sessions, wondering if it was time to hire on another coach. My client tonight had been a single mother, recovering from an abusive relationship she'd barely managed to escape from. She'd had her young daughter with her, reminding me of Tara at that age. Swinging brown pigtails and a gummy smile. The woman had been frail, terrified, and alone, desperate to find her strength again—to be a better, healthier role model for her little girl. Part of me wanted to offer my services to every victim, every beaten-down survivor, at no cost. But I had to make a living, too. I was only one person doing his damnedest to make a difference.

Blowing out a breath, I paused to let the tension roll off me before pushing forward.

When I stepped over to Halley, I greeted her with a quick nod before eyeing the teenager who appeared desperate.

She swung her gaze back to Pimple Guy.

"We could go somewhere," he said. "There's a spot at the bluffs where my friends go sometimes."

She stiffened, her hand curled around Ladybug's leash. I moved in closer and took the leash from her grip as her cheeks pinkened in the fading daylight.

When I sent her a soft smile, she let go.

Halley fidgeted, twisting back to Pimple Guy. "No. Sorry, I have plans tonight."

"Eh, you should cancel. You ditched me at the dance." He rolled back on the heels of his sneakers with a shrug. "You kinda owe me, Foster."

My hackles rose as I pretended to mind my business, letting Ladybug sniff a patch of freshly mowed grass. The late-April breeze was borderline chilly, but my blood was rising to boiling.

Halley cleared her throat. "I was sick. I couldn't help it."

"My buddy told me you didn't even want to go."

"Yeah, well, I'm not a big fan of school dances."

"So let's go to the bluffs instead."

"She said no." I couldn't help myself. Swiveling around with my hand tightly coiled around the leather lead, I flicked my eyes to Halley, then back to the kid. "Doesn't sound like she's interested."

He scowled at me. "You live here?"

"No."

"You her dad or something?"

I cringed. "No."

"Then take a hike, tough guy."

Halley looked mortified as she jolted forward, inserting her slim body between us when Pimple Guy tried to get in my face. "It's fine," she intervened. "Eric, maybe we can grab coffee next weekend. I do have plans tonight."

She didn't want to grab coffee with him.

And I wanted to break his face for pressuring her.

"Whatever." He inched backward, spitting on the lawn beside our feet. "I'll call you."

The guy finally retreated, stalking down the sidewalk with his

JNCO jeans and piss-poor attitude. I watched him disappear around the corner before slowly turning back to Halley.

She blinked at me.

"Sorry," I muttered.

I wasn't sorry.

He was a fuckass.

"I was handling it." She leveled me with a glower, moving to fold her arms in a defensive stance but popping a hand on her hip, instead. "You don't need to be chasing boys away."

"His intentions weren't pure."

"That's..." She scoff-laughed. "His intentions don't concern you."

"I was looking out for you. Something your father never did."

Her face reddened against the setting sun. "You don't know anything about my father."

"I know enough."

My gaze dipped to her left arm, still fragile and healing, before panning back up. We stared at each other as her honeyed hair spilled over each shoulder like liquid gold. Her eyes flashed, but it was more than just anger. More than aggravation.

Pain ringed her irises—a look I'd become all too familiar with.

That catastrophic shoulder massage, for one.

And then the altercation on the deck when she'd thought I was about to put my fist through her face.

Fuck.

It haunted me.

The shoulder rub had been a mistake, and the logical side of my brain had evidently jumped out the window, deserting me in my time of need. The intimate hug on the deck had been a mistake, too, but I hadn't known what else to do at the time. She'd been scared of me. Terrified and panicked, cowering like a wounded animal about to be struck down by an assassin.

It was pure instinct; her body's innate reaction to a volatile man baring his teeth at her.

I felt like shit.

Halley Foster was getting under my skin like a splinter. Poking, painful, and increasingly hard to ignore. Of course, my steady presence at this house had made the much-needed distance difficult, so I'd had to settle for digging her out of me with a dull pair of tweezers. The residual sting lingered, and she was determined to crawl back inside.

Halley jutted her tongue between her lips as her gaze settled on Ladybug and her shoulders deflated. "Are you staying the night?"

I scratched at the back of my neck. "No. Why would I?"

"With Whitney."

Frowning, I shook my head. "Whitney and I aren't together." We weren't, and we never would be again. I admired, respected, and cared about Tara's mother, but we didn't fit romantically. Ten years ago, we'd become oil and water, and it wasn't a recipe I was looking to try again. "Are you going out with Tara tonight?"

"No. I have a date."

My eyes skimmed over her, from toes to top. She was all dolled up with curls in her hair, her slender body encased in black leather that accentuated her curves. Her eyes were rimmed with kohl, her dark-berry lips lined with sadness, reminding me of the night we'd met. "A date?" I hedged. "What's his name?"

"He's a friend of Jay's. Why does it matter?"

It didn't matter, therefore, I didn't have an answer for her. "Jay's in his twenties."

"So?" Her lips pursed. "I've been with older."

I ground my teeth together.

I refused to flash back to that night on Jay's bed when my tongue was in her mouth and my fingers were buried deep inside her. She'd been soaked. Aching for me. Needy, bold, and devastatingly willing. She'd seemed experienced, and while the notion had spurred me on at the time, now it only festered in the back of my mind, clouding me with dark, toxic thoughts.

How many men has she been with?

Jesus. It didn't fucking matter.

Not at all.

We stood across from each other in tense silence while Ladybug tugged at the leash, eager to escape our silent standoff.

Halley sighed before whirling around and heading toward the front door. "I made a turkey casserole," she called over her shoulder. "Enjoy."

Then she stormed inside the house.

My breath looked like a plume of smoke when I huffed out a long sigh, letting Ladybug do her business before shuffling inside and unhooking the leash. Maybe I'd overstepped with Pimple Guy, but that shit didn't fly with me. Guilt-tripping girls into going to the bluffs—a place notorious for drugs and hookups—was where I drew the line.

Maybe it was my protective, fatherly instincts kicking in.

Or maybe I was feeling even more protective of her after the incident out on the deck. A way to right my wrongs.

Regardless, it was for her own good.

Halley was nowhere in sight when I slipped off my boots and found Whitney in the kitchen, stirring gravy in a saucepan. "Hey," I greeted.

She glanced up. "Hey. It'll just be the three of us tonight. Halley has a date."

I pressed my tongue against my cheek, wondering where they were going, what they planned to do. Halley had been living here for almost two months and I hadn't seen her socialize much, aside from mall adventures with Tara and a handful of park dates. Not that I was any different. I'd left all of my friends and social acquaintances back in Charleston, and it wasn't easy for me to make new connections. I was too busy, too guarded.

"All right." I eyed the array of food dishes on the counter. "Dinner looks good."

"I whipped up a gravy to go with the potatoes, but Halley made the casserole. She's talented. I'll admit, I'm going to be disappointed when she moves out."

I shouldn't feel the same, but some part of me wondered if I'd also be disappointed. Halley was a good cook and my daughter had never looked happier than when the two of them were playing games, watching movies together, and gossiping until dusk. Whitney seemed happier, too.

Apparently, I enjoyed splinters.

"Are you leaving after dinner?" she probed.

"Yeah. Can't stay too long. My brother's in town, on leave from Japan."

"Mm." She tensed, her features pinching with unease as her grip tightened around the handle of the spoon. "How's Radley doing these days?"

"Good. Military life suits him." I shuffled between feet, glancing down at the ivory tiles, wondering if I should have made something up about my plans.

After all, Radley was a contributing factor to our relationship breaking down.

My idiotic brother had fallen in love with her.

She was three years older than him, but he'd become smitten. It'd been a point of contention throughout the latter part of my relationship with Whit, culminating in an explosive confrontation one night outside her parents' house.

I'd accused her of cheating.

She'd slapped me.

I'd stormed out.

In the weeks that had followed, communication between us had dwindled, and the strain caused by Radley's asinine crush had become too much to weather through. Eventually, Whit and I had decided to take a break, hoping that some time apart would allow us to reassess our priorities.

But as weeks turned into months, Whitney and I had drifted further apart. It'd become crystal clear that our relationship had run its course, and the presence of my brother as a persistent third party had only complicated things. Whitney had eventually confessed that she'd slept with Radley, and that revelation had been the final blow to any hopes of a reconciliation.

I'd been pissed, and it had taken years to repair the damage between all three of us.

And while their tryst hadn't lasted, the betrayal I felt had. Five years had gone by before I'd reconnected with my only sibling. My only real family member. After losing both of our parents as teenagers, we were all each other had.

But he was content being overseas serving our country. And even though I enjoyed our occasional get-togethers, the distance worked for us.

Skimming a hand through my hair, I cleared my throat. "I'll tell him you said hi."

The statement hit too close to home, and Whit's eyes flared when she popped her head up. She blinked at me, a look of regret coasting across her face. "Thanks. What are your plans?"

"Just grabbing a drink and catching up." I wedged my shoulder against the wall. "I haven't seen him since the move to Charleston. It's been years."

My brother had invited me to a popular pub in town, and while I wasn't much for the bar scene these days, I was looking forward to seeing him.

Our relationship was complicated, but I was in my mid-thirties now. Long-term grudges didn't sit well with me, especially after experiencing how quickly time flew. Being a dad was a bucket of ice-cold water being dumped on me with every year that ticked by.

Tara was morphing into a young woman before my eyes. She was getting older every day.

And so was I.

Whitney brought dinner to the table and we sat across from each other, waiting for Tara to bound down the staircase. Five minutes later, my daughter took a seat beside me in her plaid pajamas, her hair pulled up into a high ponytail, and pecked a kiss to my cheek.

"Hey, Dad. You're looking dapper," she teased. "Hot date?"

"I'm going out with your Uncle Rad."

"Ooh, the *fun* Madsen brother. One day he'll teach us his ways."

My expression soured. "He'll teach you nothing."

"Why not? He's like Peter Pan with a sprinkling of sarcasm."

"I'll let him know you want him to wear tights."

She swatted my shoulder with a snort. "Just tell him his favorite niece says hey."

Dinner rolled on as Tara and her mother laughed at inside jokes and made plans for the weekend, the tension easing as we inhaled the casserole.

I tried to pay attention.

I tried to hang on to every word that echoed around the table.

But all I heard was the Oasis CD playing on loop, one floor above us.

CHAPTER 12

Reed

THE BAR WAS SMOKY, smelling like rich, aged whiskey and a fusion of various perfumes and colognes. My eyes scanned the dimly lit space that was jampacked with people as I searched for a familiar tousle of black hair and broad shoulders.

When I spotted him in a corner booth, sipping on a short glass of amber liquid over ice, I swerved through a group of laughing coeds and made my way over to my brother.

His eyes flicked up mid-sip, and he faltered before the glass touched his lips. A wide smile spread, full of familiarity and mischief. "Reed," he greeted, leaning back in the booth. "Long time no see, big brother."

My smile wasn't as bright, but I was glad to see him. "Hey." I slipped into the seat across from him. "You look good."

"Two whole days sober." He grinned, holding up the glass.

"A shining achievement."

"How's hero life?"

Radley slid a second beverage across the table, filled with a pale lager. Staring into the froth, I curled a hand around the sweating glass.

I didn't consider myself a hero.

I had a job, and I did that job well. In my world, the real heroes were the people I encountered every day—the survivors. The ones battling and overcoming the worst that life had thrown at them.

"The job is good. Keeps me busy and fulfilled."

Radley stretched his trademark smile, the one that always made his eyes sparkle jade and jovial. "I'm proud of you, you know. But not surprised." He skimmed the pad of his thumb across the dark stubble dotting his upper lip. "That was always your way. Making big moves, changing lives."

"I'm no saint." I took a sip of beer. "Not even close."

"Compared to me, you're the halo-wearing offspring of Mother Teresa."

"Not exactly difficult."

He barked a laugh. "Yeah. Guess I made a wrong turn somewhere and went straight to Hell." Palming his whiskey glass, he twirled it around and lowered his eyes. "You seeing anybody?"

"No." I shook my head. "Happily single."

"Just doing the fuck-and-run, then? Jay's older brother told me you were spotted getting cozy with a blonde in his bedroom not long ago. Said she was hot as hell and had legs for days."

Christ.

That was the absolute last thing I wanted going around the rumor mill.

Goddamn small towns.

Closing my eyes, I rubbed a hand over my mouth and sighed. "She was seventeen. Jay and his brother are idiots."

He shrugged like it was nothing. "This is a judgment-free zone. Age of consent *is* seventeen," Radley said, sipping his liquor before chuckling through a swallow. "Good ol' Illinois. You can't buy fireworks, but you can fuck a seventeen year old."

My eyes pinged back open and I shot him a hard glare. "Your niece is seventeen. Say that again."

He didn't.

Making a sour face, he went back to his whiskey.

Age of consent was beside the point. Halley was eighteen, so, legally, I could pursue her.

But morally?

I had a daughter only a year younger, and that was something I couldn't wrap my head around.

Conversation trickled on, veering into military life in Japan. War stories, accomplishments, bloodshed. I told him about Tara—her volley-ball achievements, friendships, and her blossoming interest in makeup and hair design. Whitney's name never came up, and while that debacle was water under the bridge these days, I was grateful for the reprieve.

An hour passed and fatigue filtered through me. After paying for our drinks, we slipped out of the bar and lingered on the sidewalk while Rad sucked on a cigarette.

I glanced at my watch. Shuffled my feet. Daydreamed about climbing into bed and sleeping for twelve hours. Maybe double.

But then a familiar floaty laugh traveled over to me, severing my goodbye. I froze, blinking away from my brother and glancing down the sidewalk toward the adjacent building.

My heart slammed to a stop.

I frowned when I spotted a shock of honey-blonde hair bobbing over someone's shoulder.

Radley followed my stare. "Mm. I noticed her, too." He *tsk*ed his tongue. "Sexy."

"I know her."

"Lucky bastard."

I shot a glare in his direction, my muscles locked and chest tight. "She's one of Tara's friends."

He squinted, his lips thinning. "She doesn't look Tara's age."

"No shit." I watched her for a moment. She was obscured by a few groups of people and a guy I didn't recognize donning shoulder-length, dirty blonde hair and a box-shaped jaw. He towered over her as she leaned back against the brick exterior of the Mexican joint next door with a disposable camera in her hands.

She flicked the little dial, biting her lip, shifting from one stilettoed foot to the other. I was well-versed in body language, using it as a guide on a regular basis for my clients, and instinct told me she was uncomfortable. Taut shoulders, wary eyes. Fidgeting and restless. The guy moved in, planting a massive hand on the wall behind her, caging her in.

Another breathy laugh fell out of her as she turned her head to the side and pressed further against the wall like she was trying to become a part of the stonework.

After the incident from earlier, I was hesitant to interfere and embarrass her again. She was an adult. They were in public.

She was fine.

Swallowing, I turned my attention back to my brother as he prattled on about one of his military buddy's recent homecomings. But I hardly heard him, my senses narrowed in on Halley a few feet away. My gaze kept floating in her direction, checking on her, making sure she was okay. Draped in black leather and yellow lamplight, she inched away from the guy and ducked underneath his arm.

"I'm getting kind of tired," I heard her say.

"It's still early."

Radley puffed on his cigarette, tossing it to the pavement and stomping out the embers. "Want to grab another round?" he asked me.

"I, uh..." My focus was shared, my worry heightening as I watched Halley start to walk away. Clearing my throat, I shook my head. "I need to head home. Early day tomorrow."

"We should do this again. Next time I'm in town."

I nodded absently, already moving in the opposite direction. "Yeah. Absolutely."

"Later, big brother. Give Tara a hug for me."

Sending him a halfhearted wave over my shoulder, I trudged closer to Halley as she took a few paces down the sidewalk.

"I'm not feeling good." Her voice pitched over the myriad of chatter from smokers dallying outside the restaurant.

"I got an apartment a mile from here," he said. "We can watch a movie and relax."

"Maybe another time."

The beast of a guy blocked her escape, a meaty hand slinking around her hip as he leaned into her and whispered something in her ear with a curling grin. I couldn't make out what he said, but I saw her reaction. She went ramrod straight, planting a palm to his big chest and pushing him back.

He didn't let up, coaxing her back against the wall and grazing his nose along her throat as his grip on her waist tightened.

Halley dropped the camera.

Started to struggle.

She had the same inherent fear on her face she'd had that night on the deck, when, for one debilitating moment, she'd flashed back to concrete knuckles and evil eyes.

Cannonballing forward, I shoved through a mass of huddled bodies until she spotted me. Halley did a double-take, freezing momentarily, the prick's face still burrowed in the crook of her neck.

"Hey." I grabbed the guy by the shoulder and hauled him away from her. "Don't touch her."

Halley wiggled free, swatting her loose hair back and trying to catch her breath, breasts heaving against her skintight bodice. She stared at me as if she was second-guessing the accuracy of her vision. Likely wondering if she'd somehow summoned a white knight or a stalker. "What...what are you doing here?" Her breathing was as unsteady as her balance, her legs wobbling underneath her.

I swallowed. "You okay?"

The guy glared at me in my periphery, sizing me up. "Can I help you?"

Ignoring him, I inserted myself between the man and Halley, pinning my attention solely on her panicked face. Wide, stricken eyes gazed up at me, her every limb trembling as she crossed her arms to subdue the shivers.

Shaking her head, she bent over to pick up the fallen camera and made a hurried trek in the opposite direction.

"Halley."

Her gait quickened, long hair fluttering behind her.

The asshole muttered profanities on the sidewalk behind me as I forged ahead, catching up to her and snatching her by the wrist.

She yelped. A little mouse narrowly dodging a hungry hawk. "Reed, I'm fine. You can go." She twisted out of my grip and charged forward. "I-I just need a minute."

I idled for a moment, studying her as she slipped into a darkened alleyway between two buildings. Something was wrong. The threat had passed, but she was still terrified. I didn't want to corner her and make it worse, but worry gnawed at me. A tingly awareness.

Pressing forward, I picked up the pace and jogged around the corner, discovering Halley leaning against the graffiti-strewn wall. Forehead to brick, she was panting heavily, her purse and camera scattered at her heels as her fingers curled into the divots.

"Halley." My tone was softer now. Reassuring.

She shook her head again, breathing escalating. "Go," she croaked out.

"I'm not going anywhere. You're not okay."

"Go...please." Each word shook as she spun back around, clutching at the hemline of her lowcut blouse. "I...I'm fine. I'll be fine."

Her actions roared louder than her words. She slid down the length of the wall, her movements frantic and erratic. I watched in growing concern as she trembled, her breaths coming in rapid, shallow gasps. Halley pressed both hands to her throat, her eyes widening with fear, desperately clawing at the invisible weight crushing her chest.

A panic attack.

My paramedic training fired and I crossed the alley, dropping to my knees across from her as I reached for her hands. "Hey, hey, shh." I soothed her, my voice measured, touch gentle. "Halley, listen to me. You're safe. You're not alone. I'm right here with you."

Each ragged inhale seemed to offer no relief, only fueling the panic further. Tears slid down her cheeks as her body shuddered atop the rubble.

I extended and splayed my palms, a silent invitation for her to take hold. "Feel the ground beneath you. Feel me." Giving her hands a squeeze, I inched in closer on the dirty pavement, locking our fingers together. She squeezed back as her terror-laced gaze met with mine.

There was nothing I could do but stay composed and keep her centered until it passed. "Can you focus on my voice?" I allowed her nails to gouge dents in the backs of my hands while pebbles and glass shards punctured my kneecaps.

As she nodded, her eyes dilated and teary, I continued to speak, guiding her through calming breathing exercises I'd learned during my medical training. "Good. You're doing good. Slow, deep breaths. In and out....in and out."

Halley's chest hissed with each taut breath, her lungs wheezy as her focus stayed locked on my face. Her eyes swam with swirling ghosts, shades of gray tinted with moonlight.

"That's it." I nodded slowly, dusting my thumb back and forth over her knuckles. "I'm right here. I've got you." I repeated the mantra, maintaining an encouraging smile as I watched the tension start to ebb. Cars and passersby whirred past the opening of the alleyway, the clamoring of engines and laughter mere background noise. When Halley finally drank in a full, lung-satisfying breath, she slumped forward into my arms with a sharp cry.

I unlinked our fingers and wrapped my arms around her, catching her. Outstretching my legs, I allowed her to crawl into my lap as we sat in the middle of the craggy asphalt and I stroked her hair.

"I-I'm sorry," she stuttered, smashing her face against my chest. "I'm broken."

"You're not broken."

"He said something my father used to say...a-and I panicked. He called me a lamb. It was like a thread snapping. A trigger. And it's stupid and embarrassing, and all I want to do is be normal, but I can't escape this helpless, awful feeling." Her words bled together, a jumble of torment. "Everywhere I go, I see him lurking in the shadows. Every time my mind wanders, I hear his voice, feel his leather belt on my skin. I'm always scared. I'm always running. But I'm running in circles, and it's exhausting, and it's endless, and I just want to be free."

I pulled her face up with both palms, gathering her tears with my thumbs. Bloodshot eyes stared back at me, her lipstick and mascara smeared. "Listen to me. When something breaks you, you pick up the pieces and put yourself back together. Maybe it's with stitches and glue sticks, but it's enough to keep going. Nobody needs to stay broken."

"I don't know what to do." She sniffled through her shivers. "And you're the last person I should be falling apart with."

"Maybe." I dusted off her wet cheeks. "But I'm the one who's here."

Halley stared down at the cracks in the pavement, the tension in her body deflating as her breathing settled to normal. "Do you ever fall apart?"

"Of course I do."

"I can't picture it," she whispered. "You're strong. Resilient."

"I'm human. Just like you." I inched back, giving her space to breathe. To process. "I don't let many people in. If I seem resilient it's because I've built walls around myself. That's not exactly healthy either. I have very few close relationships because most of them have led to heartache."

She licked the tears from her lips and glanced back up at me. "I don't want to be weak anymore."

"You are not weak." I reached for her face again, my grip on her cheeks tighter than before. "I promise you that. Get that shit out of your head."

"It is true. You just witnessed it."

"I witnessed the psychological ramifications of an abusive household," I said firmly, forcing her eyes on me. "I swear to you, Halley, you are not weak. You're recovering. And recovery takes time. I'll help you, if you need someone to talk to."

Halley's eyes glazed over as she stared at me, her tears glinting in the streetlight. Heaving in a shuddery breath, she lifted a hand and draped it over mine, her touch soft. A gentle caress.

A thank you.

She nodded, drinking in my words, my truth, and offered the smallest smile. "Are you here to save me?"

She'd asked me that same question at Jay's apartment, on the night we'd met, our backs pressed to a faded-blue couch.

Are you here to save me?

Our eyes stayed locked for another beat, a warm, confusing feeling coursing through my bloodstream. I saw her so clearly in that moment. Her pain, her agony. Her clawing need for strength. She needed someone in her corner, fighting for her. And Halley was right—it shouldn't be me.

But I was a born fighter and it was in my nature to protect. To defend. I wanted to mold her pain into perseverance; into something worthy and commendable.

I wanted to turn her into someone who could save herself.

Halley squeezed my hand. "Take me home," she said, smiling again, a heartwarming tilt of her lips. It softened my jagged edges. Wormed its way inside like a pesky invader.

Dangerous. Lethal.

A breach in my steely resolve.

Pulling to a stand, I extended my palm with a nod, helping her up.

Helping her to her feet.

I took her home.

CHAPTER 13

Halley

September, 1996

FIREWORKS PAINTED THE SKY, and I watched as the stretch of black above me came alive with streaks of emerald and violet. Labor Day weekend had officially wrapped up, and the summer season had been given a final colorful sendoff.

While the end of summer for most eighteen year olds marked shining, new adventures ahead—college, moving out, career-planning—for me, it signaled nothing but a replay.

I'd been held back.

Because of my deteriorating mental state and poor grades, catching up seemed an insurmountable challenge. It was humiliating, but I'd made the decision to repeat my senior year of high school. I had goals. Plans. I refused to be a high school dropout.

And I supposed the only plus-side to repeating senior year was that I was in the same grade as Tara now. Assuming there were no more setbacks for me, we would graduate together.

Tara cheered beside me in a lawn chair, whooping as she pumped her fist in the air. I sipped my lemonade through a straw, my legs curled up beside me on the adjacent chair.

Whitney stood in front of us, her eyes on the sky as the night went quiet. "They do such a great job with the fireworks," she mused, glancing back at us. "Reminds me of being a kid again."

I couldn't relate.

My childhood was filled with fireworks, but not the pretty kind. Instead of vivid displays bursting among the stars, it was the explosive whips of a leather belt across my back that produced stars behind my tear-filled eyes. It was the sparks of uncertainty and fear that always shadowed and defined me. The booms were echoes of raised voices and cruel words that painted a different kind of show—one that left painful claw marks on the canvas of my memories.

I forced a smile anyway. "Yeah, it was great."

"Want to go to that beach bonfire with me?" Tara popped up from her chair.

"You're going out?" Whitney turned to Tara. "It's getting late."

"C'mon, Mom, I'm almost eighteen. What's the worst that could happen?"

"Do you want me to make a list?"

Tara huffed. "I'll have Josh pick us up."

"I'm going to stay in," I told her, rearranging my face into another weak smile. "Have fun. Take pictures."

"You know I suck at that, Hals. Every time I try to take a picture, it turns out to be this weird, blurry blob that wouldn't even pass for abstract art."

I smirked. "That's because you can't stop moving. You need to focus on the moment."

"The next moment always sounds better than the one I'm in."

Again, I couldn't relate.

When you're always *fearing* the next moment, you tend to appreciate the good ones while you have them.

Whitney sighed, gathering her hair into a ponytail and securing it with a purple rubber band. "Will you call me when you get there?"

"No phones at the beach, Mom."

"Page me, then. I just want to make sure you're safe."

"Yeah, yeah, will do." Tara turned to me. "You sure you want to stay in?"

"I'm sure." There was something else I needed to do tonight.

"Okie dokie. I'll probably stay the night at Amanda's."

"Be sure to check in," Whitney called out as Tara skipped away with a wave.

"Can't wait for dinner with Dad tomorrow night." Pausing at the patio door, she waggled her eyebrows at her mother. "But I'll head to bed early so you two can have some *alone* time."

Whitney blushed, and Tara disappeared into the house.

I covered my face with my lemonade glass, hiding my own flushed cheeks.

Breathing out an embarrassed laugh, Whitney sat down in the chair Tara had been sitting in. "Sorry. She has it in her head that her father and I are going to reconnect or something."

Chugging the rest of the lemonade, I almost choked on an ice cube. "Are you?" I squeaked out.

"No. That ship has sailed."

"How come?"

"Long story. I messed up." A look washed over her face. Something like sadness. "And then I lost him."

"Lost things don't have to stay lost forever. They can be found." I wanted to believe that. Maybe I just wanted to believe that *I* could be found.

"Sometimes that's true. But I betrayed his trust. And when you lose something in the wake of betrayal, it's like trying to catch smoke with your bare hands. No matter how hard you try, it slips through the cracks, leaving you with nothing but a bitter aftertaste," she said. "And that tastes an awful lot like regret."

My insides pitched. "Regret is a heavy burden."

"It is," she murmured, her gaze distant. "And the worst part is realizing that the only person who can lift that burden is the one you let slip away."

I could almost taste the smoke; that same bitter aftertaste that tainted her words. "What happened?"

While I'd become closer with Tara's mother over the past few months, we hadn't ventured into this dangerous territory before. Tara had hinted at a yearning for her parents to make amends, but I never wanted to pry. Plus, it hurt. It hurt knowing that I had these stupid, bottled-up feelings for a man twice my age.

For a man my best friend desperately wanted to see rekindle a relationship with her *mother*.

I felt like a traitor.

An awful backstabber.

Tara and her mom had taken me in, given me safety, love, and family, and here I was, pining over the only man in the world I couldn't have.

Whitney ran her fingers through her ponytail as she leaned back in the lawn chair. "If I tell you, you'll think I'm a horrible person."

No worse than I am.

"I'd never think that." I swallowed. "You're like a mother to me."

She smiled warmly, her brown eyes glittering against the starlight. And then her smile slipped, replaced by the remnants of her regret. "I slept with his brother."

My mouth fell open. "Oh."

"Yeah." She pressed her lips together in a thin line, nodding slowly. "I was young and stupid. It's no excuse, of course, and I was older than you and Tara are now, but I was definitely stupid. I was a lot like Tara, thinking the best moments were always right around the corner. I didn't appreciate what I already had."

"That's..." I exhaled a long breath, setting aside my empty glass. "I'm sorry."

"You shouldn't be. I learned my lesson the hard way." She glanced at me. "Which I think is the only way we ever truly learn a lesson, right? It has to hurt."

"Do you, um...still have feelings for him?" I wasn't sure I wanted to know the answer, but my curious heart stole my voice.

She thought on the question but shook her head. "I'll always feel something for him. He's Tara's father, and he's a good man. A great man. But, like I said, that ship has sailed." She laughed a little, crinkling her nose in a way that made her freckles scatter. "Actually, that ship has sunk. Drowned at the bottom of the ocean. We're better apart."

I picked at the worn edges of my sandal, chewing on my tongue while stewing in her words.

"How are you doing, Halley?" she wondered.

As much as I appreciated the subject change, this one wasn't any better. "I'm doing okay. Physically, I'm stronger than ever. Running has been a great outlet for me."

"And mentally?"

My chin lifted, and our eyes met. All I could produce was a tiny headshake.

Tears glimmered in her gaze as she pressed a hand to my forearm. "I'm here for you. We all are. Me, Tara, even Reed. We're your family now. And your father is in jail. He can't hurt you anymore."

That much was true.

After months of court hearings, put in motion by Whitney Stephens, my father had been arrested and sentenced to five years in prison for domestic assault. I'd had to testify.

He hadn't looked me in the eyes. Not once.

And my own mother had been notably absent.

While the verdict had offered a small sense of relief, dark memories still seized my mind. Memories of collapsing in a disgusting alleyway after my date had hummed a haunting nickname in my ear that had taken me right back to that godforsaken house: *Lamb*.

I wasn't okay.

My father's black hold on me strengthened by the day, cackling in my ear that I would never be okay again.

Reed had been there that night, conveniently next door with his brother. I wasn't sure if that had been a mortifying twist of fate, or exactly what I'd needed at the time. I still thought about the way he'd held me, shushed my tears, stroked my hair back and calmed me down with gentle words. It was impossible not to fall even harder for him. I'd never been cradled so tenderly by the two strong arms of a man before; no father figure, no doting boyfriends. Just Reed. His arms were not meant to hold me, and yet they were the safest sanctuary in the midst of my crumbling mind.

Panic attacks were no joke. It had felt like I was dying, suffocating, drowning.

For a moment, I'd wanted to.

It would have been so easy to slip beneath the surface and float away, to retreat from the confines of my hell and find a softer place to rest my head.

But then my head had rested against his chest, his heartbeats a melodic lullaby, pulling me back to dry land.

My new favorite song.

Human beings were so damn resilient. We saw color through blackened vision, latched onto hope in hopeless places, and loved with every damaged piece of our broken-down hearts. Reed had told me I wouldn't stay broken. All I'd needed to do was put in the effort to patch my broken bits.

And that was what I planned to do.

Uncurling my legs, I stood from the lawn chair and stretched my arms over my head, reining in my courage. I glanced at Whitney perched beside me with her feet pulled up. "I'm going to go for a run."

She bit her lip. "Are you sure?"

"Yeah. I just need to clear my head."

"Take the pepper spray with you. Just in case."

I smiled softly, touched by her concern. My own mother had never questioned my safety, never wondered about my whereabouts. Never bothered to check on me at night. I'd come to terms with it. Some mothers weren't capable of providing or nurturing, or seeing beyond their own self-preservation. Love came easy for some, and for others, it was a distant illusion, forever out of reach. But, standing here, I felt a glimmer of something I had long believed to be unattainable: maternal love. It was a poignant reminder of the stark contrast between the love I had yearned for and the reality of my own upbringing. I saw a reflection of the mother I'd always wished for—the one who would hold me close, soothe my fears, and fiercely protect me from harm.

"Thank you." My eyes misted with tears. "For everything."

She smiled. "Always."

"I'll be back soon."

I padded off the deck with my heart in my throat and my pulse in my ears, praying I was strong enough to protect *them* from harm.

Love alone wasn't always enough to keep us safe.

Sometimes, it was our ultimate undoing.

It was nearly eleven p.m. when I found myself standing outside of Reed's apartment door, after waiting for someone to exit the main entrance. With a grateful smile, I'd slipped inside and then headed toward apartment number seventeen. I'd been here once before with Tara, on an evening in mid-June. I had lingered outside the doorway as Tara ran in to grab her purse that she'd forgotten, following a weekend spent with him while Whitney was out of town for work.

Now, I stared at the block of wood and number plaque, my stomach in knots.

I knocked three times.

And I waited.

Heavy footfalls approached from the other side of the door, and I inhaled a breath of courage. But that breath fell back out in a mousy squeak when Reed opened the door, sans a shirt, wearing only a pair of heather-gray sweatpants and a stunned expression.

On instinct, my gaze panned downward, taking in the definition of his sculpted abs, hard chest, and muscles glistening with the telltale evidence of sweat.

Blinking, I glanced back up.

We stared at each other for a beat.

"Hey." The confusion on his face didn't wane, so I cleared my throat, wringing my hands together in front of me. "Can I come in?"

"What are you doing here?"

Reed pressed against the door frame, his hair a disheveled, beautiful mess that mimicked the feelings sweeping through me as I dallied in the hallway.

"I wanted to talk to you about something," I told him.

"Does Whit know you're here?"

I shook my head. "She went to bed."

"Tara?"

"No. She's at a bonfire."

He stared at me for another heartbeat, his focus sweeping up the length of my body before he nodded once and stepped aside. "Come in."

I trudged inside the apartment, my shoulder brushing his bare arm as I pulled my mop of tangled hair over one shoulder. Fiddling with the split ends, I glanced around the tidied space, taking in the neutral canvas of blacks and grays. Tara was right—it needed some color pops.

When the door clicked shut, I pivoted around, watching as Reed leaned against the frame and crossed his arms. My eyes dipped to his chest again and heat bloomed in my belly, then shot south. I lingered on a jagged scar roped along the side of his abdomen, one I'd never seen before. Curiosity poked at me, and I wanted to ask him how he'd gotten it.

But he straightened back up before I could speak. "Sorry. Wasn't expecting company."

A combination of scents wafted under my nose as Reed sauntered into the adjoining room and snatched his T-shirt off a blue mat that was laid out near the kitchen—cedar from a dwindling candle flame on the coffee table, a savory aroma from a pot on the stove, and a trace of something synthetic. Almost rubbery.

"Are you hungry?" he wondered, pulling the wrinkled white shirt over his head as he reapproached. "I made soup."

"I'm okay. Thanks."

He nodded as he skimmed long fingers through his extra messy hair. "Halley—"

"I want to train with you," I blurted out.

Whatever he was about to say was cut short. Reed stopped a few feet away from me, his arm falling back down in slow motion at his side.

I lifted my chin, a surge of determination chasing away the nerves. "I never, ever want to feel helpless like that again," I continued. "I want you to teach me everything you know. Don't hold back. Turn me into someone powerful, brave, confident." Stepping forward, I watched the way his brows creased and his eyes glittered back at me with indecision. "Someone who can turn fear into strength. Vulnerability into survival."

Reed's lips parted, a sharp breath escaping.

Hesitation gripped him as he stood before me, wordless and unsure.

He was afraid of something.

And I knew what that something was.

Me.

Clearing his throat, he dropped his gaze to the floor as he rubbed his forehead. "I don't know, Halley," he breathed out. "I don't think that's a good idea."

I studied him, watching the conflict skip across his handsome face.

He felt the weight of the request slamming down on him. Heard the warning bells chiming deep within the innocent cadence of my voice.

Reed knew.

I knew, too, but I trusted our willpower far more than I should have.

"Please." Steeling my resolve, I tipped my chin higher. "I'll find a way to pay you for the sessions. I just got a job at a local animal hospital. It's only a kennel tech position, and the pay isn't great, but it's something. Whatever I can't pay you now, I will later. I promise I'll—"

"It's not about the money."

I swallowed.

He was right. It wasn't about the money at all.

Reed scrubbed a palm down his face, forehead to chin, and scratched at the bristles lining his jaw. His eyes were pinned just over my shoulder, his biceps stretching the sleeves of his shirt.

I licked my lips, inching closer. Desperate to plead my case. "My father broke me," I said, my voice fraying on the words. "He shattered my spirit, my strength, my whole damn heart. I don't even know who I am anymore. All I know is who I want to be...and it's not this girl. It's not this shadow, this terrified little *lamb* constantly looking over her shoulder for the big bad wolf to attack. To take another bite out of me. I refuse to live my life in fear, and I never again want to be *saved*."

He let out a long breath, his eyes closing as he cupped his jaw. "Halley..."

"I want this, Reed." I begged, hissing the words through my teeth. "Please. I think it's a good idea."

I watched his eyes slowly open, his gaze falling back on me.

His jaw clenched, muscles twitching.

"I *need* to do this."

Silence answered for a long time, only severed by the steady stream of traffic from outside the cracked window and the sound of my heart ping-ponging between my ribs.

"Yeah," he finally said. "Okay." He exhaled slowly, sending me a poignant look as he nodded through his surrender. "We'll train."

Something told me it was a bad idea.

And that we'd both find that out soon enough.

CHAPTER 14

Reed

SHE HIT THE MAT, hard.

"Try again," I said, a light sheen of sweat clinging to my hairline as the resounding *thud* echoed throughout the gym. She'd told me not to hold back; I'd listened. "Get up."

Scotty watched us from the sidelines, sitting against the far wall with his knees drawn up. He sipped a Gatorade, attention locked on me as I moved around Halley, my feet drawing tight circles on the blue mat.

Halley remained sprawled out beneath me, her chest heaving, expression pinched with resignation as she stared up at the high ceiling.

"Come on." I bent forward, hands clasped around my knees. "We're not done yet."

"I can't."

"You can. Get up." I wasn't pulling any punches as I reached down, snatched her by the wrist, and hauled her to her feet. "Try again."

She filled her cheeks with air and blew out a weary breath, sections of damp hair falling loose from her ponytail and dangling in front of her eyes. Shoving the strands back with both hands, she shook her arms out at her sides and regrouped.

I lunged at her.

Pinned her against the cushioned wall by the wrists.

Halley struggled, ducked, tried to rotate under me.

"Elbow over my forearm," I instructed.

"I...I can't do it," she croaked out, cheeks flushed bright red, arms quivering in my grasp.

"Wrong answer." I pressed harder, and she flailed her legs on instinct. "Use your shoulders. Drive your hips. Your power lies in your upper body."

"Reed—"

"Do you want to die today?" I shot back, holding firm. "I'm the bad guy. I'm the monster. I'm your low-life, son-of-a-bitch father here to finish what he started. Try. Fucking. Hard—"

Halley growled, the sound rumbling up her chest, into her throat, and hitting the air like a thunderous battle cry. In a burst of movement, she drove her hips and shoulders toward the inside and pried out of my grip, rotating quickly and escaping my hold.

A round of slow clapping echoed from behind us as I bit back a smile and Halley collapsed to her butt, exhausted.

Scotty stood and approached us, still clapping. "Nice job."

She drooped forward, forehead colliding with the mat as she panted through the quick-dying adrenaline.

I crouched down in front of her. "You did good."

Halley popped her head up, her gaze traveling to my face. "You're ruthless."

"You're capable."

Scotty sidled up beside me, taking a swig from his water bottle and handing Halley a fresh one. She nodded her thanks and accepted it, unscrewing the cap.

"Scotty's up next. Want to stick around and watch our session?" I loosely splayed my hands on my hips.

She sat up straight and gulped down the water, extending her legs out in front of her. "I'll stay. Thanks."

Her bronzed skin shimmered under the fluorescent lighting, and a white tank top stuck to her curves, drenched with the evidence of her hard work. She was strong, but she was nowhere near where I wanted her to be. Her sword was drawn, yet it consistently faltered in her hand.

We were two months into our weekly sessions, and while Halley was committed and determined, her self-confidence hadn't caught up to her fighting spirit. It was a flame vulnerable to the winds of her past. She doubted herself. Second-guessed her potential.

But I didn't.

I held out my hand to help her up, and she took it, curling her fingers around my larger palm and snapping to her feet. The zing of heat that flickered up my arm and bombed my chest was obnoxious, at best; I refused to acknowledge how it would feel at its worst.

Halley smoothed back the sweat-slick baby hairs framing her forehead, then exhaled a worn breath before trudging over to her duffel bag. I watched her go, wondering why she wasn't more excited, more proud of her win today. There was no bounce in her step, no confidence lifting her slumped shoulders.

"You okay?" I called out to her while Scotty did some stretches beside me on the mat.

"Yep," was all she said, her back to me.

Nodding through a sigh, I switched gears fast, putting my game face back on and whipping Scotty into shape with some new defensive moves. The hour rolled by as Halley watched us train, sitting cross-legged against the wall with piles of homework in her lap.

Scotty and I dried off with our respective towels, and then he sauntered over to Halley while I rummaged through my bag for a protein bar.

"You were awesome out there," Scotty said, collapsing beside her with the towel draped around his neck.

"Thanks." She sent him a half-smile, attention shared between Scotty and her pencil tapping against a half-scribbled notebook page. "How long have you been training?"

"Almost a year, now. Changed my life." He looked my way. "Coach is incredible. You should stick with it as long as you can."

"You look so confident."

"Took a while to get to this point. You have to really want it. Believe in yourself. You can't fake it, you know?"

She nodded absently, glancing up at me as I watched from a few feet away.

I cleared my throat. "I'll walk you home," I said to Halley, slinging the strap of my bag over my shoulder. My studio was only a mile away from Whit and Tara's house, and it was a mild November evening. Perfect for walking.

She nibbled on the pencil eraser. "You don't have to. I'm still finishing up this thesis."

"I'll wait."

Scotty said his goodbyes and slipped out the main doors, leaving Halley with her nose in the notebook. I chewed on my cheek for a moment before strolling forward and taking a seat beside her against the wall. She stiffened at my presence, her grip on the pencil tightening while she stared down at the lead-smudged paragraph.

"How's it going?" I asked, nodding at the schoolwork in her lap.

Blinking down at her handwriting, she flattened her lips as if to tell me that, obviously, it sucked. "Repeating senior year is so much fun. I'm honestly loving it."

My head fell back against the wall as I twisted toward her. "It'll be worth it. You're working hard. You're focused."

"I'm desperate." She made a face. "If I don't pass this year, I don't know what I'm going to do. It's mortifying."

"It's not. Nobody has the right to judge you unless they've been in your shoes."

Sighing miserably, she slammed the notebook shut and turned to meet my eyes. "Did you ever struggle in school?"

"I did," I admitted. "I never graduated. Whitney got pregnant on the tail end of my senior year and I dropped out and got my GED."

"Really?"

"Yeah." Pursing my lips, I studied her, my mind flickering with buried memories of those difficult years. "My dad passed away from liver cancer when I was thirteen, and then my mom died four years later in a motorcycle accident with her boyfriend. Fucked me up. I got into fights, skipped a lot of school, and didn't think there was much hope for my future."

Her eyes flared, twinkling with sentiment. "That's awful. I'm sorry."

I drew my legs up and folded my hands, pressing farther against the wall. "My brother had it worse. Drugs, petty thefts, even jail time. The only thing that pulled me from a similar fate was having my daughter. She forced me to grow up quick, gave me something to live for. I wanted to be better. For her. For her future."

Halley pressed the pencil to her chin, stewing in my words as her eyes glassed over. "Was it easy? Turning your life around?"

I huffed a laugh. "Fuck no. It was the hardest thing I ever had to do. But it was worth it. When something bigger than you—something more significant than your own bullshit—comes into play, it sobers you, and you see things through different eyes. It's like a storm clearing. Suddenly, every obstacle, every easy way out, paled in comparison to the responsibility I had to be a good dad. There were setbacks, moments of doubt, battles with my own demons. But you find a newfound sense of purpose to get you through it." We stared at each other, and I watched a myriad of emotions splay across her face. "So, no, it wasn't easy. But it was necessary. And in the end, it transformed me into the person I needed to be for her...which was a stepping stone for who I needed to be for myself."

Inhaling softly, Halley settled back against the wall and lowered her chin. "That's inspiring. Gives me hope."

"Good. Sometimes that's all we need." I smiled at her. "Sometimes it's all we have."

She nodded, taking it all in, letting my words fill her empty pockets. "My father always used to tell me that I wasn't good at doing hard things." Her voice cracked as she chomped down on her bottom lip. "Every time I fail at something, it feels like a testament to that. Like he was right all along. Repeating school, these stupid panic attacks. Even little things, like dropping a plate, or forgetting an appointment, or stumbling through training."

My brows gathered, my chest heavy. "He lied to you, Halley. You've already accomplished the hardest thing."

Cautiously, her chin tipped back up, her eyes rounding with curiosity as she glanced at me. "What's that?"

"You got back up."

She sucked in a sharp breath, her gaze clouding over. Our eyes were trapped, tangling for two beats too long as our shoulders pressed together, hips touching. Her fingers curled around the notebook and the spirals dug into her palms.

When I looked at her like this, her heart spread wide open and soul bare, she was more than Tara's friend. More than eighteen. More than a predicament, a casualty of life. A blip.

She was defiance.

A force.

A kaleidoscope in motion.

I saw things I shouldn't see when I looked at her.

Something beyond physical.

Breaking the tether, I cleared my throat and pulled to my feet, cracking my neck as I gestured for her to gather her belongings. "We should get going," I said. "It's getting late."

Halley nodded, shaking off the daze that had hijacked us both and stuffing notebooks and worksheets into her bag. She joined me near the entrance a minute later, and I stepped outside into the cool night, the sky a pepper-spray of stars. "You did good today, by the way. I'm impressed."

"Yeah, right." She folded her arms underneath her breasts. "Training was a mess. If you were anyone else, I'd be dead."

We walked side by side down the quiet sidewalk, brightened by flickering streetlamps and moonlight. A shiver rippled down her body when a fifty-degree breeze blasted us. She was only clad in a tank top and cotton shorts with no jacket, so I shrugged out of my leather coat and handed it to her. "Take it. You're freezing." I didn't wait for a rejection and draped it over her shoulders.

Halley hesitantly slipped her arms through the sleeves and let the warm leather swallow her slim frame. Her throat bobbed as she glanced up at me with only her eyes. "Thank you."

I nodded. "You can't think about the what-ifs," I told her, veering back to her original statement, our steps in perfect rhythm. "That's the shit that will end up killing you. It'll override everything you've learned, all your logic, training, and basic instincts. Fear is a disease. It's paralyzing. The only antidote is believing in your resilience. Every challenge is a chance to prove your strength."

"Right." Pursing her lips, Halley glowered like my words were a bitter pill she wasn't ready to swallow.

I needed to change that.

We continued to stride forward, and I simmered in what she'd told me the night she'd shown up at my apartment, begging for me to mold her into a fighter. Someone capable.

Don't hold back.

Taking that request at face value, I paused on the sidewalk.

She hardly had a chance to question why I'd stopped before I spun around.

I ambushed her.

Firing forward like a thief in the night, I bent over and hauled her up over my shoulder by the thighs, the duffel bag dropping to the cement, her feet shooting out behind her and kicking the air.

A quick gasp escaped her; a breathy burst of surprise.

But she didn't scream. Didn't cower.

She reacted.

Halley reached back like I'd taught her, wrapped her arm around my neck and secured her wrist. Her legs locked around my midsection, ankles crossing, and she held tightly for six seconds until I dropped to my knees on the sidewalk.

Shoving me away, she slipped out of my hold and stumbled backward, her eyes wide and glowing beneath the lamppost.

Her chest heaved.

So did mine.

We stared at each other, breathing heavily as the tension thickened, until I stretched a satisfied smile and fell back on my haunches. I flicked a hand through my hair. "Good."

Swallowing hard, Halley took a few hesitant steps toward me, half her hair sticking out of her ponytail and the jacket slipped off one shoulder. Hazel-kissed irises gazed down at me, radiating with intensity in the lowlight, as I remained kneeling below her on the sidewalk.

A smile crested on her face, sparking with the fire I'd been longing to see.

She held a hand out to me.

I took it, then climbed to my feet. Before her hand slipped from mine, I tugged her gently toward me. Our palms lingered, loosely entwined. Halley stared with a popeyed expression at our clasped hands, and I slowly pressed the underside of her palm to her still-thrumming chest.

"Feel that?" My eyes were pinned to the space between her breasts where our joined hands rested against her white tank top, the vibrations from her skittering heartbeats seeping through the pads of our fingertips.

"Fear," she whispered back.

"No." I shook my head, taking a small step closer until the toes of our shoes touched on the concrete. My thumb grazed her knuckles, my throat tightening with a heavy knot. "Power."

She inhaled sharply.

The autumn breeze stole the loose pieces of her hair, lifting them, toying with them, and a beam of soft moonlight sprinkled stardust in her eyes. Those eyes lifted to mine, held tight, and—

A car zoomed by.

I snatched my hand away from her chest, the moment severed.

For the fucking best.

I sliced sharp fingers through my hair and stepped back, knowing my place. Knowing damn well that my place was far, far away from my daughter's best friend, no matter how proud of her I was, how protective I felt, or how dedicated I was to keeping her safe and making her strong.

She did wield power.

More than I wanted her to know.

I felt it, cursed it, wanted to claw it out of me until it was a bloody heap of tattered remains lumped at our feet. Snuffed out, stomped on, devoid of any flicker of life.

Stupid.

Wrong.

Borderline catastrophic.

Halley inched the coat up over her bare shoulder and cleared her throat, her gaze floating away from my face. "Ruthless," she said, echoing her statement from earlier.

I forced a smile. "Capable."

We resumed our trek down the sidewalk as Halley crossed her arms and my hands slipped into the pockets of my sweatpants. Her own hands were hidden by the baggy black leather as she tucked them underneath her armpits.

"Are you staying for dinner tonight?" she hedged, adrenaline still coursing through her, quickening her pace.

"Yeah. Tara has a date." I grimaced at the notion. "You cooking?"

"Pierogies."

"About time."

"I feel like I made good headway just now. A reason to celebrate."

Nodding, I shot her another smile, this one less forced. I was proud of her. Not everyone could scoop up their trauma in two shaking hands and mold it into something worth holding. Her pain was clay, taking on a new form, a new shape. One day, it could become her greatest masterpiece.

And that was something to celebrate.

Whitney bumped her hip to mine as all four of us worked together in the kitchen, rolling out the remaining sections of dough. "Look at you," she beamed, her wavy-brown hair piled up on top of her head. "All you're missing is an apron."

"Mm. Think I'll pass."

Tara giggled to my right. "I bet you'd rock an apron. Christmas is around the corner, just saying."

"You wouldn't."

"It's like you don't even know me."

"Shit. You would." I groaned. "You're prematurely grounded."

My daughter jabbed an elbow to my ribs, hard enough to make me wince. The girls had a Radiohead CD playing in the background as the countertop fell victim to flour dust, butter puddles, and a slew of dirty pots and dishes.

The doorbell rang, and Tara straightened to a statue, the color draining from her face. "Oh, God...it's Josh. Josh is here. To eat food. With me."

"That was the plan," I mumbled, eyeing the door across the way and watching his shadow move behind the distorted glass.

Her fucking date.

Nothing in the parenting books and Dad manuals could prepare me for the feeling of dread that came along with watching my teenage daughter navigate the merciless world of dating.

Whit had told me she'd put her on the pill.

I wanted to puke.

"I'll get the door." I swiped my hands down the pair of blue jeans I'd changed into.

"Like hell you will. Move aside." Tara shoved past me, barreling ahead toward the foyer.

I sighed, watching her prance away as she fiddled with her freshly permed hair. "I don't like him," I muttered to Whitney.

"Of course you don't. Prince Charming could walk through that door, and you'd still say, *off with his head.*"

"Yep." I mashed the dough with more force than necessary. "Princes are overrated and never charming."

"You know what I mean."

Whitney washed her hands in the sink before sending me a smile and joining Tara at the front door.

Left alone in the kitchen with Halley—me, stewing in my toxic fatherly instincts, and Halley, filling pierogies with potato-infused filling —I pressed forward on the countertop and sent her a narrowed glance. "Thoughts on Josh."

Her chin popped up as she blinked over at me. "He's cute."

"No. Something else."

A smile slipped, and she swished a piece of rogue hair out of her eyes with a jerk of her head. "Okay, well, he's on the honor roll. He carries her books for her in the hallway at school," she told me. "Oh, and yesterday he shoved some jock up against the lockers, after the guy made a suggestive comment about her."

My eyes thinned to slits. "So, he's violent."

"Protective."

"I hate him."

Halley giggled, her easy laughter relieving my tension and softening my rigid stance. I hadn't heard her laugh much lately; she'd been so focused, driven, and serious. Preoccupied with her job at the animal hospital, schoolwork, and self-defense training. She wasn't the wilting flower I'd come to know months ago, but shadows still curled around her, suffocating her bright spirit.

I latched onto the lighter mood. "Will you be my eyes when I'm not around?"

"Your eyes?"

"Yeah. My wing-woman."

Her cheeks pinkened as she swiped a smear of flour off her cheekbone. The action only added more flour. "Nope. Sorry. My loyalty lies with Tara."

"Bet I can win you over."

"I can't be won. It's called integrity."

The side-eyed grin she sent me was as dangerous as it was charming.

"Hmm." I leaned forward on my forearms, staring at her as she sealed the dough pouches and popped them in a pan, one by one. "A challenge."

"Don't waste your energy."

A new Radiohead song began to play as cheerful voices seeped in from the other side of the house. The song was haunting. Atmospheric.

For a moment, everything else fell away. There was no laughter, no clattering glasses, no high-pitched voices—it was just me, Halley, and this Radiohead song that I was desperate to know the name of. "What song is this?"

She closed her eyes, like she was branding the melodies on her mind. *"Talk Show Host."*

"I like it."

"It's my favorite." Her hips swayed languidly to the eerie beats as pierogies sizzled in the frying pan, turning golden. Then she twisted around, reaching in front of me to grab a jar of seasoning.

Our arms brushed.

Her eyes lifted.

My attention snagged on the streak of flour dust on her cheek, and instinct took over as I raised my hand and gently brushed it away with my thumb. "You got some flour..." The words trailed off as I flicked the remaining specks of powder off her skin.

She froze, gaze dropping to the countertop as the song breathed a pulse of life into the moment.

A reckless, drawn-out heartbeat.

She swallowed.

And then she blurted out on a hitched breath, "Tara thinks Whitney is still in love with you."

I went still.

My hand fell away from her face.

A frown furled between my brows as her words sunk in, one at a time. Molasses struggling through hairline cracks. "What do you mean?"

Halley blinked down at the counter before returning her gaze to mine, her eyes glassy. She shook her head, just a fraction, as if she wasn't sure why she'd said that.

"Dad!" Tara shouted from the dining room. "Come meet Josh. My embarrassment awaits, and I know you can't resist."

I released a hard breath through my nose, palming the back of my neck as Halley stepped away and returned to the stove. Pierogies flipped inside the pan. Sizzling, crackling. The savory aroma unlocked me, and I straightened from the counter, pivoting around.

Why would Tara think that?

Pausing once, I glanced back at Halley over my shoulder, studying her flushed profile. Her eyes were glued to the pan, her grip on the spatula deathlike.

My heart was in my throat as I sauntered into the dining room, smiling tightly at my daughter who was hand-in-hand with Josh.

Whitney looked up from her seat at the table, her fingers curled around the stem of a wine glass as I approached. She took a delicate sip, her ruby-tipped nails matching the color of the wine.

Tara smiled wide and ushered me into the seat beside her mother, candlelight draped across the tablecloth.

My daughter waggled her eyebrows and winked.

Shit.

CHAPTER 15

THE SOLES of my shoes pounded the ice-capped pavement as I ran full-speed ahead down the neighborhood street. Houses were lit up like it was Candy Cane Lane. The colorful bulbs glittered through a light dusting of fresh snow, and it was just the touch of magic I needed.

I'd taken up running a few months before I'd started training. Not even a bitter, blizzard-heavy winter had been able to squash my drive; on the contrary, it'd only fueled my fire, melting every iceberg and snowy avalanche that stood in my way.

Another road block? Great, I'd plow through it. Another obstacle tossed in front of me? I'd leap the hell over it. I would turn every setback into a stepping stone until I was unbreakable.

Father wouldn't win.

His hold over me would perish. His bones would crumble under the weight of my resolve. My bruises would become trophies, my scars souvenirs.

Narratives could always be rewritten. My story thus far was nothing more than a messy first draft. I was the main character in my own life, and I refused—*refused*—to fall secondary to the villain.

My chest ached and my lungs stretched with each forward push. The tendons in my legs burned, straining and pulling.

I didn't care. I kept going.

I wasn't done yet.

I wasn't done...until I *was* done.

As I zipped around a corner with lightning speed, my foot slipped on a patch of ice. I was going too fast, turning too quickly, and my attempt to prevent a devastating nosedive resulted in an overcorrection that sent me stumbling and flailing.

I flew forward.

Face first.

Chin to concrete.

My hands shot in front of me to take the brunt of the fall, but it wasn't enough. I hit the ground as gravel and chunks of ice lodged in the heels of my palms, and my chin scraped against the pavement. It felt like I was sliding forever before I came to a stop in the middle of the quiet street.

No one was around.

It was five a.m. on Christmas morning. Anyone who wasn't still asleep was likely gathered around the tree with robes and coffee mugs, watching tiny children tear open presents.

It took three seconds for the pain to hit.

My jaw ached and throbbed, and my flesh screamed in agony. Tears exploded behind my eyes but I refused to let them fall.

Too many tears.

Too much salt had streaked down my cheeks for one lifetime.

I wouldn't succumb.

As my body pulsed with pain from head to toe, I painstakingly lifted myself from the roadway and surveyed the aftermath. My hands were mangled, blood staining the snow from white to pink where my face had crash-landed.

I was a wreck.

Hissing through my teeth, I stood fully to wobbling legs and limped the two blocks home to Tara's house. I slipped through the front door, shivering from pain and cold, and tried to stay quiet since everyone was still asleep.

Everyone except for Reed, who was seated on the couch in a T-shirt and pajama pants, after crashing on the sofa the night before in lieu of the holiday.

Crap.

I hoped to whiz by him unnoticed, but the house's stark silence was an awful traitor, and his head jerked in my direction when the floorboards creaked.

He leaped up from the couch, discarding his coffee mug. "Halley, what the fuck."

I ignored him as I aggressively toed out of my sneakers, then made a beeline for the bathroom.

"Halley," he called after me.

"I'm fine."

I wasn't fine, but I would be. I just needed to slap on a few Band-Aids and scrub the gravel from my skin. I'd be all right.

He was hot on my heels as I swerved into the hall bath and tried to shut the door in his face.

He barreled through. "What the hell happened?"

When I looked in the mirror, my heart sank—it was worse than I'd thought. "I fell," I said.

"Did you fall into a meat grinder? Jesus Christ." Reed joined me in the small bathroom, quietly closing the door behind him.

"I was running." I turned the faucet on warm and dipped my frozen, shredded hands underneath the stream of water. Glancing at my reflection, I scrubbed wet fingers over my face, erasing the drying blood caked all over my jaw. "I slipped on a patch of ice."

"Let me help."

"I got it." He reached for my hands, but I yanked them away.

His shoulders sagged. "I'm just trying to help," he said softly.

My bottom lip trembled when I finally caught his wounded gaze. I hadn't meant to be a jerk, but getting too close to Reed would be far more tragic than any stupid fall.

I was halfway in love with him—*that* fall would be the killing kind, and I'd come too far to crash and burn now.

Softening, I blinked up at him as the water trickled from the faucet. "I'm okay. Really. Nothing is broken, except for my pride."

He reached out and gently cupped my chin in his large hand, tilting my head to the side. His brows furrowed deeper, jaw ticking as he inspected the damage. Then he reached over my head to open the medicine cabinet and snatched a box of bandages and a tube of ointment off the shelf. "Is it just your hands and face?"

I swallowed through the gravelly lump in my throat as he flicked open a bandage wrapper. There was a pulsing ache along my abdomen. "Nothing serious."

As he peeled open the wrapper, I inched my tank top up to take a peek.

When my eyes landed on the full-length scrape and mottling of bruises that were already forming on my torso, my stomach turned. It was bad. Panic crept inside me as I pulled the shirt higher and higher, my fingers shaking. "I-I'm okay. I'm fine," I stammered, chanting the words to myself more than to Reed. With a squeak of anguish, I yanked the top over my head and tossed it to the floor, assessing the wounds that traveled up to the edge of my sports bra. "It stings," I breathed out.

I was standing half-naked in front of him, but the terror trumped the embarrassment.

Frazzled, I tugged a hand towel off the bar and shoved it under the running water, dampening it, squeezing out the excess liquid, then pressing it to my wound. I wheezed as my eyelids slammed shut, holding back a wave of biting tears.

Reed was inches away from me, dabbing ointment onto the padding of the bandage. "I should take you to the hospital."

My eyes pinged open. "No, please. I'll be okay. I swear nothing's broken."

He stepped forward and took over holding the rag, setting the bandage beside him on the sink. The warmth of the water had cooled, but the warmth from his proximity only heightened. Lightly patting the towel to my skin, he let the fabric soak up the remnants of blood as his gaze lifted to mine. "It's okay to break sometimes," he said. "You're allowed to be vulnerable, scared. You don't have to fight it."

I covered his hand with my trembling fingers. "I've spent my whole life being weak."

"It's not weakness. It's a strength of its own. Facing your fears, embracing your emotions—it doesn't make you weak; it makes you human."

I inhaled a shuttered breath, and somehow the feel of my hand over his overpowered the pain slicing through me. I squeezed harder, lowering my focus to our clasped hands. My thumb brushed his knuckles, and the tension congealed. I could feel it, a palpable force crammed into the tiny bathroom with us.

Then, almost as if the stroke of my thumb had unlocked something inside of him, he drank in a tight breath. The mood shifted, and his own walls felt like they were deconstructing, block by block. "You know, my brother and I...we grew up close." He untangled his hand from mine, leaving me with the rag. Reaching for the bandage again, he found my unoccupied hand. "Best friends, in every sense of the term. We played ball and board games together, swam down by the lake in the summer, went on family vacations and stayed up talking and going through baseball cards till dawn in the hotel rooms."

I held the towel to my abdomen and watched as he carefully outstretched my fingers and studied the bloodied, torn skin on the heel of my palm. His touch had me lightly swaying, undulating, almost as if the sound of his voice was the most hypnotizing melody in the world.

His eyes found mine, skimming across my face.

Reading me.

"Then we fell in with the wrong crowd during high school, after losing both of our parents. One night, he asked me to tag along to a meeting he needed to go to. Told me he owed someone money and wanted backup, just in case things got out of hand. I always had his back. Always looked out for him. So it was an easy decision."

My heart raced with every word as Reed gently fused the bandage over my palm, and I held back another hiss of pain.

"Turns out, he owed someone a lot of money," he said, teeth clenched and grinding. "Some drug dealer. He was older, massively built, covered in scars."

"What happened?" I leaned into his touch.

Reed stared at me for a heavy beat, pain creasing his brows and flickering across his face.

Then he let go of my dressed hand and reached down to lift his T-shirt.

My eyes dropped.

I gasped.

The gnarly, jagged scar shot ice through my veins, and my eyes misted at the sight. I'd seen the scar once before, at his apartment three months ago. I'd figured it was some kind of accident.

But it wasn't an accident.

"The meeting went to shit," he said. "Radley didn't have all the money, so the dealer left him with a final warning. A message. And the message was a knife to my gut that left me bleeding out and near death in a back alley in the middle of the night."

"Oh, my God."

I saw his pain.

I *felt* his pain in the same way I felt mine.

Bloody, exposed, and soul-deep.

"Point is, I've been there. I've been left for dead, spilled out across cold pavement, wondering how many breaths I had left. How many more moments...how many blips." He crooked the smallest smile. "And then when I'd survived, I had to figure out how to live through that fear and pain going forward. And that's the key—living *through* it, not *in* it. You recognize it, you channel it, you don't try to smother it. There is no weakness in fear. You just can't let it dictate your next move."

I stared at him, glassy-eyed and mystified, marinating in his words.

"I've seen the moves you've been making, Comet." His voiced dipped to a husky whisper. "I've been right in the center of them. You get back up every time you're thrown down. You're fighting for your life, in every sense of the word...and that's fucking powerful."

My breath stuttered.

I nodded slowly, my gaze drifting to his scar. Reed had gotten back up, too. He'd turned his scars into weapons. Into art. Into a story worth telling.

And now he was helping me do the same.

I lifted my hand and reached for him in a slow-motion glide, my fingertips grazing the puckered scar that looked like a small valley torn across the side of his abdomen.

He inhaled a saw-like breath at the contact.

Neither of us moved as my fingers trailed the uneven edges.

Our eyes met through the fluorescent bathroom light, his dark and intense, mine glittering with tears.

Then I pulled back, lowered the towel from my wound, and twisted around until my back was facing him. Until my disfigured spine was in full view.

I waited, chewing on my battered tongue, my eyes closed and heart split open.

He was behind me, shifting closer. And when he slid his hand across my bare back, I trembled from head to toe. I felt his palm splay across my skin as he uncovered my own harrowing secrets and stripes of belt-thrashed scars.

A warm finger traced the length of them, flitting over the borders and healing welts. I let him touch me. I'd let him touch me forever if he wanted to, realizing he'd never erase the evidence of my abuse but knowing he'd lessen the burden of it all.

"We both have scars." I tilted my chin over my shoulder, trying to catch his eyes. He was closer than I thought as his breath caressed the top of my head. "A knife. A belt. Different weapons, same wounds."

I watched his eyes flick back and forth between my face and my back. His hand continued to move and explore, languidly, up and down, journeying all the way up until his fingertips tickled the nape of my neck and caught with my hair.

My head tipped back.

I arched into his touch, my chest seizing with comfort, want, and warmth.

The ebbing adrenaline left me boneless and sagging against his chest as his hand fisted my hair. A shot of desire funneled downward, settling between my legs. We were too close. Whitney and Tara were sleeping one floor above us, and I was wearing nothing but a bra and leggings as I pressed against him, letting his heat swallow me up.

His breathing was shallow as his other hand lifted, his fingertips ever-so-softly dancing up the side of my body, grazing my scraped skin.

It didn't hurt. The pain was gone, replaced by euphoria.

The back of my head rolled against the ridges of his chest as his fingers tangled in my hair, fingertips massaging my scalp. His left hand continued its ascent up my body, skimming the side of my breast as he released a long, hoarse breath.

And then he cupped me.

He palmed my breast with one hand as my nipple hardened to a tight peak.

I moaned.

It was a raspy, begging sound. I wanted his hands all over me, awakening my deadened pieces. He told me there was a fire inside me and that all I needed was a spark. Reed was my spark.

Keep touching me, Reed.

Bring me back to life.

But instead of drawing him closer, the sound of my moan froze him out, blowing frost in his face. In the stretch of a heartbeat, he went eerily still, his hand still cupped around my breast.

Reed pulled away.

He shot back as if I were the spark, and I'd just scalded him.

"Sorry." His tone was rougher than sandpaper. "I need to go."

I turned around, confused, mortified, and helplessly turned on.

Above all, I was angry.

Angry at myself.

I watched as he backed out of the bathroom, my skin flushed, breathing labored, underwear soaked through. Before he spun around to leave, I panned my gaze south and caught the noticeable tent in his pajama pants.

He was hard.

Swollen. Huge.

Reed stabbed a hand through his hair, his eyes pinched closed, then pivoted all the way around and yanked open the bathroom door, disappearing into the hallway before I could say another word.

I stood there, shivering. Alone. Torn apart, physically and mentally. I held in the growl of lust-laced misery as I finished cleaning up and tending to my injuries. Neosporin. Bandages. It was enough to cover the outer wounds, but the flush on my cheeks and the arousal in my eyes spoke of a thousand other battles raging beneath the surface.

I splashed cool water on my face and tugged the tank top back over my head.

Then I raced from the bathroom and hauled myself up the staircase to the bedroom I shared with Tara, ignoring Reed's hunched-over stance on the couch with his head in his hands.

My best friend was fast asleep in bed, burrowed under the covers.

Only a mound of brown hair poked out on the pillowtop as her light snores penetrated the room.

Quietly, I tiptoed over to my own bed and slithered underneath the blankets. I rolled onto my back and stared up at the ceiling, my pulse pounding in my veins and between my thighs.

Without thinking, I slid one hand into the waistband of my leggings.

Oh, God.

This was so wrong.

I chomped down on my bottom lip to mask the whimper that teased my throat.

My fingers trailed lower, finding my slick flesh. I was drenched, ablaze, sickeningly aroused. My back arched slightly off the mattress as my eyes squeezed shut, and I stroked two fingers along my seam. It didn't take long for the tingling feeling to crest. I was pent-up, full of hot tension with nowhere to go. My fingers flicked hard and fast over my swollen clit, my mind racing with forbidden images of Reed's face buried between my legs.

Panting.

Squeezing my thighs until they bruised from his fingertips.

Spreading me wider.

I envisioned his tongue thrusting in and out, lapping at me, reckless and hungry, his teeth nicking me as his mouth latched onto my clit and sucked hard, and our combined moans pushed me over the finish line.

I broke, blanketed in a wash of spine-tingling, leg-buckling fireworks as I slapped a hand over my mouth. I came hard, tremors racing through me, stars flickering behind my eyes. My body hummed through the release, bowing off the bed then collapsing back down, until the feeling puttered out and I deflated.

Silence greeted me in the aftermath. Only the light drone of the space heater filled the bedroom, mingling with Tara's snores.

I covered my face with both hands.

My wounds pulsed. My skin burned hot with post-orgasm flush. My thoughts spiraled, and my eyes welled with new tears.

I'd just masturbated a few feet away from my best friend, on Christmas morning, while fantasizing about her *father*.

It was sick and twisted.

Humiliation sunk me as I tugged the blankets all the way up until I was hidden beneath them. But I knew I couldn't hide forever. Eventually, I'd need to face this trainwreck head-on.

But, in the back of my mind, I knew…

Not all collisions left you rising from the ashes.

Some just left you shattered, buried in the wreckage of your own mistakes.

CHAPTER 16

SWEAT POURED down my face like vitality-infused rain as my gloved fists pummeled the punching bag. Over the past month, Reed had transformed the back office of his studio into a dynamic workout haven. Dumbbells and kettlebells of various weights shimmered under the ceiling lights, while resistance bands hung from hooks. A workout bench was stationed near a yoga mat that was neatly laid out in another corner, awaiting its turn for the cooldown stretches that would follow my session.

My winded pants echoed off the walls as my ponytail swung side to side, muscles stretching and straining, lungs burning.

Release.

"Damn. Who pissed you off?" Scotty materialized in the doorway, his shoulder propped against the frame, arms folded.

I sent him a sidelong glance, hardly faltering as the bag pendulated in front of me. "Today?" I answered through a hard exhale. "Bob Ross."

"Impossible."

"It is possible. His trees are way too happy. It's unrealistic and offensive to the sad trees." Scotty huffed a laugh as I steadied the bag and plucked off each glove. "Speaking of too happy, why are you smiling like a serial killer who just stumbled upon his next victim?"

His overly bright smile fell, and he straightened from the doorway, slamming his hands into the pockets of his sweatpants. "Morbid analogy. Bob Ross really got to you, huh?"

"Or maybe I know from experience." I pulsed my eyebrows wickedly, then pumped a fist up and down to mimic stabbing motions.

Scotty's brows furrowed as he stared at my pumping hand.

I stilled.

It absolutely looked like I was giving the air a thorough hand-job.

Whoops.

Clearing my throat, I dropped my arm at my side and flicked a loose hair out of my eyes. "But seriously. You're in a weirdly good mood."

"Why is that weird?"

"Because you just got your ass handed to you by Coach Madsen."

He sauntered toward me, hands still hidden in his pockets. "How would you know? You were too engrossed in annihilating some vision of happy trees that didn't deserve to feel joy."

"I have ears," I said, strolling up to him. Then I deepened my voice to imitate a male cadence and stated, "*No, stop, please! I'm done, it's too much! Have mercy!*"

"That's definitely not how it went down."

I shrugged, tucking in my lips to hide my smile. "Fine, all I heard were man-grunts and growls. But you look wrecked."

"It was a good session." We met in the center of the workout room and he plopped down on the bench, staring up at me. "You're up next."

Nodding, I stretched an arm across my chest and held it there for a few seconds. "I'm ready."

"We should grab dinner afterward."

I froze, blinking down at him. "Why?"

"Why not? It's dinnertime. Food generally goes along with the concept."

"Why together?"

He hesitated, tilting his head to the side. "Again...why not?"

My jaw tensed as I dipped my chin and stewed over a response. I didn't have an answer, really. Scotty and I had gotten closer over the last six weeks, Christmas morphing into a bitter January, while February brought with it even colder temps and heavy mounds of snow. We were friends. He was twenty; only a year older than me. He was also a good guy.

A compatible potential boyfriend.

What a concept.

But my heart still recklessly ached for the thirty-five-year-old father of my best friend, who had wormed his way into our conversation and was now hovering in the doorway with a scowl.

"Thought you had dinner plans with Tara," Reed clipped.

Scotty whirled around on the bench. "Sorry, Coach. Wasn't trying to interfere."

Reed stared at me with dark eyes, his hair damp with sweat and his sleeveless dove-gray tank soaked through.

I stared back at him for a beat then swallowed, averting my gaze. "Dinner sounds great, Scotty. How about that retro diner off Seventh Street?"

Scotty blinked back to me, looking newly uncertain. "Uh, sure. If that's all right with Coach."

"Why wouldn't it be?" I zoomed past him on the bench, then bumped arms with Reed as I exited the workout room and made a beeline toward the mats. "Ready to train, Coach," I called over my shoulder. "Do your worst."

This was smart.

This was what I needed—*a distraction.* A different guy to inhabit my mind, until all thoughts of the unattainable Reed Madsen flitted from my brain like a bird leaving its nest for brighter skies.

It was something I should have done a long time ago. A few guys at school were interested, and Tara's boyfriend, Josh, had some marginally appealing friends. I supposed my tastes were more in line with older, wiser, emotionally distant men who smelled like earth and ivy, warm amber, and a plethora of compelling sexual fantasies, but that didn't matter.

I was adaptable.

Reed trudged toward me a few seconds later, all stiff, broad shoulders and hulking muscle mass. He sifted a hand through his hair and sighed.

I sank down to the mat to do a few sit-ups for the sole purpose of avoiding conversation.

"You and Scotty?" he probed, standing over me and folding his huge arms like a forbidding shadow.

Breathing in and out, I concentrated on the way my abdomen flexed and burned through the movements. "Maybe."

"That's interesting."

"It could be. Guess we'll find out."

He rubbed a hand over his jaw. "Why?"

Why?

Some better questions would be:

Why do you care? Why does it matter? Why won't you evaporate into thin air, float into somebody else's atmosphere, and let me finally breathe without choking on the idea of you?

But no part of me truly wanted that, so all I said was, "He's one of the few people on the planet who doesn't like peanut butter."

Reed's jawline went rigid as he scraped his teeth together. He watched me through ten more sit-ups before biting out, "Let's get started."

Heaving in a deep breath, I lay back on the mat for another drumbeat, staring up at the paneled ceiling while my lungs fought for a second wind. Then I jumped to my feet. We stared at each other in silence before circling the mat, eye contact holding, muscles twitching and preparing for battle.

A new wave of adrenaline surged.

My heartbeats galloped, fingers curling into fists.

Scotty strolled in and turned on music as he watched us from the sidelines.

The room vibrated and hummed with the opening chords to *Shame* by Stabbing Westward, an industrial rock song that fueled my inner flame with golden heat. I let my gaze trail from Reed's dark bangs glued to his sweat-laden forehead, to his broad chest, rippled abs, and inky, corded arms. The veins in the backs of his hands dilated along with his pupils as we continued to slowly circle each other like two hungry predators vying for domination.

He reached down and grabbed a pair of fingerless gloves, tossing me a second pair. We slipped them over our hands, and I tightened my ponytail, meeting his eyes again and measuring the distance between us. Then, in a burst of fluidity, Reed lunged forward with a lightning-fast jab. I sidestepped, feeling the rush of air as his fist whizzed by, and countered with a swift hook to his ribs. The impact resonated through my arm, and I saw a flash of acknowledgment in Reed's eyes.

The intensity escalated as we exchanged a flurry of punches, blocks, and evasive maneuvers. I ducked beneath a sweeping hook, my hair trailing through the air like a honey-tailed comet. Reed countered with a roundhouse kick, the force of which I deftly deflected with a well-timed block.

He grinned. "Good."

The mat beneath us absorbed the impact of our footwork, the sounds of shuffling and pivoting adding a percussive layer to the music. I inhaled a breath into my lungs, the air thick with an electric charge and the scent of exertion.

We moved in a synchronized dance, a fusion of martial arts and instinct. Reed executed a spinning back kick, and I responded with a low sweep, aiming to unbalance him. He leaped, avoiding contact, and landed with the grace of a wildcat.

A smirk pulled on my lips. "Not so bad yourself."

"You're predictable."

My eyes narrowed. "You're holding back."

We circled each other again, breathing heavily. I focused on his patterns, anticipating his next move. As he shot forward with a high kick, I dodged him and countered with my own.

The kick connected.

Reed staggered slightly, his eyes glinting with a twinkle of satisfaction. Seizing the opportunity, I closed the distance with a rapid combination of jabs and hooks, my fists moving with newfound speed. He attempted to block, but the force overwhelmed his defenses.

I watched as he tried to recalibrate his strategy and then used his moment of vulnerability to execute a spinning back kick, the heel of my foot connecting with his midsection.

Reed grunted, momentarily winded, and I capitalized on his lowered guard. I ambushed him with a controlled takedown, bowling his legs out from under him and watching as he landed on the mat with a *thud*.

I mounted him.

Straddling his chest, I locked our eyes together, a triumphant smirk playing on my lips. "Predictable, huh?" I taunted, my breaths measured.

My thighs clenched around him as our gazes held firm. His chest heaved underneath me, his shirt sliding up his torso as I inched forward.

My own guard collapsed, the bricks slipping out of place, one by one. I wondered how it'd feel to be in this position sans clothing, me on top of him, grinding, sliding up and down on his—

"Oof!" I gasped a surprised breath when he snatched me by the wrists and twisted our clasped hands, leveraging his strength to reverse our positions.

In an instant, I was on my back.

Reed towering over me.

Overpowering. Dominating.

In control.

Flustered, I kicked my legs underneath him, squirming with pathetic fight, a mix of defiance and surrender in my eyes. "You like being in control, don't you?" My voice was husky, laced with challenge. A thinly veiled dare.

He grinned, slow and calculated.

Without breaking eye contact, Reed shifted, his weight pinning my wrists to the mat as my back arched up, my body wanting to get closer to him, instead of wiggling free to escape his hold.

My breath hitched as he leaned in, our lips hovering dangerously close together. "Control is a delicate dance, Comet," he murmured, his voice a low timbre that pulsated through me. "And I intend to lead."

I swallowed, going lax in his grip like a pulled spring finding its release.

Flashes of Christmas morning from six weeks ago swirled through my mind.

His chest that'd been flush with my scarred back, his warm breaths beating down on me, thawing me, as his hand had palmed my breast and I'd moaned darkly, imagining those hands exposing every soiled inch of me. And then the moment that had followed; my own fingers sunk deep inside my flesh, guiding me toward a fiery pinnacle that had doused me in both humiliation and completion.

I was still flicking the ashes off my skin.

Popping my hips upward, past a ninety-degree angle, I felt Reed's grip on my wrists loosen as he shot forward, over my head, and slapped both palms on the mat to catch himself before face-planting. I quickly tilted my head to the left to avoid getting smashed by his weight, then linked my arms around his midsection, pressing my cheek to his chest. In a two-second flash, I lifted up, climbed him like a tree, and moved his arm to gain the upper hand, successfully flipping him over.

A slow smile unfolded as I embraced my victory.

On the mat, I was in control.

But I knew, if I was ever in his bed...

I'd let him destroy me.

Out of breath, I climbed off of him and rose to my feet, staring down at Reed sprawled out on the blue mat. I pushed back my damp, loose hairs and allowed the adrenaline to die out.

Reed pulled up to his knees, shoving back waves of his own disheveled hair. "You're getting really fucking good."

The compliment warmed me from head to toe, nectar sliding through my veins. He was proud of me.

I was proud, too.

"Thanks." I extended a hand to help him up.

He took my hand and slowly moved to his feet, towering back over me, unable to squash the half-smile that curled on his lips. Our eyes caught and seized, the song having morphed into another by the same band.

Reed's gaze shifted over my head to where Scotty must have been standing. A swallow bobbed in his throat as his features hardened, the smile slipping into a flat line. "See you next week," he bristled, before moving around me to the far wall, as if a switch had been flipped. "Enjoy your dinner."

I blinked, gnawing on my lip.

Scotty stalked into my line of sight, and when I twisted to face him, I noticed Reed had vanished into the adjacent workout room.

"I'm wondering if dinner could become problematic," Scotty noted, his shaggy hair pulled back into a small bun at the nape of his neck.

I frowned. "Why?"

"That looked more like foreplay than fighting."

My cheeks burned, double-flushed with post-workout exertion and embarrassment. Apparently, we hadn't been subtle. "We were training."

"Training for what exactly?"

"The same thing as you."

His face scrunched up with distaste. "Unlikely."

Sighing, I swept past him, desperate for a shower. "I'm going to freshen up. Pick me up in an hour?"

He paused, then followed after me. "Yeah? You still want to go?"

"Of course. I'm starved." I gave him my address, gathered my belongings, and glanced into the workout room where Reed was throwing punches at the swinging bag with the fuel of a dozen men.

Lingering for a beat, I watched him move. Watched his arms fly left and right, pummeling the synthetic leather with fury, power, weakness, and all the same things I felt brewing inside of me.

He pressed his forehead to the bag, stifling its movement with both hands as he went still. Then his eyes lifted in my direction. Eyebrows pinched together, face flushed and lined with beads of sweat, he sent me a tortured look as I hovered near the main door with my fingers curled around the handle.

I only let my gaze latch with his for half a heartbeat.

Then I opened the door and walked out into the cold, wintry night.

I was a matchstick.

Small, brittle, and unassuming.

But I was only one strike away from igniting.

And if I wasn't careful...I'd burn us all to the ground.

CHAPTER 17

March, 1997

"ARE you sure you'll be okay?" Whitney asked me, zipping up her coat and flicking her thick brown curls out from the collar. "I'll have my pager on, and you have Laurel's phone number. Please don't hesitate to call. Emergency. Non-emergency. Anything."

I sat on the couch with my brand new film camera that Tara and her mom had gotten me for my nineteenth birthday, my thumbs idling over the array of buttons. Setting it aside, I glanced up with a smile. "I'll be fine, I promise. You're only driving up to Green Bay. Not the moon."

"I wish we were going to the moon," Tara declared, whizzing past me with a giant suitcase, her ponytail set high and bouncing with each step—a contrast to her down-and-out mood. "You're so lucky, Hals. You don't even know. This is the worst."

"Your aunt seems really nice. You'll have fun." Truthfully, I'd only met her Aunt Laurel one time over Thanksgiving and she was verging on dreadful. But I'd never admit that. "And you haven't seen your cousins for over a year. Enjoy the bonding time."

"The last time I visited my cousins, Demon Dorothy quite literally *bonded* bubblegum to my hair while I was sleeping. The extra stretchy kind. I had to chop it off at the shoulders and it still hasn't grown all the way back."

I winced. "She was just young."

"She was fifteen."

"Well, sleep with the doors locked."

"Aunt Laurel doesn't believe in doors. Privacy is a 'secular notion.'"

I opened my mouth to counter but nothing came to mind. So I just sent her a look of pity and we wallowed together in silence.

Whitney chimed in, watching the scene from the foyer. "It's only three nights. We'll be back on Tuesday," she said, hauling her purse strap over her shoulder before pivoting toward me. "You have Laurel's number?"

"It's on the fridge, on the calendar, written in three separate notebooks, and taped to Tara's bedroom door. I also have it memorized."

She nodded, breathing out through her nose. "I really appreciate you taking care of Ladybug and watching over the house while we're gone. I know spring break is supposed to be full of fun and excitement at your age." A soft lilt infected her words. "It means a lot to me. To both of us."

Tenderness poked me between the ribs, triggering a bright smile. "I'm happy to do it. Really. Ladybug is the best company." On cue, the dog hopped up on the couch and plopped down in my lap with a contented sigh.

Whitney's eyes shimmered at the sight. "What would we do without you, Halley?"

I almost burst into tears.

Swiping a hand through Ladybug's fur, I forced back a landslide of emotions.

What would *I* do without *them*? I'd probably be on the streets. Living in a shelter. A school dropout, a lost and lonely vagrant, a directionless nobody lacking any purpose. Without Whitney and Tara, spring break wouldn't even been a blip on my radar. It would simply be another week lost in the blur of hundreds of sad, uninspiring weeks.

Tara shot me a wave as she trailed her mother out the front door. "Don't forget, there's a blizzard supposed to hit tomorrow. My dad said he'd come by to shovel at some point. You can borrow my car at any time, but the tires are bald as shit, so you might want to plan around the snow."

"Got it. Ladybug loves the snow," I said. "I'll make sure to take some pictures." Holding up the camera, I waved it in the air as they shuffled out the door.

"Bye, Hals! See you Tuesday."

"Bye," I called back.

The door snapped shut.

Silence.

With a smile still plastered on my face, I cozied up underneath a checkered quilt and continued to stroke Ladybug's fur, snapping a few photographs of her chin resting on top of my thighs.

"We're going to have a good few days," I voiced into the quiet, settling back and propping my feet up on the ottoman. "It's just you and me, Ladybug..."

Just like that, it was only me.

Ladybug was missing.

Panic had me diving into my winter boots and shoving my trembling arms into coat sleeves as I raced out onto the back deck, my head canting left and right. "Ladybug!" I shouted over the howling wind while heavy snowfall blanketed the ground in pure white, and fear pitched in my gut, turning my complexion even whiter. "Ladybug! Where are you, girl?"

The sound of eerie silence was the only response, roaring louder that my frantic, terror-laced voice.

Oh, no.

This was a nightmare. I'd let Ladybug outside to do her business during the blizzard, after she'd been whining and pacing near the patio door. The yard was fenced. Everything was secured.

But Ladybug had vanished into thin air.

My hair blew across my face as my skin froze and my legs shook. I assessed the property, even crawling underneath the deck to see if she'd sought shelter beneath the structure.

Nothing. She was nowhere.

Tracing the fence line, I checked for holes she could have shimmied through. And when I made it to the side of the house where the gate still stood locked tight, I noticed something that made my blood run colder than the frost settling in my windpipe—a hole in the gate.

A wayward tree branch, weighted by the accumulating snow, had crashed against the fence, creating a breach that had allowed Ladybug to venture outside the safety of the backyard.

"No, no, no..."

My vision was warped by the snowfall barreling down in angry slashes of white. I could hardly keep my eyes open, could hardly inhale a full breath.

Tears turned to an icy pane against my eyes as I raced back up the deck steps and hurried inside the house to grab the rest of my winter gear. I had no choice but to look for her. I would normally take Tara's car, but the tires were bald and I'd risk a crash.

I glanced at the phone hanging from the kitchen wall, biting down on my ice-cold lip as I tried to think of a plan. I didn't want to worry Tara or her mother while they visited with family over three hours away. It wasn't safe for them to drive down now, anyway.

I stared at the phone. My heart thumped between my ribs.

"Dammit," I cursed under my breath, rocketing forward and yanking the phone off the receiver. I dialed in Reed's number. He had a truck; he could help me find her.

It rang three times before he picked up. "Hello?"

"Reed? It's Halley." My voice cracked, infused with anxiety. "It's Ladybug. I let her out in the yard. It was only for a few minutes. Less than five. I—"

"What happened?"

I swallowed hard. "She...she's gone. She escaped through the fence."

A beat. "I'll be right there."

I didn't wait for him.

In an instant, I gathered my gloves and a wool cap and dashed out the front door, calling her name through the blizzard. "Ladybug!" I trudged through seven inches of snow, glancing into neighboring yards and across hills. A snowplow drove past slowly as my boots disappeared into mounds of plush white. "Ladybug!"

I was half a mile down the road when two headlights blurred up ahead, moving toward me. A flash of red seeped through the haze.

Reed's truck.

He slowed down beside me and cracked the window. "What the hell are you doing out here?"

"Looking for Ladybug." Tears streamed down my frozen cheeks. "I couldn't wait. I have to find her."

"Get in." He nodded at the passenger's side.

Tugging my hat farther down my ears, I circled the front of the truck, my feet sliding in the snow, then threw myself into the warm vehicle.

He glanced at me as I buckled my seatbelt. "We're going to find her."

All I could do was nod and hold in the sob.

Reed inched us through the neighborhood, both of our heads hanging out each window, the truck hardly going five-miles-per-hour. We shouted her name. Squinted our eyes through the snow, desperate to catch a glimpse of golden fur. Ten minutes later, we pulled up near the park that was walking distance from the house—her favorite place to chase squirrels and rubber balls.

The moment Reed put the truck in Park, I unlatched my belt and dove out of the vehicle.

"Halley!" he called after me, my name followed by a curse of frustration.

I heard him behind me, calling out as I ran full-speed ahead across the playground. "I think she's here!" I hollered over my shoulder, my words slivered by the wind.

His hand curled around my puffy coat and halted my steps, spinning me around to face him. "Hey. Take a breath."

I nodded frantically, my eyes wide and worried.

"Keep it together, all right? She didn't go far. We'll find her."

Snowflakes splashed across his dark hair. His grip on me was firm but comforting, his eyes glimmering against the hazy wash of light with earnestness.

I pulled myself together and my nod turned resolute. "Okay," I said. "I'm okay. I'm fine."

He let me go and we stalked through the woodchips hidden beneath inches of snow. I darted my gaze around the empty park while Reed went in the opposite direction, and we both shouted her name. A few minutes passed, and my terror whirled back, funneling in my chest.

She wasn't here.

The sun would be setting soon, eclipsing the daylight.

Reed jogged back over to me as we met in the middle of the park, hopelessness squeezing my lungs. "She's not here," I told him.

His eyes dimmed as he led me back over to the truck. "So we'll keep looking."

We drove around for almost an hour.

Stopping, searching, getting back in, driving some more. We were frozen to the bone, soaking wet, and defeated. All I could think about was the look on Tara's face, the horror in Whitney' eyes, when I told them I'd lost their dog.

I had one goddamn job.

Take care of Ladybug.

And I'd failed.

She could be anywhere—lying broken on the side of the road, having been hit by a car. Lost in a wooded area, seeking shelter from the snow. She could have been rescued by a neighbor or a good Samaritan, but the possibilities were endless, and given the weather conditions... *grim.*

As the sky darkened to charcoal-gray, so did my spirits. I plucked off my gloves and hat and tossed them on my lap, clawing my fingers through my tangled hair and trying in vain to avoid a breakdown. We were closer to Reed's apartment now, a few miles from the Stephens' residence, and the snow was still accumulating. It wasn't safe to be on the road.

An anguished whimper broke free.

"Halley..." Reed sat beside me with his fingers tightly coiled around the wheel, his eyes shared between me and the windshield. "Comet, hey. It'll be all right."

"I failed them," I murmured, voice strangled. "I lost their dog. After all they've done for me, I lost one of their family members."

He was quiet for a beat. "It's not your fault."

"It *is* my fault. I should have checked the fence before letting her out."

"Accidents happen."

I shook my head, rejecting his words, and fixed my attention to the window as snow continued to rain down in sideways slants.

"I'm going to pull over for a sec," he told me after a few tense beats.

"I see animal prints in the snow. Could be a fox or something, but it's worth a look."

As the truck rolled to a slow stop, I followed his gaze and spotted the trail of prints, roughly the size of a dog or coyote, that were leading toward a steep ravine. "I'll go with you."

He kept the keys in the ignition and pushed the gear shift lever into Park. "No. Wait here."

Like hell.

"Reed—"

The door slammed shut. My throat fizzed with nervous heat as I watched him stalk along the side of the empty road, illuminated by a lone streetlamp and the final streaks of daylight.

My feet tapped in parallel time, teeth clicking together.

His outline faded into the blizzard, out of sight.

Nope. I couldn't just stay put—this was *my* fault.

Heaving in a deep breath, I jumped out of the truck and raced toward where he'd evaporated into the fog as I followed the prints. I caught up to him just as he veered toward a hill rimmed by a dense tree line, my boots slipping and sliding.

He did a double-take when he felt me approaching on his right. "What the fuck?" he blared over the hissing wind. "Why don't you listen?"

My eyes narrowed to slits, part defenses, part snow compromising my vision.

"Go back to the truck. I'm handling it." He stomped ahead.

I followed. "I'm not going anywhere. I'm the reason we're even out here in the fir—"

"Christ, Halley." His brows were furrowed with frustration, hair drenched. "She's my damn dog, and I'm going to find her. It's not safe for you out here."

"She's my dog, too," I shot back. "She's my friend."

His eyes swept over me for a charged moment. "Where's your hat? Your gloves?"

"Where are yours?"

"You're being irresponsible."

"You're being a jerk. Stop talking to me like I'm a little kid."

We walked in tandem, the air fraught with friction and a slew of unsaid words teasing our tongues. He ran a hand over his face, shoving his hair back as the tips beaded with icy water droplets and we neared the edge of the embankment.

"How's it going with Scotty?" he asked me, his tone as disinterested as a rock observing a river.

I stared straight ahead, my reply more frozen than my fingers. "Fantastic."

"Really," he bit out.

"Yep. He's sweet, kind, and attentive. Treats me like an equal." I clenched my jaw. "How about you? Any lady friends lately?"

"A few."

"Good for you." Hot pressure burned behind my eyes, but I held back the flimsy dam of tears.

He stared straight ahead, his profile rigid, arms hardly swinging at his sides. We didn't say another word as we made the final trek over to the dropoff and I held my breath, my stomach weaving into knotty ropes when I moved to peer over the edge.

An arm flew out in front of me, holding me back.

Reed looked at me, right in the eyes, his expression softening unlike the storm. "I'll look."

I blinked at him, nodding gently. Lips quivering.

Then he spun around and leaned over while I burrowed my boots in the snow, fisted my hands, and squeezed my eyes shut. Time moved in slow motion, my heartbeats a reckless soundtrack. I heard my pulse in my ears as I waited; waited for him to break my heart or give me hope.

It was a feeling I was used to when it came to Reed.

"She's not here," he finally said, his words a whisper but loud enough to penetrate my thick wall of fear. "Let's head back. It's too dark, too dangerous."

I sucked in a sharp breath as he moved around me and stormed back toward the truck. "What...? No. Reed...no, we have to keep looking."

"There's no point, Halley. She probably got picked up by a neighbor or animal control. There's nothing more we can do right now."

Giving chase, I croaked out a tiny sob that was carried away with the wind. I didn't know what to say as I stared at his retreating back, the white snowfall shading the black leather of his jacket.

When we reached the darkened street, I stomped around the front of the truck, my eyes blurred by angry tears and an angrier sky. "You know, I really—"

My words cut off when a firm hand tore me backward, and my feet nearly skidded out from under me. Whiplashed, I steadied myself and glanced up, just as the hazy headlights of an incoming car zigzagged by, struggling to stay in a straight line through the snow.

A horn blared.

I choked on a breath.

Blinking rapidly, my chin tipped up, and I met with Reed's blazing eyes as I idled for a beat in the safety of his arms.

"Fucking hell," he said on a low growl, his eyes glinting against the streetlight. He held me closer, fingers curling around my upper arms. "I told you to stay in the goddamn truck."

His voice was soft gravel. Fear inched its way into his fury as his grip loosened and one hand slowly rubbed up and down my bicep. He closed his eyes and exhaled through his nose.

I relaxed for a beat, lost to his touch.

And then I shook him off me.

Glancing both ways, I carefully made my way to the passenger's side and flung myself into the vehicle. He followed. We sat together in silence before the engine revved to life, the windshield wipers swished back on, and he cautiously pulled the truck out onto the main drag.

Music spilled from the speakers, a popular eighties song. I fell back against the seat and closed my eyes, trying to ignore his proximity, trying to shove back all of the horrible images of Ladybug lost or injured in this blizzard as the wipers squeaked and my stomach pitched.

I only opened my eyes when we came to a stop and the engine died out, the sound of keys being removed from the ignition snapping me back to life.

My attention landed on a familiar apartment complex in front of us, and I frowned. "Why did you bring me here?"

He unbuckled his belt and pocketed the keys. "The roads are fucked. My place was closer."

"But—" I didn't have time to argue before he jumped out and shut the door.

There was no other choice but to follow him inside.

We made our way through the hallways, wordless, my nerves heightening when we reached apartment number seventeen. He unlocked the door and moved aside to let me enter.

Hesitantly, I stepped through the threshold, shivering from head to toe.

Am I staying the night?

Where will I sleep?

The door softly clicked closed and Reed slipped out of his jacket, toeing off his boots in the entryway. "We need to get you warmed up," he said, eyeing me as I dallied in front of him.

My leggings were soaked through, my socks soggy from snow that had inched its way inside my boots. "I...don't have a change of clothes."

His eyes trailed me, a lazy pull from top to bottom. "Tara has some clothes she left here."

I nodded, sweeping wet hair off my forehead. "Can I take a shower?"

"Not yet. You need to warm up gradually."

My throat burned as I forced another nod. "Okay. Thank you."

Our eyes held for a breath before he disappeared into one of the bedrooms and returned a minute later to find me trembling on his graphite-gray couch, my feet pulled up beside me.

Reed hesitated then moved forward, a lump of clothing and a towel draped over the crook of his arm.

I watched as he sunk to his knees in front of me and reached for my ankles, his fingers still cold as he carefully tugged the damp socks off my feet.

I gazed at him, unmoving. "What are you doing?"

"Warming you up."

My lips parted to contest, but no words slipped through. I wasn't used to being cared for, attended to with tender touches and soft caresses. So all I did was watch him as he used a bath towel to swipe the moisture from my frozen feet and calves.

Then he grazed his hands up my thighs and reached for the waistband of my leggings.

My heart pounded, breath hitching.

There was no hesitation, no awkward falters. He tugged the wet fabric down my legs, continued to dry me off, then slipped a pair of dry pajama pants over my feet. Two fuzzy socks followed, swallowing my toes painted in raspberry polish.

When my bottoms were secured, I slid them up all the way and Reed inched his body closer between my legs, hands extending toward the hem of my blouse.

His eyes lifted to mine.

They glowed with a heated mix of affection and something else. I stared at him, my own eyes hooded as my air released in puffs of nervous energy.

I slowly raised my arms over my head.

Reed swallowed, his movements even slower as he elevated on his knees between my parted legs and the blouse followed the upward glide of his hands. My tangle of hair fell back down, a chilly waterfall over my bare shoulders and bra straps. His chest heaved in and out, his own breaths shallow and frayed. Jaw ticking, he avoided my eyes as he slipped the neck of the shirt over my head and helped guide my arms through the sleeve holes.

I pulled my hair from the collar and glanced down at the T-shirt. "This isn't Tara's."

It was his Soundgarden shirt.

Gaze aimed at the front of my chest, he blinked at the logo. "Yeah," was all he said.

The scent of amber and earthy masculinity wrapped me up in a warm hug as Reed reached across the couch to snag the chocolate-brown blanket beside me. He draped it over both of my shoulders, tucking me into the cozy cocoon, his hands lingering on the fringed ends as he clasped it tight.

"Thanks." I pressed my palm to the back of his knuckles as a way to keep him close. His hand was cold and dry, so I gently massaged warmth back into his skin with my fingertips. "You're cold, too."

"I'm fine." He idled between my legs, voice rougher than grit. "Feel better?"

"Yes."

A small nod answered me as he found my eyes. "She's going to be okay," he said gently. Then he reached out and tucked a strand of wet hair behind my ear. "When she was just a puppy, she'd get loose from the yard all the time. She's good at finding escape routes. She's even better at finding a safe place to hide until she's found."

I rubbed my lips together. "I feel terrible."

"That's because your heart is so damn big." Reed reached for my hands poking out from the front crack of the blanket, cupping them between his large palms and applying friction. "You're still freezing."

I wasn't freezing. I was a melty mound of warm goo. "That feels good."

He raised our intertwined hands and blew heated breaths into his tented palms before rubbing them together again. Tingles bloomed in my fingertips like tiny razorblades and ran a marathon up the length of my arms. When Reed raised our hands again, he released another hot breath, then fully cupped my slow-warming palms as he brought them to his chin and held. His eyes closed through a long sigh, and we just sat there.

Still and silent.

I didn't speak; I just savored the moment while the moment savored us.

There was a difference between staying quiet and having nothing left to say. I had words. Plenty of them. But I wanted to be where the peace was, and sometimes that was in purging the words, and sometimes it was in withholding them. Right now, I chose the intentional quiet.

The peace resided in the things unsaid.

When his eyes finally reopened, he propped his chin on our locked hands and studied me through the dim lighting of his apartment. "I'm sorry for how I spoke to you earlier," he said, and while the words were soft and feather-light, the turmoil I saw reflected in the stormy green of his eyes was anything but. "I know you're scared. I didn't mean to make it worse."

My lashes fluttered at his gentle touch and the tingly trail his thumb left behind as he kneaded my fingers. Then I glanced at him, perched only inches away from me, and tucked my knees inward until they brushed his outer thighs. "Are you scared?"

I didn't know if I was referring to Ladybug or something else.

Maybe both.

His hands slowly untethered from mine as he dropped his chin and caged me in with both arms, pressing forward on the couch cushions on either side of me. When he glanced back up with just his eyes, his gaze was churning with new waves, new turmoil. "Halley, I'm—"

The phone rang.

I jolted in place, blinking away the daze. Reed stared at me for a heavy beat, whatever he'd wanted to say lost at sea.

He let out a sigh as he dropped back on his heels. Scrubbing a hand over his face, he sent me one last look before rising from the floor and stalking toward the edge of the kitchen where a cornflower-blue phone hung from the wall.

For an insidious drumbeat, I wondered if it was a woman...one of his *lady friends*.

"Hello?" he answered, tone clipped. Then, in the span of a few seconds, his brows unfurled and his eyes flared. "Really? Shit...yeah, thank you." He nodded. "Okay. I'll be over soon."

He hung up, and I stood from the couch, the blanket falling off my shoulders. The pajama pants were short on me, dangling just above my ankles, as Reed's shirt engulfed my slender frame. I folded my arms like a protective shield. "Everything okay?"

Reed took a step toward me, face expressionless. "That was the local animal hospital."

My whole heart bounced between my ribs as terror punched a hole in my chest.

I waited.

And then a half-smile curved his lips. "They have Ladybug. She's fine."

CHAPTER 18

Reed

LADYBUG EXPLODED through the front door of my apartment, beelining straight toward Halley as she leaped up from the couch cushions.

"Ladybug!"

I couldn't catch my grin before it let loose as I watched the reunion unfold. Golden fur blending with golden hair. Two sun-kissed arms outstretched, waiting for the dog to charge into their eager embrace. Halley dropped to her knees while Ladybug attacked her with happy tongue kisses and a swishing tail as if the two hadn't seen each other in years.

Peeling out of my snow-dusted jacket, I placed it on a wall hook then stared at them, lost to the moment, just like I was. It was sweet, innocent.

So goddamn pure.

Squealing with joy, Halley tipped backward on my light-pewter carpeting.

Turned out, an older couple had seen her wandering aimlessly at the park during the snowstorm and had driven her back to their house in hopes of finding the owner. They'd called the number on the nametag, but Halley had already left for her search-and-rescue mission. After a few hours of calling with no luck, they'd taken her to the animal hospital for safekeeping, away from their cats.

Halley had been right—she *was* at that park.

The microchip was registered under my name, considering I'd been the one to adopt Ladybug five years ago after Tara had spotted her and had to have her.

Thank fuck for that.

She straightened to her butt and scooted back, propped up against the front of my couch while the dog took up residence in her lap. Eighty pounds of matted love sprawled across the nineteen-year-old girl seated in my living room, who was wearing my favorite T-shirt and my daughter's plaid pajama bottoms.

A dark feeling sawed through me.

Dark, clawing, and painfully euphoric. I'd imagined a similar scene on a night in late June, a year and a half ago—only, minus the dog and the bevy of external bullshit.

Halley.

In my apartment.

Wearing that same smile and one of my T-shirts after a night of hot and heavy bliss.

Fantasies.

That was all it was now; a fantasy that never came to pass and would never hold any merit in the long run. It was make-believe, intangible, and the sooner I came to terms with that, the sooner I could break free of this fairy-tale narrative that continued to poison my mind.

Hands loosely planted on my hips, I moved forward as Halley's chin tipped up, her smile never waning. "You hungry?" I needed to remove myself from whatever lethal bubble we'd been sucked into before that phone had rung. "I can make something for you."

Her hazel eyes shimmered against the shitty lighting of my small apartment, giving an added glow. "Can I cook?"

"I don't have much to work with. I'm a frozen dinner guy most nights."

"I bet I can get creative." Halley unraveled herself from Ladybug's paws as she stood from the floor, her outfit as mismatched as we were. "Can I look through your ingredients?"

I shrugged. "Make yourself at home."

Fuck.

No, please don't do that.

Nodding softly, she swooped past me, smelling like peach nectar, winter frost, and me. I watched her for a few beats as she bent over to rummage through my lower cabinets before scrubbing the image from my mind and heading toward the secondary bedroom.

Tara slept in here whenever she spent the night. There were boy band posters taped to the walls and a slew of knickknacks cluttered on the dresser and nightstand, while a meshing of cheap vanilla perfume and musty carpeting filled the air. As I fluffed the recently-washed bedcovers, I glanced at a photograph in a gilded frame that was leaning against the table lamp. It was a picture of Tara and I at the park about a year ago, sparring near the basketball hoops. The image was a candid shot, but deliberately captured—perfect lighting, with the setting sun streaking through tree branches, Tara in position, grinning ear-to-ear, and me standing across from her with the barest smile and a look in my eyes that reflected pure love.

I plucked the frame from the nightstand and studied it, wondering how I'd never noticed it before.

A priceless moment, frozen in time.

Halley was the photographer, no doubt, and my affection for her soared to dangerous heights.

I set the picture back down.

After taking a few minutes to change into dry loungewear, I made my way back into the kitchen, where a pot of water was close to boiling on the stove. Halley was propped up on her tiptoes, pulling items out of an upper cabinet. A slew of ingredients littered my lack of counter space. "What did you decide on?" I asked her.

"Hodge podge pasta."

"What now?"

She sent me a sidelong grin. "You'll see."

She was in a perkier mood, thanks to Ladybug being found safe, which was always a double-edged sword.

When she was bright and happy, I was drawn to her laughter-lit smiles and the bounce in her step. When she was sullen and self-depre-cating, I was desperate to scrub the soot off her skin and bring her back to life. It was a goddamn seesaw of destructive emotion, and she was tearing me in half.

Twenty minutes later, a giant bowl of penne pasta was brought to the table, served with toasted bread and butter. I eyed the concoction warily. "There's green stuff in it."

"Green beans. Eat them," she ordered playfully, lighting one of my cedar-scented candles with a matchstick. "You should know that green stuff is good for you, given your fatherly duties and all."

I scowled.

I hated green beans.

But since they were one of the few vegetables Tara loved, I kept my freezer stocked with those frozen vegetable medleys mixed with carrots and corn.

"The only protein you had on hand was chicken, so I sauteed it in butter, added some seasonings, parmesan, and a little cream cheese." She shrugged, pulling out a chair and summoning me to do the same. "Best I could do."

It smelled delicious, and I was going to eat the hell out of it, green beans and all.

As we settled in by candlelight and cedarwood, with Ladybug lying underneath the table waiting for scraps, I tried not to focus on how much this felt like a date. Halley looked so casual in her informal clothing, her hair a beautiful mess, face scrubbed clean and makeup-less, and a smile that refused to leave her perfect mouth. It was like she belonged here, in my apartment, at my kitchen table, her hair glimmering against the brassy light fixture overhead.

Clearing my throat, I shoveled forkfuls of food into my mouth and had to hold back the moan. "Damn," I muttered through a bite.

"Good?" Her eyes were wide and waiting, the fork loosely dangling from her hand as she anticipated my reaction. "You like it?"

"I love it."

Cooking for people was important to her. It meant a lot, and that softened all the hard edges that had been whittling me down lately. The more time I spent with her, the more my attraction grew. The more my attraction grew, the more I hated myself.

And the more I hated myself, the more I transferred those feelings of self-loathing onto her.

But then there were moments like this, tender and warm.

Organic smiles, easy conversation, and a connection that felt like it wasn't *solely* based on physical draw. As the sexual attraction continued to bloom, so did this maddening nurturing feeling, like I'd be willing to move mountains for her, that I'd be content just holding her and washing away her pain until she found perfect solace in my arms.

Goddammit.

That was even worse. Unwanted attraction was deadly enough, but it was natural. With the right toxic blend of circumstances, it happened —I knew that from experience, given my own personal ordeal with Radley and Whit.

But envisioning some kind of fucking *future* with her was the real killer that would put us both in the ground.

What would Tara think? Whitney?

They'd be horrified; I had no doubt about that. Thirty-five-year-old men didn't just fall for teenagers. It was twisted and wrong, and sometimes I had to wonder if there was something wrong with *me.*

"Are you listening?"

Blinking, I lifted my chin and looked over at Halley as she swallowed down a bite of food. When I glanced at my own plate, I realized I'd somehow finished eating. And no, I definitely wasn't listening. "Sorry, I was in my head," I muttered, reaching for a piece of bread.

"Care to share?"

Hell-fucking-no. "Not really."

"Well, I was just filling you in on my photography project at school."

School.

She was still in high school. On a technicality, sure, but—

I'd zoned out again.

Swatting me on the arm to break my daze, Halley pressed an elbow to the table and propped her cheek in her hand. "Something's bothering you."

"It was just all that time out in the cold," I said, shaking away the dark thoughts. "Gave me a headache."

"Anything I can do?"

"No...tell me about your photography thing. I'm listening."

Her smile sparked back to life. "So, I'm delving into the grunge culture, the underground music scene. My pictures are geared toward bringing to life the raw energy of our time, portraying the struggles and passions of a generation on the cusp of a new millennium. I've been focusing on more intimate moments—crowded gigs in dimly lit venues, friends hanging out in vintage thrift stores, and the subtle rebellion etched in everyday expressions. It's sort of a visual narrative of a year that feels both tumultuous and liberating...frozen in the frames of my lens. You know?"

I was lost again, but not to my own intrusive thoughts. I was lost in her words, in the magic of them. In the magic she'd found in a pastime that I'd helped bring to light. Swallowing, I nodded, my eyes drinking in the joy on her face. "I think that's awesome. Glad you've found something you enjoy doing." A small smile crested, authentic and real. "You're talented."

She smiled back, even wider, her cheek still resting in her hand. "Thank you. I think I want to make a career out of it someday. Portraits, animals, events. Maybe I can travel the world."

"You don't want to stay in Illinois?" I dabbed my mouth with a napkin.

"I don't know. I feel like I have a wandering soul," she mused, gazing off over my shoulder. "There are so many moments I want to experience. It feels like a disservice to stick to one place forever."

I studied her through a slow nod.

She didn't want to lay roots in the same place that had tried to strangle her, and that made sense. When the roots you were born into shriveled and decayed, the only thing to do was to lay new roots. Build a new home, far away from the dead soil that would decompose you from the inside out.

"Anyway," she said, blinking away the daydreams. "I'll clean up."

"I got it." Pushing my chair back, I blew out the candle.

As I moved into the kitchen to put the leftovers away, I felt two arms encircle me from behind. I stiffened as her hands linked at my chest and she whispered a warm breath between my shoulder blades.

"I just wanted to say thank you," she said softly.

I swallowed hard, the feel of her pressed against me lighting me on fire. "For what?"

"Everything. For using your free time to train me, while getting nothing in return. For turning me into a fighter, making me strong and

capable. For believing in me when I didn't even believe in myself."
Nuzzling closer, she continued on, her grip on me tightening. "For
helping me look for Ladybug, then going back out to pick her up in this
blizzard. For giving me a safe place to spend the night." She sighed.
"Just...for everything."

I inhaled a breath laced with the residual smoke from the blown-out
candle but only tasted her. Vanilla beans, peach pie, and hair spun with
honey; a recipe for catastrophe.

When I lifted my hand to her clasped palms, she didn't let go. She
wanted catastrophe. She embraced it with two slim arms around my
waist and a breathy whimper that kissed my back and sent obliteration
down my spine.

This was as close as I'd ever get to her, and I was reluctant to pull
away.

"Want to watch a movie?" she suggested, finally inching back,
untwining her arms, and floating over to my living room couch as I
remained idle in the center of the kitchen.

"Yeah," I choked out, carving a hand through my hair. "All right."

Popping in a tape, I settled beside her on the couch, leaving a gap for
Ladybug to jump between us, which lessened the urge for me to scoop
her into my arms and soothe her to sleep with the stroke of my hand and
the beats of my heart.

She watched the movie.

I watched her.

Something startled me awake.

Glancing at the clock beside my bed, I rubbed the heels of my palms
over my eyes and tried to unblur my vision as the muddled numbers
came into view.

2:15.

I sighed, blinking up at the shadowy ceiling. A few drowsy seconds
ticked by when I heard a noise coming from the living room. I sat up.
There was a light on, and I knew I'd turned it off before hauling myself
to bed three hours ago.

As my senses flickered back to life, I could also make out the telltale sounds of music seeping underneath the door, something up-tempo and far too lively to be playing at two in the morning.

I swung my legs over the side of the bed, mussed both hands through my hair, and stood from the mattress. Adorned in only my sleep pants, I padded across the room and glanced down the hallway after cracking the door open.

Halley was exercising on my blue mat, wearing just a T-shirt and doing push-ups, her long hair curtaining the flush on her cheeks.

What the hell?

Frown secured, I made my way down the hall until my bare feet entered her line of sight and she halted mid-thrust.

She collapsed to her stomach, then inched up on her knees, a line of sweat curling the baby hairs that rimmed her forehead. "Shit. I woke you."

"Yeah," I admitted.

"Sorry. I couldn't sleep."

My frown deepened as I folded my arms across my chest. "Do you always take to cardio when you can't sleep?"

Licking a dot of sweat off her upper lip, she exhaled a winded breath. "No. I share a room with Tara, so I usually do it the old-fashioned way and stare blankly at the ceiling until sunrise."

"Mm." I took a small step forward, still staring down at her. "Want to train?"

Her eyes rounded at the offer. "Really?"

"We're both awake now."

"It's late," she said softly. "Or...early. I don't even know."

"It's after two a.m. But time is time, and if we're not sleeping, we might as well fill it with something productive."

She settled into my reply like she was making herself comfortable in the breadth of each word. A flicker of consent tilted her head up farther as she faced me on the mat, her fingers curling into the blue textile laid out between my kitchen and living room, and my toes a step away from the edge.

"Okay, sure." She swiped some hair from her eyes. "I'll try to go easy on you since you're all groggy and sleepy-eyed."

I feigned offense with a stony glare, but the declaration only heightened my buzz.

Sparring with her was almost as good as sex.

Pulse-stirring, rousing, and borderline erotic.

And since it'd been an embarrassingly long time since I'd had any, I would take the high where I could get it.

When Halley made a motion to stand, I stopped her. "No. Stay put."

Her eyes thinned with confusion.

I stepped onto the mat, circling her, staring down at her like she was my prey. Halley tried to lift up again, but I shook my head. "Wait for me to come to you."

Her chest heaved, billowing the baggy T-shirt that fell just below her thighs. My heart thundered in time with the song's bass as I kept my focus narrowly trained on her.

I shot forward and she reacted, raising both hands with a block before I straightened again and continued my deliberate pacing around her. Halley flicked a hand out at me, but I dodged it, half-bent over as she dropped to her butt and spun in aligned tandem, tracking my movements.

We did this for a solid minute. I was testing her focus, her reflexes, her reaction time.

She was sharp. Aware of every calculated step I took, of every swing of my arm and hitch of my breath.

I lunged forward, simulating a strike that she quickly deflected. As she shifted her weight, I circled behind her, but Halley anticipated the maneuver, spinning around to face me, our motions a synchronized rhythm of combat and strategy.

Without warning, I snatched her by the hair.

Inclined forward.

Tucked her head to my chest as she whipped her arm out to curl around my neck, an attempt at gaining the upper hand and flipping me over.

I held tight, not holding back, dropping to my knees and staying steady as her legs shot out and circled my midsection. She fell onto her back, and I followed, moving over her. Linking her ankles at the center of my spine, she used her whole weight to try and twist me, maintaining a headlock.

"Move your arm," I instructed. "Over mine."

She started flailing, and I heard the panic creeping into her shaky breaths.

"Relax, Halley." My tone was even as I held firm, not wanting to give her the easy way out. She needed to overpower me, needed to win. "Come on. Flip me over."

Grunts, pants, whimpers.

Her fuel was morphing into fear as she struggled in my grip.

I loosened up and straightened, her legs still hooked around my middle. When I lurched forward again, she reverted to a defensive move instead of offense. "Don't cross your arms."

"Reed—"

I yanked her arms apart and slammed them to the mat by the wrists. "Stop being afraid," I demanded. "Fight back. You can do this. Stop being fucking scared—"

A growl tore from her lips and she popped her hips up with renewed strength, putting me in another headlock and pivoting her body to the left with all her strength. I lost leverage and she flipped me over, straddling me with her bare thighs.

But I kept going, kept testing her abilities, refusing to let her relish in a temporary win that would do nothing but lower her guard. "That was good," I breathed out, sweat forming on my browline. I grappled with her, hauling her onto her side as our limbs tangled and our bodies intertwined like a pretzel. "Use your legs."

She huffed and heaved, moving her arms over mine, trying to swivel my hips with both of her legs. "I thought you didn't dance," she forced out, my face pressed to the crook of her neck.

I stilled for a beat, replaying her words, and then my mind reeled back to Jay's bedroom.

A pile of CDs in our laps.

Her hazel eyes sparkling, bewitching me, altering my fucking DNA.

"Do you dance?"

"Movement is art. Motion is freeing."

She tried twisting my arm as she inched her way up my torso, but I maintained control. "Is that what you think this is? Dancing?"

"Yes." She panted through the powerplay. "That's all we ever do."

The minutes ticked by.

Frustration coursed through her as she scuffled beneath me, every breath more labored, each push and tug and block losing its edge as emotion derailed instinct and knowledge.

We twisted, circled, wrestled.

Every inch of our bodies were stuck together, tied in a knot.

She released a hiss into my ear when I caged her legs in with mine. "Damn you," she cursed, on the verge of giving up. "Let me go."

"Make me," I taunted.

"I'm done. I quit."

"Not a fucking chance," I gritted out. "C'mon, Halley, harness your anger. Stay mad. Use it against me—"

"I *am* mad," she spit back, voice muffled by my shoulder. "I'm mad at you."

"You were thanking me earlier. Cooking for me, hugging me. You didn't seem mad."

"I'm both," she countered hotly. "You're mixing me all up inside. I don't know whether to hug you, strangle you, or kiss you."

A shot of heat swam through me. "Yeah?"

"Yes." She grunted, her legs linking around me again as she used her hips to try and swing me onto my back. "I hate the way you look at me like I'm a burden."

"You are." I was dousing her rekindled flame in lighter fluid because she was stronger when she was pissed off and throwing fury in my face. "You've been nothing but a burden since I laid eyes on you."

Another growl.

Another failed attempt to gain control.

"The way you talk to me." She fisted my hair with white-knuckled fingers. "Like you can boss me around, bark orders at me."

"You like it when I do."

"*No*," she seethed, breathing hellfire.

Sweat dripped off our skin as she raked her nails up the planes of my slick back, leaving claw marks behind.

Now she was fighting dirty.

And I cursed the goddamn stirring in my pants as my dick hardened, my hips involuntarily grinding against her spread thighs.

Her furious grunt died out to a whimper for the span of a second before she regrouped and battled harder. "I hate you," she snarled, thrusting upward against my erection, a contradiction to the way her arms tried in vain to shove me away. "I hate the way you spar with me like I'm your equal when you'll only ever see me as your *student*." She wheezed, struggled, her words hardly coherent as she fought for breaths and leverage. "A protege you can whip into shape so you can place me on your mantel and appreciate me from afar."

"That's where you belong." I squeezed the globes of her ass until her legs loosened on a cracked moan and I tossed her flat on her back, towering over her, my hands flying out to catch her by the wrists. I held tight, relentless, my sweat-soaked chest heaving against hers. Leaning in close, I ground out, "Far. Away. From me."

The anger fizzled out as her eyes flashed, an inch below mine, a smirk curling on her pretty, pouty lips. "You wish. But you can't stay away from me."

Grinding my pelvis against hers, I felt her damp underwear flush with my erection and swallowed my moan with more lies. "You'll never be anything to me. Nothing more than my daughter's friend. A lost little girl I met at a party, who tried to lie her way into my bed."

She squirmed against my rock-hard cock and delighted in the way I shuddered. "It kills you, doesn't it?" She lifted her chin. "That you want to fuck your daughter's best friend? A teenager, half your age."

My grip tightened to bruising, my veins popping in my arms and hands. She was trying to strip me down, defeat me with words, and it was working.

Halley's gaze dropped to my mouth as she whispered, "Tell me your plans for us that night."

My jaw locked, muscles turning to stone. I took over securing her wrists with one hand and used my other to grip her by the hair, tilting her head back.

She squeaked in surprise, gazing up at me.

Waiting.

Her eyes glinted with indignation and desire as she breathed a slow death against my lips.

My head lowered until our mouths almost touched. "I told you to never ask me that."

"I don't care. Tell me."

"No."

Halley struggled to break free, her fight funneling back as her rosy-pink cheeks puffed with a frustration-filled breath. I didn't slacken my hold, and she eventually deflated, collapsing back to the mat as I loomed over her. "Tell me what you wanted to do to me that night," she said, the anger dissipating, replaced with deadly curiosity. "I need to hear it."

I felt myself tearing through yellow tape.

My feet scuffing chalk lines.

And I embraced my own undoing as ruination filtered through my bloodstream.

"I would have taken you back to my apartment," I said darkly, teeth gritted, my fist still tangled in her hair. "And we wouldn't have made it to the bedroom before I knew what your pussy tasted like."

We both froze.

Her eyes widened to saucers, lips parting on a sharp exhale.

I couldn't believe I fucking said that.

A wave of panic surged through me with the knowing that I'd just crossed a line I could never uncross. My grip on her wrists loosened, defenses buckled.

Nineteen.

Tara's best friend.

Half my age.

My ex's makeshift foster kid.

A. Fucking. Teenager.

Swallowing hard, I stared down at her, spinning words inside my mind that could somehow untangle me from this fucked-up web.

But the shock in Halley's eyes quickly evolved into something else. Something emboldened.

Something like...*permission.*

She wiggled beneath me, arching her back and sliding her hand south as I inched up from her chest. Her hand disappeared in the space between us, and I glanced down, watching as she slipped her fingers under the hem of her shirt and into the waistband of her underwear.

Oxygen strangled me. My heart rate rocketed to a deathlike pace. I held my breath so long, I swear I saw stars.

And then she pulled her hand out of her underwear, her gaze locked and loaded on mine.

Two berry-tipped fingers came back glistening.

Soaked with arousal.

I watched, shellshocked, as she reached out and pressed her fingertips to my parted lips and I almost fucking died. My cock throbbed painfully, still nestled in the heat between her legs, aching to be released from its confinements and to thrust inside of her.

I shuttered out a breath and widened my lips, my eyelids fluttering closed.

Weakness swallowed me whole, infecting my resolve, and I didn't stand a chance.

My tongue grazed the pads of her fingertips in a slow, savoring slide, and I lapped up every ounce of her arousal, imprinting her essence onto my marrow. A low groan pinwheeled through me as her sweetness bathed my tongue, and I sucked her fingers into my mouth, rolling my hips while she let out a squeaky, mewling sound that edged us both toward annihilation.

A single taste had me tangled in tripwires.

I was fully, devastatingly aware that one misstep, one more move in the wrong direction, would have both of our worlds detonating.

Slowly, Halley slid her fingers from my mouth, dusting them along my bottom lip as she lowered her hand. With a half-lidded stare, skin flushed red, and dynamite in her eyes, she murmured huskily, "Now you know."

Now I know.

Yeah, I knew. I knew just how close I was to burying my cock inside her while simultaneously burying us both alive. Her taste was unadulterated ecstasy, honey in my veins, but something else mattered more.

Tara.

My daughter...and Halley's future.

Reality clobbered me like a frying pan to the back of the head. My brows twisted, my arms corded with full-blooded restraint, and I shot up and off of her like lightning.

I didn't look back.

Didn't spare her a single glance to see how badly I'd just burned her.

My vision clouded with red as I charged into my bedroom, slammed the door shut, then locked it behind me. I shoved my pants down my hips, dropping them to my ankles. My dick was in my hand before I could take my next breath, and I was jerking myself off like a fucking animal.

Less than twenty seconds later, jets of warm cum spurted onto my hand, my abdomen, my thighs, as a soul-shattering orgasm tore through me like the explosion I'd just narrowly dodged. I groaned, shuddered, swayed, vibrating through wave after wave of release with the taste of her pussy still coating my tongue.

Now I know.

Now I knew what it felt like to really play with fire.

And I was damn certain, that any day now, I'd go up in flames.

CHAPTER 19

Halley

I HADN'T SEEN Reed in two months.

Snow had given way to green grass and vibrant wildflowers, while I'd focused on schoolwork, photography, and everything but him. I was three weeks away from graduating, and my GPA was hovering just below a four-point-oh. Not only was I finally going to walk the stage with my best friend and accept our well-earned diplomas together, but I was also graduating *with honors*.

The thought made me giddy.

Proud.

Elated.

But everything good in my life was sullied by that sparring session that had taken place in Reed's apartment seven weeks ago when I'd pushed him over the edge and taken things too far.

I was humiliated. Sorry. Beyond regretful.

In turn, Reed had put a stop to our training sessions, having told Scotty to pass the news along to me. Reed couldn't even tell me to my face. He didn't want to see me, and I didn't blame him.

Wanting to avoid questions and probing, I had told Tara that I'd accomplished everything I wanted to accomplish with the training, therefore, there was no need to continue. Reed had other clients to train. He couldn't waste anymore time on a burden like me.

"You've been nothing but a burden since I'd laid eyes on you."

His words often funneled through me like an angry windstorm. A blizzard.

Part of me understood what he'd been doing—trying to get under my skin, rile me up, keep my fire burning through a blaze of anger.

But part of me wondered if he truly felt that way.

And that was heartbreaking.

As wispy sheets of white clouds coasted across the sky, I squinted my eyes against the sunlight leaking through, catching sight of a familiar swinging ponytail and blue scrunchie. Tara was meeting me outside of a downtown Italian café to savor the warm spring weather and to chat about our weekend plans.

After parking her car along the side street and hopping out, she greeted me with an animated wave. "Hals!"

I grinned, seated at a metal outdoor table with my camera nearby. "You're early."

"I know, right? Who am I?"

"How was volleyball practice?" I watched as she plopped down in the chair across from me.

"Fine. I'm nervous for the game tomorrow night. I'm also nervous about cosmetology school. Ack, being on the edge of eighteen is stressful."

I sent her a smile. "You're going to do amazing. Nobody does my nails and makeup like you do."

It was true. When Tara had told me she wanted to go to cosmetology school, I thought it was a brilliant idea. We both had a creative side. Art was meaning, and it could be channeled through endless avenues. Music, dancing, photography, writing. Tara and I were different in so many ways, but our hearts bled color and expression.

My friend grinned, fiddling with the ends of her hair. "Anyway, I was hoping you could help distract me."

"Willing and able."

"I want to blow off some steam at the roller rink with the fam," she said. "You should bring Scotty."

I blinked at her.

Scotty and I had gone on a few platonic dates, and I considered him a good friend. There was potential for more, but my heart was still fully invested in another man, which was, decidedly, bordering on tragic at this point. I liked Scotty; he was funny, laidback, and patient. But he knew I wasn't all-the-way available right now, so he'd been voluntarily wading in the friend zone while we spent more and more time together.

Granted, he didn't know *why* I was emotionally unavailable, but Scotty was also smart. He had a pretty good idea of who had commandeered my unrequited devotion.

Swallowing, I reached for the cola I'd ordered and took a sip from the straw. "The family, as in...your mom is coming?"

"Yup." She popped the *P*. "Dad, too."

I choked on the swallow but covered it well enough, feigning a tickle in my throat. "Oh. Isn't that awkward? Since they aren't together, I mean."

"No, it's never been awkward. Besides, I'm still getting vibes that they might reconcile."

Something told me her vibes were wrong. "Interesting."

"Yeah, it could be." She drummed her fingers on the table. "I don't know, it's kind of exciting to think about. Love winning out in the end, after all these years. I feel like it's something we all yearn for. An epic love story that defies struggle, separation, and endless hurdles." A whimsical smile shimmered in the sunlight. "And Mom and Dad don't really date, so it makes me wonder if they're waiting for each other. Not to mention, something is definitely up with my dad. He's been acting sneaky, like he's hiding something."

I pushed the second soda toward Tara as I nibbled on my straw and stumbled on words. "I don't know. He hasn't been at the house much lately."

Reed had been notably absent from the Stephens' household, giving off flags that I worried bordered on neon-red. But I'd eavesdropped on a few phone calls and gathered that his reasons had alluded to added work shifts, new clientele, and dozens of other excuses that excluded me.

Tara had been going over to his apartment instead, and that was for the best.

For all of us.

So far, nobody had questioned it, nor my role in his sudden vanishing act.

Pondering this, Tara shrugged. "Maybe Mom and Dad got into a fight. He'll come around."

Twirling my straw in a thousand different directions, I nodded slowly, my eyes cast downward. "Well, skating sounds fun. Count me in."

"How's it going with Scotty, anyway?" She smirked. "Don't think I didn't catch on to the real reasoning behind all those intimate training seshes."

Mortification scorched my face, and I fanned myself with one of the plastic menus. "It's going good. He's pretty cool."

"He's cute. And he's a little older, but not *too* old," she added, slurping down her drink. "Are you bringing him to Prom?"

"No. I'll just go stag and be your tagalong. Scotty will be in Denver that weekend for his older brother's college graduation."

"Bummer."

Eric had asked me to Prom, and part of me wanted to say yes for the sole purpose of rewiring my brain into thinking boys my age were appealing. But I didn't want to lead another guy on, so I'd turned him down. It was better to go alone.

"Does Scotty have a car? Can he meet us at the rink?" Tara leaned back in her chair and propped her sandals up on my lap.

"Yep. I'll give him a call when we get back and see if he'll be around."

"Awesome. I think this is just what we need—quality time together that doesn't revolve around end-of-school stress and college plans," she said. "Mom and Dad have been working too hard. I want to enjoy time with them before I move out and start my own life."

I wanted that, too

Too bad Reed didn't agree.

"That's where you belong. Far away from me."

His words were acid in my lungs, tainting every breath with venom.

"You're lucky." I swallowed, glancing down at Tara's painted toenails wiggling atop my knees. "You have two parents who love you."

Tara fiddled with the hem of her tank top, her smile watery. "So do you, Hals. Mom and Dad love you like their own."

Tara had no idea how much that hurt.

There was beauty in some of that hurt, knowing Whitney likely did see me as a makeshift daughter. And I was thankful for that. So damn thankful for her kind heart and giving spirit.

But there was darkness in the hurt, too.

The kind that eviscerated me from the inside out.

I blinked away the agony and forced a small smile, just as the stripes of clouds rolled across the sun, casting a dappled dance of light across the afternoon sky. Shaking the shadows away, I said, "I hope everything works out, Tara." Then I sucked down the rest of my cola, letting it cool the embers of my heart. "I really do."

I wobbled on my roller skates, my arms extended at both sides, prepared to catch my inevitable fall. Scotty was a pro, gliding beside me backward, a goofy grin on his face. I glared at him and his graceful form. "I suck at this."

"Have you ever been on roller skates before?"

"No. Is it that obvious?"

Still smiling, he snatched me by both hands to steady me as we rolled by a few skaters and I tried to keep my legs from doing the splits. "You'll get the hang of it. Hold on to me."

The lights splashed Technicolor patterns across the maple flooring. *MMMBop* poured from the speakers, triggering my own smile to bloom once I'd gotten a better handle on my balance. I glanced around the rink for Tara, spotting her doing some questionable dance moves with Josh as he circled around her, fist-pumping the air. My mood had lightened, thanks to the upbeat music, colorful swirl of lights, and my friends having the time of their lives. Even Whitney had put on skates and was slowly inching her way around the rim of the rink, hanging on to the edge for support.

Twenty minutes whirled by in a blink, and I was lost to the giddy feeling sweeping through my chest. With one hand locked with Scotty's, I peered up at him. "This is actually pretty fun."

"Of course it is. It's one-thousand percent fun. If fun had a *specific* definition, it would be this."

"Actually, it would be the satisfaction of peeling off the plastic on a new electronic device."

Staring at me through the strobes, he parted his lips to counterreply but then faltered. "I have no argument for that."

I giggled and gave his hand a squeeze as we zipped past Tara and Josh. Tara raised her hands in the air, rolling forward with ease as Josh gave us a whistle. I turned to Scotty, still feeling unbalanced and afraid to let go. "It's amazing how I can take down a grown man during self-defense training, yet I'm struggling to remain upright on these skates."

"Everything comes with practice," he said. "It took you months to gain the upper hand with Coach."

My stomach fluttered in response as my brain dredged up and sifted through the double meaning. "I guess."

"I miss you during sessions, by the way. I feel like Coach dropped you prematurely."

"He taught me everything I need to know."

"Hardly." He frowned at that, brows etched with dubiety. "When it comes to keeping yourself alive, the lessons are infinite."

I swallowed. "Self-preservation can be found in a lot of ways. It isn't always black and white."

A beat of silence rolled by as Scotty chewed on my reply and swallowed it down in fragments. "Yeah," he murmured, loosening his grip on my hand. "Suppose you're right."

As we circled the rink and neared the exit passage, I caught a familiar flash of disheveled dark hair and broad shoulders. But we'd skated by too fast, so I had to twist around to get another look. Sure enough, Reed stood near the opening, his hands stuffed into slate-gray denim pockets, and two stony eyes locked on me. We did another lap, then another, and every time we rolled by him, the look on his face softened, his gaze shimmering with something akin to misery.

Making a final round, I released Scotty's hand and attempted to make my way toward the exit. "I'm going to grab some water."

And then I was on my ass.

Both feet flew up in front of me like my skates were attached to an invisible string held by a puppet master cackling evilly from above, and I landed hard. Pain shot up my tailbone, only overpowered by the hurricane of embarrassment that rippled through me in waves.

Dammit.

When I lifted my chin, Reed was standing over me. I could see Scotty skating toward me in my periphery, but my focus was on Reed and the hand he was extending to help me up.

He reached.

We clasped.

I melted.

Long, warm fingers wrapped around my palm as he hauled me up before Scotty could come to my rescue. My feet skidded in every direction, forgetting their primary purpose of how to be feet, and I latched on to Reed's biceps to keep me steady. Both of his arms wrapped around me until I found sweet relief in balance, while my fingers curled into his hard muscle.

His hold loosened with every passing second. "You okay?" he asked softly.

I nodded. "Yep. Aside from the bruises on my butt and ego...though, I'm not sure which one hurts worse." My awkward chuckle eased through the tension between us as Reed guided me toward the exit and I grabbed onto the half-wall for stability.

Scotty was by my side in an instant. "Whoa, you good?"

"Fabulous." I rubbed my backside and made a precarious trek over to a nearby bench. Scotty carried my shoes over to me while I took a breath and watched from the corner of my eye as Tara came bounding over to her father with a full-fledged grin.

Reed was right beside me, facing the rink and smelling like cedar and sin, as Tara flung herself into his arms and he teetered back as he caught her.

"Hey, Squirt," he said through an *oof* and a chuckle.

"Have you seen Mom yet?"

"She's headed this way."

I glanced over my shoulder to take in the scene. Whitney was still holding on to the edge of the rink as she slowly made her way toward the exit where Reed and Tara stood. "Reed," she acknowledged, sounding winded. "I didn't know you were coming."

"Tara invited me."

"Huh." She nodded, a partial smile in place. "Good to see you. It's been a while since you've been by the house."

My cheeks flared with heat as I pretended to be fully absorbed in roller skate laces.

"Yeah, I've been busy." He cleared his throat, tousling his hair.

Scotty sat beside me, offering a warm smile as he nudged me with his shoulder. "You sure you're okay?" he asked quietly.

I glanced at him, and I could tell that he knew.

He knew that I wasn't okay, but it wasn't from the physical fall. It was from a different kind of fall, the kind that was going to drain me dry. This feeling was the world's longest blood draw. A needle sucking out my life force, after a nurse spent an agonizing amount of time poking and prodding, looking for a usable vein. I was bruised, sore, and weaker than ever, and I didn't even get a consolation prize in the form of a cute Band-Aid to patch me up.

But I nodded anyway, erasing the pain from my eyes. "I actually think I'm going to go back out on the rink. I refuse to let that spectacle be my grand finale."

"Well, you're nothing if not dedicated." He breathed out a laugh. "I'm gonna grab a snack. Want anything?"

"No thanks." All I wanted was the unavailable man standing near my left shoulder, who was slipping into his own pair of skates as Tara beckoned him out onto the rink.

I rolled past him, trying not to make physical contact.

Trying to remain invisible as I wobbled forward.

Tara grabbed me by the wrist, her enthusiasm nearly causing me to nosedive. "C'mon," she said, pulling me out. Then she hollered over to Reed. "Let's go, Dad! You can race Mom."

I didn't look behind me to see if they were venturing out together, holding hands, making plans to re-fall back in love and pulverize my battered heart.

My sour mood eventually evaporated into giggles with my best friend as we made the rounds and I managed to garner a semblance of finesse on the skates. It wasn't so hard. Nothing felt *too* hard after I'd already conquered the worst out of life—even letting go of him.

We raced, laughed, bopped to the music filtering out through the speakers. The lights morphed from magenta to violet, and we spent the next ten minutes savoring the adrenaline high.

Before I knew what was happening, Tara reached for Reed's hand as he came up on my left, then reached for mine, and twisted around so she was skating backward, tugging us both forward.

I nearly choked when my shoulder brushed with Reed's. He glanced down at me, the hint of a smile peeking through whatever animosity he'd been holding on to.

"Hey," he said.

I looked away, meeting Tara's eyes. "Hi."

In my friend's mind, she was gliding along with two of her favorite people. Her father and her best friend—a friend who she thought of as her father's second daughter. It was excruciating. There was a boulder in the pit of my stomach, filled with graphite and lead.

I could hardly breathe.

She let go of our hands, glancing over to where her mother was standing off near the concession counter, munching on popcorn. "Ugh. Mom is being anti-social." She grimaced. "Be right back."

Scotty was seated at a table with Josh and a group of guys from school, leaving Reed and I skating together alone.

Alone, save for the elephant on the rink in the shape of me sticking my arousal-soaked fingers in his mouth seven weeks ago.

The memory had me close to buckling, but I kept my balance, refusing to grab onto him for support.

Awkwardness crackled between us as I cleared my throat, desperate to fill the awful void. "So, um...how's training going? Any new clients?"

He stared down at his skates sliding left to right, right to left. "A few, yeah."

"That's cool."

This was the worst.

I needed air, a reprieve, an entirely new body to shapeshift into.

"Graduation is around the corner. Bet you're excited."

I nodded. "Yep."

More silence. More elephants stampeding toward us.

My resolve was threadlike, my sanity in shambles.

"Listen, Halley..." His chin dipped down. "I haven't meant to—"

"It's fine. I understand."

He glanced at me, his neck corded, veins dilated. "This is complicated."

"You don't need to spell it out for me, Reed. I totally get it."

"This can't...become anything. I hope you know that."

My fingers curled into fists at my sides, humiliation heating my neck and staining my ears red. He thought I was an idiot. I was telling him that I understood, but he was determined to pound the undeniable truth into me with a sledgehammer until I was a still-pulsing pile of unworthy bits splattered at his feet. I set my jaw, staring straight ahead, and dodging an incoming skater. "Thanks for clearing that up. I really had no idea."

"Halley."

I loathed the admonishment in his tone, but I brushed it aside and held my head high. "Look...I do owe you an apology for that night." I swallowed the rock in my throat that had caught on fire. "That was completely unacceptable behavior on my part. I'm embarrassed and ashamed. And you were right to stop our sessions. They weren't headed anywhere good."

He was quiet for a while as we skated past the common area, and my eyes briefly locked with Whitney's. I sent her a tiny smile, pretending like I was just killing time, waiting for Tara to return.

Reed ran a hand over his jaw and nodded slowly. "I thought we needed distance."

"We did." I swallowed again. "We do."

"I didn't mean to hurt you."

Frowning, I looked up at him as irritation flickered through me. "You didn't hurt me. I'm not a soft little ragdoll you need to be gentle with. I'm an adult, and I've been through far worse than this. I'll be fine."

"This is different. I never wanted to—"

"You don't need to explain."

"Halley." My name flew past his lips like a burial hymn. Two heartrending syllables hellbent on burying us both. "This is killing me."

I opened my mouth to speak but only found myself choking on the ashes of his words. Soot in my throat, cinders in my lungs. There was something raw in his declaration, a candid hitch.

Pain.

We both felt it, we both wanted to carve it out of us.

The backs of our knuckles grazed as we made another turn, and everything around me blurred. We were the paused frame in a film, a frozen moment. The slightest touch of our hands felt like color in a monochrome world. Rain on dry desert sand; sunshine melting the igloo around my heart.

When I looked up at him looking down at me, I prayed that no one saw the currents swimming between us, despite it feeling like a tangible thing.

I pulled my hand away and scratched at my knuckles, cradling my palm to my chest.

I didn't speak, didn't respond in any way—other than to flee.

Skating ahead of him, I moved as fast as I could, concentrating on my footing, trying not to slip. He didn't call after me, didn't give chase. He couldn't. It wasn't allowed, especially not here, with Tara, Whitney, and Scotty in plain view.

My chest heaved, fighting for air, as I collapsed forward against the short wall near the exit. I rolled out onto the carpeting and fell to the bench, tearing at my laces, kicking the skates off my feet as I replaced them with shoes. The moment my feet were flat on the ground, I took off, pushing through the crowd and out the main entrance doors, eager for clean air.

I ran and I ran and I ran.

I ran straight into my father.

CHAPTER 20

OXYGEN LEFT me in a silent whoosh as I crashed into a hard body.

Our stares locked.

Two dark eyes flared, looking blacker than midnight, when recognition slowly filled his shellshocked gaze.

The universe shrank to a pinpoint as I froze in place.

I was breathless, wordless.

There was a young brunette wrapped up in his meaty arm, a woman who was not my mother. They had been wandering out of the bar—situated in the strip plaza next door to the roller rink—my father puffing on a cigarette, the woman snapping a mouthful of pink bubblegum.

I glanced at her, drinking in her slow-blink of confusion, before backing away from the scene. Maybe he didn't recognize me at all. Maybe he *couldn't* recognize me because he had never truly seen me in the first place.

My soul rolled over broken glass as memories rained down on me. The scent of his whiskey breath, the snarling pitch of his voice, the crack of his leather belt against my skin.

"You've never been good at doing hard things."

"You're a disgusting disgrace, just like your mother."

"You're a whore. A waste of goddamn space."

"You'll never amount to anything, little lamb. You're a nobody."

Dozens of jagged scars on my back pulsed in remembrance, while heat needled down my arms and legs.

I shook my head, quickly, briefly.

And then I spun around and dashed away.

I heard their voices echoing behind me as I retreated back toward the rink.

"Who was that, Frank?" the woman asked.

"Dunno. Never seen her before."

This is impossible.

He was in jail.

My father was supposed to be in jail for *five years*.

My eyes were on the ground, my mind a million miles away.

I didn't understand. Nothing made sense. I—

A hand curled around my elbow.

I shrieked with pure terror.

"Jesus, Halley."

Reed's voice punctured through my paralyzed daze, and I blinked up at him, my chest billowing in and out, legs trembling. "S-sorry...I..." I didn't know what to say. My bottom lip quivered pathetically, and my eyes blurred through a screen of tears.

He stared at me, worry creasing his brows as he tried to get a read on me. Tried to make sense of my current state as I stood before him on the cement footpath, tremoring like a weak little girl.

I wanted to throw myself into his arms and let him carry me away from here.

I wanted him to save me.

God...all that training down the drain.

What a waste.

Because at the end of the day, when faced with real fear, I was going to succumb. I was going to drown in it.

Reed gave my arm a squeeze, his eyes skimming over my white-as-chalk face. "Tell me what happened."

He knew this wasn't about him; it was something else.

But I was too much of a chickenshit to tell him the truth, so all I did was shake my head.

Frown deepening, Reed swallowed hard and released my arm. Then his eyes trailed up and over my head, flitting from the parking lot to the adjacent building, until settling on something directly behind me. His jaw turned to stone, his eyes like crushed emeralds. "Who is that?"

"Nobody," I said, frazzled. "I need to go. I left my purse inside—"

"Is that your father?"

How?

How did he know that?

My father only somewhat resembled me, donning the same golden-blond hair chopped into a jagged mullet, a smaller-sized nose, and full lips that sneered instead of smiled. But his eyes were not the same, being ten shades darker than my own, and his hands were huge and punishing, with a burly frame to match. He was terrifying, and I was terrified.

Reed glanced at me, his gaze meeting with mine for a tension-filled beat, as if he were making a decision. Analyzing the data. All in the span of a single breath.

And then he was storming past me.

Oh, my God.

My eyes rounded with horror as I whipped around. "Reed!" I shouted, disbelief sinking into my gut and weighing me down.

I sprinted after him, but his strides were long and his intentions were unflappable.

He'd crossed the sidewalk before I could reach him, and I watched as his arm reeled back, his fist meeting my father's jaw as I cupped a hand over my mouth and screamed.

All hell broke loose.

Smokers scattered.

Blood sprayed, misting Father's sweat-stained white tank.

The woman beside him jumped back with a screech.

People gawked from the parking lot, some fleeing into buildings and calling for help, while I watched my father get a single clumsy hit in before Reed overpowered him.

There'd been a time in my life when I'd thought that my father was the strongest person in the world.

Indestructible. Unbeatable.

But Reed was smarter, swifter, and he knew exactly how to take down a monster. He unleashed a barrage of powerful strikes on my popeyed father, each blow landing with careful precision. Father staggered backward, stunned by the unprovoked assault.

Every move was calculated as Reed seized my father's arm and twisted it behind his back, forcing him to his knees with a guttural cry of pain. Father's face contorted in agony as Reed applied pressure, his grip unyielding.

Ignoring my father's pleas for mercy, Reed drove a knee into his back, pinning him to the ground with bone-crushing force and smashing his face to the pavement.

I couldn't believe what I was seeing.

We were in public. He was defending my honor in front of open-mouthed bystanders, but it wasn't an honor he was meant to defend.

No, no, no.

My lungs could hardly keep up with my panicked breaths as patrons barreled through the roller rink doors, newly privy to the fight that had broken out next door. To my horror, Tara, Whitney, and Scotty material-ized around me.

Tara gasped.

Scotty grabbed my hand.

Whitney charged forward, shouting for Reed to stop, stop, *stop*.

"What the hell is going on?" Tara demanded, hysteria bleeding into her words.

I dragged my fingers through my hair, tugging it all the way back as I shook my head. "My father."

In the next blink, Reed was being yanked to his feet by his arms by two other men as my father rolled onto his back, writhing on the ground, both hands covering his mangled face as one leg bent at the knee.

"You *motherfucker*," Father howled. "I'll have you arrested for this."

Everything was a blur.

Pure chaos.

I could hardly see, hear, speak. All of my senses died out, leaving me blank and rooted in place.

I couldn't say what unfolded next because I was in shock; all I'd remember was the look Reed sent me from across the footpath, his hair wild, eyes wilder, his knuckles cracked with blood. He stared at me for a potent heartbeat, saying more than he could ever convey with words.

I pressed a hand to my chest, curling my fingers into my ivory blouse and memorizing the galloping, unsteady beats of my heart—my own silent reply.

This man had just risked everything for me.

Everything.

And I wasn't even his.

Hours later, Tara and I crouched at the top of the staircase, peeking through the railing as we watched the argument unfold down below. It was like we were two curious children trying to sneak a peek at Santa Claus coming down the chimney. My fingers curled around the wrought-iron posts while Tara pressed her temple to my shoulder and we huddled together.

We listened, watched, our breaths tangled in our throats.

"I can't believe you did that," Whitney seethed through gritted teeth.

They both paced the living room, back and forth, forward and back. Reed's bandaged hands were linked behind his head, his split lip illuminated by the ceiling light.

"That piece of shit had it coming."

"Are you insane?"

"Probably."

"You're lucky you didn't get arrested. You could have been thrown in jail, Reed!" Sweeping a hand through her hair, she stilled, then crossed her arms beneath her breasts as rivers of mascara lined her cheeks. "And for what? Some macho pissing contest?"

"That's not what it was. I was protecting her," he said firmly. "I'd do the exact same fucking thing for Tara."

"*I* am protecting Halley." She slammed a flat palm to her chest. "*Me.* I'm protecting her in the legal, non-violent way. Giving her shelter, love, and safety." Her glare was sharp and cleaving. "That was not the way."

"You do it your way, I'll do it mine," he shot back.

"Are you hearing yourself?"

"Loud and clear."

Whitney let out a huff of disbelief, gaping at him with wide-eyed fury. "You pummeled a man nearly to death outside of a roller rink!"

"It was hardly a pummeling, but I appreciate the dramatic rendition."

"I can't believe you." She started pacing again, circling around him as Reed stood stock-still and dropped his arms at his sides. "Your training is rooted in *defense*, not criminal outbursts."

"I was defending Halley. That bastard wrecked her."

"He wasn't being a threat. Your actions were barbaric and unprovoked."

"His existence provoked me." Reed held his ground, eyes narrowing. "As long as he's alive, he'll be a threat. And if he ever comes within breathing distance of my girls, he's a dead man."

Whitney slowed to a stop, stiffening, her eyes lifting with a curious flash. "Your girls?"

My heart was ping-ponging between my ribs, my stomach in ropes.

The silver lining in this was that my father hadn't pressed charges.

With his criminal record—and having just been released from prison on good behavior, much to everyone's shock and disgust—it was in his best interest to let it go.

I was grateful for that.

But with whatever Reed said next, our worlds still had the potential to be rocked off their axis.

I held my breath, squeezing the railing until my knuckles bleached white.

He lowered his chin, breathing out through his nose. "Yeah."

That was all he said.

No clarification, no expansion, no context.

Whitney was a smart woman, and I was petrified she was going to see right through the red tape, then strangle us both with it.

What is he thinking?

I wanted to slap him.

I wanted to hug him tight and never let him go.

Fight draining, Whitney pointed at the front door with one hand and pinched the bridge of her nose with the other. "You should go," she said. "Go cool down. We can discuss this later."

"There's nothing more to discuss."

She glared at him. "I beg to differ."

My stomach rumbled with anxiety as Reed's muscles tightened and he opened his mouth to reply. But he didn't. No words were set free, and all he did was spin around and head to the front of the house.

Reed stormed out, the door slamming behind him and rattling the windows. Tara and I both flinched as Ladybug bounded up the staircase, shimmying herself into my lap, escaping the hostility crackling in the air one floor below us.

I watched as Whitney deflated in the middle of the living room, dropping her eyes to the floor with a shaky exhale.

"I told you," Tara whispered to me, stroking her hand up and down my spine.

I turned to look at her, my eyes puddled with tears, as Ladybug nosed my ribs for comfort. "What?"

She smiled through a sigh and pulled me close. "I told you he loved you like his own."

CHAPTER 21

Halley

TARA WAS MAKING out with Josh beside me on the couch in her baby-blue ballgown, while Josh's friend, Nolan, fidgeted to my left. He was quiet and smelled like suntan lotion and fish sticks, but I attempted conversation through the slippery sucking sounds on my opposite side. "Are you excited for the dance?" I asked him.

He swiped at his nose and nodded, leaving a large gap between us. "Sure."

That makes one of us.

Nodding a few times, I went back to staring at the wall and wishing for death.

I allowed the awkward silence to simmer for a few more beats before popping up and flattening down the smooth fabric of my black, formfitting dress. While Tara looked like a Disney princess with a glittering tiara in her hair, shimmery lotion on her skin, and a giant, fluffed skirt with sequins that could blind somebody, I was going for sleek and sophisticated.

My dress was the color of obsidian nightfall, with off-the-shoulder sleeves and a sweetheart neckline. Half of my hair was pulled up in a glitzy barrette, while the rest spilled over my bare shoulders in golden waves. I felt pretty. Womanly. My makeup was subtle, aside from the bright raspberry lipstick kissing my lips. Copperglow Berry; my favorite.

I'd been wearing it the night I met Reed, so I wasn't sure if it was blessed or cursed, but it complemented my lightly bronzed skin tone and added boldness to my otherwise understated look.

The front door opened.

I swiveled left.

And my heart bottomed out of me.

Reed spotted me instantly, a physical reaction stealing his feet as he locked up, stilled, and idled in the entryway with his eyes fixed on me. Tara was too wrapped up in kissing her boyfriend to notice him, so I latched on to the private moment and entwined myself in its grip.

His eyes were fire.

Lightning.

Embers and jade flames.

He rolled his gaze up and down the length of my body in a slow pull, and I watched his throat work and flex through a tight swallow.

I smiled softly. There was nothing else I could do.

"Picture time!" Whitney made her way into the living area with a disposable camera in hand, waving it around. "You girls look gorgeous. So unbelievably grown up."

My invisible tether with Reed snapped, its pulse flatlining. I twisted toward Tara's mom and fiddled with the pearly pendant on my necklace chain. "Thank you. I guess we do clean up nice once in a while."

Tara jumped up from the sofa, waving at her father. "I didn't even hear you come in."

I *did*.

Every atom in my body heard him and felt him.

Reed palmed the back of his neck, the creases around his eyes softening. Two dimples emerged as he studied his daughter. "Squirt...look at you."

She did a little hip-bob as the huge skirt of her dress swished side to side. "Mom took me and Hals to the salon to get our hair done. You like?" Tara flicked her fingers through her soft brown curls and waggled her eyebrows.

"You look incredible. Where's my gun?"

Tara groaned. "The only thing you're killing is my mood with those dumb Dad lines."

I giggled, turning my attention to my date as he sat like a stone on the couch. "Come on, let's get these pictures over with." While I had intended on going to the Prom alone, Tara wouldn't allow it, so she'd roped this poor sucker into being my date. He was painfully shy, but that would likely work in my favor. No pressure, no expectations. If I'd gone to the dance with Eric Solomon, I was confident I'd be channeling my self-defense training when he inevitably got too frisky with me.

Nolan inched off the couch, his face almost as red as his amber hair. "Okay."

Whitney ushered us all to the patio door. "Let's take pictures outside. The white ash tree in the backyard is blooming with those pretty flowers."

Tara and Josh strolled ahead, arm in arm, while Nolan shuffled behind them with his head down. I gathered a breath and began to walk forward.

But then two palms landed on my hips and I went deathly still. Heat broke out all across my skin, staining my chest and collarbone. I fought for air, but it was stuck in my throat like bubblegum.

Warm breath coasted along the nape of my neck as Reed leaned in and whispered, "You look...so goddamn beautiful."

My vision blurred. My legs shook under me as he gave my hips a gentle squeeze and then let go, moving around me and walking ahead to meet up with the rest of the group.

Nobody saw.

He was careful, and I only wished he'd be that careful with my heart.

We took photos by the white-blossomed tree. Tara and Josh. Me and Nolan. Tara and her parents, together and singular. Josh offered to take one of all four of us, and my pulse palpitated when Reed came up beside me while I squished my body against Tara's on my right. His arm wrapped around me, palm landing on Tara's shoulder, and his scent overpowered the spring blooms. Heady, woodsy, and clean. I swore I felt his heartbeats escalate as our bodies pressed together and his heat seeped under the fabric of my dress, sizzling my skin.

"All set!" Josh lowered the camera.

We parted. I swished a loose strand of hair out of my eyes and smoothed down my dress as the breeze tried and failed to push him out of my stratosphere.

Before we piled into the limo waiting outside, I grabbed my own camera to capture the night. Tara snatched her purse, her snow-white heels clicking against the floor as she sashayed to the entryway. Whitney said goodbye with tears in her eyes, and Reed stood off to the side, leaning against the staircase railing.

Our eyes caught briefly; his blazing, mine yearning.

I sent a smile to them both.

Reed called out to us before we filtered out the door. "Call me if you need a ride home."

He glanced at Tara first, but his gaze lingered on me.

"Don't wait by the phone or anything," Tara dismissed with an eye roll, smiling brightly before disappearing outside.

I swallowed. "We will."

He nodded once.

Whitney waved us off.

And I strolled out into the sunlight with my date.

If there was one thing I was looking forward to tonight, it was dancing.

It had been too long.

The closest I'd come to dancing lately were my training sessions with Reed, and I'd told him as much. After all, there was rhythm, balance, motion. Music played in the way our bodies moved and limbs tangled, while melodies infused our breaths and unsaid words.

Still, I wanted a dance floor. Disco lights. My favorite songs spilling from giant speakers while Tara and I laughed the night away and reveled in the carefree atmosphere.

So, when the limo stopped in front of a house miles away from the Prom, my intuition pitched. Anxiety churned as I took in the unfamiliar two-story home.

Glancing across the seats at Tara, I frowned. "Who else are we picking up?"

She sent me a mischief-laced grin. "Nobody. This is where we're going."

"What?"

"C'mon, Hals. Prom is boring. Eric is having a huge house party instead."

I blinked at her, my heart sinking. I didn't want to go to a house party. There would be nothing but drinking and sex, and I wanted nothing to do with that type of fun.

I'd had my fill of watching other people drink. I'd grown tired of promiscuous sex to numb my pain. This was the last thing I wanted to do.

"I don't want to go," I said. "Can you take me back?"

"Halley, this is going to be a blast."

"I don't want to. Please, Tara, take me back."

She nibbled on her shimmer-glossed lip, her eyes shining with confliction. "Halley...we don't need to stay long, okay? I promised some of my friends I'd be here. But we can leave early. I promise. I don't want you to be uncomfortable." She sent me a soft smile. "I really wanted to have a fun night with you. We've been so busy with school lately."

I could tell she meant it. She cared about my well-being more than this party, but I also knew she was excited to go. I didn't want to be the one to hold her back or spoil her night.

Inhaling a compliant breath, I nodded and gathered my purse and camera. "Okay. I'll stay for a little bit."

"Yes!" Tara leaped over two laps to ambush me with a big hug. "We're going to have the best time. Way better than a school dance."

I hugged her back and forced an agreeable smile as the four of us filed out of the limo. Nolan hadn't said a word the whole time, but his eyes were twinkling when he glanced at the brightly lit brick house. Sighing, I allowed Tara to link our arms together and lead us through the front door, while daylight melted from the sky, leaving splashes of tangerine and blush behind.

I wrinkled my nose when we stepped inside.

Noise.

Everywhere.

A beer keg, loud R&B music, girls in skin-tight dresses inhaling Jello shots. My skin crawled with sealed-up memories springing back to life.

I was reminded of years past when I'd escape to nearby house parties as a way of blending in and feeling normal. But normalcy was always elusive, a mirage on an endless horizon. Same as peace. Those two concepts were constantly being redefined.

This way of life *used* to be my peace; my refuge.

Now, the only vision that sprouted in my heart when I thought of peace was a man with pale-green eyes and dimples he gave away like wishes. It was his steadfast belief in me that blanketed me in the truest sense of sanctuary.

But that was a mirage, too.

I spent the next hour scoping out good lighting and taking pictures with my camera, while following Tara around like a shadow. She did her best to include me, to zap her enthusiasm into my lackluster bones, but I struggled to fake it.

Eventually, I slipped away from her and found a quiet place to relax in the basement den, where only a few stragglers were drinking beer and chatting about sports.

The quiet didn't last long.

Only a few minutes passed before Eric and one of his friends found me seated on a rust-hued loveseat as I did my best to remain invisible.

"Yo, Foster," Eric hollered over to me.

I was in no mood. While his enormous pimple had vanished, his off-putting existence in general had not. "Hey, Eric."

"You were supposed to be my date. Who's the redhead?"

"Nolan."

"Never seen that kid before."

"He's gone to school with us for years."

Eric sniffed, strolling closer with his hands stuffed inside the baggy pockets of his black slacks. "You got a thing for the wimpy wallflowers?"

"I don't have a thing for you, if that's what you're getting at."

"You've never even given me a chance."

"I'm not required to," I said with a sigh. Already feeling annoyed, I stood from the loveseat and forced a tight-lipped smile before moving around him.

He snatched me by the forearm.

I froze.

The hairs on the back of my neck jumped.

Eric gave me a quick tug toward him and leered. "Heard you were fast."

Heartbeats galloping, I twisted my head to glare at him. "I'm not easy, if that's what that means."

"Dom says different."

I tried to remember Dom, but those early high school years were an embarrassing, traumatic blur. Still glaring, I tipped my chin up as I wrenched my arm out of his grip. "Do I look easy to you?"

His clear-blue eyes raked over my body, holding heavily on my cleavage. He licked his lips. "Not really. But you look like you'd be hella worth the headache."

Disgusted, I shook my head and stepped forward.

He grabbed me again.

The bastard put his hand on me, curling his grimy fingers around my elbow, and I reacted. My instincts kicked in before I could think it through, and I spun around and aimed a swift and controlled strike to the side of his knee.

Eric buckled, dropping to the floor. "What the hell?"

I winced at my overreaction. "Sorry."

"You crazy bitch," he barked, his face breaking out with pink splotches.

His friend cackled with laughter beside us. "Shit, Solomon. You just got served by a chick in a Prom dress."

"Fuck you."

Swallowing down my embarrassment, I darted over to the couch to gather my belongings and then made a hasty retreat. I was still vibrating with adrenaline as I hauled myself up the basement stairs and went searching for a phone.

"Call me if you need a ride home."

I needed a ride.

I need him.

While my relationship with Reed was brimming with unresolved tension and a mess of complicated forces determined to keep us apart, it was primarily built upon something else: trust.

I trusted him.

More than anyone.

Every time I'd step onto his mats, I would give him another piece of that trust, until one day, he'd earned the entirety of my vulnerable, closed-off heart. Trust hung in the air like a delicate thread, connecting us in a way nothing else could. It was the unspoken promise that he would catch me when I stumbled, breathe courage into me when I doubted myself, and guide me through every dark back alley of my past until I slowly made my way to the other side.

And I knew that any time I called...he would come.

The main level was teeming with rowdy teenagers as I made my way down a long hall and slinked into one of the bedrooms. I spotted a phone sitting on a nightstand and bit back my nerves. With his phone number memorized, I dialed it in, tapping my foot as I sat on the edge of the bed.

It rang twice before he picked up. "Hello?"

I squeezed the bodice of my dress in a clammy hand and slammed my eyes shut. "It's me."

A beat. "Halley?"

"Can you pick me up?"

There was a long pause, and I imagined him scrubbing a hand over his face, playing the potential repercussions of my request over and over in his mind.

But he didn't sound annoyed or unsure. "Of course. Did something happen?"

"Nothing major," I said, still toying with my neckline. "I'm at a house party. Can you write down the address?"

"A house party?" He sounded pissed.

I gulped, thinking of a way I could explain everything to him without throwing Tara under the bus. "Um, yeah...we left the dance to hang out with some friends. It's not a big deal, but Tara's having fun, and I didn't want to drag her home early."

"Are you okay?"

I folded in my lips, hiding the smile he couldn't see. "I'm okay."

"Give me the address. I'll head out now."

Rambling off the address, I added, "Can you park at the end of the cul-de-sac? I don't want Tara to see your truck."

"Yeah," he said. "See you soon."

Fifteen minutes later, I watched his truck roll past the house, coming to a stop a few yards away. I slung my purse and camera straps over my shoulder and made the unsteady trek over to his vehicle in my too-high heels. The taillights glowed red as engine fumes wafted around me. My heartbeats kicked up speed when I rounded the side of the truck and yanked open the passenger door.

Reed was leaning back in his seat, an elbow resting on the console as he stared out the windshield. "You're sure Tara's all right? I don't need to worry?"

Ungracefully, I hopped inside, my legs twisted up in the contoured dress. Reaching over to shut the door, I settled into my seat and snapped my belt into place. "She's fine. She's not drinking or anything," I told him. "She was playing pool with Josh and some friends when I left."

His gaze dragged over to me, eyes panning up the length of my body and landing on my face. "Why did you call me?"

My jaw tightened as I pulled away from his stare. There were a thousand different reasons why I'd called him, but I only gave him one. "This guy Eric got handsy with me and I freaked out," I confessed, my cheeks flaming. "My training instincts fired, and I sort of...kicked him."

I was too mortified to meet his eyes.

"Did he hurt you?"

"No," I said. "All he did was grab my arm. I overreacted."

"No, you didn't. Nobody has the right to ever put their hands on you without your permission. Got it?"

When I finally glanced at him, he was staring at me with conviction, with earnestness. I rubbed my lips together and nodded. "Got it."

Our gazes held for another beat before Reed put the truck in Drive and circled around the cul-de-sac before pulling out of the subdivision. I stared out the window at the coal-black sky and shadowy moon. Trees and houses streaked by, and my chest ached as we sat in silence. I wasn't sure what to say, how to feel...how I was *allowed* to feel. There were so many things that needed to be said, but my tongue was tied in knots, and so was my heart.

A few minutes ticked by, and I frowned when Reed pulled the truck into a vacant parking lot that overlooked the lake. I didn't move, didn't speak. I just waited, silent and still, as he killed the engine and inhaled a deep breath. My pulse pounded in my throat when I slowly turned to look at him.

His head was tilted back against the headrest, his eyes closed.

"Why did we stop?" I wondered.

There was no response for a while, and I allowed the wordless beats between us to culminate into a crescendo. My breaths were a steady soundtrack, filling the space with anxious harmonies.

As we sat there, Reed lifted his hand from his lap and carried it over to mine. He took it inside his big, calloused palm, then intertwined our fingers together, squeezing gently, and I swore, I knew—*this* was the moment I fell in love with him.

My eyes watered as the feeling siphoned every last drop of hopelessness out of me.

It was a perfect, frozen-in-time blip.

The best one yet.

I stared at his profile as his eyes fluttered open, his chest heaving with emotion as his brows creased and his jaw tightened.

Reed finally turned his head to look at me as he brushed a thumb across my knuckles. "I needed a moment with you," he said, every word braided with torment. "Just for a minute."

My body trembled, caught between knowing I should remain in my seat but wanting to leap across the console into his arms. "You have me."

It was a wicked lie. He'd never truly have me. These little moments were all we were allowed.

I let him hold my hand as twilight faded into night and stars twinkled above us like tiny lanterns. The lake's surface sparkled in the distance, reminding me of the first time we'd met—when I'd been lost, and Reed had unknowingly saved me.

I blinked over at him as he gazed out at the water. The semblance of light seeping into the truck brightened the slow-fading bruise still painted on his jaw from my father. Swallowing, I parted my lips to speak. "That day...at the roller rink," I started. "How did you know that was my father?"

Reed inhaled a breath as he glanced at me. "I just knew."

My brows furrowed curiously.

"That look on your face, like you'd just seen a ghost," he continued. "I know you, Halley. And I knew there was only one thing in this world that could shake you up like that."

I grazed the pads of my fingertips over his knuckles. Evidence of the fight still lingered in a dappling of healing cuts. "You didn't have to do that."

"I know."

"You risked too much."

"You're worth it." Shifting in his seat, he inched forward, his grip on my hand tensing. "No one's ever stood up for you like that before, have they? No one's ever fought. And that's bullshit. You deserve to have someone in your corner, fighting like hell for you. For your honor, your worth. I want to be that person." He stared at me with an intensity that etched lines across his entire face. "I'll be that guy...even if that's all I'll ever be."

Something came over me.

A needy, clawing urge rippled through me with sharp teeth, like a dark possession.

I sucked in a breath and leaned over the console. Reed's own breath faltered as he let go of my hand and lifted it to my cheek. His words had been tameless, but his touch was gentle. A caress. A kiss in the form of the back of his fingers against my jaw.

My neck bowed. My lips drew apart as a moan-like sound danced up my throat and infected the air around us with everything wrong and everything right.

Reed's grip on me turned feral, his fingers splaying and curling around the side of my neck as he tugged me closer. I felt his lips graze my throat. Whatever entity had taken me over wanted Reed and only Reed and didn't care about the consequences.

His thumb extended, pressing along my bottom lip and unhooking my jaw. "You have so much power." His words breathed fire on my skin. "I wanted to give you all of it. I wanted to watch it take you over, consume you."

"Reed." My head was tilted back, my hands raising to fist the lapels of his leather jacket as I brought him closer.

"But, goddammit, I gave you too much." He opened his mouth wider, a hot, wet trail coursing up the length of my throat until his lips were a millimeter away from mine. "I gave you power over me."

Then he closed the gap.

A light kiss.

Whisper-soft.

He was giving me a taste, but I wanted a feast.

Whimpering, I stole more, parting my lips and tracing his with the tip of my tongue. Reed panted softly, a shiver rippling through him as he fought against the draw.

"Please." I peppered more kisses to his bottom lip, my hands curling around his neck.

"God, Halley. We can't." He wasn't moving away; he was only strengthening his grip on me, like his words weren't formidable enough to keep him away.

I felt his weakness, the shake in his resolve. The cracks split wider and wider, allowing me to slip inside. Arching back, I lowered his face to the swell of my breasts. I lured him with temptation. Begged for him to crumble and submit.

Reed trembled, inhaling deeply, grazing his nose along the heaving swells as his head swung side to side like he *hated* himself for this.

Lashes fluttering, he released a groan of surrender. Shot back up my body. Snatched me by the back of the head and hauled me forward.

He kissed me. Viciously.

Fire tore through me as I grabbed his face between my hands, pulling him closer, taking him deeper. Mouths wide open, he lashed his tongue against mine, one hand wrapped around my throat while his other arm circled around me and dragged me across the console.

It was foolish, wrong, senseless. Everything and more.

Moans poured out with pure relief and purer passion. Our tongues twisted, tasting, yearning for something deeper. He smelled of smoky oak and amber, tasted like mint. An elixir that had me sinking into him, gripping him desperately, dragging my nails down his face and neck.

Reed's hand coasted up my back and landed in my hair, his fingers curling into a fist as he yanked my head back and his mouth slid down the center of my throat, his tongue diving into the space between my breasts.

He groaned loudly, unrestrained, the leather of his coat cooling my scorching skin. "*Fuck*, Halley..."

I was vibrating in his arms, my underwear pooling with need. I raked my fingers through his hair and squeezed, my chest surging beneath his mouth. "More." My dress was suffocating me, my own skin strangling me.

"We *can't* have more." But his lips made their way back to mine. He kissed me again, harder, more punishing, like he was cursing the air we breathed and the world that turned while we stood still. He flicked his tongue against the roof of my mouth and caught my bottom lip between his teeth before pulling away. Grasping my cheeks, his fingers dug into me. Our foreheads pressed together as he gritted out, "This is all we'll ever have."

I shook my head, tears blooming. "Keep kissing me." My mouth reached for his, but he dodged me. "Reed, please."

"Halley, no. We can't take it any further."

"We can…"

"Not if I plan on surviving this."

My eyelids fluttered closed as his words trampled through me. He'd told me at the roller rink that this was killing him. He had feelings, and they went beyond physical desire. While I lived my life in little moments and intervals, savoring each one for what it was, Reed was looking ahead. He saw how our future played out. He knew exactly what was coming.

And it wasn't a happily ever after.

It wasn't a fairy tale glimmering with wedding bells and baby bumps.

It was pain.

It was me on one side of the waterline, and him on the other.

Tara would never forgive me. The betrayal would eat us both alive, and I had just started living. How could we ever have a future? If we were to get married, that would make me…

Tara's stepmother.

The notion had me inching away, my fingers slowly letting go of his hair. I nodded, understanding. Knowing he was right.

"I'm sorry." He fell back into his seat and scrubbed both hands up and down his face. "I shouldn't have done that."

I settled back on my own side and swiped away the tangling of hair that had come loose from my barrette, staring out at the water, my chin quivering. This was my fault. If I'd never lied to him about my age that night, this connection never would have seeped inside of us, hollowing out our vital parts. He would have just been Tara's father.

"I'm sorry, too," I said softly, crossing my arms and leaning back. "For everything."

We simmered in the thick tension, the silence that said so much.

And then the tears started falling.

Sliding down my cheeks and clouding my eyes.

"You're crying," he said, after a long beat had trudged by.

I nodded and squeaked out, "Yes."

"Because I kissed you? Or because I stopped?"

Swiping the salt off my cheekbones, I turned to look at him, his face bathed in moonglow and dashboard light. Then I swallowed, heaving in a broken breath. "Because...I didn't get to dance."

I almost laughed.

But I was too sad to laugh.

He frowned in confusion, studying me. "What do you mean?"

I shrugged, forcing a small smile. "Prom," I told him. "We didn't dance."

His eyes skimmed my face as he continued to read me, drinking in my silly tears. Then he nodded once, reached over my lap, and popped open the glove compartment. I tilted my knees to the side and watched as he sifted around for something before pulling out a cassette tape.

He slipped it into the tape deck, fiddling with some buttons, and turned the volume all the way up on the dial. "Come on," he said before opening his door and stepping outside.

I sat there frozen for a moment as music spilled from the speakers.

A slower, dreamy song.

I didn't recognize it...until I did.

It was a cover of *Save the Last Dance for Me*. I remembered sitting on Jay's bed, mentioning the song to him while we sorted through CDs.

"There's a really good cover of that song by Harry Nilsson," he'd said to me.

The tears dried up on my cheeks as the concrete in my chest melted into slush. A smile pulled on my lips, and I pushed open my door, sliding out as my heels connected with earth. I joined him on the side of the truck while the lake rippled and shimmered behind us—the perfect backdrop.

The song was loud, spilling out through Reed's open door.

He stood before me, draped in a moonlit hug. The breeze caught my hair, and it took flight all around me, in time with my heart. I moved toward him, slowly, carefully.

Reed extended his hand. "Dance with me."

Our palms locked, and he pulled me to his chest.

His hand planted gently at the small of my back as I curled my fingers around his bicep, and we swayed in a perfect, lovelorn rhythm.

My cheek to his chest.

His heartbeats vibrating through me.

Side to side, lazy circles, our touches tender and soft.

I was lost.

Chords and notes awakened every piece of me as he sang the chorus into my hair, his voice a low, gritty serenade.

I held him tighter, burrowed deeper. Intimacy warmed me, cradling me in its unfit arms. I wanted to dance tonight, but I never expected this. I never expected his body pressed to mine, our fingers and souls intertwined.

And I realized, with every painful inch of me, that I would never dance like this again.

Stars twinkled down on us with unanswered wishes, only offering a smattering of spotlight. Reed pressed his lips to my hairline, and I closed my eyes, savoring the few minutes we had left.

I knew that when I left his arms tonight, I would never get them back. These arms would never swoop me backward on an altar as we shared a forever kiss. They would never hold me in the middle of the night when I awoke from a nightmare. They would never cushion our newborn baby as he gazed down at a pink or blue swaddle with love in his eyes.

I wanted all of those things.

But I wanted them with the wrong man.

Reed rested his cheek on the top of my head as his hand stroked up and down my back, leaving warm shivers behind. "You like this song?" he murmured into my hair.

A tear slipped down my cheek as the final chords rang out. I nuzzled my face to his chest, wrapped my arms around him, and whispered back, "It's my favorite."

CHAPTER 22

Halley

I GAZED out the window as Reed drove me back to the Stephens' house, my hands tightly woven in my lap as the cassette tape played a handful of unfamiliar songs that did little to curb my love-born curse. Silence festered while streaks of streetlight and porch lamp sailed by in dizzy ribbons, blurring the lines inside of me that separated logical reasoning from emotional demand.

My head and my heart.

I wondered what it would be like to live in a world where the head always won out.

Smart, steady...*safe.*

I was both envious and averse to such a life.

Reed sighed, puncturing the bubble of heady quietude engulfing us as I twirled my thumbs and bobbed my knees, my skin and lips still tingling from his kisses. I braved a glance at him, unsurprised to find him with one hand cupping his jaw, his opposite wrist slung over the wheel. "You can drop me off around the corner." My voice was damn-near shrieky as it carved through the silence. "Whitney will have questions if she sees your truck. I'll tell her a friend dropped me off."

He nodded tightly. "All right."

I wanted to say more.

I wanted to purge and sing, but nothing good had ever come from our misfit dance. We were a song that howled with arrhythmic heart-beats and a never-ending bridge.

But I wanted us to be the chorus.

The good part.

The catchy part that stayed with you forever.

Slinking lower in the seat, I released my own sigh into the bleak void as we turned off onto a barren road and cut across town. Five more minutes, and I'd be home in bed, condemned to dream about everything left unsaid and undone. I hated finalities more than I hated loose ends. Loose ends could still be sewn into pretty things. Things my hands could hold. Things my heart could keep and love.

"Halley."

My eyes watered at the sound of my name hitting the air like false hope. "Reed."

He hesitated. "You okay?"

"I will be." I popped my shoulders with a halfhearted shrug. The other half of my heart was too broken to participate. "You don't have to worry about me."

"You know I do."

We glanced at each other through the shadows as headlights barreled toward us, illuminating his tortured expression. My lips parted to speak, to wipe that wretched look off his face, but my attention whirled back to the windshield when my periphery caught sight of those headlights swerving right toward us.

It was staggering how a moment could change so fast. In the blink of an eye.

A kiss.

A moonlit dance.

A scream.

"Reed!" His name was now nothing but daggers and dread as his head whipped forward and the truck shot right.

"*Shit.*" He jerked the wheel with one hand while the other lashed out, his arm a shield across my chest, and we started spinning.

I screamed again as he slammed on the brakes and the other car skidded past us, still swerving precariously in the opposite direction, narrowly missing us by a millimeter. The world outside distorted with chaos as the truck careened out of control, tires screeching against the unforgiving pavement. Reed's reflexes were a whirlwind of desperate maneuvers, his hand gripping the wheel as he tried to maintain control while still holding me back against the seat like I was the most valuable thing. With each spin, my heart hammered against my ribcage, and I latched on to his arm and the door handle. Terror gripped me. My eyes squeezed shut. All I could do was brace myself for the aftermath of flying over a ravine, or combusting into flames, or flipping over into a ditch.

Breathing my last breath.

But then, as abruptly as it had begun, the spinning ceased, leaving us suspended in a moment of eerie stillness. The acrid scent of burnt rubber hung heavy in the air, mingling with the metallic tang of fear. Adrenaline and shock coursed through me as I turned to Reed, his face etched with a mixture of relief and disbelief. We were shaken but alive. The truck idled in one piece, still upright on all four tires. No flames, no collision, no shattered glass.

We were facing the opposite way, and his arm was still extended across my heaving chest.

"Jesus Christ." His arm fell, dropping to my lap. He squeezed my thigh like he was making sure I was still with him, still whole. "Are you all right?"

My heart was a grenade, nearing imminent explosion. I grabbed his hand and held tight, trying to calm myself, as if the pressure of my fingernails digging into his skin could alleviate the pressure around my ribs. "I-I think so."

"Halley, I'm sorry. That asshole came into my lane and—"

I unbuckled my seatbelt and threw myself into his arms over the console. He didn't hesitate, wrapping me up in his embrace as I inhaled leather and soap, ridding myself of the scent of angry rubber and near-death. Gathering me close, Reed buried his face in the crook of my neck, breathing heavily as we both came down from the rush of panic.

"You're okay." He peppered kisses along my throat. "I got you. You're okay."

A car drove by at a snail's pace but kept going, not bothering to check on us. My heart still pounded, ricocheting off of his, while soft music played, doing what it could to ease my tremors.

When I inched back, his eyes were glowing with worry and torment.

I pressed a quivering hand to his cheek like a thank you; a thank you for keeping me safe and protected. "Are *you* okay?"

He nodded slowly, his throat working through a swallow. "If you are."

We couldn't stay diagonal in the middle of the street forever, so I pulled away and relatched my belt, a silent request for him to keep driving. Another frazzled moment passed before he sucked in a breath and turned us around, continuing forward. The truck was no longer sideways in the roadway, but everything inside of me was. Images of splintering glass and blood-soaked skin consumed me as the truck crawled down the gravelly road. Panic still lingered in my chest and pulsed in my veins, while my limbs shook with slow-dying shock.

We could have died.

I could have lost him—*really* lost him.

It was the only thing on my mind as we pulled into Reed's complex ten minutes later, the drive over filled with treacherous silence after he'd turned off the music. The trek inside his apartment was also silent, and I wasn't sure why he'd brought me here—*again*—instead of to Whitney's house, but I was undoubtedly grateful for it anyway. I didn't want to be alone. I couldn't bear the thought of not being close to him moments after nearly losing him to a metal-crunched bloodbath.

Shivering, I followed him into the apartment on autopilot, slipping out of my high heels and tossing my purse and camera to the entryway floor. I wobbled on jelly-like legs. My breathing escalated. Reed sliced a hand through his hair, then shook out of his leather coat and let it fall beside my items. He rubbed at his forehead like he was begging his mind to form words. I didn't know what to say either. In the wake almost dying, the only words that sounded marginally appropriate were a solemn acknowledgment of the fragile line between life and death that we had just bridged. A "thank you" to the universe for a second chance.

A *thank God you're still here.*

Our eyes met from a few feet away. I inhaled, exhaled, my breaths wheezy and fraught. Tears glistened and clouded my vision as I watched him step toward me, landing on the entry mat, a reach away. Did he feel it, too? This energy spooling around us, something bigger than us both. Heavier than our circumstances and our unfair fate.

I shook my head a little. For no reason, for every reason. Tears burned hotter, welling up like someone had stuffed a sock in a drain and turned the faucet on. The water had nowhere to go, other than to overflow.

Cupping a hand over my mouth, I kept shaking my head as the tears fell down. Everything came to a peak, until down was the only direction left.

Reed caught me as my knees failed me and I crumpled, landing in his arms. A soft-landing. The only landing that could keep my fraying pieces in place. I clutched the front of his muted-gray T-shirt in both fists, smashing my face to his chest and sobbing.

"Comet," he murmured, his breath as warm as that nickname as it danced across the top of my head. He gathered my limp curls in two hands and held me close while I unraveled, string by string. "Shh. We're okay."

"Are we?" I croaked out.

"Yes."

I needed the lie right now, so I allowed it to soothe me. My nose nuzzled against the fabric of his shirt, my breaths sporadic and shaky. He walked us backward until my spine was flush with the apartment door, and I fell back as my chin tipped up, my fingers still clasping soft cotton.

Extending a hand, Reed reached behind me to flick the lock, securing us inside.

My shoulder blades grazed against the cool wood, my eyes unwilling to leave his. He swallowed, his focus dipping to my mouth as he blinked twice, then lifted both hands to cup my cheeks in a tender grip. I loosened in his arms, becoming dead weight, while his hands clenched tighter. His eyes panned back up and tangled with mine, and we stared at each other, our bodies and gazes holding, alighting, brimming with electrical currents and indecision.

Neither of us wanted to let go. Neither of us wanted to end this before we had a taste of what it could become.

"You should get to bed." He glanced back down at my mouth. "Take the guest room."

"Okay." My pulse unsteadied as my hands journeyed up his chest and wrested his shoulders, and Reed's grip on my cheeks turned firm and bruising. A contradiction to our fruitless words. I tilted my head back, my lips parting with a tiny whimper when he curled one hand around my neck.

All of his staunch reasoning and well-intentioned plans became background noise. A distant, aimless hum. None of it compared to this feeling. This falling.

He leaned in closer, breathing meaningless words against my mouth. "I shouldn't have brought you here."

"I know."

I knew, and he knew, but neither of us cared.

All that mattered was that we *were* here. Alive and hot-blooded. *Together.*

"Why did you?" I arched my back against the door, craning my neck, cinching his shoulders so hard my nails would leave marks. Our pelvises brushed and I felt his erection straining against his jeans. Another mewl slipped past my lips as I ground against him and trailed my hands up his neck, pulling him closer. Our mouths touched, a graze, a gavel slamming down on our fate.

Either path we chose felt like death, but this death was sweeter.

I saw his resolve draining the longer we held.

Reed's jaw clenched tight, cheeks flickering with suppressed feelings. "I needed to be close to you. Watch you sleep, watch you breathing."

"Living," I exhaled.

"That's right."

"Life is living." My voice quaked as I echoed his words to me from that first night at the lake. "If you're not living exactly the way you want to live, then what's the point?"

Our foreheads melded together, his mouth a toe-lift away.

Boldness shot through me as I pulled all the way up and flicked my tongue against his bottom lip. "Tell me goodnight, Reed."

He stared at me, locking on a breath.

The world fell away.

Reason disintegrated.

Longing dominated the raging war. Temptation was a rallying cry, roaring in our ears.

He snapped.

Whatever line he'd drawn in the sand was flushed away by the tide as he pounced on me.

Before I could process anything, his hands were linking both of my thighs around his hips as he hauled me up the door and our mouths collided.

Yes.

A stunned cry caught in my throat as I grabbed his hair, sucked his tongue into my mouth, and jutted against his erection. A groan vibrated through me—his, mine—as he fisted my knotted curls in his hands, while my dress rode up my thighs and I crossed my ankles at his lower back.

Licking every inch of my mouth, he only pulled away to unzip the back of my dress, tearing it down my body until my breasts were exposed.

My moan echoed through the empty apartment when his mouth clamped around my breast and sucked hard, his teeth nicking my nipple before he dove over to the other. "Reed...oh, God..."

My fingernails clawed the nape of his neck as my body writhed against him, seeking friction. I nearly pulled his hair from the roots when he laved my nipple into a tight bud, groaning hotly as he devoured me. Wetness drenched my thighs, seeping through my lace underwear.

I needed him inside me.

Reed spun me away from the door before carrying me across the living room and dropping me on the blue mat laid out across the carpeting. I shimmied out of my dress and underwear as he whipped his belt from the loops, unzipped his jeans, and shoved the denim and boxers down his hips, kicking them free. He climbed over me, and the moment our mouths fused back together, a cocktail of wet tongues, nips and bites, I reached down between us and fisted his cock.

Huge, rock-hard, pulsing in my hand.

"*Fuck*," he cursed through a hoarse moan, his face falling away from my mouth and burrowing against my neck.

I stroked him up and down, the tip sliding against my pussy as he bucked into my palm, his muscle-corded arms caging me in as he kept himself propped up.

Then he shot down my body.

Wrenched my knees apart.

And plunged his tongue between my legs.

My lower body jerked up against his mouth and I let out a high-pitched mewl, while Reed linked his arms under my thighs to hold me steady.

The sounds he made as he ate me—animalistic, hungry, insatiable.

If he stretched me any wider, he'd snap me in two.

I gripped his hair, my pelvis heaving skyward as I begged and gasped and moaned, shuddering with every violent thrust of his tongue.

No one had ever done this to me before.

My insides immediately unfurled with a primal, clawing feeling that started in my womb and zapped hot, blinding starlight all the way down to my toes. I jolted off the mat with a sharp cry, digging the heels of my feet into his back as my vision blackened and the world slipped away.

He lapped, sucked, tongued me until I collapsed to a trembling heap beneath him.

But I didn't have a chance to recover before he drew up to his knees, grabbed me by the hair, and yanked me upright.

"Suck me," he rasped out, his chin and lips glistening with my orgasm.

His cock hovered in front of my face, thick and throbbing, lined with blue veins and leaking from the tip. Moving closer, I wrapped my hand around him and took him into my mouth as he palmed the back of my head and guided his hips forward.

Gagging when he went flush with the back of my throat, I inched back a fraction as he let out a prolonged groan.

I hollowed out my cheeks and sucked him.

"Christ...fuck, *yes*." His fingers braided through my hair, making a fist, as his other hand stroked the base of his cock.

He was too big to fit fully in my mouth, and my pussy pulsed, imagining how he'd feel deep inside me. How he'd fill me, own me, ruin me for anyone else.

My watery eyes lifted while I sucked, my hands holding on to his muscled thighs. I watched his head tip back, his lips parting with raw pleasure.

He glanced back down at me with a half-lidded gaze, combing my hair off my forehead, almost lovingly; tenderly. "I could come down your throat right now." Eyes glinting with heat, he shuddered and tensed.

Then he tugged me away from him and glided the tip of his thick cock against my lips. "But I need to be inside you."

Beads of salty precum bathed my tongue as I licked the head, circling around and around, tasting and savoring every drop.

A visceral sound bowled through him, and Reed tossed me onto my back again. I hit the mat, my breasts bouncing, my legs spreading apart as his body covered mine.

I knew he wouldn't be gentle.

I knew he'd take control, make it rough, *destroy* me—body and soul. And I welcomed every bruise, every bite mark, every scar he'd leave behind.

Slipping my fingers under the hem of his shirt, I frantically tugged it up over his head, removing the final barrier between us. We were skin to skin as he fell on top of me, stealing another harsh kiss as his cock teased the soaked juncture between my thighs. His teeth snagged my bottom lip and tugged, and I cried out, clawing my nails down his back.

As he pushed up, Reed cupped my knees with both hands and shoved them forward, until I was completely spread and exposed. His eyes dipped downward, skimming over my swollen pussy. Pink and glistening, eager to take him in.

Breathing raggedly, he gripped his cock, pumping a few times with his fist as he centered himself with my hole. One white-knuckled hand was still clamped around my knee as he pushed inside me, just an inch, an agonizing slow slide. Reed's mouth fell open as he watched us come together, watched me stretch and yield to his thickness. My fingertips dug into the mat on either side of me as I panted, on the brink of another orgasm before he even filled me to the hilt.

"Jesus, Halley..." Hissing out my name, he leaned farther over me, planting one hand on the mat as he pulled out, then slid back in halfway. "You're so fucking tight."

I nearly buckled, arching my back and palming my breast. My hips lifted off the floor, my body greedy and begging for him to go deeper. "More," I cried out. "Please, Reed."

He groaned, a gritty, virile sound. "Keep begging for my dick, and this won't last long."

"I need you..." I bucked my hips, taking him inside me farther, almost all the way, until he finally slammed home and collapsed over me. Both of his hands pressed to the mat on either side of me, my knees nearly hitting my chin, and he thrust hard.

I cried out, a threadbare whimper, and his eyes rolled up as his eyelids fluttered closed. He rutted into me again, harder, hitting places deep inside me as I wrapped my arms around his neck and held him closer. Face buried in the crook of my neck, Reed pistoned his hips forward, faster, each stroke more punishing than the last, his grunts and groans mingling with the sounds of skin slapping together, a slippery, raw, sweat-soaked fusion. "Yes, yes...God, *yes*," I chanted.

"You feel so fucking good." The words rumbled against my throat as he sucked the sensitive skin between his teeth, then trailed his tongue up to my earlobe. He nipped it before growling, "Soaked for me. Tight and perfect."

My legs coiled around his back, and my body met his rhythm, that tingly, soul-defying feeling blooming inside me for a second time.

"Come for me again." Raising his head, he tugged my hair back, our faces a centimeter apart. His lips hovered over mine, grazing, teasing, as his hips ground into me. "You're so beautiful. So goddamn gorgeous."

His words were soft, his thrusts rough and merciless as he fucked me.

We were beautiful.

A beautiful, forsaken mess.

"Please," I keened.

The barest smirk tilted his lips as he felt me vibrating beneath him, needy, desperate for that pinnacle. Reaching under me, he held me up by the ass and angled his cock higher and deeper, his movements picking up speed.

My eyes shot open as another orgasm slammed into me with lightning force, without warning, and his tongue plunged into my mouth, stifling my cry.

I held him, gripped him, cherished him as I blissfully unraveled, with galaxies in my eyes and stardust in my lungs.

"That's it," he breathed against my open mouth. "That's it, Halley."

Falling back onto me, Reed cupped a hand over the top of my head to anchor himself as he buried his face in my hair and his body took over.

He rutted into me hard, each thrust more graceless than the last as he teased the edge of release. "Ah...*fuck*." He tensed, shuddering violently through a hoarse moan as his neck arched back, spurts of hot cum pulsing through his cock and spilling inside me. Pleasure twisted his face and unlocked his jaw as he groaned through his climax.

All I could do was hold on to him as we came back down, my fingers sliding through his slick hair, my cheek pressed to his when he collapsed.

It was over.

I didn't want it to be over.

Everything had happened so fast. Ended even faster.

Drops of sweat rolled down his temples and neck as he deflated on top of me, still sheathed inside and twitching through the final shockwaves. Both of us were panting, our choppy breaths the only soundtrack to my whirlwind thoughts.

We had sex.

In his apartment.

On his training mat.

Emotion bubbled to the surface as we lay there in silence, entwined and wholly bare. The scent of sex, sweat, and synthetic rubber wafted around me, and a lone light flickered above us, a dull spotlight illuminating our crime.

I was sticky, satisfied...and sad.

Refusing to be the girl who blubbered after mind-blowing sex, I forced back a rush of tears and turned my head to the side, away from him.

But he reached for me, covered my cheek with his hand and forced our eyes to meet. A rough thumb grazed my cheekbone, his gaze shimmering with tenderness.

With apology.

"Reed." My eyes pooled with unwanted tears as I inhaled a ragged breath. "Tell me this changes things."

I had to know.

I had to know there was hope for us. This wasn't a spur-of-the-moment mistake, a weak blip, or a lapse in judgment. There was something here. Something powerful.

A life worth living.

And yet, I already knew what he was going to say.

I'm sorry.

We shouldn't have done this.

Nothing changes.

Reed closed his eyes, but his eyes didn't need to be open for me to see right through him. Despite the fact that he was still hard inside of me, still cupping my cheek and dusting his thumb across my skin, the truth resided in everything he didn't say.

My feet defeatedly trailed down his backside, his thighs, calves, until they plopped down to the mat and my whole body drained of fight, my hopes shrinking to fragile embers.

I fought back tears. I fought back anger.

I needed to go.

"Get up." I rasped out the words, my voice small. "Please."

His eyes fluttered back open. They glinted with promises he wanted to make but couldn't keep. Fairy tales he wanted to weave into happily ever afters.

Pain so raw it hurt to look at.

But he obeyed my wishes and pulled himself off me, while I covered my breasts with both arms, glancing around for my scattered clothing, my thighs damp from our combined release. I couldn't meet his eyes while he stepped into his boxers and plucked my dress and underwear off the floor, handing them to me.

Sitting up, I yanked the dress over my head, hauled the lace up my legs, and remained silent. Reed paced the living room with his hands in his hair, a blur in my periphery.

When I was dressed—my zipper unzipped and my dreams undone —I stalked over to my discarded heels, covered in nicks, scratches, and bite marks. My skin was pink and blotchy. An ache throbbed between my legs and ribs, a subtle reminder of what we'd been too stupid to resist and too weak to pursue any further. We hadn't even used protection, but I was too tongue-tied and sucker-punched by the turn of events to broach the subject.

I just need to go.

Frazzled, I snatched up my purse and camera, flattened my chaotic hair, and reached for the doorknob.

Reed called out to me, his voice cracking on my name. "Halley, wait."

If I opened my mouth, I would cry, and I refused to cry. I hadn't even cried after sex with those nameless, faceless men, after they'd pumped into me a few times and rolled over, leaving me pleasureless and used up. And that was because I'd been numb to it.

"I can't stay," I said.

"Where are you going?"

He hadn't expected me to leave. I had no car to drive, no sneakers to run in. Nothing but adrenaline and pain fueling my escape. "Home."

I unlocked the door and raced into the hallway, then out through the main doors, the humid night and half-moon guiding me the four miles back to Tara's house. Ripping off my heels, my bare feet pounded the pavement while hot tears burned my eyes, muddling my vision. I ran. I ran with pebbles in my soles and glass in my lungs. I still felt his body pressed to mine, felt him between my legs, felt his tongue on my flesh, engraving his essence into me. I'd never be able to scrub him off my skin.

I ran the whole way home until I buckled in the front yard and dropped to my knees, out of breath, out of hope, my fingers fisting the grass blades.

My insides howled and bled.

Tears burst from my eyes, carving devastation down my cheeks.

I sunk into the earth and begged for it to bury me.

One thing was certain—I wasn't numb anymore.

And oh, how I wished I was.

CHAPTER 23

Halley

TARA TURNED eighteen the day before our high school graduation.

Blue water sparkled before me as I stared out at the slow-rippling surface, the shoreline teeming with Tara's circle of friends celebrating her birthday with a luau-themed beach party. Sugar Ray's *Fly* mingled with loud laughter as four girls smacked a volleyball back and forth, one of them diving into the lake to retrieve it after it'd gone rogue.

A melancholy smile tipped my lips. I sat by myself, watching the summer Saturday unfold, sipping a cherry Coke while my skin sizzled beneath a cloudless sky. My emotions were all over the place. I felt a pull to join the fun and distract myself from the Reed "incident" from a week ago, but my legs refused to budge, anchoring me to the sand.

I hadn't seen or spoken to him since it happened, and it was my fault for running away before we had a chance to discuss things. But I also knew there was nothing worth discussing. It was easier to pretend it never happened than to breathe more life to something that had the power to unravel every other thread stitching me together.

When the song ended and the radio DJ cut in, Tara raced toward me with braided pigtails in her hair and multiple colorful leis around her neck. "Hals!" she called out, her smile beaming as bright as the midday sun. She always said my name like that, like happiness, like happiness caught in a granite bubble that would never leak.

Shielding my eyes from a sun flare, I watched her zigzag toward me, a cloud of sand kicking up at her heels. "You look like you're having fun," I said as she approached.

Tara snagged a Coke from the cooler and plopped down beside me. "Unlike you." Her eyes narrowed. "What's up? You're sitting by yourself in the land of the lonesome."

"It's the land of the loungey," I corrected, loath to admit my self-inflicted misery. "I'm just waiting for Scotty."

"Dad should be here soon to drop off presents."

I tensed up as a shot of anxiety stabbed me in the gut. "I didn't realize he was coming."

"He's not staying." Her shoulder lifted before a new thought stole her expression. "Oh! Mom told me you and Scotty finally...you know."

I froze.

She wiggled her eyebrows. "Details, Hals. Tell me everything."

Mortification competed with my slow-blooming sunburn, flooding my skin in itchy heat. "She told you that?"

"Duh. We tell each other everything." Tara leaned back on one hand and sipped her pop. "She got you a prescription for the *whoopsie* pill and then put you on the patch. Smart. I can't imagine a little Halley running around." She squinted her eyes at the sun, deep in thought. "I mean, I can, and she'd be adorable as crap, but you've got dreams to live out first, you know?"

Oh, my God.

I fell backward in the sand and draped an arm over my eyes. "I can't believe she told you about my sex life." My sex life made of lies, no less.

She followed, dropping beside me. Our hair blended together, gold and chestnut. "It's not a big deal. Josh and I are doing it. Mom got me on the patch a while ago." Her face changed when she glanced at me. "I think Scotty will be good for you. I never understood your interest in older men. They're nothing but trouble."

My heartbeats accelerated. "How so?"

"Just trust me."

Looking away, I fiddled with the string on my bikini bottoms. "I don't know. I feel weird that you know about that. It's personal."

"Not in our household." She wrinkled her nose with teasing. "The Stephens family is an open book. And you're basically one of us."

I wasn't one of them.

I was the traitor, the turncoat, the Judas.

"Hey, speaking of dreams, what are your thoughts on getting an apartment together?"

"What?"

"Josh offered, but I'd rather live with you. Chicks before dicks." Giggling, she canted her head toward me. "I can't imagine starting college and moving on without you."

I met her gaze across the sand. "I have some money saved up from the animal hospital, but not enough for monthly rent. Can you afford your own place?"

"Mom's been helping me save. I was thinking we could get a two-bedroom. You and I can share a room, and someone else can take the other one. Between the three of us, I think we'd be fine."

I nodded, contemplating the offer.

Tara was going to community college, which didn't have dorms. I figured she'd be living at home until she secured a full-time job in her line of work.

As for me...well, I had no idea what I was doing with my life. Scotty was heading to South Carolina in the fall, after Reed had offered him an opportunity to teach self-defense courses at his east-coast studio under the assistance of his old friend. He would be getting an apartment while he saved up for a more permanent place.

The twist?

Scotty had suggested I go with him. He said he wouldn't charge me rent until I was on my feet.

The offer was tempting.

Traveling and sight-seeing had always been on my bucket list, so getting handed an opportunity to live near the ocean—and miles away from my ocean of issues—was something I needed to seriously consider.

But I didn't want to leave Tara.

I didn't want to leave her father, either.

Love always had the upper hand.

"What's the matter?" Tara wondered at my delayed reply. "Did you have other plans?"

"Nothing concrete," I said quickly. "But what if something happened between us?"

She frowned. "What do you mean?"

I mean...what if you found out that I fucked your dad?

My face heated, and I swallowed hard. "What if something got in the way of our friendship? What if I did something to make you hate me?"

Silence slipped between us, only severed by squeals and laughter drifting from the shore. Tara pulled up on her elbows, staring down at me with confusion. "Halley...nothing will ever come between us. No fight in the world could make me hate you."

"You don't know that."

"Yes, I do. You're like a sister to me. You're my best friend—my *family*—and you've been through more crazy shit than anyone I've ever met. If you can survive the worst out of life, so can we. We'll get through anything together," she said with surety. "Even if you start to snore."

I sniffled, emotion sinking its way inside. "I don't snore."

"Good." Grinning, she bopped my shoulder with hers. "That was the worst thing I could think of, so there's literally nothing to worry about."

"You swear?"

Tara yanked me upright by my wrist and locked our eyes together, drawing out the moment. "Look into these eyes, Halley. Stare deep into my murky green depths that resemble swamp guts and discover the truth hidden within."

A giggle slipped out.

"You're laughing, but this is serious," she said, unable to mask her own laughter. "I swear on Jared Leto's sexy-ass soul that nothing will ever come between us. We'll pinkie-swear on it."

She snagged my pinkie finger and held tight. My smile stuck as I nodded, and our hands bobbed up and down. "Okay."

"Great. It's settled, then. We'll get an apartment and one day raise little Josh and Scotty babies together."

The elation deteriorated and I ducked my chin, releasing her finger.

"But not anytime soon," she added. "Try to keep your ovaries in check for a few more years, even though Scotty's walking this way, and he does look good without a shirt."

Blinking rapidly, I glanced up and found Scotty headed toward us. "Um...I'll be right back."

Tara smacked me on the bikini bottoms and hollered to my retreating back, "Keep it in your polka-dotted swimsuit, Hals!"

Scotty strolled over to me, swiping his long hair back. "What was that all about?" He glanced over my shoulder at Tara, who was darting back to the netless volleyball game.

"Oh, nothing important. Can we talk?" The question spewed out of me before I could gather the reins. I needed to confide in somebody, and I trusted Scotty.

Nerves raced through me as he met my eyes, evidently noting the terror that resided inside them.

"You look like you're about to puke."

"Probability is high." I coiled my hand around his wrist and dragged him through the sand, over to a tent covering a spread of finger foods and munchies. "Are you good at keeping secrets?"

"Uh, sure." He trailed behind me until we both came to a stop and looked at each other. "What's this about? You're kind of freaking me out."

"I'm the one freaking out."

"Okay," he said, eyes thinning. "Tell me."

Flapping my arms like a bird fighting gravity, I finally collected my wits and skimmed my fingers through my hair, staring down at his ruddy-brown sandals. "I slept with Reed."

Silence.

A barbed-wire knot formed in the pit of my stomach as I glanced up at him, my cheeks burning.

His eyes bulged. "*What?*"

"Coach Madsen."

"I know who Reed is." Scotty stared at me, dumfounded, cupping a hand around his jaw and scratching at the copper stubble growing in. "Damn, Halley."

I folded my arms and dug my toes into the sand. "I know."

"What were you thinking? He's Tara's father *and* your training coach. I knew there was some weird tension between the two of you, but..." Shaking his head, he breathed out a heavy sigh. "Holy shit. I didn't think you'd ever go there."

Shame nibbled at my insides and shook my words. "I don't know what to do. Everything's a mess."

"When did it happen?"

"Last week. Tara doesn't know," I croaked out. "She thinks I slept with you."

His body went rigid, his eyes glazing over with something like pain. "All right." Jabbing his tongue against his cheek, he sighed again. "Why are you telling me this?"

"I...I don't know. I trust you. And I was hoping that if Tara ever said anything...you'd cover for me?" I was being so selfish. Scotty had feelings for me, I knew that, and I was using him to hold on to my depraved secrets that centered around another man. It was an awful, cruel thing to do. "God, I'm really sorry. Never mind. That was a terrible thing to ask you. I'm such a bitch."

"You're not a bitch."

"Forget I said that," I rambled on. "I'll deal with it on my own. If everything implodes, it's my own fault, and I'll figure it out—"

"Halley." Scotty grabbed my shoulders and bent to eye-level. "I won't say anything. I got your back, okay? Breathe."

My eyes watered as I inhaled a breath, hoping to tame my ebbing panic attack. I didn't deserve his friendship or loyalty, but I was undoubtedly grateful for it. "I'm sorry. I'm sure you hate me now, but you're one of my only friends, and I had to tell someone. I need...advice, I guess."

"You know I don't hate you." A muscle in his cheek twitched. "But you won't like my advice."

I sighed, my face falling. "You think I'm being stupid."

"I think you're being reckless," he said. "I think you're playing with a fire too powerful for you to control. Honestly, Coach is the stupid one. And my advice is to cut ties before you both burn."

Gritting my teeth, I rubbed my lips together. "It's more than physical," I tried to reason. "We met two years ago, before I knew he was Tara's father. I was in a bad place then, and I lied about my age. A connection kind of blossomed, and now we're in too deep to just cut it out of us."

He shook his head slowly, his brows knitting together as he processed my bomb. "What's your endgame here? Are you just fooling around and having fun, or do you have real feelings for this guy?"

My heart jumped, a reminder of all the feelings I was too weak to stomp out. "Real feelings," I murmured. "I hate this, but it feels impossible to walk away."

"It's going to feel a hell of a lot worse when you're faced with no choice *but* to walk away. Tara will find out. And she's not going to forgive you. Then you'll be walking away from them both."

His words danced through me with steel-toed boots.

Tears rushed to my eyes as I envisioned a future spun with betrayal, heartbreak, and ultimately, loneliness. Everything I'd tried so hard to escape from. I'd been running and running, and it felt as if I'd run three-hundred-and-sixty degrees, landing right back where I'd started. Different circumstances, same result.

I inhaled a breath. "What if Tara's okay with it?"

His brows shot up. "You really believe that?"

"I don't know what I believe. It's hard to make soul-crushing decisions on a hunch when things might play out in a positive way."

"I mean, I'm not a psychic, but all signs point to everything going to shit."

"But, why?" I demanded, frustration fueling me. "Why is this so wrong? We're both consenting adults. Sure, there's an age gap, but so what? Why does everything have to be so hard?"

A new presence warmed my skin at the same time Scotty's eyes flicked over my shoulder and he took a step away from me, pushing a hand through his hair. My heartbeats jackknifed as my mouth snapped closed, despite being too cowardly to turn around. I flinched when two gift-wrapped packages plopped down on the picnic table beside me, but I kept my eyes on the sand and my heart in my chest so it wouldn't give us both away.

Tara's voice floated over to me, her footsteps following. "Hey, Dad!" she called out, jogging closer in her ruby-red one-piece.

Cautiously, I pivoted around, my arms crossed over my bikini top. Reed turned toward Tara as she entered the tent and threw her arms around her father for a hug.

"Hey, Squirt." A smile flickered to life the moment she was in his arms. "Having fun?"

"Sure am." She stepped back and did a little curtsy. "I'm trying to get Halley in the water, but she's allergic to fun today. Maybe you can convince her."

I willed a spontaneous lightning bolt to strike the tent and bury my shame in a fatal avalanche. Forcing an awkward chuckle, I choked out a hello to Reed. "Hey."

He stared at me, his smile faltering, as he palmed the back of his neck. "How's it going, Halley?"

So casual.

He offered no indication of being inside of me only a week ago, bringing me to double orgasm, as he'd thrusted and moaned and chanted my name like it was his greatest undoing.

Tara was completely oblivious, and I wasn't sure if that made everything better or worse.

Scotty intervened, shaking Reed's hand in greeting. "Good to see you, Coach."

"Yeah. You, too."

My eyes instinctively panned back to Reed's when he glanced at me again, and the brief contact felt like a moderate earthquake rumbling in my chest.

Looking away, he nodded at Tara. "I was just stopping by with gifts. Can't stay."

"Keys to a new convertible, I'm guessing?" Tara snatched up a blue-foiled box and shook it. "Sounds like socks. I'll definitely be gifting you that apron for your birthday. Hot pink."

I was still staring at Reed, completely checked out, when Scotty reached for my hand. "I'm gonna go for a swim. Join me?"

Blinking away from the obscenely attractive source of my turmoil, I tried to center my unruly thoughts. "Sure." Anything was better than this blistering corner of hell.

Waving them off with a weak goodbye, I followed Scotty over to the water, no words passing between us. There was nothing more to say. He linked our fingers together, and the gesture was a small comfort as we waded into the shallow water and my toes burrowed into cool sludge.

My gaze skated across the beach as the breeze caught my hair and draped it over my face. Reed stood just outside the tent, watching me from afar, looking plagued and haunted. He couldn't shutter the curtains, couldn't drop the blinds over his eyes.

I saw it all. Felt it.
We didn't smile, didn't blink.
We just stared at each other.
Me on one side of the waterline, and him on the other.

CHAPTER 24

Halley

TARA SKIPPED beside me through the sand, her braids drenched with lake water. "Sorry to call you back here," she said to Reed. "We're out of pop and chips. Can you make a store run?"

I stared at my nails attached to prune-like fingers as Tara dragged me over to her father, who had just returned to the beach after excessive pages from Tara.

Two hours had rolled by and I was mentally exhausted. Scotty had taken off a few minutes ago, leaving me drained and limp as I stewed in my brief interaction with Reed from earlier. Sunset was approaching, carving out a canvas of vibrant colors in the sky that did little to brighten my spirits.

Reed sauntered over to us from his truck, still clad in his grunge-band T-shirt and navy-and-white swim trunks, fixing his focus solely on Tara. "You're not ready to wrap it up?" He glanced at his watch. "Getting late."

"It's not even dark yet." She huffed, like the notion was preposterous. "Suzie set up a net, so we're going to play a round of volleyball until sundown. Can you get the stuff?"

Sighing, he flicked a hand through his windblown hair and nodded. "Yeah, all right. Tell me what you want me to grab."

Tara rattled off a grocery list that included Willy Wonka's entire chocolate factory while I stood like a stone beside her and counted the wrinkles on my hands.

"Want to be on my team?" she asked me, breaking through my zoned-out daze.

"Oh." I blinked. "I was thinking of taking off. I'm getting tired."

"So lame."

"Sorry. I can walk home. It's not far."

"You're wearing sandals. You'll murder your feet."

"I'm fine. It's not that far and I can—"

"I'll drop you off at the house."

Reed's offer slammed into me, rearing my head up as my eyes locked on his. My face heated, and I was thankful for the sunburn flush that had graciously stained my cheekbones. "Um, you don't have to do that."

"It's on the way. Come on."

The reddest of red flags fluttered in front of my vision as I watched Reed spin around and stalk back toward his truck. What a terrible idea. We had no business being alone together only a week after our spontaneous, spine-tingling, utterly illicit and detrimental sexual encounter.

But I had no words to fight him. Tara was dallying beside me, extending her arms for a goodbye hug and sending me a smile.

"Thanks for sticking around so long," she said, releasing me from the hug. "I know you weren't really feeling it."

"I was. Sorry if I was boring. I think I'm about to get my period," I lied.

"Yuck. Totally understandable."

Before I turned around and bounded toward an awkward ride with her dad, she reached for me one more time and hooked our pinkie fingers together.

Emotion seized me. It almost felt like our goodbye hug had grown wings, preparing to fly me far, far away from my best friend.

"See you back at the house!" She swiveled around, dashing back toward her friends as the setting sun splashed tangerine hues across her hair.

Swallowing hard, I stepped into my denim cut-off shorts and pulled them up over my bathing suit, then toed into my beach-dusted sandals. My trek toward the parking lot was steeped in nerves as I practiced potential conversations in my head. Reed was already in the driver's seat, the engine rumbling, his head tipped back against the headrest.

I avoided eye contact through the windshield and slipped in beside him. We sat in silence for a few beats before he put the truck in Reverse and pulled out of the lot.

Five minutes later, we were at the grocery store.

Frowning, I glanced at the building, then at Reed. "I thought you were dropping me off at the house?"

His jaw was tight, eyes unreadable. "Figured we should talk."

I scratched at my collarbone, where new heat lingered in rosy patches. "That sounds painful."

He muttered a "yeah," then pushed open the door and stepped out, until I had no choice but to follow him inside and hope no one could see the scarlet letter branded on my chest.

Grabbing a cart, Reed shuffled forward and glanced over his shoulder at me while I trailed him. "You all right?"

"Peachy."

He sighed. "Halley."

My face flamed under the fluorescent lights. "Reed." I inched closer and folded my arms, realizing my bikini-clad cleavage was on full display for the shoppers. "I don't know what you want me to say."

"I want you to say whatever you're thinking," he said. "You ran out on me before we could discuss anything. I was worried about you walking back to the house alone."

"I couldn't stay." I scratched behind my ear, one arm still draped across my breasts. "And there was nothing to discuss. I was mortified."

He fell silent for a breath. "There's plenty to discuss."

"It was just sex." My words were flippant, but my pulse was doing backflips. "It's not like I haven't had sex before."

"*Just* sex," he parroted flatly, hands curling around the bar of the shopping cart as he perused the shelves. "Felt like more to me."

It *was* more.

It was everything and more.

Hope shimmied up my chest and sprinkled its magic over my heart like pixie dust. "Emotions were high. Life and death situations can muddle sound reason." I glanced around, hoping no one of relevance was in earshot. "Nothing changes, remember?"

Shaking his head, he pressed forward on the cart. "I never said that."

"Heavily implied."

"You didn't give me a chance to talk, Halley. I was still fucking inside you when you checked out and then bolted from the apartment."

Molten heat doused me from toes to top as I glanced at him, my eyes wide.

He swallowed, pausing the cart with a sigh of frustration. "Are you, uh..." Clearing his throat, he stared blankly at a bag of potato chips. "Protected?"

I wanted the squeaky linoleum floors to morph into quicksand and swallow me whole. "Yes. You don't have to worry about having two children, eighteen years apart."

Reed blinked over at me and ran his tongue along his upper lip before sending me a tight nod, then continuing forward. "You don't have to worry about anything either. I haven't been with anyone in a long time."

My breath caught. I was trudging through that blizzard again, his words icing over my heart.

"Any lady friends lately?"

"A few."

I gawked at him. "But you told me—"

"I lied."

Silence followed, and I tightened my arms around myself as we circled the aisles. I had convinced myself that Reed was out there sleeping around, meeting attractive women in bars and clubs, and scrubbing me from his mind like I was week-old dirt. After all, he was a gorgeous, mid-thirties bachelor who had a stable career, his own place, and the prettiest green eyes that could reel any woman in. Even the random shoppers that strolled by were unable to keep their eyes off of him.

It didn't make sense that he'd be celibate.

My curiosity got the better of me, and I asked timidly, "How long?"

Hoisting a twelve-pack of Coke off a bottom shelf, he slid it onto the bottom of the cart and straightened, looking right at me. "How long have I been caught up on you and unable to even look at another woman?" His tone was void of emotion, but his words were passion-doused daggers. "A year and a half."

I paled, rendered speechless once again.

Reed swallowed and dipped his gaze, returning to the front of the cart and rolling it forward. The next ten minutes slugged by in itchy silence as I processed his revelation and spun it every which way inside my mind.

When we found a line and started filling the belt with items, I was still dumbstruck.

"Halley," he said softly.

I shook my head as we inched up the checkout line, hardly able to keep my emotions in check.

A year and a half.

"Comet...look at me." He twisted toward me as the scanner pinged with items sliding across the surface. When my eyes finally lifted and glued to his, he leaned forward and said with all the conviction in the world, "I wanted it. I wanted it more than I wanted air."

Waiting, I stared up at him, expectation blooming in the pit of my stomach.

Ping, ping, ping.

"But it can never happen again."

The balloon popped. I deflated before him and looked away, my jaw set and my soul withering. "Yeah," I whispered. "I know."

"Oh, God...*yes.*" My forehead was pressed to Reed's, my arms circled around his neck. The swell of my breasts bounced inside the cups of my clamshell-pink bikini as I rode him in the front seat of his pickup truck.

His T-shirt was still on, but his swim trunks were halfway down his legs, clinging to his muscled thighs. Dipping his head, he yanked down my bikini top and covered one of my breasts with his mouth, devouring my nipple through ragged groans as I bobbed up and down on his lap.

We were being reckless.

Dangerous.

The truck was parked in an empty corner of an industrial parking lot, away from traffic and passersby, but we weren't being careful.

Someone could spot us, call the cops, have us arrested for public indecency...and then what?

All hell would break loose.

Yet, somehow, none of that compared to the absolute *heaven* I felt when he was inside me.

Dusk filtered in through the windows, a chalky gray haze swirling with sparks. I gouged my nails into the nape of his neck and fisted his hair with the other as my head craned back and the erotic melody of our bodies slapping together drove me toward ecstasy.

"*Fuck*," he ground out, laving his tongue up my chest, my throat, until our mouths locked.

Sloppy, wet kisses fueled us, and a song on the radio did little to pierce the sounds of our moans. I cried out as his tongue idled in my mouth, his eyes closing, lips parted with euphoria. My hips picked up speed, and he squeezed the globes of my ass to anchor me as he began to come undone.

We panted through the pinnacle, his hand reaching between us, fingers rubbing my clit to take me over the edge. My knees dug into his hips as my grip on him turned vicelike. My body tensed and vibrated, while shimmery light danced behind my eyes and an orgasm yanked me under.

I buried my face in the crook of his neck to stifle my cry as he fisted my hair and drove his hips up, grunting through his own release.

"Halley, Halley...*fuck*." He broke apart, spilling into me, his whole body going rigid as he held on to me until his grip on my hair loosened and he collapsed back against the seat.

I remained draped across his chest, my heavy breaths warming the skin of his throat. When I pressed a tiny kiss to his pulse point, he shuddered, both arms wrapping around me to keep me flush against him. I felt his chest heaving up and down, his heartbeats in my ear. Stickiness coated my inner thighs as warm molasses filtered through my veins.

For the barest moment, I was content. Safe, alive, and adored.

I allowed the moment to last longer than the first time, savoring the feel of him hard inside me, filling me in every way. Sighing, I kissed my way up his neck and jaw, hesitating when I reached his still-parted lips.

Reed combed my hair back with both hands, then cupped my face, his thumbs grazing gently over my flushed cheeks. "Don't run away from me this time," he pleaded softly, his eyes skimming across my face before he sealed our lips together for a gentle kiss.

Exhaling, I buckled atop his chest, my cheek plastered to his beating heart while he stroked my hair, my back, palming the base of my neck. "I don't know what to do," I confessed as puddles gathered in my eyes.

He pulled me closer, held me tighter, and said nothing.

A tear slipped loose. "You're supposed to know. You're supposed to have the answers."

"Why?"

"Because you're older."

Simmering in my claim, Reed inched me up until we were face to face again. "Older doesn't translate to wiser, and age doesn't guarantee answers." He cradled my cheek in his palm as I nuzzled into his touch. "With age, comes certainty. You grow to know exactly what you want. But that doesn't always mean it's wise or right, and then that certainty becomes a curse."

"What are you certain about?" I swallowed, my fingers curling into his T-shirt.

Reed continued to massage his palm up and down my spine as his eyes glassed over with sentiment. His lashes fluttered, and he exhaled through his nose, whispering back, "I'm certain it's going to hurt like hell when this is over."

CHAPTER 25

Reed

TARA STOLE one of my french fries as we sat across from each other in a diner booth while mid-June sunshine streamed in from the adjacent window. It brightened her smile and lit her up, highlighting the truth I'd been struggling to digest over the last two weeks: my little girl was now a high school graduate.

She was a legal adult; a grown woman.

It felt impossible...but here we were.

I leaned forward, both of my forearms pressed to the tabletop, and tilted my head. I studied her through the melancholy. There was a dreary cloud coasting over my head, because I knew that these moments together were going to be fewer and further between.

And paired with my new extracurricular activities, these moments may diminish to fleeting glimpses, overshadowed by the weight of my secrets.

Tara munched on a fry, swallowing it down before her eyebrows dipped. "What? You're looking at me like I traded faces with a baboon."

I frowned. "I don't like baboons."

"I know. That's my point."

"I would never look at a baboon like I look at you. There's only pride and unconditional love in these eyes."

"You look like I just stomped all over your heart with my creepy, hand-like baboon feet."

I physically shuddered at the mental image. "I was just thinking about how fast time has gone by. How much you've grown up."

She nodded slowly, processing, then shoveled a few more fries into her mouth. "Well, you *were* thinking about that. Now you're just thinking about baboons."

Smirking, I flicked a french fry across the table and it bopped her on the nose.

"Rude!" She broke out into giggles and tossed a handful at me. "You know I'm not above public food fights."

"Oh, I know. Your seventh birthday party still finds me in my nightmares."

"Cake. Everywhere."

"So much."

Her features softened, her emerald eyes sparkling against the window light. Long hair fell over her shoulders in cocoa-brown waves, and her eyelashes were long and curving, just like mine. Tara had my bone structure; an angular jaw, dimples, and full lips. While her eyes were my color, they were shaped like Whitney's. They shared the same button nose, too.

She was so damn perfect.

My little girl.

"I feel like you invited me out to lunch to get sappy with me," Tara said through a bite of food, dipping one of her fries into a chocolate milkshake. "Am I right?"

"Yes."

"Oh, boy." She sighed and collapsed backward in the booth. "I saw your tears during my graduation ceremony. I had a feeling this was coming."

"Those weren't tears. The wind was in my eyes."

"We were inside."

"There was wind."

Pursing her lips to the side, she let a smile break free. "I'm still your little girl, Dad."

Fuck.

The wind was back.

Sniffing away the emotion, I scratched my jaw and nodded. "When you're a parent, you're consciously aware that these days are ahead, destined to find you. You try to prepare, and you think you'll be ready, but it's not possible. These moments always seem so damn far away at the time, and then—*bam*. No more piggyback rides, no more swimming lessons, no more birthday cake painting the walls. It's like I blinked and you were older."

Tara pushed her plate aside and stared down at the table, her own eyes wet and glimmering. "Do you feel like you missed out on stuff? Being separated from Mom?"

"I feel like we did a good job of making it work. There's sacrifice in every decision." My teeth clenched through a tight swallow. "If we had stayed together, we would've been bitter and unhappy, and then other parts of our lives would have suffered. You would have resented us both."

"I can't imagine resenting either of you."

I folded my hands together. "You won't fully grasp that unless you ever experience it—which, I hope you don't. I hope you find someone who complements you in every way, who gives you strength and courage, who fights for you tooth and nail, no matter the consequences, and who loves every single piece of you. Even the sad pieces. Even the ugly pieces you try to keep buried."

Lost in thought, she curled a hand around her soda glass and nodded. "You guys didn't love each other's ugly pieces enough to stay together."

Spinning a reply over in my mind, I glanced down at my hands, knowing that these hands weren't capable of keeping all the pieces together sometimes. Even the beautiful ones. "You know I still have a lot of love and respect for your mother. That'll never change. But, I think that when someone you care about betrays you, nothing can glue those broken bits back together," I explained. "Think of that puzzle we were working on for weeks, a few years back."

"Sure. The Mickey Mouse one."

"Ladybug was still just a puppy and she chewed up one of the pieces. We had the whole puzzle put together, but that one piece was bent and smashed, so it never fit into the space. You were so mad. You said it would never be a perfect puzzle because of that broken piece, no matter how much I tried to flatten it out and squeeze it into place."

The analogy flickered in her eyes, and she looked away, biting her lip.

"I'm just saying, some things are great while they last. We had fun putting the pieces together, just like your mom and I had a lot of great moments throughout our relationship. But the end result is still the same: a broken puzzle."

Inhaling a shaky breath, she stared out the window, fisting her hands together in her lap. "Yeah, I get that. I guess I had it in my head that you two still loved each other and wanted to try again."

"That love is a residual feeling built around you."

"Makes sense," she said. "Halley thought I was reading into things. Apparently, she was right." Shrugging, she sent me a sheepish smile. "I just want you to be happy. Both of you. You guys are always working, always alone. Is there someone else?"

My chest buckled at the question.

Muscles locking, heart jumping, I squeezed my hands together and blinked across the table. I wasn't able to hold back the brief flare of my eyes, nor the truth that flashed inside of them.

Her dark brows lifted with intrigue. She gasped. "There is. Who is she?"

"Nobody." I'd said it too quickly, my voice drowning in treacherous grit. "There's no one."

"You're such a liar."

"I'm not with anybody, Tara."

It was partly true. Halley and I weren't together—*not really*. We were just having sex, and that came with an expiration date.

Wrinkling her nose, she blew a piece of hair out of her eyes then swatted it back. Her focus thinned as she gazed out the window, stewing in the implication that I'd been ill-prepared to hide. "You can tell me, you know. It won't break me."

She had no idea how wrong she was.

I propped my chin on my cupped hands, my elbows digging into the table almost as hard as my teeth were digging into the inner lining of my cheek. "I know."

"I'll support you, no matter who she is."

My eyes fell shut as white-hot guilt filtered through my bloodstream, a sickly feeling that had my veins shriveling and my heart rotting a hole in my chest. "You know I love you more than anything, right?" I confessed, my voice hitching with a devastating crack.

I needed to say it. I needed her to know.

Tara blinked back over at me, her cheeks glowing pink, and her gaze widening at the emotion pouring out of me. "Of course I know." She reached for my hand over the table and squeezed. "I love you, too. You're kind of the best dad ever."

The light returned to my eyes as I leaned forward. "I wasn't aware of any competition."

"No need for contenders. Everyone knows you would dominate."

I grinned. "They just know I'd beat the crap out of them for top spot."

Off her giggles, the conversation wheeled back to a more palatable place, and we resumed our playful banter and french fry fight.

Still, the guilt lingered.

Guilt in the form of betrayal; something I'd just given my daughter a lecture on.

Guilt in the form of weakness.

Guilt in the form of her best friend.

My *Wonderwall.*

But the wall between us was anything but wonderful. And I feared we were all one loose brick away from that wall crashing down and putting us six feet under.

CHAPTER 26

Reed

THERE WERE the kinds of messes that took a dishrag to clean up, and some that required a mop and a bucket. Some messes spilled over and compromised other areas, which turned a minor inconvenience into prickling aggravation. And then there were grade-A, next-level catastrophes that left you sifting through the wreckage, contemplating every misstep, every wrong turn, that led you there.

We weren't any of those things.

We were just plain fucked.

This wasn't a stain on the carpet that could be scrubbed away, and it wasn't even a gut job that required hours upon hours of manual labor to fix what was broken; it was a relentless flood, drowning everything in its path. And as I stared at her sun-kissed limbs tangled in my silver bed sheets, her hair a golden river splashed across my pillowtop, I wondered how we could possibly ever reach the surface and breathe clean air again.

Sunshine trickled in through the bedroom window of my apartment, showering pale-yellow stripes across her cheek. She was so damn gorgeous. Sweet innocence curled around her, mingling with sinful memories from the night before.

We'd been sleeping together for two weeks.

I wasn't proud of it, and I sure as fuck wasn't expecting anything more to come from it. This was all we were going to get.

I placed a hot cup of coffee on the nightstand and crawled onto the mattress, wrapping an arm around her and tugging her to my bare chest. I'd been doing my damned hardest not to let emotion stifle reason, and to allow this to be exactly what it was: a forbidden affair that would live in the shadows and never see the light of day. I'd never take her out to dinner, hold her hand in public, or put a ring on her finger.

I had laid my intentions out, loud and clear, and Halley claimed to be content with the terms. But I knew that even the best-laid plans were often butchered and left splattered across a murder-scene floor.

Halley stirred awake, making a breathy, squeaky sound that jump-started my heart. She twisted toward me, her long lashes fanning out and tickling her brow. A drowsy smile stretched when I skimmed my hand over her abdomen and pressed a kiss to her temple.

"Morning," she said groggily, her voice sleep-ridden gravel. "You're up early."

"It's after seven. You should probably get going."

Stretching her arms over her head, her belly flattened and tightened beneath my palm, and I grazed my hand up between her breasts until I captured her throat and tilted her mouth to mine.

She deflated the moment our lips brushed, circling both arms around my neck and pulling me on top of her. "I don't want to go." Careful fingers mussed my uncombed hair. "I like it here."

"I like you here." Our lips touched again, just a feather-soft graze.

"I told Tara I was sleeping over at Scotty's. She won't expect me back till lunchtime."

My eyes closed, my throat rolling. "It's dangerous. We shouldn't be doing this here," I told her. "Tara has a key to my apartment."

She nodded, even though her expression soured. "I guess we can resort to seedy motels and shady corners of parking lots."

Fuck. I didn't want that, either. I wanted her here, in my bed, in my home, imprinting her golden light on every lackluster inch of my world. "You look best in my bed." My dick hardened from half-hard to rock-solid as I kissed my way down her throat. "But it's not safe."

"Maybe I can stay a little longer?" The heel of her foot crooked around my ankle, then traveled up the length of my calf. "I still want to do things."

"Yeah?" My tongue flicked her pulse point, where a light bruise shaded her skin from the night before. "What things?"

She reached a hand between us, cupping the erection tenting my boxers. "Coffee." She gave me a firm squeeze until I shuddered against her. "Breakfast." Her hand stroked me through the thin fabric. "A shower."

"Mmm." I groaned, slipping down her body and palming both breasts in my hands as she arched up. I sucked a dusky nipple into my mouth until it budded, swirling my tongue around the peak. "Later."

"Okay," she panted, vibrating beneath me. "I'm adaptable."

With one quick motion, I rotated our positions until I was flat on my back and she was straddling me. She gasped in surprise as I hauled her up my torso, my chest, until her pussy was hovering over my mouth. "Coffee's on the nightstand," I ground out, kissing her neatly trimmed patch of curls. "Breakfast can wait." When she tried to lower herself onto my mouth, I held her up, just out of reach, her pelvis swiveling with frustration. "And I do plan to fuck you in the shower." My tongue lightly flicked her clit, making her writhe and moan above me. "But first, you're going to ride my face."

Curling my hands around her hips, I hauled her down on my mouth and devoured her. Halley cried out, bowing her back as her knees caged my head and dug into the pillow. I plunged my tongue in and out of her with hungry, vicious strokes, holding her to me as she clamped onto the headboard with both hands and thrust against my face.

I ate her like a starving man, like she was my last meal, knowing she'd forever be the most priceless delicacy I'd ever taste. She was responsive, so eager for me to take control and have my way with her. She'd let me do anything.

Even break her heart.

She always came fast this way, so it was only a minute before she shook, panted, and quivered, one of her hands sinking into my hair and squeezing tight. I sucked her clit hard, my tongue sliding in and out of her, and she shattered like broken glass, moaning my name, begging for more, and collapsed on top of me with her forehead landing on the headboard.

I didn't give her time to recover before I slid out from under her and repositioned her on her hands and knees. Hiking her up by the hips, I yanked my boxers down my thighs until my cock sprung free, already throbbing with need and beading at the tip.

I kneeled behind her as her hands fisted the bed covers and her face planted on the pillow, dragging my swollen head up and down her slick entrance.

She moaned, bucking her ass against me, greedy and demanding. "Reed..."

Hearing my name keen from her lips always unleashed a beast inside me; a primal, possessive feeling that carved its way through me, lighting a fire in my blood. I slammed into her, my knuckles going white as my fingertips bruised her slim waist.

This was how it always was.

Brutal, carnal, fast.

I realized we hardly ever had sex face to face, save for those first two encounters. I took her doggy-style, let her ride me, or drove into her with me on my knees and Halley on her back with her legs hooked over my shoulders. Intimacy would be our undoing. Too much eye contact, slow kisses, soft touches, and gentle strokes—those were the things that would make it damn near impossible to walk away.

And I had to walk.

There was no other choice.

But not yet...

I fucked her like I always did, with anger and frustration fusing with twisted lust, rejecting the tendrils of affection that tried to seep inside. Halley whimpered below me as I tugged her up by the hair and bathed her neck in hot, wet kisses, inhaling her scent as she took me over the peak. With her back flush with my chest, I circled an arm around her and clutched her breast, hating that it was always over too soon, never long enough, no matter how hard I tried to prolong the inevitable.

Groaning through a sharp climax, I buried my face in her soft hair and rode out the waves, spilling into her. My teeth nicked her shoulder as she buzzed and swayed against me and a delicate sweat sheened on her skin, glistening in the window light. When I pulled out of her, she dropped to the mattress, panting through the adrenaline.

Making a satisfied humming sound, she rolled over as I yanked my boxers up. Another languid smile tipped her lips, and she stretched again, her perfect body splayed before me. Her eyes were glassy and adoring as she gazed up at me with flushed cheeks and disheveled hair, like I was her soulmate, instead of what I really was.

Halley plopped back onto her stomach, wholly satiated, until her bare back was facing me.

I stared at her scars.

A swirl of undisguised tenderness bloomed inside my chest, turning my stone heart to sand. Against my better judgment, I bent forward and splayed my palm atop her spine, then trailed my index finger over the puckered edges of her battle wounds. She hissed out a breath, stilling beneath me. My own scar pulsed like it was drawn to hers, like we were in some sort of secret club together. A partner in pain. A companion in violence. Two warriors braving the storm, hand in hand.

Halley made a whimpering sound as I continued to trace and touch, empathy stifling reason. The deepest parts of me wanted to protect her from the evils of the world, to keep her by my side and defend her, always, body and spirit. But those parts of me also knew that the only way to protect her was to let her slip through my fingers. I needed to saw through the steely binds and let her go.

Turning over, Halley peered up at me as my hand landed on her hip. "I like when you touch me like that."

I idled on my knees beside her, the sweat cooling on my skin. "Like what?"

"Like I'm yours."

My heart shrank.

She *was* mine.

She would always be mine.

But not everything we were given was meant to be kept.

She saw me retreating, saw me burrowing back into the emotionless corner of my mind and slipping the mask back on. Pulling to a sitting position, Halley spoke before I could cut the thread. "Take a picture," she said.

I frowned. "What?"

A smile brightened her mouth as she crawled over the mattress, leaned over, and snatched her camera off the floor. "A picture. To save the moment."

Halley was particular about her moments. She didn't take photos on a whim, didn't capture unworthy things. This was a moment she wanted to preserve.

She handed me the camera, and I stared at it like it was a foreign language textbook.

"You just press the button," she said, still smiling. "Right here."

Pushing the camera toward me, she moved in closer and showed me what to do. It was heavy in my hands, an uncharted relic. I brushed the strap away from the lens and lifted the camera body to my face, peering through the eyehole and watching as she flopped backward on the bed, tugging the bedsheet up her chest. She made a silly face that pulled a laugh out of me.

"Take it," she ordered playfully.

"You're moving too much."

"Those are the best ones."

I centered the frame as she tickled my thigh with her toes and I flinched. She collapsed backward with a laugh, her cheeks still flushed, hair askew.

It was beautiful, this moment. Our ugly reality fell away as I snapped the picture, just as her teeth flashed white, her eyes closed, and her hair blanketed my pillow in streams of honey.

I couldn't draw out the tenderness any longer. It would consume me. Discarding the camera on the mattress, I sighed, the beauty fading to black. "Breakfast?" I hedged, crawling off the bed.

"Sure." Her smile slowly buckled in my periphery as I reached for the lukewarm coffee.

I handed her the russet-colored mug and watched as she took a small sip. The smile returned, half as bright as it once was.

"You already know how I like my coffee."

Scratching my hair, I offered a dismissive shrug. "I've seen you make it at the house."

Dark roast, a splash of milk, and a teaspoon of honey.

It didn't mean anything.

Knowing how she liked her coffee, her favorite songs, her deepest fears and dreams, the way her breath hitched on my name whenever my tongue was between her legs, and her assortment of smiles dependent on her mood, only meant that I was observant.

Halley scooted off the bed and made her way to the bathroom to clean up, meeting me in the kitchen a few minutes later as I pulled a few boxes of cereal out of a cabinet.

I glanced at her wearing only my T-shirt, my jaw tightening as my eyes rolled down her bare legs. I cleared my throat and turned back to the cabinets. "Cereal good?"

"Yep. Unless you want me to cook something."

"We can keep it simple."

Watching her cook magic in my kitchen while wearing nothing but my T-shirt wasn't going to do my sanity any favors.

Halley hopped up behind me on the small island top and swung her legs back and forth, her hair falling in chaotic waves over her shoulders. She flipped on the radio and a pop song filled the kitchen. I tried to ignore the way her lips moved as she sang along to the song, only partly in key, and snagged two bowls and spoons from the cupboard before grabbing the milk.

Her eyes lit up as she watched me pour the cereal. "Rice Krispies. The Christmas kind."

"I stocked up over the holiday. Pretty sure cereal lasts forever."

Hazel irises glimmered with specks of green when I carried a bowl over to her. "I remember buying you a box on Christmas Eve."

I ate my cereal standing up, leaning back against the counter across from her in my running shorts, still sans a shirt. "Yeah, you did."

"Then you tried to pay for all my groceries and *still* snuck money in my pocket, even though you lost the bet. You're a good man."

A good man.

The title gnawed at me with rotting teeth. Pretty sure good men didn't fuck around with their daughter's friends and lie about it.

I was definitely a piece of shit.

"Mm," I said tersely.

We ate our cereal in silence, stealing glances, dodging some, both of us lost in our own heads. Before I could think of something to say, the song morphed.

Fucking *Wonderwall.*

Her smile twinkled back to life when the first few chords rang out, and I recalled a chilly afternoon out on Whit's deck, shortly after her flu bug had passed. She'd looked halfway in love with me at that point, so

I'd had no choice but to reroute things, telling her I'd originally gotten the CD for someone else. A lie, of course. Only *her* face had flashed through my mind when I'd been browsing through albums at the record store.

One specific CD for one specific girl.

I'd told myself it was innocent, but here we were.

Sighing at the memory, I chewed through another bite of cereal and mulled over my words, a darkness scratching its way inside. "Looking back, I wonder where exactly I fucked up, you know?" I wondered aloud. "Maybe it was buying you that damn CD. The little moments. Definitely the training sessions." Jaw clenched, I glanced down at the floor tiles. "Feels like every step took me in the wrong direction and we ended up here. In this goddamn purgatory."

Halley's brows gathered between her eyes, the smile wiped off her face. "That's not how I see it. I like to think everything happens for a reason."

"That's an imaginary concept designed to make you feel better about your life and help you sleep at night. Santa Claus, angels, wishes, fate. They're not real. They're coping mechanisms."

Her frown deepened. "You sound so cynical."

"Maybe I am. I'm a thirty-six-year-old man fooling around with a teenager." The hitch of her breath had guilt joining in on my pity party, and I closed my eyes, exhaling a slow breath.

Halley hesitated before jumping down from the counter and stepping over to me. "Regardless of what this can or can't be, please don't diminish what it is."

My eyes opened and narrowed. "What exactly do you think this is?"

Her delicate palms slid up the length of my torso and landed on my chest. "Something beautiful."

More fantasies.

More pretty lies to help her sleep at night.

"Beautiful things don't last," I said, trying to remain stiff and sharp-edged but tenderizing against her touch. I wanted to reach for the lie, too; weave it and mold it into something honest, something worth keeping, but I was too aware of everything it wasn't.

"I know. But they can still be beautiful while they're here."

Halley lifted up on her tiptoes for a kiss, and I was helpless to the magnetism. I lowered my head and caressed her lips with mine, stupidly allowing the soft moment to warp my darkness with streaks of light, with glimpses of a fairy tale that would never come to be. I deflated on a sigh, on a dream, on a wish for so much more.

But I couldn't let it last, couldn't draw it out. I couldn't give it a pulse. If I breathed any more life into it, it would outlive us both.

Pulling away, I turned my back to her and set my bowl on the countertop, pressing forward as my arms tensed and my muscles twitched with bitten-back emotion. "You should hop in the shower and get ready to head out," I said, stoning my voice. "It's getting late."

Her body heat buzzed against my back as she idled behind me, exhaling a breath. "I could. Or I could kick your butt at Resident Evil."

I was grateful I wasn't facing her, as I was unable to prevent the smile from slipping.

She was always breaching me, always digging her way back inside.

A stubborn sliver.

Pivoting around, I tried to erase the smile in time, but she saw it. She latched onto it, clung to it, stored it away, and I was defenseless. "Shower," I stated.

"Video games."

My lips pursed to the side.

Then, at the same time, we both raised a hand and slammed it to our opposite palm.

One, two—

Halley did paper.

I did rock.

Grinning with victory, she stepped forward, inched up for a kiss, and reached down between us to grip the growing bulge in my shorts. "Paper covers rock."

She kicked my ass at Mortal Kombat, and then I took her one more time in the shower like I'd promised. I watched her on her knees with equal parts agony and ecstasy as she sucked me to near completion before I hauled her up the tiled wall and buried myself between her thighs. Our wet bodies tangled, danced, and yearned, slipping and sliding with no traction to keep us bound together for long. Water spewed from the showerhead, drenching us in hard jets, trying to wash us clean.

But even after I released inside her and then took my time to lather her in soap bubbles, gently shampoo her hair, and cradle her against my chest until the water ran cool, neither of us felt cleansed.

There were too many layers.

Too much dirt piling up, just beneath the surface.

And as I said goodbye and watched her dejectedly leave my apartment an hour later, her eyes glistening with unshed tears, I knew nothing in the world could erase the stains of our sins.

More importantly, nothing could ever wash away the haunting residue of what we would become.

CHAPTER 27

Halley

AFTER SPENDING the afternoon touring apartments with Whitney and Tara, I paced the common grounds of a nearby complex with my camera in my hands, taking pictures of the vibrant rose bushes and lush landscaping. A little bird's nest was hidden in the foliage, so I crouched down, angled the camera, and snapped a picture that was draped in half-shade and half-muted sunlight. Zooming in closer, I was able to capture a mama bird dropping food into the tiny, wide-open mouths of three baby robins.

A smile gleamed on my lips, and I couldn't wait to process my film at the local art center. It had a public darkroom I'd visited a few times with Scotty, who enjoyed tagging along after coffee and lunch dates to witness my creative side take over. There were so many new photos I was dying to see and relive, my goal being to make a big scrapbook of my life's sweeter moments.

As I straightened in place, a woman wearing an eclectic, multicolored pantsuit exited through the main doors, smiling at me as she passed. "Hey, darlin'. Moving in?"

I smiled back. "Not currently. We're on the hunt for an apartment. My friend and her mom are still inside talking to the leasing agent."

"It would be nice to see some new faces around here," she said, approaching me in the grass and extending a hand. "I'm Monique."

We shook. "Halley."

"Are you a photographer?"

"In-the-making, I guess you could say. But I'd love to make a career out of it."

Nodding, the woman skimmed a hand through her short cropped hair. Amethyst nails and lipstick dazzled against warm dark skin. "I see you've met Annie and the kids."

I blinked, glancing around the empty common area. "Who?"

"Our bird family." She pointed to the nest, her dark-brown eyes glimmering. "Not that I'm trying to scare you off, but they're by far the most likeable residents. They keep to themselves. Zero noise complaints."

A giggle fell out as I glanced at the nest, then back to Monique. "Have you lived here long?"

"Nope. I'm what they call a nomad. I don't stay in one place for more than a few years." She hauled her purse strap over her shoulder. "Gets boring."

"That's understandable."

"Listen, I run the banquet hall off Leming Street. We specialize in weddings and events. I'll give you my card in case you're looking for some work," she told me. "We hire on a few extra photographers during the busy season. Assistant jobs, mostly, but the pay is competitive."

My eyes popped at the invitation, my pulse stuttering. "Really?"

"If you can handle the heat. It's a ruthless line of work, and some prefer to capture the Annies of the world. But if you're open to it, I'd love to bring you in for an interview." Monique reached into her front pocket and pulled out a small rectangular card, handing it to me.

"Thank you," I breathed out, glancing at the cursive lettering. "That's kind of you."

"I'm a peach when I want to be. But peaches go sour, and you don't want to be standing in the line of fire when Becky the Bride has a meltdown and tries to harass me into a full refund because her wedding flowers weren't the exact shade of blush she envisioned." She snorted a laugh. "I mean, seriously? I've navigated flower markets with military precision, battling unpredictable bloom seasons, only to be taken down by the wrath of a bride who swears the difference between 'blush' and 'bashful' ruined her entire day."

I cringed, biting my lip.

"Anyway, if your cup of tea includes a few shots of whiskey, maybe you'll work out."

Laughing softly, I bobbed my head, sliding the card into my back pocket. "Honestly, I've made it through worse things," I assured her.

"Yeah." Her soulful eyes gave me a full sweep. "Something tells me maybe you have."

We shared another smile before Monique retreated, sending a wave over her shoulder.

"See you around, Halley."

"Bye," I called back, just as Tara bounded down the cement steps with her mother on her heels.

Tara jogged over to me in the grass, a lollipop secured between her teeth and cheek. "This is the one," she said with a squeal.

"Yeah?" My eyes brightened, skipping over to Whitney. "We're getting it?"

"I just paid the security deposit. You move in next month."

"Oh, my God."

"Oh, my *God*," Tara parroted with double the enthusiasm. "I am so ready for this."

We leaped at each other, spinning around in the grass, our hair flying in every direction as Annie fluttered from the nest and soared skyward over the treetops.

An apartment with my best friend.

A potential new job.

A down payment for a junky car stuffed in the top drawer of my nightstand.

Things were falling into place, finally—a rarity in my once dismal, directionless life.

Without a mother's warm embrace, I had Whitney.

Without a sibling to confide in, I had Tara.

As for a real boyfriend to share the triumph...well, that was missing.

So the minute we arrived home, I jumped from the car, raced through the front door, and picked up the phone to call Scotty.

My heart was being held together with taffy and floss, my bones made of parchment paper.

As excited as I was, I wasn't ready.

For any of this.

The following weekend, a boombox blasted from the deck as the scent of smoky barbecue wafted from heated grates, filling the air with summertime magic.

Reed sat slumped in a lounge chair, wearing sunglasses and a faded black baseball cap, a beer bottle dangling between his knees. He was facing my direction as I swept by him, but I couldn't tell if he was looking at me, thanks to the sunglasses. Probably deliberate.

I sent him a smile anyway, just to be nice, just because I smiled at everyone, so it wouldn't have made sense to not smile at him, too.

He fidgeted in place, bringing the nozzle to his lips and downing the rest of the beer, his unoccupied hand twitching against his thigh.

"Want me to get you anything?" I asked him, aimlessly shuffling pasta salad bowls around on the table.

Eyes still shadowed by dark lenses, Reed leaned forward on his elbows. "I'm good."

An inflatable pool was blown up in the backyard, and Tara and a few friends rimmed the edges, cooling off beneath the scorching sun, their squeals and splashes floating to my ears. I glanced over at the group as they kicked puddles at each other.

"You should be over there having fun, not acting as the waitstaff." His tone was acidic, his posture stiff.

I pivoted back to the table to hide my scowl. It was true I'd been running around all day, helping, assisting, cooking, and cleaning. But I enjoyed being useful. Especially when it came to people who didn't get off on using me like my own parents had. Hospitality was my love language.

"Helping makes me happy." Reaching into the fruit bowl, I popped a strawberry into my mouth. The tangy juice sluiced over my tongue as I glanced back at Reed over my shoulder.

He chugged down the rest of the beer in a few swallows and discarded the bottle, attention aimed at the wooden deck planks.

One of Whitney's male co-workers helped man the grill, twirling hotdogs and flipping burgers, his demeanor far less frigid than Reed's. Whitney idled beside him with a wine cooler, their laughter mingling with the music.

Their interactions were flirty.

Part of me wondered if that was why Reed was in a mood. Maybe it had nothing to do with me and everything to do with his ex-girlfriend and some guy making eyes at each other.

"I'm going to restock the cooler," I muttered to Whitney as I whooshed past her, swiping my hands down the light cottony fabric of my sundress.

She nodded with a smile before returning her attention to her friend.

I slipped inside to grab more refreshments, closing the sliding door behind me and stifling the sounds of The Offspring. My lavender dress kissed my knees and my hair sat high on my head, coiled into a messy bun that bobbed with every barefooted step across the hardwood floors.

Tara's family always hosted a summer barbeque, and there was even more to celebrate than usual this year—we'd officially started packing, weeks away from moving into our new apartment. It was a slow-going process as we picked out new furniture and stowed away beloved knick-knacks into bins and boxes, but excitement was starting to claw its way through my apprehension.

And as the days drifted by and summer trickled on, I wondered how this new chapter would unfold. My feelings for Reed hadn't lessened, not even a little. We'd managed to sneak away for a handful of private rendezvous that carved out new holes in my heart, leaving me hollow.

Every kiss was full of passion, yet over far too soon.

Sex was rough, abrupt, and urgent.

Reed hardly ever made eye contact. Never held me through the aftermath, or whispered pretty words into my ear. I was starting to wonder how much longer I could withstand our "arrangement."

I glanced around the quiet house, humming under my breath as I made a pit stop to the bathroom first.

Washing my hands and readjusting my hair in the mirror, I noted that my summerlong sunburn had faded into a warm shade of bronze, making my eyes look lighter. My skin still gleamed with suntan lotion, and a smattering of freckles were sprinkled across the bridge of my nose and cheekbones. A smile tilted my lips as I gave myself a final onceover, dried my hands, then pulled open the door to head into the kitchen.

But my retreat was compromised when Reed barged inside the bathroom, shut and locked the door behind him, and proceeded to haul me up onto the sink counter before I could intake a breath.

"Reed—"

His mouth crashed to mine, and my legs instinctively linked around his hips.

Our tongues slashed together, filling each other's mouths; hot, wet, desperate.

"Comet," he murmured huskily, dragging his lips down my jaw and nipping my throat. "You're killing me in this dress."

I gasped when his hand disappeared up my sundress and yanked my underwear to the side. "We – we shouldn't...oh, God..." Two fingers plunged inside me as I collapsed back against the mirror and spread my legs wider. My moan filled the small space, and his palm shot up to cover my mouth, muffling my cries, his other hand still pumping deep and hard.

"Need to watch you come," he rasped out, replacing the hand over my mouth with his tongue.

He tasted like citrus beer, and I wondered if he was buzzed. Reed was always careful when we were at the house; this was anything but careful. His kisses were clumsier, his balance teetering, and he didn't seem to mind that his family's laughter was seeping through the thin walls.

I wrapped my arms around his neck as my pelvis jutted off the counter, his thumb rubbing and teasing my clit, the slippery sounds of my arousal weaving him into a frenzy. His baseball cap slipped off his head when my hands sank into his hair and squeezed the strands, while the scent of barbeque smoke and amber musk assaulted my senses.

"Goddamn," he breathed against my mouth, pressing our foreheads together. "The things you do to me."

His eyes were fixed on mine, the intimate contact ballooning my heart. With two fingers still buried inside, curling and stretching me, I felt the coil of need unravel.

"You smell like coconuts and summertime." He dragged his nose against mine and inhaled sharply, his eyelids fluttering. Inserting a third finger and thrusting hard, he continued to rub my clit, drawing me closer to the edge. "You have no idea how hard it is to be in the same room as you and not touch you, hold your hand, tell everyone you're mine."

Yes.

This was what I needed, wanted, craved.

These words, this passion emanating off of him in volatile waves.

I bowed my back, arching into his touch as his body pressed forward, draping me in warmth, our foreheads colliding back together.

"Reed..." I bucked against his hand as starbursts rocketed through me, blurring my vision and heating my skin. Detonating into shimmering fragments, I tried desperately to keep the scratchy cry lodged in my throat.

"That's my girl." He looked utterly transfixed as he massaged my clit, and I rode out the waves. "I love watching you come apart. So beautiful."

Reed flung open his belt and unhooked his jeans, and I mewled with need, reaching to tug down his pants and boxers until his erection bobbed free. My hand gripped him and stroked hard, causing his brows to pinch, his mouth drooping open as a soft groan rumbled in his throat.

"Every moment with you fucking hurts." His voice was pure grit, words cracking and breaking. "Every moment *without* you...hurts so much more."

"You have me, Reed. Take me."

My cheeks were flaming with desire, my eyes misting with love.

I wanted him to see me right here, right now, spread before him like a treasure. I wanted him to keep me as one. As his favorite.

As his only.

Forever.

He slid my underwear down my thighs until it dangled off my ankle, and then he lifted me higher and pushed forward, the thick crown of his cock slipping inside me. My head dropped back against the mirror before he cupped it in the palm of his hand and pulled my face to his.

Tenderly.

Lovingly.

Our mouths hovered, a centimeter apart, his warm breath pluming against my parted lips.

He held my gaze as he pushed all the way inside, gripping me beneath the thighs as I squirmed and adjusted to his girth. My spaghetti straps dipped off my shoulders, the swell of my breasts bouncing as he started thrusting, in and out, slow and steady.

A dense cloud formed around us. A beautiful haze of wrong and right, nothing and everything, could be, wouldn't be, shouldn't be.

Is.

My eyes were locked on his, unmoving, unblinking, as currents churned between us.

His hand journeyed up to grip my throat like a delicate claim as he pumped into me, and I tried in vain to rid myself of this lovelorn affliction. But he was in my bones, in my blood, and there was nothing I could say or do to carve him out of all of my essential pieces.

I would die with him a part of me.

Sound drowned out as we remained secured in our flimsy bubble. He never looked away. Never faltered, never broke contact. He was with me.

Even as he released, his body tensing up and legs shaking, Reed kept our eyes locked together and offered me another part of himself that made everything so much harder.

It was harder because now I had even more to lose.

We stayed connected for a few more restless heartbeats, panting against each other's mouth. His hand lifted to cup my cheek, his thumb dusting over my jaw.

I stared at him, awestruck, dumbstruck, lovestruck.

Stricken and skewered in every way.

Then a feeling mauled through my chest and up my windpipe, turning tangible the moment my words leaked out.

"I love you," I whispered.

Reed tensed, slow-blinking at me, my confession seeping inside him like sludge. His gaze skimmed my face as he drank in those three destructive words, one by one, swallowing them down, until their sweetness turned sour and poisoned the moment.

I watched his features collapse, his hooded eyes losing a little of their light.

I shouldn't have said it.

I shouldn't have handed him my heart right here on this goddamn bathroom sink.

Reaching for him, I tried to pull him back into our magical bubble, but the bubble had popped, and he was gone.

I'd already lost him.

Reed pulled out of me and lowered his head, yanking his boxers and jeans back up and methodically relatching his belt. My eyes snapped closed, and I cursed my stupid tongue for reminding him of everything that would never come to be.

"I'm sorry," I said, my jaw clenching through the threatening tears.

He scrubbed a hand over his face, top to bottom. "Don't apologize. I shouldn't have..." Releasing a long sigh, he swallowed hard and shook his head as his eyes danced away from me. "I should go."

All I could do was nod through the heartbreak.

Reed hesitated for another beat before stalking forward and tugging my face to his with one hand curling around the nape of my neck.

He kissed me. No tongue but all fire. Our mouths lingered as his other hand fumbled for something in his back pocket then swept across my hip.

When he pulled back, he didn't spare me another glance before plucking his hat off the floor, opening the door, and slipping out into the hall.

I sat idle on the sink.

Breathless, boneless.

A quiet hum filled the bathroom, replacing the echoes of our kisses and moans. We were running out of time while running in circles, and the air around me was thinning, the niggling of hope slowly draining away.

I hopped off the counter and splashed cool water on my face, then yanked my underwear back up and readjusted my dress, keeping the emotions at bay.

But something tugged at me.

Blinking at my reflection, I slid my hand into the pocket of my dress and sifted around inside. My heart galloped, skipped. Silken petals tickled my fingertips as I removed my hand and outstretched my fingers, peering down at my open-faced palm.

A stem of blue morning glories.

CHAPTER 28

Reed

I BRAVED a family dinner at the house the following week, after running out of excuses to decline. We were all adults. I could pretend my kisses with Halley had never happened, and our limb-tangled rendezvous had never happened, and that her whimpers and moans weren't an erotic soundtrack to every internal thought that swept through my mind, even though they were seared on my soul with a hot-iron brand.

It was only a few hours.

I could pretend.

But it was damn hard to pretend I was immune to the way my blood heated with possessiveness and nauseating jealousy when I discovered Scotty seated at the dining room table next to Halley, his shoulder pressed to hers, his enamored eyes on her flushed profile as she sipped a glass of water.

I sat across from her. Tried desperately to avoid her glassy-eyed glances and soft laughter that seeped into all of my vulnerable pockets. I tuned out their conversation, ignored his arm slung around her, and blocked out every sound, movement, and stolen look, until everything around me turned to static.

Only when Tara jabbed her elbow into my ribs, did I tear through my self-built bubble and plaster a smile on my face. "What was that?"

"How much wine have you had?" she griped.

I looked at my glass. It was empty, but I didn't remember taking a single sip.

Not enough.

"Just a glass. Sorry, work is on the brain."

Whitney sat at the end of the table, sipping her own glass of Merlot. "Tara was just telling us about her first client."

"Client?" I blinked at my daughter, feeling terrible for zoning out.

She beamed with pride. "My friend Chrissy is a bridesmaid in her sister's wedding. She hired me to do her hair and makeup. Fifty bucks."

"A paid fucking gig?"

"Reed." Whitney shot me a warning glare. "Plenty of adjective alternatives."

I didn't care. I was fucking proud. "That's incredible, Squirt. I'm fucking proud."

"*Reed,*" Whitney scolded.

Tara and Halley both laughed before Tara continued. "Yep. And Halley's getting paid, too. She's photographing the wedding."

My head twisted toward Halley who was gulping down the glass of ice water, her skin turning pink. "Yeah?" Then I cleared my throat, worried the word had fallen out too soft, too intimate. "That's awesome, Comet. Proud of you both."

A beat of silence washed over the table, and it took several more stretched-out beats for me to realize why. I looked at Tara, catching her furrowed brow of confusion while feeling Whit's eyes on me from the other end of the table.

"Comet?" Tara scrunched up her nose.

Shit.

Fucking-shit-fuck.

I did everything in my power to prevent myself from choking on nothing.

"Uh...yeah. Like Halley's Comet," I said, playing it off the best I could. On the inside, my ribcage was trying to smother me. "You're Squirt, and she's Comet."

"Gotcha." Tara bobbed her head, accepting the answer.

Halley sunk lower in her chair, her cheeks staining with more color as she avoided eye contact with me and stared down at her hand clasped around the glass.

"Huh. Cute." Whitney honed in on her wine as she swirled it in aimless circles. "So, Halley, are you and Scotty officially together?"

I fidgeted in my seat and scratched the back of my neck, cursing the idiotic slip. Tara was oblivious, but I knew Whit's tells. I was going to be interrogated, and the anxiety was nibbling away at my sanity. Wishing I could zap more wine into my empty glass with mind voodoo and desperation, I glanced across the table at Halley as she latched onto the redirection.

I was also pathetically eager to hear her response.

"Um, nothing too serious." Her eyes shimmered with apology as she peered over at Scotty. "We're just having fun."

Scotty's smile was flat and lifeless. It was no secret that he was smitten with the woman beside him, and that hurt. Scotty was a good kid—one of the best—and he didn't deserve to be the third wheel in our triangle of tragedy. Every session we had together, her name came up. Every time her name came up, he couldn't shake the grin, or fake indifference.

He'd told me he'd invited her to the east coast with him and offered her the extra room in his apartment, and all I'd been able to do was smile pleasantly as my heart teetered on a gravel ledge.

Guilt tackled me from every direction.

Clearing his throat, Scotty skimmed his fingers up Halley's arm and stretched a hard-fought smile. "Yeah, we're taking it slow," he said. "Nice guys might finish last, but I like to think the wait is worth it."

The wink he sent her made her blush, and my chest fizzed with anxious heat. Stupid, unjustified jealousy, paired with shame. I felt trapped. Four walls on all sides of me, closing me in, filling with water. The edging suffocation smothered reason as I slumped back in the chair and rubbed my forehead.

"Well, you're welcome over any time," Whitney continued, her attention shared between Scotty, Halley, and my own unraveling. "It's great to see Halley making new connections."

"She's strong. A fighter. Watching her train was inspiring."

"I can imagine." Whit slowly panned her eyes over to me and that's where they settled, her smile tight. "Why did you two stop training again?"

I tapped my foot under the table and folded my arms. "I just thought—"

"It was my call," Halley interrupted, noting my fidgeting. "I really wanted to focus on school and graduating with high grades. Mr. Madsen taught me a lot, and I felt like he'd given me all the tools and lessons I needed."

Mr. Madsen.

And here I was worried that Halley might slip up, might look at me too long or say the wrong thing. But she was convincing, giving no indication that my dick had been inside of her last night and that I'd spent the better part of two years doing everything in my power to keep her out of my bed.

Only to fail miserably.

Halley had dropped by the studio yesterday after my evening training session, and then I'd fucked her in the workout room beneath the resistance bands. I was weak. Powerless. A victim to this unbreakable draw.

Before she'd left, Halley had handed me a photograph—the one I'd taken last month of her grinning ear-to-ear, her naked limbs tangled in my silvery bed sheets. There was no question of where she'd been or who she'd been with. And her flushed cheeks and sex-mussed hair portrayed exactly what we'd been doing.

I'd tossed it the moment I'd gotten home, burying it in my garbage can.

The risk was too high, the evidence too damning.

Whitney nodded, taking a small sip of wine as she mulled over Halley's response. "That makes sense. I'm glad it all worked out."

"It was a great experience."

Conversation trickled on, veering from elaborate summer plans, to one of Whit's social work cases. I did my best to follow along, to smile and react at all the appropriate times, but dark clouds manifested in my gut, spewing cold rain all over my insides. I needed shelter, but everywhere I turned another stormfront rolled in, shading my world in gray.

As the girls cleared off the table twenty minutes later, Whitney signaled me into the kitchen. "Help me with the dishes?"

My throat closed up as oxygen dwindled, and I was certain that if I attempted a verbal response, I'd sound like I just inhaled a gallon of helium.

Halley interjected. "I can do it."

"No. Enjoy dessert with Tara and Scotty," she said. "I made cherry pie."

I caught Halley's eyes for a heavy beat before pushing out my chair and sauntering into the kitchen like a pint-sized deviant on the brink of scolding.

Joining Whitney at the sink, I moved in beside her to help her dry off dishes as she rinsed them under the faucet with soap and a sponge. She sent me a sidelong glance while I stacked dinner plates into a pile and reached for another.

"I'd say dinner was a success," she stated, looking back down into the dish bath. "The girls are happy. Scotty is a great guy."

"Yeah." I nodded, pretending to be immersed in my task while awaiting my sentencing.

Laughter sprinkled into the kitchen. I pivoted around to see Halley taking pictures of Ladybug running circles around her feet as the dog clutched a hambone in her mouth. Scotty tried to pry the bone away, but Ladybug held tight, her butt swishing furiously from side to side.

Whitney made a humming noise beside me, twisting off the faucet and shaking water droplets from her hands. She leaned forward on the sink, eyes aimed downward. "Comet?"

Icicles bucketed down on me.

I knew what she was hinting at because I wasn't an idiot.

Or, maybe I was, but I was an observant idiot.

"It's just a nickname," I said, lowering my voice.

"Are you sure?"

"What does that mean?"

Her throat rolled through a tight swallow. "Nothing." Blinking rapidly, she swiveled back around to the sink. "Forget it."

I reached for a dishrag and dried my hands, the mood thick with unsaid words and tension that teased the brink of imminent destruction. It wasn't the time or place for this conversation, with our daughter and Halley a few feet away, but I wanted to know what was going through her mind. I needed to assess impending damage control and debate my next move.

Pressing forward on my hands, I stole a glance at her profile. Her doe-like features were pinched, freckles wrinkled with all the things she was too scared to ask me. "Tell me what you're thinking."

She huffed. "That's never ended well."

"Whit."

Rolling her tongue across her teeth, she dipped her head. "All that time training together," she said softly, warily. "And then that reckless, impulsive assault on her father that I'm still scratching my head over. Now, a nickname?" Cautiously, she canted her head toward me until our eyes locked. "Tell me nothing is going on there, Reed."

Needle-pointed guilt stabbed at me, and there was a part of me that would rather die a liar than whatever the hell the truth would make me.

But I had to find the balance.

I couldn't give her the whole ugly truth, but it wasn't in my nature to tell a bold-faced lie.

I set a plate down and turned around, leaning back against the counter and crossing my arms. Whitney was watching me, her chestnut eyes trying to unravel my threads, until a clearer picture was revealed. "Listen," I began gently. "We did develop a bond during training. Of course we did. Those sessions are built upon a strong level of trust, so it's impossible not to draw connection out of that. I care about Halley. It's remarkable what she's survived and what she's capable of becoming."

Her slender throat worked through another swallow as she continued to read me. "So, she's like a daughter to you?"

My heartbeats sputtered, shredded tires on ice. She was trying to decipher the exact nature of the connection we shared, while desperately wanting to believe it was familial. But I couldn't shove her in that direction. Morally, I couldn't allow her to think our relationship was rooted in a father-daughter dynamic. "No," I admitted. "It's about respect. I respect her as a woman, a fighter, and a survivor."

Whitney ran a hand through her hair, analyzing my words, studying me for a long bated breath before slowly blowing it out. Whatever expression I'd managed to school my face into seemed to have worked. And it was all true.

"Okay." She scratched her collarbone, fidgeting in place. "Sorry for the inquisition."

"You don't need to apologize. You care about Halley, and I'll never villainize you for making her best interest a priority."

I would do the same.

I will do the same.

"I do care about her. I've witnessed a lot. I've heard her crying into Ladybug's fur when she thinks no one is listening. I've seen the fear in her eyes when there's a knock at the front door, or when the phone rings, or when I drop something and she nearly hits the ceiling. There's been long talks where she spills her heart to me and I take her in my arms and promise her she's going to be okay." Her eyes watered, glinting underneath the kitchen lights. "I just want the best for her. The world has been so cruel."

"I want that, too." Sighing deeply, I slung one arm around her shoulders and pulled her to me. Whitney stiffened for a beat, caught off guard by the hug, until she relaxed against me and breathed a soft exhale against my chest. "You're doing an incredible job. Those girls have all the tools to create beautiful, fulfilling lives, and that's because of you. I hope you know that."

She nodded. "Thank you."

A presence moved in behind me and my skin tingled with familiarity. Letting go of Whit, I turned around to find Halley reaching into the refrigerator for whipped cream. She didn't look at me right away, didn't acknowledge either of us. Not at first.

But then her gaze flicked up, for just a millisecond; for the span of half a breath. Our eyes caught, and it felt as though we were breathing a thousand wayward breaths. Each one suffocating. Each one void of oxygen. The back of my neck heated, my fists clenched, and whatever piss-poor version of truth I'd led Whitney to believe only a moment ago dissolved into ashes.

Shutting the fridge door, Halley darted her gaze away from me, her posture stiff like a board, then whirled back around and flitted out of the kitchen, returning to the table.

I cupped my jaw.

A heavy, grating moment slugged by as I waited, my back to Whitney.

I just waited.

Whitney moved around me and pressed her hand to my forearm. She didn't look at me, and I didn't look at her, and there was nothing I could do but wait for her words to slice me down.

"I need you to think long and hard about whatever it is you're doing," she said, her tone low and leveling. "Or about to do."

Swallowing, I twisted to face her, everything I was so desperate to hide shining back at her within the guilty glimmer of my eyes. Despite my efforts to shield myself, Whitney's words cut through the bullshit, exposing the raw truth I couldn't seem to bury. "Whit..."

"Don't, Reed." She shook her head, telling me she already knew. She didn't know everything, but she knew something. "You're a grown man, and she's an adult. It's not my place to tell you what to do. But it *is* my place to protect our daughter."

My breath hitched. "I would never hurt Tara."

Her eyes flashed as she chewed on her lip. "You'd be surprised how easily good intentions can turn rotten. Every single one of us is capable of hurting the people we love most." Emotion infected her words as she inhaled sharply. "Trust me. I know."

I didn't get a chance to respond before she whooshed past me into the dining room, joining the rest of the group at the table with a force-fed smile on her face. "How's the pie?"

Fuck. Me.

I needed to break this tether.

This bind.

Whitney wasn't ignorant to it, no matter how hard I tried to reroute things in a more savory direction. She'd soon discover the full extent of my depraved truth, and then it would only be a matter of time before Tara did, too.

I couldn't let that happen.

My daughter was my foundation. With every misstep and heavy-footed stumble, I was making cracks. And if I didn't start patching these holes, she'd slip right through.

We all would.

CHAPTER 29

Halley

I STEPPED through the main door of Reed's studio later that week, greeted by the sound of feet hitting the mat. Energy swirled around me as grunts and kicks echoed off the walls and a pop song poured from a nearby boombox. It was late June, almost two years to the date since I'd first laid eyes on Reed Madsen.

He didn't look the same as he did that night. The creases around his eyes were slightly more prominent, and the color of his jade irises had darkened some. He was even more built now than he was then, a wall of muscle and strength. A wall, in general. Too sound and too well-constructed to break through. Shadows followed him around these days, and sometimes I wondered if they had left me for him. Maybe they'd grown bored with me. Tired and uninspired by my tedious gloom.

I quietly closed the door behind me as I watched him train with a middle-aged woman with hair spun with light-amber frizz. Beads of sweat rolled down her cheeks and nose like they were playing connect the dots with her freckles. I observed the sparring session with equal parts melancholy and nostalgia. While I missed training with Reed, I didn't miss the debilitating feeling that came along with our dodges and blows.

Reed's eyes flicked my way, the image of me taking a seat along the wall catching him off guard for a moment, long enough for the woman to aim a hairline strike that had him teetering back.

She squealed with victory, her gloved hands shooting toward the ceiling, unknowing that I'd been the one to distract him.

You're welcome, lady.

A few more minutes passed before Reed turned off the music and plucked off his gloves. "Nice job, Sandra. Same time next week?"

"Thanks, Coach. I'll be running a few minutes late, but I'll be here."

"Sounds good."

I nibbled my thumbnail and zoned out on my chipped red polish. Scotty had told me that Reed wanted to see me tonight. Wanted to talk to me about something. I wasn't sure what that something was, but curiosity had me trudging through a blanket of humidity as I'd jogged the mile over. Sweat still clung to every inch of me, so I billowed the tank top off my stomach to let my skin breathe.

Poor Scotty.

He'd become our middleman since Reed wasn't able to call the house or show up at the front door to request a private meeting with me. That would only prompt questions, and questions would incite answers we couldn't give.

Scotty had choked down his pain, still treating me with kindness and friendship. It was almost like he was patiently waiting for whatever this was to peter out so I'd look at him in the same way he looked at me.

In the same way I looked at Reed.

Reed chugged down a bottle of water as the woman gathered her purse, sent me a bright smile, then disappeared out the entrance. The sound of the door clapping shut was like a metaphorical door closing on my fantastical daydreams.

There was a dark, solemn look in his eyes that had anxiety swirling in my gut.

Is this it?

Was he going to point a pistol at my chest and pull the trigger?

I bit my lip as he stared across the room at me. "Hey," I greeted, my voice already strewn with bullet holes.

"Hey." Capping the water bottle, he set it down beside him and flipped off a few of the lights, until only a dim glow bathed the room. "Thanks for meeting with me."

"So formal." I chuckled, not knowing what else to say or do. Folding my arms, I sauntered over to him. We met in the middle of the studio, and I kicked off my sneakers, toeing them aside and stepping onto the mat. "What did you want to talk about?"

"You. Us."

My face flamed with premature heartbreak. "I figured as much."

He wore a mask.

Stony eyes stared back at me as if he'd doused himself in concrete, and I couldn't tell what he was thinking or feeling. I couldn't read him. Even a scalpel wouldn't chip away the veil.

"Listen, Halley," he continued, planting his hands on his hips. Dark hair glinted under the lone light, still damp with sweat. "This is hard, so I want to make this quick."

I swallowed, the anxiety growing toothed wings. "Quick?"

A drumbeat pounded between us.

A sharp inhale.

And then...

"I'm moving back to Charleston."

I blanched.

My lungs shriveled up, and my heart slammed to a full stop so long I feared it would never rev back to life. It felt like he'd taken his wet concrete and poured it all over me until I was sealed up tight, buried alive, and gasping for breath.

"What?" I whispered.

"It's for the best."

"For whom?"

He didn't even blink. "For all of us."

My arms hung defeatedly at my sides as I broke our stare and gazed at the sterile wall behind him. Shock infected me. I wasn't emotionless, but I was frozen. There was no argument I could throw back at him, because every logical part of me knew this wasn't going anywhere.

It was smart for him to leave before we dug ourselves two side-by-side graves.

And yet the tears still came in the form of hot, fiery pressure scorching my eyes. "I don't know what to say."

Reed exhaled through his nose, nostrils flaring. The only sign that he was marginally affected by this. "There's nothing to say. It's done. I'm staying with a friend while I get back on my feet. I'll be in charge of the studio again, training Scotty as an assistant coach."

"Does Tara know?" I croaked out. "Whitney?"

He shook his head. "Not yet."

"Are you sure this is the right move? I just mean...you've been building your life here. You have a career, a family—"

"I'm sure."

My fingers curled into fists as a wave of devastation rippled through me. Tears stung and clawed, neon heat blurring my vision as panic pierced my chest, bending my ribs in half. "No." My head swung side to side. "No, I'll go. This is silly. You can't just uproot your life when I'm the lifeless one. I have nothing keeping me here. No real home, no purpose." Warm salt trickled down my cheeks as my lips quivered. "Please...let *me* go."

Finally, gradually, his face twisted with something other than cool indifference. Pain leaked through, shimmering in his eyes, creasing his forehead and brows. Reed took a step toward me and cupped my wet cheeks in his hands. "I am letting you go, Comet."

The dam broke inside me.

Breakage tore up my stomach and weaved a splintered labyrinth up my chest until it bulldozed through my lungs and throat. A war cry flew past my lips, agony fused with anger, as I fisted the front of his faded-navy tank, unsure if I wanted to pull him closer or shove him out of my pinwheeling orbit.

"Halley." Pressing a kiss to my forehead, his lips lingered, parting through a shaky exhale. "I'm sorry. This is just the way it needs to be."

No.

Lies.

This wasn't the way; it wasn't the way at all.

Anger won out, and I shoved him away from me. "This is your solution?" I demanded, vibrating with feeling. All feeling, every feeling. "You're just...leaving?"

He linked his hands behind his head and closed his eyes. "I have to."

"You don't *have* to. You're taking the easy way out."

Two molten-green eyes pinged back open, flaring with what looked like fury. He stepped forward again, his face inches from mine. "The easy way out?" His tone was as deadly as his stare.

I cowered back but tipped my chin. "Yes."

A slow nod was his reply as he simmered and churned in my response, glancing down at the blue mat like a prelude to more words that would butcher me into mincemeat.

But he said nothing.

My brows furrowed, and I crossed my arms defensively. "Whatever you're thinking, just say it."

He turned away, his hands still interlocked behind his head as every muscle in his back rippled with tension.

"Say it, Reed. Tell me what's on your mind. Please, enlighten me." I was instigating him, poking and prodding, but this hurricane of rage was far easier to digest than the chasm of grief threatening to swallow me. "Tell me why you think running away from your problems is better than facing—"

"Because you've fucked me all up inside!" He whirled back around, both hands sliding into his hair and fisting hard. "Do you realize that? One little lie, and you opened up a doorway to hell. You allowed me to let my guard down, to let this goddamn connection seep in, and now I can't shake it. I can't shake *you*. If I had known your real age, I would've walked away the second you told me. You fucking *cursed* me, Halley."

The tears kept welling, kept falling down my cheeks in trails of vulnerability. "So, this is my fault?" I shot forward, my fingers bruising my biceps to keep my hands from reaching for him. "This isn't all on me. You're being weak."

One eyebrow flicked up, as if daring me to say that again. "I'd rather be weak than *wrecked*," he ground out. "And that's exactly what's going to happen if we take this any further. We'll all be fucking wrecked."

"You don't know that."

"I do know that. You're dead wrong if you think you can't destroy me with a single look," he rasped. "That's why I need to go. I need to put distance between us. Thousands of miles of it, before I ruin both of our lives." Heaving in a deep breath, he pressed his hands together like a prayer and leaned forward, trying to talk reason through the madness. "Tell me what you think is going to happen if we keep doing this. If Tara finds out. Tell me what's going through that pretty little head of yours, because I can assure you, it's not what's going through mine."

"I...I don't know," I answered helplessly. "Maybe you're underestimating her. Maybe she'll be fine."

"I know my daughter. Nothing about this will ever be *fine*."

"Maybe it will be. Maybe—"

"You. Are. My. Daughter's. Age." He jabbed a finger in my face like an exclamation point to every word. "I'm sick for even thinking about you like this. It's twisted. It's fucked. And I'm completely helpless when I'm around you. Tara is going to be blindsided. She'll look at you like a traitor instead of friend. Is that what you want? To destroy the one person who took you in—who sees you as a *sister*—who gave you friendship and love and loyalty when you had nothing?"

I gouged the heels of my palms into my eyes and shook my head. "I don't want to hurt her," I sobbed. "But I don't want to *hurt*. And this hurts. So much."

"I know," he said, tone softening. "But it'll hurt a hell of a lot more if I don't leave. Tara is my little girl, and I know in my heart she would forgive me one day, but I don't think she'd *ever* look at you the same. And that's not something I can live with."

"Reed..."

"Halley, please, try to see the bigger picture here. You need to see this for what it is and not for what you desperately want it to be." Stepping closer and sounding broken, he finished with, "I told you I would always fight for you, and I meant that. This is how I'm doing it."

I choked out another sob and lowered my hands from my eyes, gazing up at him with all the bare-boned truth I could muster. "I love you," I confessed painfully. "You can't pull me from rock bottom and then send me right back."

My heart was a splattered mess between us, the love inside of it spitting and snarling for one last beat. He could scoop it up in his palms, mold it into something beautiful, something better, and return it to the bleeding cavern inside my chest.

Or he could stomp it out.

Snuff the flickering of life out of it with just one look, one word, one step in the opposite direction.

Reed's eyes slowly closed as he drew in a long breath, like he was debating what to do with the most precious piece of me. "Halley, this is infatuation. This is the thrill of sneaking around with an off-limits man who is twice your age."

Goodbye, Heart.

His words chewed through me, acid corroding flesh. A dagger with dull blades sawing through my bones. I wrapped both arms around my stomach as if that could keep my pain tucked inside. "How dare you say that to me," I gritted out, teeth grinding against metal.

"It's the truth."

"That's *your* truth. It's not mine."

"It's the only truth."

"No." I glared those dull daggers right back at him. "How dare you rearrange my feelings into something that makes you feel better about walking away. How dare you talk to me like I'm a child—like I'm a lost, pathetic little girl who doesn't have the mental capacity to know what she wants. How dare you make me feel these things and then twist them into something dirty. You made me finally *feel* something, Reed, something other than this godforsaken pit of worthlessness and loneliness, and now you're—"

Reed snatched me by the biceps and spun me around, walking me backward until I was pushed up against the cushioned wall and his face was centimeters from mine. Trailing his hands up my arms, he gently cupped my cheeks, tenderizing the hard steel I was molding around us. "I feel those things, too," he said, chest heaving, voice hitching. "I feel it, Comet. I do. But it's not what you think." His forehead fell to mine as he sucked in a fraught breath. "It's a goddamn death sentence."

Anger battled it out with treacherous pain. I knew he was right, but it was too easy to be hateful and bitter when my heart had become nothing more than rubble clogging my ribcage.

Mascara-laced tears streaked down my cheeks as I shoved him away from me. "Fine. Go."

He palmed his hair back, slick with sweat from exertion and heartache. "Don't make this harder."

"Don't tell me how I'm supposed to respond to the things *you're* setting in motion."

"I never wanted it to go this far. I never wanted to hurt you."

"Well, you failed." My shield went up, my weapon drawn. I was mad. So irrevocably mad. "You just had to be so perfect. My white knight. My rescuer. You had to be everything I've dreamed about, every wish I've made on falling stars and birthday candles and pennies in mall fountains, and you had to make me fall in love with you." Words spilled out of me, assaulting him like an ambush. "How could I not? It was so damn easy. You made it easy."

His brow was wrinkled, features taut and brimming with tension. "Nothing about this is easy."

"Falling for you has been the easiest thing I've ever done," I confessed through the anguish. "Everything else? Painful. Torturous. Difficult beyond belief. But loving you..." The anger died out, flatlining to a dead pulse. "Effortless."

Tears rimmed his eyes, his emerald irises glowing with heartbreak as he drank in my pain and let it funnel through him. Stepping forward, he tried to reach for me again, but I dodged him. There was no comfort here.

No more soft-landings.

"Don't," I said, moving backward. "I can't."

"Halley—"

"Just go. Leave. Pretend none of this ever happened and toss me away, just like my parents did, just like—"

"Whitney knows."

My words clipped off, nosediving off a craggy bluff.

I gaped at him, eyes rounding with shock.

Whitney. Knows.

"What?" I swallowed. "How?"

"Because she's observant. Because we haven't been as careful as you think. Because she knows me better than anyone and has had a front-row seat to our relationship for the past two years." Reed squeezed the back of his neck, staring down at the floor. "Pick one."

Ice filtered through my veins, freezing my hostility. Fear leaked through—fear that my love for one man had ultimately derailed the only other love in my life. "Oh, God...I-I didn't know."

"Now you do. That's why I'm leaving. Tara is going to find out, and I can't let that happen. I can't do that to her." He inhaled a cracked breath and shook his head with defeat. "I can't do that to you."

His words slowly trickled through me.

A clearer picture formed.

With it came a new image of Reed—not as a villain or a coward—but as the man he promised me he'd be. The fighter. The warrior.

"You deserve to have someone in your corner, fighting like hell for you. For your honor, your worth. I want to be that person. I'll be that guy... even if that's all I'll ever be."

This was his way.

This was the *only* way.

While pieces fell into place, other pieces broke into tiny fragments. All of my stupid hopes and daydreams shattered at my feet.

Reed was a realist. He knew there was only one way out of this, and that was him putting true distance between us. Miles of it. States, borders, highways, and mountains.

We weren't done. Our story wasn't over, and yet "The End" was stamped in black ink across the pages. I knew it was for the best, but the best didn't always feel better.

We would forever be a half-written song.

Finally, ruefully, I nodded my surrender. If he was going to be strong, then I'd be strong, too. I would prove my father wrong and do this really hard thing with my back against the wall, my knees shaking and buckling, and my heart in splintered tatters.

I can do this.

"Okay," I told him in two broken-down syllables. "You're right."

He smiled the saddest smile. "I don't want to be right."

"I don't want us to be wrong."

When he reached for me again, I let him. I let him cup my damp cheeks between his palms and press his lips to mine, our kiss infused with salt and pain. Our foreheads touched, our noses grazed, and I said softly, "Are you here to save me?"

Another kiss landed on my hairline, and he lingered there, squeezing me tighter, exhaling ragged breaths against my skin. "You never needed saving, Halley. You were never lost."

"I was," I cried. "I was lost when you found me, and I'll be lost when you leave me."

"No." He kissed my forehead, my tear-tipped lashes, my quivering upper lip. "You were searching for something you already had."

As his hand splayed across my chest—my *heart*—I collapsed into a heap of devastation against him, burying my face into the crook of his neck and wishing I would never have to leave the solace of his arms.

It was fascinating the way human beings tended to living things; how we could nurture something so fiercely, all while knowing it was going to die. Just a little more water, we'd say. Better sunlight. A silent wish for a few more good days. But it didn't matter. Every hearty, thriving thing carried with it the certainty of an expiration date.

Nothing lived forever.

Even love.

And still, we allowed it to bloom. We breathed life into it, while simultaneously whispering our last goodbye.

Some goodbyes just came far too soon.

CHAPTER 30

Halley

OUTSIDE THE WINDOW, through vertical blinds, all the ink slowly leaked from the sky as the sun began to rise, turning it cerulean blue. Tara and I lay sprawled together in our new queen-size bed that her mother had purchased for us, staring up at a galaxy of glow-in-the-dark stars on the ceiling. Per Tara, nobody ever grew too old for glow-in-the-dark ceiling stars.

We hadn't slept; we'd stayed up all night, talking, reminiscing, laughing through tears.

After tumbling through the front door for our first full night of sleep at the new apartment, we'd made a chef-worthy dinner of Spaghetti-O's and double-chocolate ice cream sundaes, then jumped on the bed, screaming the lyrics to every song on the *Jagged Little Pill* CD in our pajamas, while glueing constellation stickers to the popcorn ceiling.

It had been a good night.

Memorable, innocent, carefree. The calm before the storm.

And maybe that was why I hadn't slept, couldn't compel my eyes to close for longer than a few fretful heartbeats. I was savoring. I was sampling. I was pretending that what was would always be.

While my best friend spoke of the future with bare-boned joy, my ribs splintered with gritty shards of grief. Boxes were half-unpacked, unlike Reed's stacked boxes—filled to the brim, littering his own apartment. A fresh beginning. A tragic end. All at the same time.

And that was a tragedy in of itself.

Tara linked our fingers together as birdsong trickled in through the cracked window on a breeze. "Will you miss him?" she asked softly.

Darkness faded from the sky and jumped ship to my heart. Rudders cracked, masts tore, and waves crested and surged, swallowing my reply.

All I did was squeeze her hand and nod.

Reed was leaving at the end of the month. Three more weeks. The hours ticked down like a splintering thread, unraveling my strength, little by little, while June faded into a stormy July.

Reed had finally broken the news of his departure to Tara and Whitney. It had been a tension-filled evening, and the mood that had washed over the dinner table had turned colder than the uneaten food. Tara had been confused and disappointed by the revelation, while Whitney had said it would be a good change of scenery for him. New ventures, new goals.

All I'd heard was: *a new woman to pursue.*

Surely, she'd been thinking it.

Days later, Tara was still trying to make sense of the sudden bombshell.

"I can't believe he's leaving," Tara continued, the light mood compromised by a topic that hurt more than my decadelong abuse. "It feels so random."

"Maybe there's more to the story."

I shouldn't have said it, shouldn't have put ideas and gnawing whispers in her head. It would only lend itself to answerless questions.

"Like what?" she asked.

"I don't know."

Tara sighed, our two-toned tangle of hair splashed across the cream pillow. "It's weird. Family has always come first for Dad. Unless..." Trailing off, she stuttered out a breath and canted her head toward me. "Do you think it's because of a woman?"

I blinked up at the faux stars and made a billion silent wishes. My heart crumbled, the debris slithering through me and settling in the pit of my stomach. "Maybe."

She let go of my hand and wrenched the covers up to her chin, thinking it over. "I had a feeling he was seeing someone. I figured she was local, but maybe he started something out in Charleston and wants to try again."

Everything inside of me curled and shriveled up, my mouth going dry.

All I could muster was, "Yeah."

Another sigh escaped her, longer, heavier. "I should talk to him before he leaves. See what's going on." Her nose wrinkled with reflection. "Mom thinks it's strictly for work, but I know him better than that. He has a good job here."

I marinated in her words, silent and stiff. More light filtered in through the blinds, bathing us in dawn's first blush. Fatigue washed over me, a consequence of the sleepless night and my restless mind, and I turned onto my side, gazing at her profile across the pillow.

I didn't want her to talk to him about *that*—but there was nothing else I could say. "That's a good idea."

We spent the next hour going through some of the photographs I'd developed, a welcome levity slicing through the sour mood. She flipped through the stack, one after the other, her smile brightening with added color.

There was a picture of Tara with a cheesy grin, a pencil clamped between her teeth. A self-taken photo of both of us making a kissy face at the camera in the front seat of her car. Whitney reading by the fireplace, her lips turned up with wonder. Ladybug on her back in the snow, paws lifted like she was trying to morph into a *T. rex*. Reed and Tara on Prom night, followed by another of them hugging, her glittery curls in motion. I'd taken the camera from Whitney, trying to capture a less-posed moment.

She lingered on that one. "This is a great shot," she said, emotion infecting her voice. "I don't remember you taking it. Dad doesn't like being in pictures."

"That's why I took it." My words were a fusion of nostalgia and melancholy. "No matter what happens, we'll always have these moments. They're more than memories this way. Memories fray and falter, but pictures don't. They just are. You never have to question them."

"Can I keep some of these?"

"Of course."

I made sure to give Reed the photograph of me, blissfully sunny-eyed and lovesick, sprawled out across his bed sheets. A forever memento. No matter what happened between us, he'd always have concrete proof that I was real. That I was once his.

I never wanted to be the memory that frayed or faltered.

Tara stacked the photos beside her on the nightstand, then soon fell asleep while the sun fully rose. I just lay there, stewing in the unknowns of my cloudy, murky future. I couldn't turn my mind off. Couldn't turn the pain off.

Maybe there was no calm before the storm.

There was only the storm, the aftershocks, and our broken bones scattered in its wake.

My smile was as close to beaming as it could be as I pranced out the double doors and into the late-summer sunshine. A camera strap dangled around my neck and a backpack bounced between my shoulder blades. I'd just completed my first training stint at the banquet hall in preparation to help capture a wedding in two weeks.

The day had been filled with excitement as I'd proudly showcased my passion, impressing Monique and the rest of the staff. My knowledge was vast, considering I'd accumulated plenty of hours at libraries, dark-rooms, and photo labs over the past year, eager to intake everything I possibly could. Lighting, camera settings, composition. Exposure, shutter speed, aperture. Every shot required careful consideration and precision, making each photograph a labor of love and craftsmanship.

I took pride in my work, and I was confident it showed.

My new used Camry sat idle in the parking lot, an ugly shade of taupe decorated with rust and old bumper sticker residue. I'd saved every penny from my prior animal hospital job, earning enough for a down payment on the junky vehicle, while also having a little left over to put toward rent. Tara and I had already found a roommate to take the second bedroom.

Things were looking up.

And then *I* looked up—and spotted Tara leaning back against a cherry-red convertible, waving at me across the parking lot.

My smile widened. "Hey," I greeted, approaching her in my sandals and pale-yellow sundress. "What are you doing here? And whose car is that?"

"Josh's." Her eyebrows waggled. "He let me borrow it while I get my brakes fixed, so I'm heading over to Dad's apartment to talk about the move. Want to come with?"

I blinked at her, anxiety curling like a fist around my lungs. "Oh."

This was not a conversation I wanted to be privy to. I'd rather be a fly on the wall. An inconspicuous ant skittering across the carpet, taking in the sights and sounds without being noticed. Witnessing Reed's tall tales and fabrications firsthand, all while knowing I was the reason for his exit, was a torture I wasn't mentally prepared to deal with.

Trying to sway her in a more palatable direction, I gripped both straps of my bookbag. "Are you sure you don't want to go alone? This feels like a private moment."

"No way. You're part of the family," she said, laughing like my statement was outrageous. "Besides, you need to take a ride in this thing. It's lifechanging."

My nose scrunched up, and I scratched at my cheek. "I just think—"

"Come *on*." She snagged me by the wrist and hauled me forward. "I only have these wheels for the day. Let's break some speed limit laws on the way over, then I'll drive you back to get your car."

Out of arguments, I trudged around the front of the convertible and hopped inside the passenger seat, my whole body sagging with surrender. I tossed my items in the back and buckled my belt, glancing at Tara as she revved the engine. Her eyes sparkled with vibrant green flecks. Her glossy lips twitched with anticipation.

And then we were careening out of the parking lot, the wind in our hair, the sun warming our faces, and for a brief moment, I allowed the sweetness to find me.

The open road stretched out before us as Tara flipped on the radio to full-volume and fell back against the seat. *Gangsta's Paradise* blasted through the speakers mid-song, and we both tried to ramble out the lyrics, laughing through our tied tongues and mismatched words. She punched the air with her fist, the motions heightening with each beat. I giggled until my belly ached.

A sense of peace found me, and I realized that maybe there was no calm before the storm...because there was no storm.

There was only an endless summer, ripe with possibilities, unbreakable friendship, and memories of a love story that would forever keep me warm. Every love story served a purpose, but not every purpose was the same. Reed tended to my wounds when I was broken-down and damaged. He molded my fear into strength. He gave me tools, wisdom, and hope for better days.

He found me when I was lost.

Now, only I held the power to chart my own course and find my way back to myself.

I was breathless when we pulled into Reed's apartment complex. Winded from laughter and living. Unbuckling my belt, I jumped out of the car, the smile still glued to my cheeks by each corner of my mouth.

Tara swooped ahead of me, gesturing me forward, and we headed down the familiar hallway to apartment seventeen. I refused to let the burdens of my fear and poor choices hinder my epiphany. All I could do was stand by Tara's side and be her courage, while swallowing down my nerves.

"Dad?" Tara popped the key into the keyhole and pushed open the door. "Dad, it's me. You home?"

Following behind her, I glanced around the near-barren apartment, making sure there was no evidence of me littered on the couch, strewn across the floor, or twisted in the bed sheets. I swallowed, noting Reed was mostly packed. He'd scrubbed me from his space.

"Damn." Tara peeked into the empty rooms. "He must be at the studio."

A sigh of relief fell out as I fiddled with my hair and stared down at my toenails. "Guess so."

"It's weird seeing all these boxes," she said, entering the second bedroom and flipping on the light switch. "Feels so real."

It did feel real.

We felt real.

And now we were quickly becoming nothing more than memories, slipping through my fingers like grains of sand.

I pressed a hand to her bicep and gave her a comforting squeeze. "It'll be okay. He'll come visit us. And it'll be fun to take cross-country road trips and dip our toes in the ocean."

She nodded. "I suppose he could've picked worse places to live." Tara stepped fully inside the room, assessing the tidy space. The twin bed was made, a few posters still stuck to plaster. A photograph of Tara and Reed sparring at the park rested beside a lamp on the nightstand, one of the only personal mementos still unpacked.

Tara's profile softened with a smile as she honed in on the picture frame. "I love this one. Thank you for taking it."

Memories from that spring morning washed over me like a breeze, back when I'd been seated on the park bench with Ladybug curled around my feet. "I have lots more. We can hang them around the house."

She grinned. "True. He can't complain about being in pictures if he's not here to look at them."

I watched as Tara reached into the pocket of her cut-off jean shorts and pulled something out. She unfolded another picture—the one of her and Reed on prom night, standing beneath the white ash tree.

Tara's head was tipped sideways in the shot, pressed to his broad shoulder, his arm wrapped around her waist as they posed for the camera. They were both smiling; indelibly happy.

Tara sighed, studying the photograph and flattening out the crease along the center. Plucking the gilded frame off the nightstand, she turned it over and unhooked the back piece of cardboard. "I'm updating this. I look way better when I'm not dripping with sweat. I can smell my B.O. from here."

Chuckling, I slipped my hands into the pockets of my sundress and rocked back on my sandals. "He'll love it."

"I know. Dad always..."

Her words trailed off.

I was staring out the window at a little trio of bluejays floating through leafy branches when my attention returned to Tara and her sudden silence. Her face morphed from carefree and gleeful into a look that had my insides pitching and my knees wobbling. "What is it?"

She turned her back to me, her head bowed forward as she stared down at something.

"Tara, what?" My heart started pounding. My airways tightened, the light mood thickening with black tension. "Tara—"

"What the hell is this?"

She whipped around, her hair flying over her shoulder as her cheeks turned scarlet.

In slow motion, I let my eyes fall to her outstretched hand.

And my world shattered.

The floor beneath my feet turned to quicksand.

I was freefalling.

My gaze panned back up, and our eyes locked.

I couldn't speak, couldn't think, couldn't breathe.

Because hidden behind the photo of Tara and Reed...was the photograph of *me*.

Naked. Cheeks flushed.

Tangled in his bed sheets.

In her father's bed.

"I..." Nothing felt real. I was in a time warp, trapped in a moment where everything stood still yet raced past me at the speed of light. "That was just..."

Tara glanced back down at the photograph, her eyes as wide as saucers. A gasp fell out. A croak. A horrible sound I'd never forget, like everything had just unblurred, and the picture in her shaking hand had come into full focus.

The truth held physical form and was devastatingly undeniable: her father was having a sexual relationship with her best friend.

"Oh, my God," she breathed out, shellshocked, dumfounded, horrified. "You...you're sleeping with him?"

My stomach curdled.

Nausea spewed bile against the back of my throat.

Weak, pathetic words squeaked past my lips. "It's...it's not like that." My skin sweated, my hands shook. I swung my head back and forth as if to dislodge the photograph from her mind. I tried to reach for it, to snatch it away, but she wrenched her arm back. Tears blanketed my vision. "Tara..."

"This...this is *you*." She jabbed the image through the air like a gavel against a sound block. "This is you. In my dad's bed."

"Tara," I cried, choking on her name. "It's not what you think, it's not, I..." Sucking in a sharp breath, I voiced my confession: "I love him."

Her eyes flared twice their size. "You what?"

She needed to know this was *real*. This wasn't a fling or a charade. This was love.

Nodding through my heartbreak, I swiped at my cheeks. "I do. I love him."

"No..." She gawked at me, her gaze flitting across my face, assessing my truth bomb, wading through the cataclysmic aftermath, and processing it all with buckshot in her skin.

I stepped toward her.

She moved away.

My hand extended, a plea for pardon, as I silently begged her to see this for what it was.

But she kept inching away, plodding backward.

And with a sharp sob, Tara tossed the picture frame to the nightstand and raced past me, out of the bedroom, still clutching the photograph of me.

She darted from the apartment.

I stood like a statue in the center of the room, unable to accept what had just happened. I glanced at the discarded frame that was still filled with the original picture. Innocence veiling a deadly secret. I shouldn't have given him that photo of me, shouldn't have been so stupid to think that concrete evidence of our sins wouldn't be uncovered.

Scraping my fingernails through my hair, I dashed from the room and followed Tara out to the parking lot, tears dangling from my jaw and dampening my neck. She was already in the driver's seat, her hands curled white around the wheel.

I jumped in and ambushed her with apologies. "Tara, please. I'm so sorry. Please don't hate me. It just happened—it-it just happened and I couldn't stop it, and we just—"

"Don't."

Pressing a hand to my chest, I twisted the fabric of my dress between my fingers. "Let me explain."

She swallowed and started the engine. "You don't need to explain."

The car jerked, and we jolted forward, cruising out of the parking lot at double the speed limit. The drive was made in silence. Itchy, crawling silence. Every time an excuse or explanation skipped across my tongue, I swallowed it down, unable to string the words together.

What could I do? How could I fix this?

My mind reeled with vicious thoughts. My limbs trembled as the tears fell, fell, fell, and I swore only a few seconds had passed us by before we were pulling into Whitney's driveway.

I tried again. "Tara, listen to me—"

She hauled herself out of the convertible and slammed the door on my words. I watched as she stormed up the walkway, into the house, and I just sat there miserably, broken, completely lost.

When I gathered up the fragments of my strength, I followed her inside, catching sight of Whitney staring up toward the second floor where Tara must have escaped to.

She frowned, glancing at me. "What's going on?"

I shook my head, a battle cry teasing my throat. "Nothing." Then I darted up the stairs, two at a time, mumbling behind me, "Everything."

Tara was sitting on her old bed—now a guest room bed—when I entered, her fingers coiled around the fuchsia-blossomed bedspread, the picture of me sitting beside her. I stared at it, cursed it, wanted to rip it into tiny shreds and toss it to the wind. But it was doomed to blow back in my face, an eternal reminder of my betrayal. "Tara...I'm so sorry." I cupped a hand around my mouth as my shoulders shook with grief. "Please, forgive me. I never meant to hurt you."

Her eyes lifted, slowly, sluggishly, her brows gathering between her eyes.

She was silent. Stiff.

I stepped toward her, riddled with desperation. "I wanted to tell you so many times. You have no idea how much it was killing me. I promise, I never wanted to—"

Tara jumped up from the bed, slicing my words at the quick.

At first I thought she was going to slap me, shove me, slaughter me with her wrath.

But I froze when she raced toward me, pulled me into her arms, and wrapped me up in a firm hug instead.

My whole body went rigid.

Shock infected me.

My ill-timed heartbeats skittered with a shot of hope, with the realization that maybe I'd assumed the worst. Maybe Reed and I hadn't given her enough credit to understand us, to come to terms with our relationship.

Maybe...

We're going to be okay.

Drinking in a relieved breath, I closed my eyes and held her tight, sinking into the warmth of her embrace. "God, I'm sorry." I pressed my temple to her shoulder. "I'm so sorry I didn't tell you sooner. I wanted to. So badly."

"Shh." She shushed me, stroking my hair. "You have nothing to be sorry for."

I smiled, tears puddling in my eyes.

Thank God.

This whole time, we'd been wrong about her. All that pain and heartbreak for nothing.

Tara was smart.

She understood.

"You've been through so much, Hals," she continued, skimming a soothing hand up and down my back and tugging me closer. "I can't even fathom it."

I nodded, tears trickling down my cheeks. "I know."

We stayed like that for a drawn-out heartbeat, for one precious moment, where she was my best friend and I was hers, and nothing would ever come between us.

But then she inched back.

Tara stared at me, her gaze hardening to unburnished stone.

She squeezed my biceps, her jaw clenching, expression creasing with new fury. "Listen to me," she stated, her tone steeped with ice. "This is *not* your fault."

Sniffling, I gazed back at her, confusion settling in my gut. "What do you—"

"This is my father's fault."

I blinked, my stomach lurching. My lungs constricting.

Tara snagged my pinkie finger like a promise and squeezed tight.

And then she finished with words worse than death.

"He groomed you, Halley," she said darkly. "And he won't get away with it."

CHAPTER 31

Reed

"DADDY, I'M SCARED."

The sun beat down on her Care Bears helmet, while two brown pigtails fell over the shoulders of her denim overalls. I held my hands over her tiny fists as they clung with terror to the handlebars. "Don't be scared, Squirt. I'm right here."

"But you're letting go. I don't want you to let go."

"I have to let go eventually. How will you learn?"

She pouted, her button nose wrinkling. "I can learn tomorrow."

"Why not right now?"

"It's too scary right now. Look, it might rain."

I glanced skyward, squinting my eyes at the golden globe of sunshine hovering overhead without a cloud in sight. "No rain. Only sunny skies and a father who's about to be really damn proud."

Tara's feet idled on either side of the bicycle as she let out a long sigh. "Mommy says that's a bad word."

A chuckle slipped out, and I crouched down beside her on the sidewalk, waiting for her to look at me. When our eyes met, I cupped her scraped knee with a smile. "Hey," I said, my voice full of reassurance. "You're going to be really brave today."

"I don't feel brave."

"That's because you're afraid. Being afraid always comes first. That's the first step to being brave."

She studied me, her big green eyes glistening with tears. "Why are all of my friends braver? I'm six. Everyone can ride without training wheels except for me."

"Bravery isn't about comparing yourself to others," I said gently. "It's about facing your fears, no matter how big or small they may seem. You're trying, even though you might fall. And you're going to get back up again. That's the bravest thing of all."

A little tongue poked out between her lips as she processed my words. "You won't ever let me go, right?"

"Not yet," I murmured. "Not right away."

"Never, Daddy. Never let me go."

I tried not to read into her innocent words and brushed a thumb over her neon-pink Band-Aid. Pulling to a stand, I steadied her bike and prompted her feet onto the pedals. Wispy streamers dangled from the handlebars as a little bell chimed with gallantry when I gave it a flick. "I won't let you go, Squirt. You're stuck with me."

A smile bloomed, and Tara schooled her expression with resolve. "Okay," she said, inhaling a deep breath. "Let's go!"

I held on to her as we pushed forward, my steps gaining speed as the tires rolled. Her eyes rounded, the breeze picked up, and a warm feeling trickled through me, pulsing with pride and love. "You've got this. You're doing great."

"Ahh! Don't let go!" she called out, the bike wobbling side to side as it cut across sidewalk cracks, her pigtails flailing behind her. "I'm going to do it, Daddy. Just don't let go yet!"

My eyes watered as I stood in the middle of the sidewalk, both of my arms lifting toward the sky.

I'd let go ten seconds ago.

She was already doing it.

I parked my truck in front of the house, then scrubbed a hand over my face. My skin was layered with cool sweat, still sticky from my training session. Whit had called me at the studio twenty minutes ago, alerting me of a "situation" and to hurry over to the house. I'd cut my session short, apologizing to my client and half-running through the parking lot to my truck.

Considering I wasn't ordered to the nearest hospital, I tried to settle my racing heart, hoping it was something manageable. A leaky pipe. A clogged toilet. Maybe Ladybug had eaten something she shouldn't have and the girls needed help getting her to the vet.

Whitney wouldn't tell me what was wrong.

All she'd said was, "Reed, I need you at the house. We have a situation."

Her tone was flat, unflinching. I knew Whit, so I knew that when she spoke with little emotion, something was wrong. It was the same cool inflection she'd had when Tara had been bitten by the neighbor's cat on her ninth birthday. Given Whitney's blasé attitude, I'd assumed it was a minor nick. Instead, there was horror-movie-level blood loss, swelling, and redness casing up the length of her arm.

Now, I could only wonder if I was about to walk into a pinprick or a bloodbath as I stared at the old two-story house with cream shutters and a blue door, imagining what *situation* lurked on the other side of it.

Pocketing my keys, I exited the truck and jogged up the familiar walkway to the front door with my heartbeats thundering in my ears. I hesitated before twisting the knob and shuffling inside.

Deep breath.

Swallowing, I stepped through the threshold and glanced around the living area. "Hey, what's..." My words tapered off. Frozen in place, I scanned all three ashen faces staring back at me as fear crept inside my bones. "What happened?"

Instinct had me searching for Ladybug, thinking the worst, but the golden furball was sprawled out on the couch with her snout tucked between her paws. She didn't run to me, didn't shimmy her butt or wag her tail. Even the dog sensed the cloud of dread hovering over the room.

I blinked several times, closing the door and stepping forward. Silence greeted me. Whitney stood off to the side with her arms crossed, her red-rimmed eyes the only indication she was upset. Halley sat beside Ladybug on the couch, slouched over, her head in her hands.

And Tara...

"How could you?" My daughter stormed across the room and beelined toward me, her expression a mask of indignation, her eyes razorblades. "How *could* you?" she repeated, sharper than the last.

Stunned, I shook my head as confusion rippled through me. "What's going on?"

Tara glared at me. "You tell me." Then she stalked forward, lessening the gap between us, and slammed something against my chest. "Explain."

My eyes were glued to her face.

I couldn't move, couldn't breathe.

"Explain!" she demanded, her fists balled at her sides.

I forced the haze to evaporate and glanced down at a photograph I'd been unknowingly clinging to. I stared at it. Processed it. Registered the gravity of what I'd just walked into as the image trembled between my fingers.

Fuck.

Me.

A barrage of guilt, horror, and devastation rained down as I slowly looked back up and locked eyes with Tara. Stupidly—and for bullshit sentimental reasons—I'd dug the damn photograph out of the garbage can right before trash day, recovering it, then hiding it behind another picture.

A catastrophic judgment call.

I bit down on my tongue, a film clouding my vision. "Squirt..."

"I am not your *Squirt.*"

My muscles locked, breath stalling in my throat like I was being held underwater. This was *not* how I'd intended for this to unfold. This was the worst-case scenario.

This was my nightmare.

Tara lunged at me and shoved at my chest with both hands. "You're a monster. You're *sick.* How could you do this to her? What is wrong with you?" Anger mingled with pain as tears dribbled down her bright-red cheeks. "How long were you lusting after my best friend? How long were you *grooming* her?"

"Tara!" Whitney whipped forward and snagged our daughter by the elbow. "Calm down. Think about what you're saying."

"I seem to be the *only* person thinking clearly right now. God, this is the Stacy situation all over again," Tara shot back, genuine emotion rocking her words.

Whitney paused, frowning. "This is not the same."

"Yes, it is. Open your eyes."

My lips parted to speak, but nothing came out.

Only a gravelly sound of despair.

Off my paralyzed silence, Halley stumbled from the couch and hurried toward us, inserting herself between me and Tara. "No. No, Tara, please don't turn this into something it's not."

The photograph fluttered from my feeble fingers and landed at our feet. All I could manage was another headshake as Halley tried to defend my honor, while I just stood there, shellshocked and numb. I was letting her down. I was letting everyone down.

Tara's face twisted with disgust. "Don't, Hals. Don't justify his behavior. He's a full-grown man, and you're practically a child. You were traumatized and abused. He took advantage of you."

"Stop it!" Halley squeezed both fists, her cheeks flaming. "I'm an *adult*. This was mutual. I pursued him, and he tried to stop it. This isn't his fault."

Her eyebrows hiked up. "That is exactly something a victim would say." Tara swiveled around to face her mother, her hair catching between her lips. "Mom, come on. You've spent your entire life dealing with social work cases. You witnessed firsthand what happened in Charleston. Halley is a *victim*."

Whitney's eyes glimmered with tears. "I understand why you would feel that way, but this isn't the same thing. I know your father. *You* know your father. Let's try to be rational here and look at this for what it is. It's different."

"Listen to yourselves!" Tara's arms flew up at her sides. "Halley was vulnerable and desperate for affection. He preyed on that."

"He didn't prey on me!" Halley interfered, close to sobbing. "Stop talking like I'm a clueless idiot who can't think for herself. We fell in *love*, Tara. Love isn't always black and white. It's murky, gray, and complicated. Nobody planned this. We met before I even knew he was your father."

Tara's mouth snapped closed as she glanced between us, processing the claim. "What do you mean?"

"I mean, I met him at a party two summers ago. A total coincidence. I had no idea he was related to you."

My zoned-out eyes ping-ponged between all three faces. Three blurry, blacked-out faces. Sound was warped and muddled, my brain a hollow organ. Only my pounding pulse gave way to proof of life.

Tara stiffened, tears streaming down in rivulets of betrayal. "Two summers ago?"

"Yes. You and I had only just become friends and I didn't know he was your father."

Hot-lava rage flickered in Tara's eyes. "Two summers ago you were *seventeen*."

Halley fumbled for a reply, blinking rapidly as she peered up at me, silently begging for help.

My forehead creased, my head still swinging, rejecting everything. "No, it...it wasn't like that," I finally said, feeling like a third party in my own body. "It's not what you think."

"He speaks," Tara bristled.

Whitney cut in. "Just for fact purposes, the age of consent in Illinois is seventeen. There is no crime here, Tara, regardless of your moral stance on the matter. I'm not saying I approve of any of this, but your father is not a felon by any means."

"I don't care about the laws!" Tara scoffed. "Wrong is wrong."

I inhaled a breath then let it out, hoping words came with it. "Listen...things only escalated recently," I tried, sounding pathetic, sounding frail. "Yes, I did meet Halley when she was seventeen, before I knew she was your friend. A connection formed. But I kept my distance."

"Right. Roping her into private training sessions, pretending it was for her own benefit, was totally keeping your distance."

"That was *my* idea," Halley interfered.

I swallowed. "I care about her. A lot."

"You only care about yourself. If you cared about Halley, you wouldn't have put your damn hands on her. If you cared about me and Mom, we wouldn't be standing here right now, dealing with this mess you created."

Slivers of truth bled into the madness as everything jumbled to distortion. Wrong, right, black, white, lust, love.

Fuck.

Nothing had prepared me for this reaction from Tara. She thought I was a monster. A disgusting creep.

Am I?

Holy shit. This was a fucking mess.

"Tara, just try to—"

"Don't tell me what to do!" She was seething. Raging. "You lost that privilege the moment you started fantasizing about a seventeen-year-old girl."

"Stop!" Halley sobbed. "This is crazy. This is so far from the truth..." Turning to face me, she latched on to my useless, lifeless arm and shook me hard. "Reed, tell her. Tell her this is real. It's not a crime. I'm not a victim. This is love, and it's pure, and it's beautiful." She shook me again. "Tell her you didn't know I was seventeen when we met and that I lied to you. I told you I was older. Then I chased you down, kissed you, begged for you to train me so I could be close to you. I did this. I'm responsible. *Me.*"

Another lull of silence festered as Halley's onslaught of words soaked in.

Tara frowned, her eyes narrowing with consideration and disdain, her steadfast belief in her best friend gaining holes. She sucked in a breath. "Is that true?"

"Yes," Halley said.

Gaze freezing with ice, Tara stared at Halley, her loyalty cracking. Shreds of doubt blossoming. "You lied to him so you could sleep with him?"

I choked.

Panic crawled through me as I glanced between Halley and Tara. Halley cowered back, new fears blooming to life. The fear of losing her best friend. Losing her found family.

Slowly, I panned my attention back to my daughter, drinking in her broken, conflicted face.

Memories unfurled with light and love. Sweet, tender moments. Childhood laughter, late-night homework sessions, sparring at the park, bonding over television sitcoms while eating pints of ice cream on the living room floor. Birthday parties, ocean waves, family dinners, bedtime stories.

But everything was eclipsed by a promise.

A promise to the woman on my left that I'd always fight for her. Protect her. Keep her safe, so no one could ever hurt her again.

I hurt her.

I set this in motion because I was weak. Because I fell for her, despite the flashing neon-fucking-red signs telling me to turn back now.

Tara would forgive me one day.

I knew she would.

The storm would pass, the waves would placate, and our family would get through this.

But Halley?

She had no one. No one else to guide her through the seas of uncertainty, through the high tides of recovery.

She'd already lost one family; I couldn't let her lose another.

A feeling came over me.

A painful, all-knowing feeling.

Bravery. Stupidity. A mix of both.

Aiming my eyes at the floor, I found my voice and used it to tell the greatest lie. "You're right, Tara," I whispered, the haunting hum of my broken words loud enough to crumble mountains.

Halley's grip on my arm loosened.

A look of pure blindside splashed across her face. "What?"

"You're right. About everything." I turned to Tara, trying to keep myself from buckling. "I did this. I took advantage of Halley when she was vulnerable, and I hate myself for it."

"Reed..." Halley blanched before my eyes. "No."

I kept going.

I had to keep going because there was no way out of this for us, no matter which road we took. But there was still a way out for Halley. For her heart. I'd absolve her of these sins. "I could tell she had a crush on me," I said. "I was lonely, weak, and selfish. Halley is beautiful, and I lost control."

Halley gouged her fingernails into my bicep, her pleas shrieking with disbelief. "No! He's lying." She whirled around to Tara and Whitney, her face in ruins. "He's lying, I swear."

"I'm not lying."

Whitney closed her eyes, her fingers sliding through her hair. "Reed, stop. Just stop talking."

"None of this is Halley's fault," I continued, stoning my resolve, forcing the words out as my stomach did somersaults, and I nearly bent over and retched. "I knew better. I knew it was wrong, but I did it anyway. Regardless of the consequences. Those training sessions were my idea. It was an excuse to be around her because I couldn't stay away."

My daughter's hand shot up and clamped around her mouth, her eyes squeezing shut.

"Don't blame Halley." I pleaded with Tara as I broke apart and died inside. "Please. She doesn't deserve any of this. Blame me. I'm the bad guy. I made her believe we had something real so I could keep her in my bed. I'm not proud of it. I'm ashamed. But that's the fucking truth."

My limbs trembled, my mouth cotton-ball dry. Nausea spun and churned, and all I wanted to do was shout from the rooftops that I loved this woman, and she loved me.

But Tara would never buy it.

She'd crucify Halley. I saw it all over her ghost-white face.

And that would crucify me.

Tara's shoulders tremored, her face paling to ash. She gaped at me, sickened and horror-struck, then removed her hand to speak. Shattering me into pieces.

"You're disgusting." Her teeth chattered from the strength of her revulsion. "You're disgusting, and I hate you."

Tears rimmed my eyes as my voice quavered. "I understand. I hate myself, too."

A single, salient beat passed as I watched my little girl digest all the things I'd just forced her to believe, before she flew past me to the foyer and raced outside, leaving the front door swinging on its hinges like a wrecking ball.

Halley lifted her chin, her eyes meeting with mine. We gazed at each other, apology flickering across my face, scorn molded into hers. Her features collapsed with hysteria, tears pouring down her cheeks. She shook her head, horrified by the lies I'd just expelled like water.

With a wretched cry, Halley let go of my arm and charged out the front door, slamming it behind her.

The windowpanes rattled.

An engine whirred to life.

Tires squealed out of the driveway.

Only wreckage was left behind as everything went silent, blanketing the room in the eerie quiet that permeated after a hurricane stormed through. A post-apocalyptic hum.

Ladybug crawled off the couch and trudged toward me, landing atop my feet with a defeated sigh, while Whitney looked at me with incredulity from across the room.

Her voice vibrated as she murmured, "What the hell did you just do?"

I gazed out the window, imagining a six-year-old Tara riding her bike without training wheels for the first time as her pride-like giggles echoed in my ears and gave me the greatest sense of peace. Twelve years ago, I made a promise to my daughter that I'd never let her go.

Then I made another promise.

A promise to the woman I love that I would always fight for her, even if it was the only thing I'd ever be allowed to do.

But promises were like petals in the wind.

Easily scattered.

Hard to hold.

I couldn't keep them both.

A tear trickled down my cheek as I swallowed the ashes of my sins.

What the hell did I just do?

I exhaled.

Closed my eyes.

"What I had to."

CHAPTER 32

MY KNUCKLES BRUISED with the weight of my knocks as I slammed a fist to Reed's front door for the twentieth time. "I'm not leaving," I shouted, uncaring that neighbors were poking their heads from cracked doors with invisible buckets of popcorn. I was making a scene. *Good.* "Open the door, Reed. I'm not going anywhere until you talk to me."

I knew he was inside; I saw his truck in the parking lot. He was ignoring me, hoping I'd grow tired of pounding and hollering like a madwoman in his hallway. Not a chance.

All he did was turn his music on.

Loud, shrieky metal music.

Son of a bitch.

Five minutes crawled by, and I was still here. He underestimated how stubborn I could be.

Knock, pound, knock.

"I swear to God I will curl up and go to sleep on this shitty maroon carpeting tonight if you don't—"

The music shut off and the door whipped open.

I staggered back, not from the motion itself, but from the disheveled, bone-weary look in his eyes. Dark circles, chalky skin, hair sticking up in every direction. My gaze rolled down his body, taking in his wrinkled white tank and sweatpants that hung from his solid frame like a flag flown at half-mast.

My resolve weakened. Empathy leaked through as my eyes flicked back up and met with pure sorrow.

He mistook my moment of vulnerability for surrender and tried to shut the door in my face.

I shot my hand out and barged inside, shaking off the sympathy. "Finally," I mumbled.

Reed idled in the threshold, one hand curled around the door frame, the other planted on the wall as he hunched forward, his back to me. "What," was all he said.

What.

What?

My chest heaved as the anger funneled back in crimson waves. "I have plenty of *whats*," I hissed. "What was that? What the hell were you trying to accomplish with that ridiculous charade? What made you think more lies and deceit would fix this? What—"

"You shouldn't be here." Whirling around, he shut the door and collapsed against it, his head slamming to wood, eyes falling closed. "You need to leave."

"I'm not going anywhere."

His eyes fluttered back open. "Yes, you are. You're going to the east coast with Scotty."

My jaw dropped, all my words chopped to bits. Only a humorless bark of laughter slipped through. "No, I'm not."

Reed's face remained expressionless, as if all the passion he was trying to conjure up had fizzled out in the aftermath of a soul-sucking defeat. "I think it's for the best. You wanted to travel, see the world. You deserve that."

"You don't get to decide what I deserve. And you certainly don't get to rip the rug out from under me, then roll me up in it and toss me off the nearest cliff."

He scrubbed a hand down his face. "You're being dramatic."

"*I'm* being dramatic?" I gawked at him, my head rearing back. "A few hours ago, you delivered a show-stopping performance that brought everybody to their knees. It was Oscar-worthy. Truly."

A glare was his response, but it wasn't hateful, wasn't angry.

It was just...detached.

Painfully distant.

I took a step forward, trying my hardest to spin my fury into conviction. "Reed, please. We need to talk about this."

"There's nothing to talk about. It's done."

"It's not done. It's only beginning. And maybe if you had tried to convince Tara that what we had was real, we'd have an *actual* beginning to work with." Tears welled, despite my yearning for strength. "What were you thinking?"

Finally, something other than apathy shimmered in his eyes. Reed pulled up from the door and hovered in front of me, his brows creasing with pain. "I was thinking about *you*, Halley," he said. "Something I should have thought about from day one. Yes, I twisted the truth, but not everything was a lie. I *was* weak. I *was* selfish. And now I have to suffer the consequences of those actions."

"Reed..." I stepped toward him, closer, melting the icy gap between us. "Love is weak. Love is selfish. It's not this fairy-tale illusion of candy hearts and paper flowers. It's messy and painful. But it's always worth it."

He dropped his eyes. "You keep saying that word."

"What word?"

"Love." He spit it out like he'd chewed it up first.

I blinked at him, tears still threatening. "Well, do you?"

A long sigh commandeered the mountain between us, and Reed fisted his hair with both hands as he moved around me, into the living room. "I don't know what you want me to say, Halley."

"The truth."

"That's counterintuitive."

"It's not," I whispered.

Pacing the room, back and forth, forward and back, he shook his head. "Tell me what you want. Tell me what you want me to say that will make this better."

"No," I volleyed back. "I only want you to say what *you* want to say. Do you love me? It's a yes or no question. It's an easy answer you can—"

"*Yes*." Reed stopped pacing, coming to a dead stop a few feet away. He stared at me, jaw clenched tight, hands balled even tighter. "Yes, Halley, I'm in love with you. I think I proved that when I threw myself under the bus and completely destroyed my relationship with my daughter to protect you. To keep her from hating *you*," he gritted out. "So, yes...I love you. I love you fiercely, wholly, selfishly and unselfishly, more than I *ever* fucking should. I love everything about you, from your smile, to your perfect heart, to the way your hair always slips from your ponytail when you're running or sparring and hides those eyes I've been enamored with since the moment I first saw you. I love how you take every picture like it's the only one you'll ever take, how you love like it's simply a way of life, and how you cook from your soul because it makes everyone around you so goddamn happy. I love the strength you pulled from nothing, from bare bones and rock bottom, and how you choose to dance through life with grace and courage, finding music in every sound-less shadow, when anyone else would have laid down and died." He choked out the last words, emotion catching in his throat as his chest puffed with the weight of each breath. "Now...tell me how that changes anything."

I gaped at him.

Jaw dropped, heart sunk.

Every inch of me was submerged in warm water as I drowned myself in his words. Color drained in my periphery, sapped from each newly gray pocket and hollow crevice. But he was bright. He was vivid. Reed was a dazzling mural, a splash of watercolors in a sepia world.

I hadn't realized I'd been holding on to all my air until a burst of breath fell out, dousing us both in sunlight. I wanted to curl up, live here, stay forever in this moment of pure contentment.

Reed loved me.

That changed *everything*.

But the tragic look in his eyes told me he didn't believe it did.

I rushed forward, spilling into his arms like my bones were made of putty. My face smashed to his chest and I breathed him in, memorizing the scent of his skin and the echo of his confession. "You love me," I near-sobbed, my tears dampening his shirt.

Slowly, despite everything inside of him telling him to remain stiff and lifeless, he raised both arms and wrapped them around me, pulling me closer. Love did that. It zapped your heart when it'd rather give out, and it possessed your arms when they wanted to droop instead of hold. He was defenseless. Love made us all so damn defenseless.

"You know I love you. But that's not always enough."

"It has to be. We'll make it so."

"We don't have that kind of power, Comet. We don't fit."

I shook my head against him. "We fit in every way that matters."

Palming the back of my head, he pressed a hard kiss to my forehead before inching me away. He held me at arm's length, both hands curled around my biceps as he bent to eye-level. "Listen to me. If I saw a way out of this, I'd take it. I'd fucking reach for it and keep you in my arms forever. But that's not how the cards fell. You're nineteen years old, and I'm thirty-six," he said. "Your life is just beginning. You need to be brave enough to start over."

My face crumpled with agony. "I want to start over with *you*."

"How?" The question was full of thorns and barbs. "I can't marry you. I'm not having any more babies. I'm pushing *forty*, Halley, and you're on the brink of a bright, fulfilling future."

"I don't need marriage and babies," I reasoned.

"You say that now."

"I'll say it forever. None of that matters."

"Stop. Please, stop and think." He squeezed me tighter. "All your dreams. Your plans. You can't toss them to the wind on a feeling that never should have existed in the first place. Feelings change and ebb, but lost time is irreversible. You're going to wake up one day and realize you threw everything away, and for what? A relationship with your best friend's dad that no one will ever condone, let alone nurture?"

My body shook with tremors, my lips wobbling as I tried to speak. Nothing came out. Words turned to dust on my tongue.

He latched onto my hesitation. "Go to Charleston," he pleaded. "Swim in the ocean, take pictures, walk down the aisle in a white gown, and raise beautiful children who see you as the center of their universe. I want that for you. I *need* that for you." Pain carved its way into his words as he tried in vain to keep the shudder out of his voice. "If you don't go, I will...but I think you should. It's what's right. And I know you see that, too, even though it's really fucking hard."

I shook my head side to side, rejecting what I *did* know was right. The proof resided in everything he'd just said. Our relationship was doomed. Severed at the roots before it ever had a chance to grow.

I knew he was right. But all I wanted was right now.

Right here. With him.

I lived my life in present moments, because there used to be days when I didn't know how many I'd have left. A fist to my face could have been the last. Glass in my artery could have caused me to bleed out. Days locked in my bedroom with no food might have led to my slow, painful demise.

The future was a privilege. Dreams were a luxury.

I cherished the right now.

And that was Reed.

He was tangible, warm, and mine. Seeing beyond what I held so dear felt like a violation of my heart. It hurt. It stung and chafed in places I didn't know existed.

Reed cupped my wet cheeks between his palms and pressed a kiss to my lips. "Go, Halley," he whispered against my mouth. "Go with Scotty. Go *because* I love you. Go because it'll kill me if you don't do everything in your power to live a life you won't regret."

I kissed him harder, forcing his mouth to part to deepen our hold. He exhaled a groan when our tongues touched, a soft flick of yearning.

He fused our foreheads together, canting his head left and right like it was taking all of his effort not to crack. "Halley—"

"I'll go," I cried out. "I will. I'll go."

His eyes snapped closed as I said the words he both longed, and loathed, to hear. He nodded, every muscle twitching and tense.

"It's better if I go and you stay," I said, gasping for breath and strength. "You need to fix things with Tara. Rebuild your relationship while I try to build some semblance of a life without you."

He kept nodding, his eyes squeezed shut as tears leaked out.

"I hate this, but you're right." I reached up to dab a tear from the corner of his eye with my thumb. "Maybe one day I'll find love with another man the way I found it with you. I'll try to take pictures that aren't all black and white. I'll swim in the ocean, all while wishing you were on the same side of the waterline with me. I'll try, Reed," I rasped out. "I promise I'll try."

He inhaled a ragged sigh. "Good."

I lifted on my tiptoes and pulled his face to mine, releasing a final request against his lips. "Just let me lose myself one more time."

A beat passed as our mouths idled, warm breath mingling as one.

Then he gave in on a needy groan and tugged me to him.

Our mouths locked again, both opening at the same time as our tongues tangled together, desperation fueling us. He gripped my hair, cupped my jaw, pressing closer like he could forge a home inside of me. I'd let him. I'd let him gut me from top to bottom and build anew.

The kiss grew vibrant wings, our hands dipping everywhere, my leg curling around his hip, his arms hoisting me up. With a quick tug, I was in the air, linking my ankles behind his back as he carried me to the bedroom. Reed lay me on the bed, carefully, like I was a precious thing, and trailed both hands up my thighs until my dress was inching its way up and over my head. He discarded his clothes and crawled over me as I slid my underwear down and off.

My knees parted, an invitation. A petition for forever.

But I knew, all we had was this.

Our last dance.

I wrapped my arms around his neck as he settled on top of me, skin to skin. Eye to eye. He was inside me before I could take a breath, moving like warm molasses, savoring the sweetness of our final moment.

It was slow, careful, tender.

There was no urgency because there was nothing else waiting for us on the other side of it.

My hands sifted through his soft hair, branding the texture on my fingertips. My feet grazed over his lower back, sliding across his skin. His strokes deepened as he tried to reach my innermost parts. Our hearts pounded together in synchronized rhythm, matching his thrusts, and my eyes remained open the whole time, hazel fixed to the prettiest color green I'd ever seen.

I saw the sadness. I saw the love. I saw a crystal-clear future reflected in his gaze that neither of us would ever live out.

His mouth parted on a low moan, one hand dusting down my hip until he was palming my thigh. Squeezing. Memorizing, just like me. He peppered kisses to my throat, my collarbone, my cheeks and nose, my lips that trembled with lust and loss. There was magic in the air. Magic and mourning bleeding into our bones.

When his fingers caressed the space where our bodies joined, I arched back, unwilling to let go. I wasn't ready. I knew the pinnacle was nothing but a head-first dive off this love-grown cliff.

Reed rubbed harder, thrust faster, deeper, edging me closer to the drop-off.

I clutched at him. Fought. Fingernails and teeth. With everything I had left.

But then he leaned over and released precious words into my ear, his fingers working me, his body filling me with everything I'd ever need. His breath warmed the shell of my ear as he said softly, "I love you so much."

I broke.

I couldn't hold on, my legs gave out, my feet lost traction, and I slipped into the blinding light, into the shimmery, star-studded void where my soul took flight and our love felt everlasting, my moan a sere-nade to goodbye.

Reed followed with a final thrust, gripping me with a ferocity that felt powerful enough to keep us together. He buried his face against my neck, kissing the delicate skin as he unraveled, meeting me in that eternal place where time stopped and everything else evaporated into fog.

Tears flooded me.

I sobbed beneath him, spent and sucked dry. He gathered me in his arms and held me through the heartbreak, shushing my tears with kisses and gentle words.

It wasn't enough.

It will have to be enough.

The following moments were a blur as we untangled and slipped back into our clothes, my loveless future dangling in the bleak chasm between us. There was nothing left to say.

It was time to go.

As I trudged over to his front door with a knot in my throat and my eyes bone-dry, he called out to me before I walked out of his life.

"Do you think you can someday?"

I hesitated, my hand loosely curled around the doorknob. Glancing over my shoulder, tear stains burned lines down my cheeks as I breathed out, "Can I what?"

Reed swallowed, the gesture causing his lips to tremble, his eyes to water. "Love again."

I closed my eyes and imagined the future I'd always wanted: a man to love, a house that felt like a home, children laughing and playing at my feet while I cooked dinner. An idyllic, wholesome life I knew I deserved.

A life with a man who wasn't Reed.

Lowering my head, I twisted the knob and yanked open the door.

I gave him my final words.

I offered him the only truth I could pull from the tangled threads of my heart.

"As much as a girl can love the next best thing."

CHAPTER 33

Halley

DEPRESSION HAD CARVED a black-tar tunnel through my insides. Bleakness oozed. Misery prevailed. I'd only lived in this apartment with Tara for a few weeks, and now I was packing up still-cluttered boxes with everything I would need to start anew, hundreds of miles away.

But, I supposed the last few weeks between these drab white walls had still felt more substantial than it'd ever felt living in my childhood home. So, I was making progress.

Tara whizzed by me, eating a bowl of oatmeal, as I sat cross-legged in the middle of the living room. I could hardly lift my head to glance at her. Everything was difficult. Even tiny, inconsequential gestures. A smile, a wave, a look that sparkled instead of dulled.

She came to a stop, standing over me as she licked the back of the spoon. "Did you give your notice to the banquet hall?"

Nodding, I stuffed clothing into the shoddy cardboard, uncaring that my carefully folded items had already unraveled. "I gave Monique my two-weeks."

"How did she take the news?"

"Monique has two emotions: overly enthusiastic and firecracker-mad. Thankfully, she was the former."

Tara frowned. "She's glad you're leaving?"

"No, but I told her I was going to start up my own photography business in South Carolina. So she's happy for me." It wasn't a lie, but it was a hopeful exaggeration. I'd be lucky if I left my bed for weeks, let alone prioritized new business ventures.

But...someday.

Someday I'd start living again.

Tara took a cautious step forward, then dropped to the floor, lowering to her knees in front of me as she discarded the oatmeal. "I'm really going to miss you, but this will be good for you, Hals."

My face remained expressionless as I tossed a pair of sandals into the overcrammed box. I couldn't scrounge up the effort to force a smile, but I didn't want to throw my anger at her, either.

The truth?

I *was* angry.

I was pissed off and fuming.

There wasn't a single part of me that sympathized or understood Tara's feelings in regard to her father. How she could accuse him of *grooming* me—of being a monster and a predator—was beyond my comprehension. My anger and confusion had only heightened in the days since everything imploded, while we lived together, slept in the same bed, and participated in lackluster conversation that did little to soften my edges.

It didn't make sense.

Never, in my wildest dreams, did I imagine the scenario playing out like this. I thought, surely, Tara would hate *me*. Blame *me*.

Never Reed.

Never her own dad.

It was almost funny how I was so concerned with Tara turning her back on me, cutting me out of her life, slapping the label of "traitor" on me...when, in reality, I was the one doing that very thing to her.

"I know," was the only response I could muster.

Tara sighed. "Mom has a lot of connections with therapists and psychologists, you know. Maybe it would be smart to talk to someone before you leave. So you can start over with a clear head."

I froze. My hand halted midway to the box, my fingers squeezing a tie-dye T-shirt with bleached knuckles. She thought I was broken. She thought I'd been brainwashed by a man who'd only ever had my best interest in mind. Who'd only ever loved, cared, nurtured, and provided for me.

For both of us.

It sickened me.

Teeth clenched tight, I shook my head, releasing the shirt and watching it splash across the pile of outfits in vivid color. I slammed the folds on the box, hiding it all away. "I don't need to talk to anyone, Tara. I'm not a victim. I'm not defective."

"Hals, this is more complicated than you realize."

"I don't even know what you're talking about. I don't want to have this conversation again."

"That's because you don't understand. You can't see the truth yet." Her features buckled, sadness seeping into her eyes. "I don't want you to leave like this. I want to fix things."

There was only one way to fix this, and that was for *Tara* to see the truth. To scrub the rot from her mind and see what was right in front of her, clear as day. Slowly, I panned my eyes up, my lightless ones peering into glistening jade. "Then fix it," I said flatly. "Tell me you jumped to ridiculous conclusions. Admit that you latched onto the most heinous, unrealistic explanation in a moment of blindside and you regret ever branding your father a monster."

Darkness flickered across her face, dimming her eyes. "I can't do that."

"Then that's that." I pulled myself up and stalked out of the room.

She gave chase. "Halley, stop. Wait."

"I need to get ready for work. There's a wedding this afternoon."

"I'm on *your* side," she called out, her voice heightening with desperation.

I balled my fists to stones and whirled around, facing her in the center of the hallway. "You're not on my side. If you were, you'd put your misguided beliefs aside for one goddamn second and try to *understand* me. Your dad didn't take advantage of me. He saw me. As an equal. As a woman."

"I do understand you. Believe me, I do." A huff of frustration expelled from her lips. "I'm not blaming you for feeling that way, or for you believing wholeheartedly that you love him. He manipulated your feelings. Older men have a way of doing that."

"That's bullshit," I spit out. "You've always been the one to say I'm so much older, so much wiser than you. Why can't you trust that now? Why can't you trust that I'm a woman capable of reasonable thoughts? I'm a victim, yes, but Reed has never been my abuser. He's been my savior. And maybe I do need therapy, but it has nothing to do with him and has everything to do with my disgusting, worthless father who almost put me in the ground before I ever had a chance to experience true love."

Out of breath, I shoved pieces of hair out of my face, then slammed the heels of my palms to my eyes to prevent the tears from leaking out.

"Halley..." Tara shuffled closer, extending her arms for a hug. "I love you. You're like a sister to me. I swore nothing would ever come between us, and I meant that. Don't let it be this."

I shook my head, dodging her comfort. "You're making everything worse," I whispered brokenly. "Why can't you try to see it from my point of view?"

"Because he admitted it himself." Her face twisted with grief and disappointment. "Why would he do that?"

I inhaled a tear-filled breath. "He did it for me. He was protecting me, just like he said he always would. In his mind, you hating *him* was better than you hating *me*, and part of me will never forgive him for that."

She hesitated, looking away. A few beats rolled by as she considered her next words. "Listen...I know from experience that sometimes the people we trust most are capable of things we never thought possible. It happens; it does. And I refuse to be an enabling bystander again, wearing rose-colored glasses, justifying something that's wrong, just because he's a family member." She swallowed. "Just because I love him."

Studying her, I fell silent, mulling over her words and searching for the deeper truth. "Again?" I echoed. Tara was holding back. Keeping something from me. "What experience?"

Her eyes remained fixated on the far wall, her complexion turning ashy.

My brain spun back in time.

The confrontation with Reed had been horrifying and unexpected. I'd been so lost to the heart-wrenching feelings, the anger, the disbelief, I hadn't stopped to consider the little moments. The breadcrumbs sprinkled in, adding a new layer to an already nightmarish fallout.

Charleston.

Something had happened in Charleston.

Stacy.

"Tara." I took a step forward, softening my voice. "Tell me what happened in Charleston."

She lifted her head, her eyes flaring. "I...I can't."

"You have to. I need more context." I stared at her, pleadingly. "It doesn't make sense that you'd slap a label like that on your father when he's only ever loved you, unconditionally."

She blinked at me.

And just like that, her features crumpled.

Tara draped both hands over her face and hunched over, tears drenching her fingertips. "It was my fault," she sobbed.

Empathy soared to the surface, overriding my resentment. My best friend was hurting, and I didn't know why. I bridged the gap between us and pulled her into my arms. "Tell me." I comforted her with gentle touches as she vibrated with sadness. "Please. I need to understand."

"She was my best friend and I failed her."

"Who? Stacy?"

She nodded.

"I don't believe that. You're an amazing friend."

"It's true." Sniffling, she popped her head up, swiping beneath her eyes. "There was this teacher. Mr. Baker. He taught sophomore English class and would leave us little sonnets and poems sometimes, hidden in our folders. I thought it was sweet. He was handsome and charming, and because he was older, I assumed he was just being nice. Fatherly. He had a daughter, so it made sense at the time."

My chest panged as I held my breath, processing her words.

"Stacy was my best friend. She sat next to me in homeroom and made me feel like we'd known each other our whole lives. Just like you." Tara rubbed at her nose, her eyes bloodshot, lashes damp. "She was struggling in English class, and Mr. Baker offered to tutor her after school. She told me she felt uncomfortable, but I convinced her to do it. He was so kind, so attentive. I never thought..."

Oh, God...

A sour feeling swirled in my gut as the pieces fell into place.

"Months went on, and Stacy started acting mopey and withdrawn. She said her grades were bad. I didn't think anything of it. But she stopped wanting to hang out with me. With everyone. She always had plans, other things to do." Her breath quivered as she inhaled. "One day, I saw her reading a note in the bathroom. I took it from her and she freaked out. It was from Mr. Baker. But it wasn't innocent, Halley. It was awful. Disgusting. I couldn't believe it."

Tears slid down my face, my eyes closing. "Tara..."

"It was a fucked-up *love* letter. From our teacher. It was sick. He talked about making plans, a future, and referenced something sexual they had done." Chest heaving, and fire spitting from her eyes, she hissed out, "She was fifteen!"

I shook my head, reached for her hand, and squeezed. "That wasn't your fault."

Tara pulled back, crossing her arms. "It was. I told her to tutor with him. I trusted him because he was older and attractive. I was so stupid, Hals. And I swore I would *never* let something like that happen again." Pushing a hair off her face, she glanced at me. "I understand what you're feeling. Stacy thought she loved Mr. Baker, and he knew exactly how to manipulate her because she was young, vulnerable, and needy for affection. I refuse to turn my back on a friend again—on a *victim*. When I say I'm on your side, I truly mean that."

I rubbed at my forehead, debating my next move.

Even though my heart broke and my tears fell faster, I needed Tara to understand that this wasn't the same. Not at all.

I wasn't Stacy.

Reed wasn't Mr. Baker.

"This is different, Tara." Urgency tinged my words. I had to rewire her faulty way of thinking. "It's not the same because you *know* your dad. You know he's a good man."

"I thought I knew him," she croaked out, picking at the skin around her thumbnail. She sighed, hopelessly. "God, I can't believe he would do this."

I grabbed her by the shoulders and forced her eyes on me. "Look at me. I swear to you, your father never manipulated me. Forget what he told you—he was taking the blame to keep you from turning your back on *me*. I was the one who pursued him, I was the one who lied about my age, and I was the one who begged for him to train me, even though he told me it was a bad idea. He tried to stop this from happening."

She squeezed her eyes shut, more tears slipping out.

"We fell in love," I confessed, my voice cracking. "Real love. He saw me as a woman, as an equal, as a partner. Age doesn't matter. They're just numbers. There is no crime here."

Tara sucked in a long breath and withdrew, moving away as she tightened her arms across her chest. "I can't accept it, Halley. It doesn't make sense."

"It doesn't make sense because you're looking for parallels in a completely different situation."

She stared down at the floor, her body stiff, and all she said was, "I'm sorry."

Defeat sunk me. Exhaustion soaked into my bones, leaving me dry.

Closing my eyes, I stepped backward, wishing I could crawl under the bed covers and sleep the day away. Sleep the rest of my life away. "I have to get ready for work. Please...just think about it," I pleaded. "I need you to try to understand."

Tara said nothing.

Didn't call me back.

She stood statue-still in the middle of the hallway, her eyes glued to the carpet beneath her feet.

Tears still falling, I walked into the bedroom and closed the door, praying, wishing, begging she could make sense of this.

Two weeks had passed and nothing made sense.

Scotty helped me carry the final boxes to his van as I robotically trailed behind him with a scrapbook in my hands. We'd stopped by the Stephens' house before leaving town to gather the few boxes that hadn't made their way over to the apartment yet.

And to say goodbye.

Although I now grasped the root of Tara's reaction more clearly, stemming from the lingering guilt of her past that she'd been carrying around for years, we had yet to make any progress in seeing eye-to-eye. Tara couldn't scrub the similarities from her mind, which meant I was leaving with this painful crater still wedged between us.

I swallowed, my throat stinging like a beehive. Tara and Whitney stood on the front porch with crestfallen expressions while I pivoted back around and faced them from the edge of the driveway.

This was real. This was happening.

I had sold my Camry, figuring I'd need the extra cash to get back on my feet, and now I was driving off into a daunting unknown with nothing but some flimsy boxes and a hole in my chest. My attention panned to Tara as she took a seat on the porch step and stared at me from afar, her ponytail swinging in the early-August breeze.

The sky turned gray, her skin sun-faded. Even her eyes were a somber shade of green. I wondered if my own eyes were playing tricks on me, muting all color to match my mood.

Inhaling a deep breath, I moved forward, just as Scotty reached for my hand. I glanced at him.

"Hey," he said gently, dusting a thumb over my knuckles. "I'll be in the van while you say your goodbyes."

"Okay."

"Unless you need me."

I shook my head. The only man I needed was holed up in his apartment, far away from my knee-buckling departure. "I'll be fine. Just give me a minute."

"Sure thing."

He let go of my hand and I was on my own. I slogged up the driveway, shoulders sagged and legs wobbling. The moment I looked back up, tears flooded my eyes with a waterfall of grief. My face crumpled, and I clasped a hand over my mouth to keep the wail from pouring out.

Tara jumped up and ran to me. She pulled me into her arms and buried her face against my shoulder, sobbing her heart out. Pushing my bitterness aside, I held on to her. This was more important, this sad goodbye, and she was still my best friend. She was still the girl who held my hand through the worst years of my life and dusted off my crumbly heart.

"I'm going to miss you so much."

"I'll miss you, too," I choked. "I'll keep in touch."

Inching up, Tara swiped the water from her eyes and nodded. "You better."

I sniffled, my hair stuck to my cheeks. "Can you promise me something?"

She crooked her pinkie finger and secured it with mine, nodding. "Anything."

I held up the scrapbook and handed it to her.

"What's this?" Her blue-tipped fingers danced over the peach cover that featured a singular photo of us sitting by the lake. Whitney had taken it the prior summer as we sucked on red-white-and-blue popsicles, staring at each other with goofy grins and drowning in laughter. "A photo album?"

"Sort of. I've been working on this scrapbook for a while. I want you to have it." She went to open it, but I stopped her. "Later. After I'm gone."

"Okay." Her eyes flicked up to mine as she asked, "But what's the promise?"

My eyes watered as I pictured Reed.

His handsome face skipped across my mind in full color, a permanent photograph in my mind. His voice, his laughter, a precious melody.

My favorite song.

I smiled sadly, more tears trickling from my eyes. "Try."

It took a moment for the statement to process. When it did, her eyes flashed. "I—"

"Promise me you'll try."

Try to understand. Try to see him as the man he is; the good, noble, loving man who raised you right. Try to put love above all else. Please try. For me. For him.

For you.

My silent plea crackled between us as our eyes locked and Tara fisted the scrapbook with two hands. More tears spilled down her flushed cheeks as she glanced away and gave me a single nod.

It was a promise I would forever hold her to.

"I love you, Hals."

"I love you, too."

Soft smiles tipped our lips as Whitney approached us from the walkway. Tara stepped aside as Whitney moved in, pulling me into a warm embrace. She smelled of cinnamon and cake. Sweet, comforting. I wrapped my arms around her and squeezed her tight, unleashing my eternal gratitude into her ear. "Thank you for everything," I said. "For giving me a home. A real home. For two beautiful years that I will never, ever forget."

"Oh, Halley." She broke down, her body vibrating against me. "You're precious to me. It's been my greatest honor having you here with us. You *made* our house a home."

I knew in that moment that I could do hard things.

After all, I loved Reed Madsen.

I loved him with every ventricle and chamber of my broken-down, barely beating heart.

And now I was walking away.

From all of them.

It was the hardest thing I'd ever done. My years of abuse and torment paled in comparison to this feeling. This heart-crushing feeling of voluntarily leaving behind something so pure. These people were my family. They were my heart.

Whitney pulled back and cupped my cheeks. "I'll talk to her," she promised, stroking my face. "It'll be okay. We'll get through this."

My lips trembled. "You know the truth, right?"

"I know that forgiveness, growth, and understanding can be found in even the darkest circumstances. I know that love has power. Power to break and ruin, and power to rebuild." She wiped away a tear. "I know that what is meant to be, *will* be. You can't rush it. You can't fake it. You just need to wait for the storm to pass and pick up the pieces when the time is right."

"We never meant to hurt anybody," I said softly.

"I know that, too. Trust me, I've been there. I've made awful choices, and those choices had consequences. There is no right or wrong here. There is only what is and what will be. You'll be stronger for it, Halley. So will Tara. You're both young. It's never too late to forgive and recover."

I hugged her again, inhaling her sugary scent and her words of solace. "You don't hate him?"

That mattered.

That matters most.

"I don't hate him," she said. "I'm disappointed it turned out like this, but that's life. And life is too short to hate the people we care about. Tara will realize that soon enough."

I allowed her wisdom to spread through me, offering a semblance of relief amid the pain. All I could do was hope that all the fractures I'd set in motion could be sealed in my absence. Love would reign. Everything would be okay.

With time.

As I pulled away, the front door cracked open and a final farewell greeted me in the shape of four paws and a swishing tail. I broke down again, collapsing to my knees as Ladybug barreled toward me and sank into my arms.

I held her extra close, stroking her fur, releasing my tears into her golden coat. I thanked her for being my friend. My steadfast companion. A constant reminder that unconditional love could be found in many forms. "Be a good girl, Ladybug," I said, drenching her fur with wetness. "Take care of Tara and Whitney." My heart spasmed, bled, splintered. "Take care of Reed."

I kissed the top of her head and scratched between her ears.

Then I told her goodbye.

As I twisted around with a strangled sob, I glanced behind me one last time. Tara and Whitney waved me off while Ladybug sat in the middle of the driveway, her paws dancing up and down like she wanted to run to me but knew she couldn't. She whined, a squeaky little sound that shot beams of devastation to my heart.

She knew.

She knew I wasn't coming back.

And in the back of my mind, I knew, too—this would be the last time I'd ever see her.

As we rolled down the familiar neighborhood road, and the Stephens' home became smaller and smaller in the rearview mirror, a feeling came over me.

I shot up in my seat, my chest squeezing, heart pounding. "Can we make a quick stop?"

Scotty turned the radio dial down and sent me a brief glance. "Sure. Where to?"

"Just a few streets over."

I guided him onto Bradshaw Avenue. Towering, branchy trees lined the old street as little ranch houses came into view. Gravel driveways, withered light posts, a child riding a pink plastic trike. Familiarity burned holes in my bones as I drank in the remnants of my childhood.

When I stopped him in front of the small ruddy-bricked house, my pulse jumped and my mind dizzied. For a moment, panic inched its way inside me. Awful memories bloomed like poisonous flowers in the garden of my mind, their thorns sinking into my flesh.

I swallowed, staring at the cracked bricks and dilapidated doorframe. "I used to live here."

Scotty was silent for a beat. "You want to say goodbye?"

I blinked through the foggy glass. "I don't know."

I hadn't stepped foot on this street in the two years I'd been away. It was too painful, too triggering. I was petrified my father would be lurking behind trees and bushes, eager to swoop me up and carry me back to that hellhole.

My mother had never reached out. Never called, never visited me. There were days when the notion had festered in my blood like a disease. But, as Whitney had said, what was meant to be, would be. Only time could paint the clearest picture, and time had showed me in striking pigments that my mother didn't deserve me. She wasn't worthy of my love.

Once upon a time, I thought I missed her.

But it was *she* who'd missed out on *me*.

Not all mothers were meant to be caretakers.

Not all monsters were meant to be rehabilitated.

And not all love stories were meant to last.

Finally, I dropped back to my seat and shook my head, turning to Scotty as I buckled my seatbelt. "I'm ready now."

CHAPTER 34

Halley

"YOU'VE GOT MAIL."

I popped my head up from the slew of boxes strewn across the second bedroom of Scotty's apartment.

My apartment.

The window was cracked, the hot August air doing little to cool the muggy space cursed with defective air conditioning. Car horns blared from the busy street, and I did my best to pretend they were the melodic lull of ocean waves. Unfortunately, living by the beach cost a pretty penny here in Charleston, so it was a solid fifteen minutes to sand and shorelines.

Sweat cased my hairline as I tightened my ponytail and pulled to a stand, meeting Scotty in the bedroom doorway. We'd driven into town four days ago, and I was still slowly unpacking. Doing anything was hard enough when there was a dark cloud hanging over my head, but filling rooms with decorations and colorful knickknacks felt like a Herculean task.

I managed a small smile, glancing at the priority mail package in Scotty's hand. "That's for me?"

"Yep." He nodded, handing it to me. "No return address. Doesn't weigh anything."

"Hmm. Mysterious." Thanking him, I took the padded envelope and retreated back into the room while he shuffled into the kitchen to whip up a pot of spaghetti.

I hopped onto the lilac bed covers and crossed my legs, peering down at the address label.

My heart stuttered.

I recognized the handwriting.

With a closed-up throat and a jack-hammering pulse, I tore through the package with my fingernails and jabbed a hand inside. Something soft tickled my fingertips. Fuzzy and plush. I shimmied it out of the bubble wrap, then glanced down at the item resting in my palm.

It was a Beanie Baby.

A blush-pink bunny rabbit.

I gasped, my eyes watering as I looked back inside the packaging and discovered a note. Eager to read his words, to imagine his voice in the privacy of my mind, I fingered the cream sheet of stationary and tugged it free, my hands shaking.

Through a wall of tears, I read.

Comet,

You told me a story once. You were standing in the kitchen making a taco casserole, wearing a fuzzy sweater that matched your eyes. It was a story about a bunny. When you were young, a little rabbit had found its way into your garage, injured and bleeding. You wanted to save it. You wanted to give it a second chance at life. Unfortunately, the story didn't end well, and I wished so hard that I could go back in time and help you save that bunny.

Since my powers are limited, I did what I could.

Meet Hoppity.

I hope that when you look at it, hold it, set it on your shelf, you think of me. I hope it serves as a constant reminder of your beautiful heart and the way it changes people. The way it changed me. You changed me, Halley, in all the best ways.

Let this be your second chance at life. Take risks. Take opportunities.

Take pictures that hang in galleries one day, so everyone can see your talent, your beauty, your immeasurable worth.

Fight. Fight for you, for your future. Not with fists and kicks, but with what you've always fought best with: love.

The night I met you, you sat down in a cold lake and said, "You're welcome." I said I didn't thank you for anything and you replied with, "You might one day."

You were right.

Thank you, Halley Foster.

You've made me a better man.

Reed

Tears bucketed down like rainfall as I clutched the letter in one hand and Hoppity in the other. I fell backward on the bedspread with the plush toy plastered to my heart, my body shaking like a stormfront had belted right through my soul.

I grieved.

I grieved hard. Messily. Painfully.

And I allowed the crushing moment to span for one whole hour, even when Scotty came to check on me, even when he crawled into bed beside me and held me in his arms, trying his best to soothe a bleeding heart that could only be healed by one man who was hundreds of miles away.

I let him.

I let him hold me, hush me, swipe away my tears as my pain petered out and left me drained.

Then I regrouped.

I brushed off the remaining shards of my shattered dreams and made a promise to myself that I would be strong, brave, formidable.

I can do this.

Days rolled into weeks. Weeks into months. Scotty took me to the ocean every weekend, and I would dunk my feet into cool water, letting each dip wash away another fragment of my fear.

As the sun began to set on a warm October evening, a shiver rolled through me as I stared out at the churning salt water.

Deep, dark waves crested, hypnotizing me.

It was fascinating how beautiful things could look so frightening when you were up close.

But then, the very things that frightened you could be beautiful, too.

If you looked a little closer.

I turned to Scotty as he waded a few feet away, his profile splashed with golden sunlight. He found my eyes, his smile broadening against the hazy lowlight, triggering my own.

Blinking back toward the water, I stared out at the aquamarine abyss with new eyes, with eyes scrubbed clean, and I drank in a salt-spun breath.

Then I did exactly what Reed told me to do—I fought.

CHAPTER 35

Halley

August, 1999

"WELCOME. YOU'VE GOT MAIL." The announcement was followed by the sound of a squeaky door opening.

I plopped down in the rolling chair, sorting through notifications while Scotty rummaged around the shelves behind me, dusting and organizing. Over the past year, Reed's east-coast training studio had flourished, with Scotty at the helm, me as the administrator and assistant coach, and a slew of accomplished trainers who helped make this business thrive.

Life had been busy.

Busy, fruitful, and shockingly fulfilling.

While most of my weekdays were spent here, my weekends were almost entirely filled with wedding photography. Photography was my passion, and love was my philosophy—my calling. Combining two of the most important elements of me had been nothing short of therapy.

In a gratifying twist of fate, Monique had stayed true to her self-imposed title of nomad, joining me in Charleston eight months after I'd left Illinois. Together we'd started up a two-person photography business, earning clients through word of mouth, shining referrals, and paper fliers taped around town and in local cafés and coffee shops. We made a good team.

And the fact that I was able to help train fellow survivors at the studio—a full-circle career achievement that paralleled my own recovery process—was the ultimate validation and a testament to my resilience.

Nothing had been easy. Rewarding and necessary, sure, but never easy. Those first six months post-move had been harrowing, heart-wrenching, and hard as hell. Scotty had been a steadfast friend and companion through it all, and while I had attempted to spin our platonic relationship into something more, that soul-sizzling, heart-stealing connection had never managed to bloom.

I'd tried; I truly did. But romantic love could not be forced, and my affections began and ended with friendship.

We'd kissed. We'd gone on dinner dates and sea-swirled walks along the beach, hand in hand. I had done my best to mimic that sparkle in his eyes whenever he looked at me. Yet nothing beyond gratitude and luke-warm feeling ever stirred inside me.

Scotty was understanding; a true friend. And over the past year, he'd settled down with another woman named Angela, well on his way to forging his own love story.

I hoped his ended more happily than mine.

"I'm thinking oysters and ocean waves after work," Scotty said, breaking into my daydreams. "Ang has a friend in town. We can make it a group thing."

I scrolled over the newest e-mail and printed it out as a reminder to set up the consultation. "Sounds good to me."

"You hate oysters."

"I don't hate them. I just need to hold my nose while I eat them so I don't taste them."

"Smear them in peanut butter."

My frown went to war with my glare. A formidable battle. "I hate you."

"Less than peanut butter. I'll take a win when I see one."

"When are you proposing?"

"About that." He pressed a hand over his heart and heaved in a melodramatic sigh. "You complete me, Halley. Marry me."

I smirked, tossing a pink eraser at him and relishing in the way it bopped off his nose, making him flinch.

He scratched at the lingering tickle. "Fine. As soon as Ang stops making anti-marriage comments, I'm going for it." Another sigh left him, more defeated than theatrical. "It's really putting a wrench in my plans. Specifically, the ring-shaped plan sitting in my nightstand drawer."

"That does complicate things." I swiveled back to the computer and tapped a pencil to my chin. "But don't worry. You've stashed away the evidence in the most unassuming place. She will never, ever find it there, so your secret is safe and she will be none the wiser."

"You're such a brat."

"Why we're friends."

We did a secret handshake. Because we were seven.

Our conversation was interrupted by the AOL chat messenger ding when I switched over to my personal account. A giddy smile crested, and I swiveled back around to face the computer, already knowing who it was.

I reached for the mouse, my grin widening.

> **Tara:** Met this guy in a chatroom. His screen name is Bloody-morrow187. Theories?
>
> **Me:** Hmm. Tomorrow will be quite grisly, and he has 187 hatchets in his murder-garage to prove it.
>
> **Tara:** No.
>
> **Me:** Maybe he's British. Tomorrow will be a buggering 187 degrees – bloody hell!
>
> **Tara:** You're so weird.
>
> **Me:** Not as weird as the British serial killer who's courting you via the interwebs.
>
> **Tara:** BRB – he's talking to me.

Tara disappeared for twenty minutes before I was alerted of a new message. I pulled up the chat box and skimmed.

> **Tara:** Update! The screen name is based on an urban legend of a woman who was slaughtered on a street called Morrow. Her bloody ghost was spotted walking down

the street if you honked your horn on a bridge three
times. 187 was the call sign for murder.
Me: Told you!!
Tara: Dang it.
Me: You're still talking to him, aren't you?
Tara: ;)

Chuckling under my breath, I rolled back in the chair when Tara disappeared again, then closed out the chat box and switched back to our company account. Tara and Josh had ended things amicably ten months ago, so she was on the prowl, roping me into her many dating adventures from nearly one-thousand miles away. Tara had visited once with Whitney, our only in-person encounter since the moment I'd driven out of their driveway, my furry, golden friend watching me leave from the edge of the driveway, her image shrinking in the rear view mirror but never in my memories.

For my twentieth birthday, the Stephens' women had had a custom canvas of Ladybug and I hand-painted and shipped. Opening that gift was the hardest I'd cried since the day I received a Beanie Baby bunny in the mail with a note that still resides underneath my pillow.

I missed them.

I missed them all desperately.

But internet chats and e-mail updates with Tara, and long, heart-healing phone calls with Whitney, had lessened the burden of my pain.

I was a work in progress.

An admirable second draft, well on her way to a finished product.

Scotty left the office, gearing up for his next session, and I shuffled around the room watering plants and digging a yogurt out of the fridge.

Back to work.

E-mails piled up with clients rescheduling appointments, as well as potential new clients seeking information, looking to take advantage of our first free training session.

I returned phone calls, scribbled notes, and sipped my coffee, popping spoonfuls of blueberry yogurt into my mouth between tasks. As I moved the mouse to close out the screen, a new e-mail chimed to life with a subject line that stated, "Upcoming Visit."

I froze.

My eyes lingered on the familiar e-mail address, my insides tangling into knots.

Reed.

Two years had trudged by, and I still couldn't keep the tremble out of my hand or the shiver out of my bones. Reed checked in from time to time, helping Scotty operate the Charleston location from afar, behind the scenes. He helped with budget and marketing, mostly, but we were in the architectural stage of adding on a new addition, so he'd been in more frequent contact recently.

I opened up his e-mail, tapping both feet under the desk as I held my breath.

Hey—

I'm coming into town next week to finalize the design with the architect. I'll be flying in on Monday. Just a heads up.

Reed

Acid burned cavities in my throat.

It wasn't like we hadn't communicated over the years, considering I worked for his company and manned the communication aspects of the job. But every time I read over his words, or listened to the rich baritone of his voice on the other end of the phone line, time had a way of narrowing to nothing, all my hard-fought progress withering to dust.

Be strong, Halley.

Stay strong.

I shot back a quick, impersonal response that conveyed none of the still-open wounds carved into my essence and closed out the screen.

Thank you. We're looking forward to the visit.

—Halley

In my imagination and varicolored daydreams, if I ever saw Reed again, I'd be a picture of regal beauty, dolled-up to the max with curls in my hair, ruby stain on my lips, and wearing the sexiest dress fresh off the rack. My strut toward him would be a slow-motion glide of seduction and grace.

He'd be mesmerized, no doubt.

In reality, I was flat on my back after taking a miscalculated kick to the stomach by Mrs. Bronson, sweating profusely from every crevice as I wheezed out a lung. My hair was in shambles, my face painted in blood-red splotches, and my athletic shorts were riding up my ass.

Cartoon birds flitted behind my eyes as the ceiling blurred and a distorted face came into view above me. I blanched the moment the birds evaporated and the image cleared.

"Reed?"

An amused smile hinted as he stared down at me. "Hi, Halley."

"Oh, my God." I hauled myself up, popping to my feet and swiping my chaotic hair back as drops of sweat trickled down my forehead. "I thought you were flying in on Monday."

"I came in a day early."

I stunk.

I was within inches of the man I loved for the first time in years, and I smelled like year-old gym shoes.

Mrs. Bronson apologized profusely from behind me, her cigarette-parched vocal cords blowing smoke through our unexpected reunion. "Sorry, sorry," she rambled out. "I went to that happy place you told me to go to and you suddenly morphed into my ex, Ronny. Nothing personal."

"Um..." I glanced at her, trying to catch my breath as I begged my pores to douse themselves in feminine, floral notes. "No worries. I'll see you next week, same time?"

"With bells on." She winked at Reed as she moved around us, off the mats.

Reed was still smiling when I turned back to face him, the tilt of his lips softening; less amusement, more star-struck affection. We stared at each other for a few beats, my pulse pitter-pattering as I drank him in. He was thirty-eight now, but he was aging well, wearing only a hint of silver in his dark goatee. A golden-bronze hue colored his complexion, making his light-green eyes all the more striking. He wore a winter-gray T-shirt like a second skin, paired with charcoal jeans and familiar black combat boots that swallowed his feet. Muscles strained, his jaw ticked, and the smile faded the longer our eyes held, erasing the dimples I'd come to cherish.

We spoke at the same time. "It's great to see—"

"You look—"

I laughed, ducking my head. "I look horrifying. I'm sorry for that."

"No." His voice was a mere whisper. He squinted like he was studying a lost relic, flicking a hand through his hair as he murmured, "You look exactly like how I remember you. Just..."

"Just what?"

His eyes rolled over me, head to toe. "Older."

It sounded like a compliment, so I blushed and lifted my gaze to his. "Unlike you. Do you age?"

"Only in my back."

A chuckle vibrated past my lips before dying out. I didn't know what to do with my hands, my mouth, or my heart. My arms swung awkwardly as I fumbled for something else to say. "So, we haven't burned the studio down yet."

"I'm impressed." Reed folded his arms, looking fidgety. The toe of his boot scuffed across the shiny floor as his jaw ticked. "Your form is good."

"My form?" My form. Sparring. Training. *Business.* "Right." I cleared my throat, dragging my gaze to the far wall for no other reason than to avoid getting sucked into his pale-jade stare. "I did learn from the best."

He was staring at me in my periphery. Hard lines, firm muscle, stiff stance. But softness emanated from the places where it counted—within the hair's-breadth parting of his full lips, the muted glow of his irises, and the whispery exhale that mellowed out his chest.

He was striking.

Stunning.

Standing right in front of me.

My hands curled, tension infiltrating my muscles and joints. "Well, I'm sure you have a lot to do. I don't want to keep you."

Lies.

I wanted to keep him. Forever. For always.

Reed's lips opened a fraction more, but the words he wanted to say dissolved. I watched them draw lines in the space between us, penning his deepest secrets, before evaporating into nothingness. "Yeah...I need to go over those designs."

"Of course." I coughed because that was what people did when they avoided saying the hard things. "It was really great to see you."

Then I ducked my chin and shuffled past him with no destination in mind. No long-stretching road, no detailed map, no compass would ever lead me back to him. It didn't matter where I went.

But his arm snaked out and snagged my wrist before I moved out of sight. Our eyes met. I held my breath and swallowed, every inch of me focused on his fingers coiled around my trembling wrist.

"Did you, um..." He blinked several times, lost in the eye contact. "Did you receive the package I sent you? The letter?"

Emotion stomped on my chest, bruising me deep. I nodded lightly. "Yes. Thank you."

His lips twitched before his hand dropped away from me in a slow-motion slide. "Yeah," he said. "You're welcome."

And that was it.

With a roll of his neck, he pivoted away, heading toward the office. I watched him go with a knife between my ribs, then turned in the opposite direction.

"You know what?" Reed spun back around and stalked toward me, scrubbing a hand over his jaw. "Fuck it."

"Fuck it?" I blinked, spinning around to face him. "Fuck what?"

"This. It's stupid. You're here, and I'm here, and we have history."

"Okay," I breathed out.

"I miss you."

My eyebrows hiked up, meeting my hairline. "I...miss you, too."

"Good. Have dinner with me tonight."

I went quiet.

Oh.

Comets and shooting stars barreled through my chest, settling in my throat as I squeaked out a gasp of surprise. "Oh."

"If you're not busy."

"I'm not."

"And if you're not..." He glanced at the office over his shoulder as if imagining Scotty on the other side of the closed door.

I shook my head at the implication. "I'm not."

He swallowed, relief tenderizing the tension-riddled lines on his face. "All right." Reed took a few paces back, his eyes still coasting over every inch of me. "There's a little seaside grille in Folly Beach called Rita's. Meet me at seven."

My lips flopped like a fish as I stuttered out a reply and watched him walk away. "I-I'll be there."

His half-smile saw me off, and he disappeared inside the office.

I stood there, dumbstruck. Vibrating with shock. Hope soared like a baby bird's first sky-bound flight, wings of promise fluttering inside me.

Reed and I had ventured through the best and worst out of life. Love, pain, laughter, soul-bared intimacy, and the saddest goodbye. But there was one thing we'd never done before. Never got to experience. Something so simple, so common, the idea of it stole the breath from my lungs.

A date.

CHAPTER 36

Halley

WHEN I SAW HIM AGAIN, five hours later, the shellshock hadn't thinned.

Reed Madsen had evaporated from my orbit like a meteor streaking across the night sky, leaving behind a trail of stardust that clung to my core, impossible to scrub away no matter how hard I tried. Now he'd returned like a thief in the night, leaving me breathless and wanting within the span of a single heartbeat.

As I approached, I spotted him leaning against the wood-planked exterior, perched beside an aqua-bordered entry door. Fingers tucked into denim pockets and eyes charged like a storm-licked sea, Reed gazed at me with tragic longing as I sauntered down the sidewalk and into his line of sight.

This was a terrible idea.

Truly idiotic.

Yet neither of us seemed to care as our own brand of magnetism pulled us together for what felt like a reunion of souls.

He hugged me. No hesitation, no awkward falters. Everything else fell away—time, age, social propriety. It was just me tucked inside the warmth of his arms, where I was always meant to be.

Reed exhaled a breath against my ear, tugging me closer, his large palm cradling the back of my head. "It's so good to see you." He wasn't pulling away. "Sorry this was sudden. I wanted to cut to the chase earlier before I lost my nerve."

My body buzzed and melted at the same time. "I'm glad you did. I probably would've talked in circles about nothing until the days drifted by and you were gone again."

Painstakingly, he inched back, his hands taking their time to trail down my arms and return to his sides. His eyes held hotly to mine, torture and affection creasing his browline. "It's hard to believe I'm looking at you. Something other than a photograph or memory." Then those eyes crawled down my body, drifting from the curve of my neck to my shimmer-dusted cleavage, all the way down my bronzed legs. When they flicked back up, his gaze glittered with dark lust. "Take a walk with me?"

I blinked away from his thigh-clenching stare, glancing over at the restaurant in my black, thigh-length cocktail dress and chic ankle boots. "I thought—"

"I know. I've just always wanted to do this."

"Do what?"

He reached out and clasped my hand, linking our fingers together. "Hold your hand in public."

My breath burst out in a puff of wonderment.

I nodded and we started walking down the crowded, seaside street with salt and laughter mingling in the air. Words couldn't find me. Only feeling. Only the sensation of his palm squeezing mine, our steps a perfect rhythm.

This isn't a date. We're just friends.

This can't be a date.

Friends held hands.

Scotty and I held hands.

It didn't have to mean anything...because it *couldn't* mean anything.

But the mantra folded in half as his thumb dusted over my knuckles, our fingers intertwined in a way that felt like more. Emotion burned holes in my chest. Love blazed hot, the fire far from cindered.

"I don't know what to say," I admitted as we dodged other couples, dogs on short leashes, and a slew of baby strollers. "I think my words are broken."

He glanced at me, tangerine highlights from the low-hanging sun brightening his dark hair. "You don't have to say anything."

"I should. There's so much to say." I sighed, squinting my eyes at the orange globe hovering on the horizon. "How are you?"

"Never been better."

"I mean...before. Before you came here. How's your business? Your life back home?"

He stared straight ahead, his cheek twitching. "Doesn't feel like home these days."

"How's, um..." My eyes closed, pain sinking inside. "How are things with Tara?"

The grip of his hand strengthened, and I could almost hear his pulse kick up. "Strained," he said.

God...still?

It had been two years.

Reed was never a topic of discussion between Tara and me. I refused to bring him up, hoping, praying, silently begging for her to broach the painful subject that haunted all of us. She never did.

Had she looked through the scrapbook? Drank in those pages filled with love and truth?

I didn't know.

She had never mentioned it.

I swallowed, clinging to his hand. "I'm sorry."

"Whitney told me everything." He glanced down at the sidewalk and stroked his chin with two fingers. "I'd known a little at the time—a teacher getting fired, a strained friendship. I knew Tara was going through something, but I never sought out details. I was busy getting my business off the ground, and I regret not being more present. More in tune. If I'd had known..." Reed's eyes glassed over as he exhaled through his nose. "I never would have put those ideas in her head."

Our palms squeezed.

My heart clenched like a fist around an iron weight.

"Anyway...I just keep hoping every day brings with it the potential for a fresh start. Forgiveness. Healing." His eyes narrowed with thought. "I've seen her. I think she's trying. But it's not the same, and there's still this divide between us. A dark cloud. Whitney says she's making progress, but it's hard to see it that way from my side."

We turned a corner, headed toward the beach. The breeze stole his hair, spinning it into a disheveled, glorious mess I ached to sift my fingers through. "I'm still hopeful. If I can be standing here after everything I went through, so can she."

A smile tipped his lips as he switched gears. "You're doing amazing things, Halley. I saw your website. Your wedding photography. It's just incredible."

A shimmery beam dazzled through me at the compliment, lightening my mood. "It's been everything I ever dreamed about. Capturing forever moments; love in motion. The smiles, the speeches, the carefully selected flowers and trinkets that decorate tabletops." I peered up at him, unable to tame my smile. "My favorite part of the whole wedding is when the groom catches sight of his bride walking down the aisle for the first time. While Monique is concentrating on her, I'm focused on him. The tears in his eyes. The unmistakable love splashed across his face. It can't be staged. It's just so...raw. So magical."

He smiled sadly as the pavement beneath our feet morphed into sand. "Do you want that?"

I wavered for a moment. "Love?"

"A wedding."

"Oh." I glanced ahead, a landscape of blue-green water coming closer into view. "I don't know. It's not something I think about."

His eyes narrowed with consideration. "Interesting."

"I don't photograph weddings and ever wish it were me in the white dress with flowers in my hair. I'm fully absorbed in *their* moment. *Their* joy."

As we ventured toward the waterline, Reed stopped, releasing my hand and digging into his pocket. My eyes followed the movement, waiting, wondering.

Then he pulled out a little stem of vibrant blue flowers.

Morning glories.

My breath shook as he lifted the blossoms in the air and tucked them behind my ear, pushing my hair to the side and adjusting the stem into place.

A grin crested on his mouth. So bright it outshined the backdrop behind us that glittered with golden sunlight on water. "You look pretty with flowers in your hair."

I didn't know much, but I knew for certain that my heart wouldn't make it through the night without imminent implosion.

I was toast.

Fiddling with the fragile blooms, I forced back tears. "Flowers. Hand-holding. A long walk on the beach." I bit down on my lip. "This feels like a date, Reed."

He took my hand again and ushered me forward. "It's just a day." Our arms swung with levity, the dark clouds fading into clearer skies. "A really good day."

Food trucks and charming shacks crooning with live music lined the shore, the scent of deep-fried treats and savory snacks infusing the air. I stared out at the rippling water, foolishly imagining more days just like this. More really good days.

Reed guided me toward the row of food trucks as people shoveled barbecue and overstuffed tacos into their mouths from paper trays.

My stomach tightened with hunger pangs. "Should we eat?"

"You cooking?" He sent me a sparkling sidelong glance that put the ocean to shame. "I miss that."

"Ah. Maybe my grandmother was right."

"How's that?"

"The best way to a person's heart is through their stomach."

He nodded slowly, tugging me into one of the food lines. "Maybe. But you found a way in before I ever tasted your food."

Warm flush soaked into my skin.

Yep.

I was absolutely toast.

My smile was now plastered to my face with superglue as we dallied at the end of the line, our shoulders brushing. "Tell me about the studio," I said, changing the subject before I disintegrated and became one with the sand. "Do you have a lot of clients?"

He nodded again. "Business is booming. Keeps me busy. Distracted."

"Have you made friends?"

"I have."

"Good. You were always such a recluse."

"I'd left most of my friends in Charleston, so it was hard starting over once I moved back to Illinois. My daughter certainly didn't get her social butterfly persona from me."

I tried not to flinch at the mention of Tara. "I'm glad you're not alone," I mused before an insidious, clawing feeling inched its way between my ribs. "Are you, um...seeing anybody?"

A lump formed in my throat, and my chest thundered with anxious black heat.

He swallowed, glancing away. "Nothing's worked out."

I rubbed my lips together. "Sorry to hear."

"What about you?"

"Same."

"Anything happen with Scotty?"

"I tried." Shrugging, I dug the toe of my black boot into the sand. "It didn't go anywhere. We're better off as friends."

He studied me, taking in my answer. "Does he agree?"

"He does now. We're really close and still share an apartment together. I'm saving up to get my own place, and he's been in a long-term relationship for a year. He's happy. He even bought a ring."

"That's great." Reed scratched the back of his neck as we inched up the line. "I'm happy for him."

It *was* great.

So many things were great.

But Reed and I were both single, staring starry-eyed at each other, and standing together on an ocean-rimmed beach, yet we lived a thousand miles away, the mountain between us even vaster.

That wasn't great. It was painful.

As we approached the window, I crossed my arms and glanced at the menu. My breath caught when I noticed the signage. "Pierogies?"

A knowing grin teased his lips. "Homemade. The best kind."

Airiness danced between us again as we collected our orders and strolled across the crowded shore, melted butter and onion seizing my senses. I shoved a forkful in my mouth, moaning. "Ohmigod," I mumbled through the giant bite. "Heaven."

Reed chewed through his own bite, his eyes twinkling as they settled on my giddy face. "I concur."

Music filtered around us as we ate our food, both our strides and conversation losing their tension. He told me survivor stories about his clients, the lush condo he leased in May that overlooked the down-town scenery, and Ladybug's harrowing love story with the neighbor dog.

"A chihuahua?" My eyes bulged. "An unforeseen plot twist."

"He bit her on the cheek and then had instant regret. Whitney found the two of them curled up next to the shed that afternoon, the chihuahua licking her wound until dusk." He chuckled. "They've been inseparable ever since."

I was partly amused, but mostly touched. So touched that another prickle of tears teased my eyeballs. Sniffling, I forced a laugh as we discarded our empty food trays into the nearby trash can. "Now that I would have loved to have taken a picture of."

We made it to the edge of the water, where dry sand turned to sludge. My boots sunk into the muck as a gust of wind whipped through, blowing my freshly washed hair into chaotic ribbons across my face. I was so fixated on the way the sun made love to the water, I hadn't noticed Reed digging through his wallet.

A photograph emerged in front of my face. I blinked down, pushing a section of hair to the side, my eyes landing on a picture of Ladybug and her new friend, Nico.

Oh, my heart.

Memories soared as high as my emotions. I plucked the photo from his hand and studied the image, dragging my fingertips over the outline of my fuzzy best friend. Nico was nestled against her belly, one of her huge golden paws secured around the tiny creature. Their eyes were closed. Utter contentment.

Nodding through a wave of heartache, I fisted the picture and handed it back.

"Keep it," he said. "I took it for you."

My gaze lifted, wide and awestruck. "You did?"

"Yeah." Hands in his pockets, he rolled back on his heels. "I take a lot of pictures now. I have a shoebox full of them. I plan to mail them all to you one day."

"What?" I blinked away tears, a watery smile blooming. "Reed..."

"It keeps you close. Like you're right there with me, pressing the button."

I turned back to the water, folding in my lips to keep the sound from falling out. The anguish. Then I tucked the picture inside my purse that was strapped across my torso.

"You should get your feet wet."

"You should come with me."

Reed glanced at the water, his brows gathering as he slid his thumb across his lower lip. "Maybe another time."

His words from that first night at the lake coursed through me—when I'd invited him into the water, and he'd declined.

My voice lowered with sorrow as I echoed back, "Liar."

I toed out of my boots anyway, dropped my purse to the sand, and sauntered forward, the cool water sloshing against my bare feet. Drawing them in. Drawing me away from Reed.

He stood still at the shoreline, watching me submerge, his black boots barely teasing the shallow tide. I turned to face him and walked backward, yelping when the tide grew wings and crashed against the backs of my thighs. A laugh fell out of me, and he laughed, too.

Fifteen feet away, we stared at each other as I allowed the ocean to suck me in while Reed's adoring smile did everything it could to keep me standing upright. Seawater lapped at my hips, drenching the bottom of my dress. My toes curled into the spongy floor. I flapped my arms, splashing the air with droplets and twirling in circles as sunlight painted my body in vivid colors. Fuchsia, orange, and amber. His eyes reflected the same colors.

Shivering and soaked, I padded back to the shore, meeting him on dry land.

Reed reached for me the moment I was within arm's length as a song played from a cobblestone patio draped in string lights. "Dance with me."

I pretended it was our song. Composed just for us.

I let him hold me as he wrapped both arms around my waist and pulled me to his chest. We swayed lightly to acoustic guitar strings and the remnants of the setting sun while warmth settled in, eclipsing the ocean's chill. I was at home again. Not in Illinois, but in Reed's glittering galaxy.

A comet landing in the arms of its favorite star.

He sighed heavily, dropping his face to the crook of my neck, his stubble tickling my soft skin. His arms tightened. My heart ballooned.

We danced, undulating side to side, in unsteady circles, with wet sand beneath our feet and salt on our skin. Tears and ocean mist.

"This was all I wanted tonight, Halley. Just this. Something we never got to experience." His words were warm honey against my ear. "Everything between us was built upon respect and genuine connection, but it was only able to be harnessed in the physical sense. Behind closed doors. Kept in the shadows." Reed slid a palm up and down my spine, his thumb grazing the zipper of my dress. "It killed me that you left, and we never got this. Not once."

Public affection.

Transparent love, out in the open.

A fuck-you to the universe that we were right and they were wrong.

Age didn't matter. Numbers meant nothing in the grand scheme of destiny.

"I still want this," I murmured against the heather-gray cotton molded to his chest, the fabric tormenting me with masculine, familiar scents. "I'll always want this."

"I know." He kissed the column of my neck. "Me, too."

But...

There was always a *but*.

We both knew what it was. Tara hadn't forgiven him yet. She hadn't accepted that we were more than a clandestine affair; more than a repeat of her harrowing past experience.

Something that never should have been.

And until that day came, we would never have a chance to *be*.

As the sun fully set behind the horizon, we'd somehow drifted toward a little gazebo away from the crowded beach. He took my hand in his and ushered me inside the wooden, screened-in pavilion that was shrouded in dusk, noise from the crowds sounding miles away.

The moment we were tucked inside, he kissed me.

I wasn't expecting it.

I wasn't anticipating his mouth on mine, parting my lips with his eager tongue. My body sagged against him, turning to dough, my tapered moan swallowed by his. He pressed me against the timbered wall, cupping my cheeks between both hands and devouring me. I latched on to the front of his shirt, gripping tightly, tugging him closer as my leg lifted up his thigh. Our faces angled, tasting deeper. Taking everything. Nips, groans, licks. He was intoxicating, and I wasn't sure why he thought this was a good idea. Reed was leaving. Going back to Illinois, to his life without me. We'd be separated in a day's time, banished to our homeless homes on opposite ends of the earth.

His mouth lowered to nick my jaw, then settled on my throat, his tongue sheathing a trail of wet heat up to my ear as he nibbled the lobe and whispered my nickname. "Comet."

He'd only intended for this to be a kiss. What more could it be?

But he should have known better. My thighs spread on instinct, my leg lifting higher, offering an invitation he couldn't refuse. Temptation.

Our mouths were still locked as he grazed a hand up my inner thigh and pushed my underwear aside beneath my dress. I jolted, gasped, my head falling back against the gazebo planks. "Reed..."

He kissed me again, my mouth falling open as our tongues clumsily and blissfully danced. Two fingers slipped inside me. Caressing, claiming. I held on for dear life, my nails digging into the planks of his chest, my back anchored to the wall as voices floated over to us from the beach. Music played. Waves crested, a soundtrack to our stolen moment.

Reed rubbed my clit with his thumb, two fingers still buried inside. Wetness soaked him, leaking down my ocean-damp thighs.

It didn't take long. It never took long for me to break, splinter, shatter against his touch. Dizzying white heat blanketed my vision as an orgasm slammed into me, leaving me slumped and heart-heavy against the shelter's wall. Reed gathered me in his arms as I came down from the high, releasing apologies into my ear.

Apologies.

No celebrations, no fireworks, no beginning to our happily ever after.

Only a goodbye, setting as quickly as the August sun.

I hugged him harder than ever before, tears tracking grief down my cheekbones. The morning glories had slipped from my ear, now splattered at our feet in broken buds.

Mourning.

Glory.

Both bleeding together with despair.

"I love you." Reed tried in vain to erase my tear stains with his desperate kisses. But they'd carved holes. Left scars. "I love you, Halley," he gritted out. "I'll never stop."

We lowered to a nearby bench, and he scooped me into his lap, cradling me as all the light was sucked from the night sky. That was where we stayed for another hour. Weeping and wishing.

Delaying another painful goodbye.

I saw Reed one last time at the studio before he left town twenty-four hours later and headed back to Illinois. I'd known it was temporary. Every piece of me had known it, except for the most important piece. That piece ached and sobbed, begging for a different outcome.

I'd come a long way over the last two years, and I wanted so badly to say I was okay. That I'd moved on. But, while I could confidently say I'd moved on in so many ways—from my past traumas, my insecurities, my bone-deep fears—the love I held for Reed hadn't budged. It was a constant presence, anchored inside me. Steadfast and stubborn.

All I could do was wait.

Reed had given me a lifeline.

But I wanted a lifetime.

CHAPTER 37

Reed

HOLLOWNESS FESTERED in the months after I'd returned home from Charleston. Business went on as usual, the studio hovering at the forefront of my distractions. A friend had roped me into regular weekend boating trips while the weather clung to warmer temperatures, and my brother had made it into town, temporarily occupying my runaway thoughts for a few days with drinks at bars and afternoon golf outings.

I'd recently turned thirty-nine; I guessed that meant I golfed now.

But it didn't interest me.

Nothing did.

And at the very bottom of my interest list were the come-hither invitations from one of my training clients who was dabbling in jiu-jitsu. I was a session away from encouraging her to find another studio. While life dragged by in shades of dishwater-gray, nothing unsettled me more than the thought of being intimate with another woman.

A woman who wasn't her.

Halley possessed my mind like a relentless storm. When I closed my eyes, I pictured her standing waist-deep in the ocean, her hair a golden halo around her face, her eyes shimmering with sunset swirl. Puckered skin from the cool mist. Full, parted lips, begging to be kissed.

I was a fucking idiot for kissing her. For taking something that wasn't mine, for touching her in places that were no longer meant for me. For giving us both a deadly ray of hope. She'd been too willing, too responsive. Too goddamn beautiful. It was a recipe for disaster, and that disaster had followed me home.

Over the past year, I'd transformed half of the back room into an office, where I spent weeknights detailing workflow spreadsheets for both locations. A computer sat atop a paper-strewn desk in the corner, only sharing the space with a cup of pens, a stapler, and a single pewter frame that held a photograph of Tara and Halley sitting by the fireplace on Christmas Eve.

I glanced at it, missing them both.

Craving Tara's hugs and Halley's kisses.

My mind zoned out, just as a notification dinged to life on the screen. A chat box. I pivoted forward in the rolling chair, my heart skipping at the unexpected message.

Halley: Late night at the office?

We hadn't messaged like this before. There had only been impersonal, work-centric e-mails that did little to subdue the sharp ache between my ribs. I hadn't thought about making personal contact. It felt too real, too intimate. Too goddamn painful.

But that was...*before*. Before our visit, when my fingers had found their way between her legs, love confessions had spilled from my unworthy lips, and my tongue had knotted with hers while a salt breeze fused with tears.

Blinking at the instant message, I lifted a hand, positioning my fingers over the keys. A slew of poetic words whirled through my brain. They didn't make it to my fingertips.

Me: Hey.

Lame as fuck.

Halley: Hey yourself.
Me: Sorry. You caught me off guard.
Halley: In a good way or bad way?

> Me: Good. Always good.

A solid minute passed while I waited for more conversation that I would inevitably butcher.

> Halley: Since your greeting led me to believe you're gearing
>   up for some rich, insightful, soul-baring conversation, I
>   can only follow-up with something equally fitting: How's
>   the weather?

I grinned, chewing on my cheek as I imagined her sitting cross-legged in her desk chair, her sun-kissed hair piled on her head, pajamas swallowing her slim frame.

> Me: It's not picture-book sunsets over sparkling water while
>   splashes of color paint your face and your laughter out-
>   sings the ocean waves. But I'm enduring.
> Halley: Ooh, there he is. Much better :)
> Me: I miss you.
> Halley: Even better yet. I always knew you were secretly a
>   romantic.
> Me: Because I swept you off your feet? Literally. Countless
>   times.
> Halley: LOL. The scissor sweep! But no, it's because of the
>   Beanie Baby sitting on my desk. Hoppity knows the
>   truth.
> Me: :) How are you? Any weddings lately?
> Halley: We're wrapping up the busy season next weekend
>   and only have a few more in the books until April. I'm
>   going to e-mail you a new favorite picture I took. Hold
>   please.

I held.

Held on to my breath, my heart, my hopes.

A new e-mail chimed, and I switched over to my inbox and opened it up. It was a low-quality image of a mother and daughter dancing. The bride's head was tipped back with laughter while the mother's face scrunched with emotion, tears falling down her cheeks. It was beautiful. Candid. A testament to Halley's keen eye, talent, and unmatched heart.

> Me: It's incredible.
> Halley: Thank you for pushing me in this direction. A dream come true.
> Me: Rock, paper, scissors foreshadowed this, remember? If I won, you were going to chase your dreams—wings spread, eyes on the sky, no looking back. I won.
> Halley: Feels like I won. :)

And yet...it felt like we'd both lost.

Lost something vital. Something fundamental.

Sadness trickled in, dampening my schoolyard smile. She was one-thousand miles away. Too far to touch, to hold, to cradle in my arms and lull to sleep with the beats of my heart.

I drummed my fingers on the desk before sending a reply as a knot hollowed out my throat.

> Me: I'm going to head home and make dinner.
> Halley: Have some pierogies for me!
> Me: Not the same without you. Rice Krispies it is.
> Halley: The Christmas edition?
> Me: You know it.
> Halley: Goodnight, Reed.
> Me: We should do this again some time.
> Halley: We should. Maybe the weather will get better. Sunny skies ahead.
> Me: The forecast is looking up. Goodnight, Comet.

Signing off, I lingered at the desk for a few more gloomy minutes before gathering my keys and heading back home. Late-October chill nibbled at my skin as I jogged from the studio over to my condo a mile away, my somber thoughts drifting to my daughter. The last two years had been painful, trying to maintain a semblance of a relationship with Tara, while her cold shoulder and glaring eyes cut me into pieces.

I truly thought it wouldn't take this long for her to see the light.

The truth.

To open her heart to me again and view me as something other than a nefarious monster.

A lunch date six months ago had been arranged with little progress coming from her. But she'd showed up, slumped in the diner booth across from me, making squiggly designs in her ketchup as itchy silence scratched between us. Whitney had encouraged her to go. To make amends. And I'd fucking tried so hard to reroute her pain into acceptance with ill-timed jokes, forced smiles, and questions about beauty school, only to be sliced down by cool indifference.

She'd been a brick wall.

But...she had come.

And that had been the tiniest beam of sunlight in my cold, shadowy world.

As I approached my front door and sifted around for my keys, I was surprised to find that it was already unlocked when I reached for the handle.

Weird.

Cautiously, I cracked open the door and peeked inside, freezing in place when a silhouette came into view, seated stiffly on my couch.

I blinked, convinced I was imagining her. "Tara?"

Sullen emerald eyes lifted to my face, the twinkle long-since faded. She sat like a stone, waiting for me to enter the condo.

With a hard swallow, I pushed inside, closing the door behind me and pocketing my keys. I studied her, lost for words. Having no clue why she'd be here.

It had to be an emergency.

Whitney or Ladybug.

Fear creeped into my bones as the color drained from my face. "What happened?"

She frowned, her eyes narrowing. "A lot has happened."

"Did someone get hurt?"

"Yes."

My eyes assessed her from toes to top before I realized she wasn't talking about physical injury. I stepped forward, my throat fizzing with stinging heat. "What are you doing here?"

She looked away. "I don't know. Mom said you were depressed. She was giving me a guilt trip."

"I'm not depressed." I was.

"No?" Slowly, her gaze found me again, still devoid of the glimmering light I craved. "Never mind, then. False alarm."

When she moved to stand, I whipped forward, extending my hand. "No. Wait. I don't want you to go."

"It was stupid to come."

"We can talk through it."

"Words won't help." She picked at the sleeve of her fuzzy ivory sweater. "I just wanted to make sure you weren't about to down a bottle of pills or something."

My brows pinched together. "I'm not suicidal."

She shrugged. "Cool. I'll let Mom know." Tara remained seated, still fidgeting with her sweater, her feet tapping in opposite time.

I crossed my arms, my heart pounding with hope. She hadn't seen my new condo yet, but I'd left a key for her with Whitney, wishing one day she'd walk through the door and fall into my arms again. "You were worried about me," I decided, unable to keep the sliver of warmth out of my voice.

A huff fell out like bitterness. "Don't get all excited. I just don't want to see you dead."

"Thanks."

"I should've had Mom check on you."

Hesitantly, I crossed the room, idling a few feet away from her. "But you didn't. You came."

Another apathetic shrug.

I scratched at my hair and sighed. "Talk to me. Tell me what's on your mind. We can get through this. We can—"

"Did you see her?"

My throat closed up, a line of sweat forming on my hairline. "Yes."

"And?"

"And nothing. I had to fly in and meet with the architect and contractors."

"Convenient."

"Necessary."

Her lips pursed to the side as she glanced at me. "You still love her, don't you?"

The question sent a flame through me. My skin heated, my heart scorched, and only the truth spilled out like a river bursting its banks. "More than I can say."

Tara stared at me, her expression creasing with every emotion.

"How do you feel about that?" I prompted.

She blinked at me. "How do I feel knowing my father is having sex with my best friend?"

I lowered my eyes to the charcoal-gray rug beneath my boots. "Was."

"Was what?"

"I *was* sleeping with her. That's been over for two years."

"Because of me."

"Yes," I confirmed softly. "Because of you."

Tara lunged up from the couch, swinging her head back and forth, her brown hair spilling over her shoulders. "That's not fair. Why do I feel like the bad guy here when you were the one fooling around with a seventeen year old behind everyone's back?"

"She was nineteen."

"Seventeen when you met. That's fucked-up, Dad."

Dad.

I hadn't heard that title in years. One little syllable had the power to bring me to my knees. My eyes watered, the rest of her spiel becoming background static.

Biting her lip, she took in my expression, a softness coasting across her face. Then she shook it off. "I never thought you'd still love her after all this time."

"Why? You do."

Her eyes flared, almost like she'd never taken the time to put the pieces together like that. I'd been the damaged piece. The chewed-up, broken piece that didn't fit into the puzzle. Everyone was allowed to love Halley except for me.

"That's different," she said.

"How is it different?"

"You know how it's different. You're double her age." Swallowing, she glanced away. "I realize you didn't know all the details about Stacy. I told Mom, but I never told you. But that doesn't change the situation. I can't ignore the parallels and how it makes me feel."

My mind wheeled back in time to standing in that living room with Halley latched on to my arm, begging me to defend what we both knew was real. But it hadn't been the time for truth. If I hadn't done what I did then, Tara would have abandoned us both.

I'd been certain of it.

Now, two years later, the truth felt like the only thing left to say.

I took one more step forward, watching as Tara crossed her arms, defensively. I had to break through her shield. "Tara, listen to me." My voice lowered, imploring her to listen. "I love Halley because it's impossible not to. It wasn't planned. It wasn't even wanted. It just happened. And I'm sorry this affected you so profoundly; I'm so damn sorry for that. I had no idea how deep the situation went back in Charleston. If I had, I would have done it all differently. I wouldn't have filled your head with that untrue shit." I closed my eyes, breathing out through my nose. "But I see what *you* see. A strong, capable, resilient woman. I never viewed her as a teenager or a broken soul who needed fixing. She just needed guidance. Love. Someone to believe in her. And that was you, me, and your mother. My love just came with consequences."

Tara's eyes flicked over my face, her lips twitching. "I've tried, Dad. I've been trying so hard to understand this. I promised Halley I would, and I didn't lie. I just..." Tears welled in her eyes. "I didn't realize how hard it would be. I'd been so clueless to what happened with Stacy and our teacher, so stupidly ignorant, and I promised myself I would never allow that to happen again. Not to anyone, especially my friend."

"Tara, it's not the same. God, it's not even close."

"You *hurt* me." She gritted her teeth, trying to hold back her heartbreak. "I trusted you. More than anyone in the world."

My shoulders slackened. Two years of tension slipped away at the sound of her voice breaking, her words cracking. Finally, something other than steely detachment poured out of her, and all I wanted to do was mold it into something sweeter. Something we could use to make this right.

I lifted a hand and stepped forward.

She jumped back. "No, I'm not okay yet," she said brokenly. "And I'm not trying to be petty or selfish or unforgiving—I swear to you, I'm not. I realize it's been a long time. Years. It's just really hard to trust in this after everything I've been through."

"I understand. Everything about this is hard." Tears blurred my vision as I pressed my hands together like a prayer, a desperate petition. "But easy love is overrated. Hard love means you have to fight, and when you're fighting, it means you have something worth fighting for. And that's beautiful. That's everything." I ran my tongue along my top teeth. "I want you to fight. For me. For us. For our relationship that I miss so damn much."

"I don't know how to just accept this," she confessed. "I thought it was over. When she left, I thought you'd start dating again—start over with someone else. Someone your own age. At the time, I truly believed Halley was nothing more than some twisted fantasy you needed to satisfy a disgusting itch."

Mind-numbing pain trickled through me as my face collapsed. "You know me better than that."

"I thought I did." She shrugged, hopelessly. "I think that's why this hurts so much. You blindsided me. You lied. Snuck around behind my back for two years."

"Tara, I had no clue how to deal with it. Every day that passed, the harder I fell for her. And the harder I fell, the more I buried myself deeper. Betraying you was the last thing I ever wanted."

"But you did it anyway." A tear trickled from the corner of her eye, drawing a grief-stricken line down her cheek. "And then you allowed me to believe you were a monster. A creep. It took months of long talks with Mom—of legitimate *therapy*—to understand why you did that."

My own tears burned, drowning me in heartache.

But nothing sucker-punched me more than her next words.

"You were choosing her."

I choked on my breath.

Stared at my daughter with devastation carved across my face.

I'd made a knee-jerk decision in that moment, and I'd chosen to protect Halley's heart over my daughter's, believing so entirely that Tara would understand one day. Forgive me. Use the tools and wisdom she'd acquired from a privileged, love-drenched life to heal her wounds. Halley had never had that. She'd come from nothing, and my own selfish decisions had left her with nothing but packed bags and a daunting, unknown future.

But I hadn't known the weight of Tara's trauma.

Her own burdens that haunted her.

Her pain.

In hindsight, I could have done something differently. Tried to find the balance in disorder. Thought harder, fought harder. Maybe I could have saved them both from the damaging repercussions of my actions.

But in the game of forbidden love, someone always lost.

I just never thought it would be all of us.

Tara looked away off my silence, dropping her chin, her eyes squeezing shut as more tears spilled out. She shook her head. Inhaled a shuddery breath.

I had no more words of solace to give. No more explanations to offer. She already knew that I loved Halley—time had opened her eyes to that truth.

But I feared nothing I could say would ever convince Tara that I loved her just as much.

And that was my fault.

That was my eternal cross to bear.

I rubbed a hand over my face, defeat weakening my bones. "Tell me how to fix this."

Tara swiped away the remnants of her sorrow and straightened her stance. "I don't know, Dad. This isn't my fourth-grade science project. You can't just run to the store when the glue runs out and save the day."

"There has to be something." My words bled with rawness. With pleading. "You're my little girl."

"I'll always be your little girl." Tara gathered her purse from the couch and breezed past me, muttering a final statement over her shoulder that twisted the blade in my chest, all the way through. "And you'll always be the man who broke my heart."

CHAPTER 38

MOM WAS SEATED at my tiny kitchen table with a glass of wine when I slipped into the apartment and kicked off my shoes. Her head popped up at my entrance, her eyes glimmering with hope.

Sorry, Mom.

Hope doesn't live here. You broke into the wrong apartment.

I tried to remain inconspicuous despite my lumbering retreat to the bedroom, unable to meet her eyes. The last thing I wanted to do was talk about this. Again.

"Tara."

"I'm tired," I called back. "I don't know why you're here."

"Yes, you do." She stood from the chair, the legs squeaking against yellowing tile. "How did it go?"

Sighing, I paused in the center of the hallway and flicked my hair out of my eyes. "He's not dead." Then I attempted another escape.

She stopped me. "Tara. Let's talk."

"Sounds worse than a lecture from Aunt Laurel about the importance of color-coordinating your prayer shawls for the church bazaar."

"I'm serious," she said, swirling her wine glass before taking a hearty gulp. "This is important."

It *was* important.

That was why it hurt so much. And when something hurt, I avoided it instead of dealing with it. I distracted myself with shiny, pretty things, eager to bury the pain and move forward, focusing on anything else. Everyone had their coping mechanisms. Mine had served me well enough.

But I recognized her tone. She wasn't going to let up. She'd follow me into the bedroom and try to talk sense into me while I daydreamed about burrowing under the bed covers and waking up to a new day, where my mother wasn't hovering over me, forcing parental wisdom down my throat.

I huffed and spun around to face her, my face a mask of irritation. "I'm twenty years old. I don't appreciate you showing up at my apartment without an invitation."

"You gave me a key."

"For emergencies."

"This is an emergency."

My eyes narrowed. "Dad screwing my best friend isn't an emergency. It was a stunning lack of judgment on his part that I don't feel like rehashing for the billionth time. I'm tired. Please leave."

She stared at me with knowing acorn eyes. Warmth resided there. It always did, no matter what crass words spilled from my mouth. No matter how incorrigible I could be. She was always warm and soft. Reassuring in a way that severed my defenses and had me wanting to run into her arms, regardless of my anger or bitterness.

Halley never had that. Not until she lived with us.

It was hard for me to imagine a life without a mom like mine, so that was what had me trudging forward, sighing with surrender, and loosening the chip on my shoulder. "I tried," I murmured. "I tried to understand. To accept. But it feels impossible."

A smile tipped her lips as she gestured me toward the table. "Sit."

Ruefully, I obeyed, inching closer to the kitchen. That was when my attention landed on something sprawled across the tabletop. Something that had my jaw clenching, my fists balling, my heart kicking up speed. "Where did you find that?"

She glanced at it. "It's been collecting dust under your bed for two years."

"That's mine."

"Have you looked through it?"

I swallowed, folding my arms. "No."

"Why not?"

"That doesn't matter." Acid stung the back of my throat as an itchy feeling crawled over my skin. "I'll look at it when I'm ready. You don't get to decide when I'm ready."

"I'll look through it with you. Maybe that will help."

"Help with what?" I scoffed. "Is there a time machine inside? Can you erase the last few years?"

Mom sat back down and gestured toward the empty chair beside her, discarding the wine glass. "No need for a time machine. Erasing the past doesn't do us any favors. If everything had an easy way out, we'd be a brittle, complacent species." She arched an eyebrow. "Sit."

My hands uncurled.

Damn her.

Damn her and her motherly wisdom.

She'd always been the sensible one. Now she was almost forty, so she had time on her side—time and experience to weave into life lessons that she couldn't wait to shove down my throat.

I didn't appreciate it, but I would listen. I owed her that much.

Pulling out the chair, I plopped down like a petulant child and planted my chin in my hand. I stared at the wall. I wasn't going to make this easy on her. Nope.

"I remember taking this picture," she noted, grazing her index finger over the image on the front cover of Halley and I at the lake. "It was only a few months after Halley moved in. I knew in that moment she was going to have a better life. A good life."

Softening, I looked over at the photograph. "You did an amazing job."

"So did you. I commend you for standing by her side through all of that."

"The transition?"

"The fallout." Her eyes thinned, studying the picture. "Anyone else would have painted her the villain. The betrayer. Girls can be catty and self-absorbed. You were brave. A true friend."

A true friend.

A resentful daughter.

I wasn't perfect.

Mom opened the scrapbook, and my eyes fell away again. I wasn't sure what I was afraid of.

The truth?

Yeah, that was it. I was content living with my anger, trapped between self-constructed walls. It felt safer than opening myself up to soul-crushing epiphanies. I wasn't built for that sort of thing.

"Tara, please look." Mom reached for my hand and clasped our palms together. "Halley gave this to you for a reason. This is her truth—her journey—through her eyes."

My own eyes misted, bitten with talon-tipped tears. I slowly panned my gaze to the open book and peered at the pages. Ivory cardstock. Multicolored doodles. Stickers and notes.

Pictures.

So many vivid pictures. Some that I recall. Some I never knew about.

I drank in a cracked breath and moved in closer, skimming over each carefully assembled page. It was the story of us. Our lives in Technicolor brilliance. Beach days. Homework huddles. Game nights, holidays, parties, barbeques. Prom night.

I studied that one, honing in on the way Dad was squished in next to Halley, and her head was dipped toward his shoulder. An unsuspecting moment I never would have given a second glance to. But now, with context, I saw something there.

I kept going.

Flipping pages. Burning images into my mind.

There were a few taken at Dad's apartment. Part of me wanted to spew hostility all over the secret, stolen moments, but I pushed my animosity aside. Dad was sitting on the couch with a video game controller in his hands. He was looking at the television screen with a smirk on his face, knowing Halley was sneaking memories in his periphery. It was playful. Sweet. An everyday moment I had soured with my wrath and misconstrued beliefs.

Mom continued to hold my hand. A steady presence, keeping my broken bits from unraveling.

More photos glimmered from sketched pages.

Halley in bed with Ladybug—I had taken that one. Golden hair and fur blended as one as they slept soundly. Halley's pink cast kept a clunky hold on our beloved pet, a reminder of everything she'd been through. Everything she'd survived.

Another photo of me and my father sent a wave of emotion funneling through me. I was asleep on his shoulder. Curled up and peaceful after an afternoon of sparring at the park. His arm was slung around me, his head tipped back against the couch cushions, eyes closed. I didn't think he knew the picture had been taken. Caught and captured, forever immortalized.

I missed that. I missed his warm, safe arms around me, protecting me, even as I slept. Dreamful and free from burdens.

And then there was a photo of just my dad.

Sitting on a park bench, his hair caught in a breeze. Bones the Beanie Baby was a blur clutched in his hand, partially cut off in the frame. He was looking at the camera with the barest smile, his eyes as close to sparkling as I'd ever seen them.

Looking right at Halley.

The photo was rimmed with a heart in blue Sharpie, and beside it, three words bled into the cardstock:

He sees me.

My breath caught.

It was so raw. A candid, real-life moment. There was feeling there. Tangible feeling I could almost reach out and touch. I felt it in my chest, in the tainted chambers of my closed-off heart. Life seeped inside of it, relighting the shriveled-up organ. Defibrillator paddles sparked it anew.

Warm tears rushed down my cheeks in rivers of remorse.

All this time.

Years had flown by while everyone else had moved on with life and I'd remained idle. Idle and stagnant, too comfortable in my hatred. Too stubborn in my staunch beliefs.

I'd painted my father a monster in my mind, and he hadn't steered me any differently. Maybe he was waiting for me to see the truth. Words were useless when falling on deaf ears. Only I was able to allow the honesty inside...when I was ready.

Am I ready?

God, I wanted to be. I was so done with this. I was over living with this pain that constantly possessed me, day in and day out. It wasn't comfortable. It wasn't safe.

It was poison.

My mother squeezed my hand, dusting a thumb over my knuckles. "Do you see it?" she asked me.

I chewed on my lip, sinking the heel of my palm into my eye socket as the other eye leaked more tears. "See what?"

"What you need to."

I nodded because I did. I saw it. I saw everything and more. "How did you accept this so easily?" I croaked out, my words shaken by grief.

Mom sighed, swallowing down her own pain. "Forgiveness comes a lot easier when you've had practice. I spent years learning to forgive myself. I was the betrayer once. I was the enemy. Life is fragile, choices are reckless, and forgiveness is always hard-fought. Your father isn't perfect, and neither am I. Neither are you. Neither is Halley. Imperfections are what bind us together. Our common thread. We're all capable of screwing up, but we're all capable of forgiving, too. That's what makes us stronger humans."

I sniffled, still bobbing my head, letting her words touch all of my cold, sealed-tight places. "They really love each other, don't they?"

She smiled gently. "What do you think?"

"I think I made it a lot harder for both of them. I ruined something beautiful when beautiful things in life are so fleeting. Halley moved away because of me. Dad stayed behind because of me."

The verity of my willful convictions haunted me. They had given me power once. Resentment held power. Negative energy held power. People mistook that power for feeling, but all it really did was *suck away* the feeling and drain us dry. I was barren. A shell.

"Do you think it's too late?" I wondered, lifting my bloodshot eyes to my mother.

She didn't even flinch. "Do you?"

"You keep answering my questions with questions."

"That's how we find answers."

My gaze panned back to the scrapbook, where the answers lived. Where they dwelled in dormancy, lurking, lingering, waiting to be harnessed and molded into action.

I did hold power.

Power to destroy and power to heal.

I thought about the puzzle Dad and I had done, years back. The one with the gummed-up, crooked piece. That puzzle would never be perfect. It would never be exactly what I'd envisioned it to be. But it was still a finished puzzle, with every piece stitched together, just the way it was *supposed* to be.

I would put the final piece into place.

Imperfect.

Flawed but complete.

And then, finally...

A new puzzle could begin.

CHAPTER 39

Reed

THERE WAS a knock at my door.

Pulling up from the training mat in my bedroom, I jumped to my feet and searched for a clean T-shirt as I swiped a sheen of sweat off my face with a towel. "Coming." I flipped off the radio, assuming it was my elderly neighbor asking me to turn the music down.

Draping the towel over my shoulder, I sauntered to the front door and tugged it open.

Nothing.

Nobody was there.

I blinked, glancing around the vacant hallway. Then, shaking my head with a sigh, I moved back to close the door.

But something stole my attention the moment I dropped my eyes.

My heart rate tripled.

It was a photograph of me. A picture taped to cream-colored cardstock, decorated with blue marker and flowing words. Beside it was a little note.

I bent over, my pulse in overdrive, and plucked the pages off the floor.

Curious, disbelieving eyes roved over the picture as I registered what it was.

Halley's handwriting stared back at me: *He sees me.*

It was the picture she'd taken on a spring day, long ago, in the early stages of our budding relationship that would tip us sideways and rock my world. I was sitting on a park bench as she flaunted a disposable camera in front of my face. Her foray into photography. She'd managed to capture an authentic reaction, despite my efforts to remain stone-walled and expressionless. A tilt to my lips. A twinkle in my eye.

The beginning of the end.

My eyes watered as I studied her doodles and words.

He sees me.

I did see her. From the moment my eyes had landed on the sad girl in the lake, staring out at a bleak, dark canvas of water, I had done more than notice her. I'd seen her pain. Her misdirection. Her hopelessness. I'd felt it. She'd seeped inside of me and never left.

I exhaled a long breath as my attention turned to the accompanying note.

Whitney?

A frown creased my brows and my heart jumped again.

No...

Tara.

It was my daughter's handwriting. A few words were scribbled onto a scrap of lined notebook paper. Words that stole my breath.

I see it too, Dad.

That was all it said.

But it was more than I could hope for. More than I ever thought possible.

It was an olive branch.

A first step.

A stand-down.

A little white flag fluttering with forgiveness.

I cupped a hand over my jaw and reread her words over and over, until I slumped to the floor, years of stress, hardship, and bone-deep heartache evaporating like mist under the warm sun.

It was enough.

CHAPTER 40

Halley

THE MOON HUNG from the night sky, surrounded by jewels. A shiver rolled through me as the ocean lapped at my ankles, the mid-fifties chill of late November causing my skin to pucker. I folded my arms. There was a sadness tucked inside of me, cradled by the melody of soft-cresting waves.

I often came here when I needed peace.

A place to let my mind wander.

When I was younger, I'd venture off to the lake and stand just like this, imagining a life beyond the ripples and swells. A bright, vivid future, miles away from the horrors of my unforgiving cell at home. So many secrets dwelled beneath the surface. We'd compare notes, the water and me, and it had always allowed me to feel less alone.

Tonight, the last thing I expected was an ally.

"Are you lost?"

I whirled around, water sloshing at my legs and disbelief pounding between my ribs.

What?

It couldn't be.

I was imagining him.

Blinking rapidly, I pressed a hand to my chest, squeezing reality back into my heart. I gaped, jaw-dropped and legs-wobbling. "Reed."

He stood on the shore, his hands hidden in the pockets of his dark-wash jeans. He'd be too far away for me to make out the color of his eyes, but I'd already memorized the precise shade of pale-verdant green.

We gazed at each other across the barren beach.

When he took a small step forward, I swallowed hard, in a daze. "Do I look lost?"

"A little."

"What are you doing here?"

Reed tilted his head to the side, studying me through the night shadows. "Scotty told me you were here. That you go to the ocean alone every Friday night."

"That doesn't answer my question."

"Yes, it does." He smiled.

No...*it didn't*.

I couldn't possibly know why he was here.

Licking a salty drop of seawater from my lip, I shook my head. "You're here for work."

"Try again."

"Something with the studio. The building design. I—"

"No."

Tears muddled my vision. "Reed..."

Still smiling, he took a seat along the shoreline, drawing his knees up as his fingers sifted through damp sand. "I'm having a strange sense of déjà vu."

I was having a heart attack.

Instinct and knee-crippling shock had me lowering into the water, sitting a few feet across from him as I splayed my legs and stared at the way the moonlight glimmered in his eyes.

My voice shrank to nothing. My limbs vibrated with ocean frost and incredulity.

"I spent the day looking for an apartment."

"A what?"

"An apartment. In downtown. I found something that could work for now, a few miles from the studio. It could use some color pops. A woman's touch."

"Please speak in English."

He grinned, his dimples shooting Cupid's arrows to my heart. "I'm moving here, Halley."

"You're not."

"I am. As soon as my lease is up on my condo back home."

"Stop," I sobbed. "Why are you saying this?"

He was messing with me. Cruelly playing with my barely beating heart.

Tears streamed down my cheeks as I brought my legs up, pressing my face between my knees.

"I'm saying this because it's true," he said. "Because I've been wanting to say it for over two years. Because I want it more than I want to breathe."

"Reed." I choked on his name, on his words, on his imaginary presence. This couldn't be real. There was no hope for us. Yet, he was hinting at promises and serendipity and a future I so desperately ached for with such conviction, all I could do was cry. "But we're doomed. We're not meant to be."

"Why?"

"Because...Tara. She would never—"

"She gave me her blessing, Halley."

My head snapped up, my blood pumping with hot-lava hope. "What?" I gawked at him, searching for the lie. The trick. "That's not possible."

"It is possible. I'm here. I'm here because there's nowhere else I'd rather be."

"She would never approve. Never be okay with this." My head shook, my palms fisting ocean sludge. "It's been *years*."

"Years have a way of making things look a lot clearer," he told me. "We talked. We cried. Tara may never fully accept it, but she understands this is real. She doesn't want to be the forever wedge between us. She loves you. We both love you. And even though that love was built differently, it comes from the same place." Heaving in a deep breath, Reed stood. He rose from the sand-blanketed shore and took a step toward the water, placing a hand over his heart. "It comes from here."

My chin lifted, my eyes glued to him as I watched him plod into the water. An inch at a time. A new barrier crumbling between us. Shallow tide kissed the toes of his boots as he pressed forward, until the ocean swallowed his feet to the ankles.

Both of us. Together.

On the same side of the waterline.

I couldn't move. I was paralyzed, hypnotized. Spellbound by his careful approach, his body sinking deeper into the water. And then he sat down, right across from me, caging me in with two long legs.

I leaped at him.

Water sprayed and splashed, mingling with my tears, as I launched myself into his arms and he caught me before we tipped backward and submerged, just for a moment. But I was already drowning. Sinking with shellshock and love so pure I couldn't breathe.

He held me close, wrapping both arms around me and peppering kisses into my hair.

I pulled back to cup his cheeks between my hands, then sifted my fingers through soft brown-black hair. His eyes glittered, the shadows gone for good. "You're here to save me," I breathed out.

Warm lips brushed against mine as he whispered, "Maybe you're here to save me." Then he pulled me to my feet and spun me around, his smile engraved like it had been carved with rare diamonds. "Dance with me."

Laughter poured out of me as he twirled me in the water.

I clung to him, my fingers digging into his arms, never wanting to let go.

Never needing to let go.

Reed hummed the chorus of *Wonderwall*, knowing there were no more walls standing between us.

No more barricades.

Just the open expanse of our shared horizon, painted with the colors of hard-fought love.

We danced.

We swayed beneath the moon, the stars, the vastness of possibility, water drenching our legs and a well-deserved future soaking our minds.

He held me. He dipped me.

And when he pulled me back to his chest, he murmured softly, "Do you like this song?"

Tears of joy flooded me as I pressed my cheek to his chest and listened to every perfectly timed heartbeat, serenading precious melodies against my ear. "It's my favorite."

EPILOGUE

Halley

June, 2005

LADYBUG BOUNDED through the front door of our quaint bungalow, her timeworn, snow-white muzzle connecting with my face for over-eager kisses. At thirteen years old, she was far from feeble, still brimming with puppy energy and unconditional love.

There was a time when I thought I'd never see her again. But things in life that were meant to stay always managed to find their way back to us.

I held her close and kissed her snout, drinking in memories and baby powder softness.

"Mommy! Auntie Tara is here!"

As Ladybug collapsed into my lap, my best friend sauntered through the door with two giant suitcases, Whitney trailing behind her.

"Longest. Drive. Ever."

I grinned up at Tara, scratching behind Ladybug's ears. "But worth it?"

"Depends on what you're cooking."

"A casserole."

Her eyes narrowed with consideration. "And wine?"

"Yes, please," Whitney cut in, shimmying out of her jacket.

"Wine. Mexican casserole." My eyebrows waggled. "And whiskey bread pudding for dessert."

Tara's eyes bulged. "Jesus. Sold. Then we're immediately going to the ocean. You can't stop me."

I stood from the floor and swiped golden fuzz off my leggings as Reed sauntered out of the kitchen with a scowl on his face, decked out in his usual attire of a T-shirt and dark jeans.

But it was the extra item he was wearing that had Tara snorting a laugh behind her hand. "Nice."

Tara had stayed true to her promise from years back of gifting Reed an apron.

It was pink.

He wasn't happy about it.

But he'd dig it out of the closet every time Tara came to visit, which was twice a year. Summer and Christmastime.

Sighing with a self-deprecating shrug, Reed rearranged his face, until a beaming grin shimmered back. "Hey, Squirt." He glanced at Whitney. "Whit."

She smiled a greeting.

Tara shuffled forward, releasing her suitcases and accepting the warm hug he extended. "Good to see you, Dad," she said, holding him close.

My eyes misted at the sight.

The years had been kind to all of us. Difficult, at first, but filled with compassion, healing, and understanding, nonetheless. When Reed had packed up his condo and moved to the east coast to be with me, I had no idea how the future would play out. Would Tara hold on to her resentment? Would it burst back to life in shades of black and gray?

Those first few months had been anxiety-ridden and daunting.

But as time had passed, and Tara had communicated amiably, without any lingering doubt or hostility, our lives had begun to take on fresh meaning. A new outlook.

Love won out like a steady flame.

As I moved the suitcases to the side, our adopted babies rushed to the foyer, all squeals and smiles. "Hi, Grandma!"

"Hi, Auntie Tara!"

Both women bent over, scooping up a respective child in their arms.

Tara held our daughter close, their brown hair blending as one. "You got bigger."

"I'm almost five."

"I was five once. It was great." She set our daughter down and mussed our son's hair as he lay sprawled against Whitney's chest. "I missed you little rascals."

"We missed you, too."

"That's the truth," I said. "They talk about you every day."

"Of course they do. I'm the best."

Our pinkie fingers linked together as we shared a tender smile and the two children ran into the bedroom to show Tara their new toys.

A deep-rooted part of me had always wanted to foster children one day. The forgotten. The unloved. The homeless and abused. It was a blooming desire that grew wings with every passing day. Reed was fully supportive of the idea, so a year into our whirlwind relationship, we fostered newborn twins that had been pulled from a drug-addled home: a girl and a boy.

Mina and Jayce.

Mina meant "love," and Jayce meant "to heal."

Of course, my heart hadn't been built for giving up two precious bundles of pure love, so it wasn't long before we were signing the adoption papers. Once the kids grew older, I wanted nothing more than to keep fostering, keep nurturing, keep sharing my home with sweet, lost souls.

I'd been lost once.

Sometimes all it took was a helping hand to guide us in the right direction. To allow us to find ourselves again.

When Tara and Whitney joined the kids in the bedroom, I ambled into the kitchen, where Reed was checking on the casserole. I came up behind him and wrapped my arms around his middle, pressing my cheek to the warmth of his back. "Mmm. You smell good."

"I showered."

"I remember."

He swiveled in my arms with a wink, then pressed a kiss to my forehead.

"I might want to shower again later," I confessed.

"Yeah?" His eyebrows arched as lust glinted in his eyes. "You're insatiable."

"I'm in love."

He pulled me to him, resting his chin on top of my head and stroking a hand down my spine. Tingles erupted, blooming like the balloon of happiness in my chest. "I always knew we had that kind of love," he told me, sighing with an air of solace.

"What kind of love?" I was putty in his arms, a sagging, boneless heap.

Reed swayed me gently, side to side. "The growing old together kind."

My eyes closed.

Tears prickled as my heart soared.

While I'd never felt the *need* to get married, knowing our love story burned brighter than wedding bells and legal binds, Reed had asked me to marry him in the fall of 2000. Of course, I'd said yes. It was a simple ceremony at a local lake with our closest friends and family, and Monique had been overjoyed to capture our blissful day, leaving me on the other side of the camera for once. Now, we had gold rings on our fingers, a home we owned and cherished, and two precious babies who blessed us daily.

We had it all.

Growing old with the one you love was an underrated treasure. Aging was frightening. Death was an ominous certainty that nipped at our ankles. But the journey to the other side of this life with someone who held your heart, who shared your dreams and fears, who knew you in the deepest corners of your soul, was a privilege beyond measure. It was a promise of companionship through every storm. And as Reed's words encompassed me like a comforting embrace, I knew that no matter what lay ahead, we would face it together.

I was good at doing hard things.

And the hardest things in life gave way to the greatest rewards.

We ate dinner as a family, a CD playing from the speakers in the living room. *Stop Crying Your Heart Out* by Oasis was a well-loved soundtrack to our meal—our children's favorite song on the album. Luckily, I'd stopped crying my heart out a long time ago, so the song only brought a smile to my face as we shared stories, laughter, and plans for the future.

When supper was finished, we gathered in the living room beside a stack of photo albums, featuring old pictures passed down from Whitney, as well as my photography portfolio.

And our own book of family memories.

Mina flipped through the leather-bound album, her chubby finger pointing at every picture. "That's Daddy." Her chocolate-brown eyes widened with awe as she glanced at another image of us together. "Mommy and Daddy at the beach."

"That's right." I smiled, my soul alight and filled to the brim. "We were going for a swim. It was the day before we brought you home, and we wanted to celebrate with a dip in the ocean. One last day of just the two of us before our home got bigger and our lives changed for the better."

"What's this one?" Mina wondered.

I glanced at it. "That was when your dad and I opened up a third location for our training studio in Washington."

"The fighting place?" Jayce inquired.

"Yes. The fighting place." I chuckled, pinching his arm. "We help people become strong and brave. Just like you."

Jayce leaned over to study another photograph of Reed watching me walk down the grassy aisle in my modest ivory dress. It was my favorite picture taken that day. The way Reed's eyes had glistened with tears and love, the elated smile stretched on his mouth, the crease between his brows, wrinkled with every emotion. A priceless moment, forever immortalized.

His love for me.

Clear as day, never to be questioned.

"Hey, Mommy?" Jayce inquired, his brown eyes skimming over the page of wedding photos.

"Hmm?"

"How did you and Daddy fall in love?"

I blinked.

My gaze trailed over to Reed as he sat beside me, squeezing my hand. We shared a look. A knowing, love-steeped look that sent tingles to my heart and a warm shiver down my spine.

I turned back to the kids as Reed's arm wrapped around me and tugged me close. With a contented sigh, I dropped my temple to the breadth of his shoulder, closed my eyes, and replied softly, "I'll tell you when you're older."

The End

*Thank you for reading **Older**—I hope you enjoyed the forbidden ride!*
If you're looking for more love in hopeless places, feel free to check out the
rest of my angsty, slow-burn romances.

ALSO BY JENNIFER HARTMANN

STILL BEATING

#1 Amazon Bestseller in three categories!

When Cora leaves her sister's birthday party, she doesn't expect to wake up in shackles in a madman's basement.

To make matters worse, her arch nemesis and ultimate thorn in her side, Dean, shares the space in his own set of chains. The two people who always thought they'd end up killing each other must now work together if they want to survive.

LOTUS

To the rest of the world, he was the little boy who went missing on the Fourth of July.

To Sydney, he was everything.

Twenty-two years later, he's back.

This is Oliver Lynch's story...

This is their story.

THE STARS ARE ON OUR SIDE

Tabitha Brighton's name made national headlines when she was kidnapped by the infamous serial killer known as the Matchmaker.

Two years later, she's ready to tell her story, while Gabe—the new man in her life—will do whatever it takes to keep her from slipping back into the shadows.

THE WRONG HEART

Audie Awards Romance Finalist 2021!

When my husband died, he left my broken heart behind.

He left another heart behind, too—his.

I know it's wrong. I shouldn't be contacting the recipient of my husband's heart. I don't even expect him to reply...

But there's a desperate, twisted part of me that hopes he will.

After all, the only thing I have left of my husband is inside him.

JUNE FIRST

Want to know what happens to a man who barely claws his way out of a tragedy, only to fall right into the arms of the one girl in the world he can never have?

Another tragedy, that's what.

THE THORNS REMAIN

Vengeance was the goal, and Josie Grant was his way in.

He never meant to fall in love with her.

Now...there's no way out.

THE DUET SERIES — ARIA & CODA

When the lead singer of his rock band starts falling for a pretty waitress, Noah will do whatever it takes to make sure she doesn't get in the way of their dreams.

But it would be easier if that waitress didn't accidentally spill her darkest secrets to him one night, triggering a profound connection neither of them saw coming.

THE HEARTSONG DUET – AN OPTIMIST'S GUIDE TO HEARTBREAK & A PESSIMIST'S GUIDE TO LOVE

Lucy can't seem to let go of two important people from her childhood. On a whim, she purchases the house that used to belong to her best friends, Emma and Cal.

The bittersweet memories have her tracking Cal down almost a decade later and applying for a job at his auto repair shop.

Only, Cal is no longer the sweet, goofy boy next door... he's gruff, built, tattooed, and wants nothing more than to forget the same past that Lucy is longing to reclaim.

CLAWS AND FEATHERS

Small town cop, Cooper, is intrigued by the mysterious new girl who walks into his father's bar, but the last thing he expects is for her to go missing that same night.

Finding Abby is just the beginning. The only way to truly save her is to unravel her secrets—a task that proves to be more challenging than he could ever anticipate.

ENTROPY

By 9:03 A.M. Monday, bank manager Indie Chase thinks her day can't get worse.

She's wrong.

Dax Reed is a reluctantly retired pro hockey player with a past he'd rather forget, well on his way to doing so when everything goes to hell.

Together, they're caught in a robbery that's going to take everything they have to survive.

It's going to take trust.

It's going to take strength.

It might even take...*each other*.

COMING SOON

<u>CATCH THE SUN</u>

Releasing July 16th, 2024

As feelings blossom between childhood friends, Ella and Max, new tragedy strikes their small town, darkness threatening to tip the delicate balance of friendship, love, and something else entirely. In order to find the light, they'll have to navigate the shadows.

And to catch the sun...they must first endure the flames.

PLAYLIST

Listen to the playlist **HERE**

"Wonderwall" – Oasis
"Black" – Pearl Jam
"Until I Fall Away" – Gin Blossoms
"Gramarye" – Remy Zero
"All I Want" – Toad The Wet Sprocket
"Eve" – Neulore
"Talk show Host" – Radiohead
"One Headlight" – The Wallflowers
"Higher Than Reason" – Unbelievable Truth
"Weak And Powerless" – A Perfect Circle
"Would?" – Alice In Chains
"Save Yourself" – Stabbing Westward
"Everlong" – Foo Fighters
"Algiers" – The Afghan Whigs
"Save the Last Dance for Me" – Harry Nilsson
"Dancing In The Dark" – biz colletti
"Don't Look Back in Anger" – Oasis
"Until I Wake Up" – Dishwalla

"Name" – The Goo Goo Dolls
"Loosen Your Hold" – South
"Stop Crying Your Heart Out" – Oasis
"Take A Picture" – Filter
"Wonderwall" – Boyce Avenue

CONNECT

Give me a follow!
Reader Group: Queen of Harts: Jennifer Hartmann's Reader Group
Instagram: @author.jenniferhartmann
Facebook: @jenhartmannauthor

Twitter: @authorjhartmann

TikTok: @jenniferhartmannauthor

Merch, Newsletter, and More:
www.jenniferhartmannauthor.com

ABOUT THE AUTHOR

Jennifer Hartmann resides in northern Illinois with her own personal romance hero and three children. When she is not writing angsty love stories, she is likely pondering all the ways she can break your heart and piece it back together again. She enjoys sunsets (because mornings are hard), bike riding, traveling, bingeing *Buffy the Vampire Slayer* reruns, and that time of day when coffee gets replaced by wine. She loves tacos. She also really, really wants to pet your dog. XOXO.

Made in the USA
Middletown, DE
06 September 2024